# Like Cassettes
by Jason Sauls

*For the incredible people in my life who mirror the characters in this story. You are like my favorite songs and I remember the words to all the best ones.*

*And for my Mom, the first person to tell me I should write a book someday.*

"Cassette" (definition): *A compact case containing a length of tape that runs between two small reels; used for recording and playback.*

# Prologue - September 1990

The first time Analisa, or Anna for short, saw him was when he didn't know he was being watched.

Her family had just moved from Kenosha, Wisconsin to Concord, California and the movers were unloading the truck into their new house. She would be starting at her new high school in a few days. It was not a move she'd wanted. No one she could think of would want to move to a new school in their senior year. Even friends in Kenosha that hated school in general had sympathized with her situation.

Anna was mature enough to know that her father's new job was a big deal and that he worked extremely hard to land it. She believed her parents when they told her his position with a bigger law firm out west was a great opportunity.

"This will make it so much easier for us to put you and your sister through college" was highest on the list of things they'd said dozens of times in explaining why the move needed to happen, even as they admitted the timing for her was terrible.

If she'd needed any proof that they weren't lying about the money part, the new house was it. Even with her parents having complained multiple times about how much more expensive houses were in California versus Wisconsin the Concord home was still bigger and newer than their house in Kenosha. It had a larger garage, three bathrooms instead of two, a nicer kitchen, and some other features that clearly made her parents happy. Anna claimed the larger of the two bedrooms meant for her and Jackie, her younger sister. And her new room was also a little larger than the one she'd had back home. The only thing smaller in the new house was the backyard. She was alone in the new backyard, standing on the patio for the first time when she heard the argument over the fence.

"That is not where I shot from!" a male voice cried.

"Yes it was!" said another.

By the time Anna walked across the small grass area and peered over the fence the other boy, holding a basketball, was walking to some invisible spot she assumed he was talking about.

"I shot it from here," he explained. "Now take the shot."

7

The other boy, who appeared to be a few years younger, bounced the ball a few times and then took his shot at the basket and missed.

"That's 'S'. You're almost out."

She worried they might see her but continued watching. The older boy dribbled from the far end of their backyard half court, stopped, bounced the ball off the side of the house, retrieved it, and then shot it. It went in.

"Your shot," he said, handing over the ball.

The younger boy attempted to duplicate all the moves and missed once again.

"You're out," the older boy said.

"Rematch?" the other asked.

"Nah, I gotta get ready to go out."

"You and the boozehounds?" the younger one asked.

From her view, Anna thought she saw the older boy give the younger one a stern look. Her educated guess was they were brothers.

"Chill out. I'm not gonna narc on you," the younger one said.

His comment confirmed the relationship in Anna's mind. They were definitely brothers.

The boys walked across their yard and then into their house. Anna walked away from her spy duty with two thoughts. First, she was envious of the basketball court because it was the kind of thing that she thought would have made her like the new house a lot more and maybe even make her less upset with her parents. Second, she wondered if these two neighbor boys were or weren't like the boys she knew back home. She thought maybe she heard a little more California in their voices but also recognized it might be her own preconceptions. She felt bad for the younger brother because the older one seemed like he was a bit of a jerk or a know-it-all or both. Or maybe they were just brothers that way. As an older sister she knew she wasn't always as nice as she should be to Jackie. The younger boy looked to be, at the very least, high school age and she guessed he was maybe a junior or senior. He was the one who had caught more of her attention, as she speculated he was closer to her age. She wondered if he went to the high school she would soon be attending. She assumed he probably did, given that they were in the same neighborhood. But maybe he went to a private school? Or, she thought, maybe they were both going to be at her new school or maybe they were

"It's got so many great songs," she said, before adding, "And I'm glad we're still friends."

# Chapter One - October 1990

## *"Strangers When We Meet"*

The first time Cal met her was after English class. He vaguely remembered her being introduced as a new student from somewhere or other a week or so before. And their first conversation was not even really talking. It was disagreeing with each other from across the room during a class wide discussion about *The Great Gatsby*. Their teacher, Ms. Cook had asked whether her students thought Daisy Buchanan was a strong person or a weak person.

"What I'm saying," the new girl argued, "is that Daisy was *trying* to be strong and *trying* to be independent during a time when that was a very foreign concept for women."

"And yet," Cal countered, "She still ultimately makes the safe choice, which is the weaker choice. If she was strong she would have just *left*. You don't stay in a situation you hate if you're in love with someone else."

"But you *did* in the 1920s. People still do that today," the new girl countered. "It was patriarchy then and its patriarchy now. I don't understand how you can just ignore the context of the culture at the time. Or even now!"

Cal, as good an English student as he was, wasn't quite sure what patriarchy even meant. He glanced at Reed sitting next to him for some kind of support but all Reed gave him was a smirk and shoulder shrug that said, "I am not even going to help you with this." And this girl, whose name Cal couldn't remember, seemed a bit angry with him. And he hated when any girl was angry with him.

Before Cal could get his next words out Ms. Cook came to the rescue and shifted the conversation to other questions, calling on other students. On the way out of class Cal walked by this new girl, who looked at him with the kind of contempt he usually only saw on the face of someone who was upset about a joke or a misunderstanding.

"Hi," she said.

"Hey," he said, wondering if he should smile but a bit terrified to do so, before adding, "Thanks for the...debate, I guess?"

"Do you do debate? Like a debate team?" she asked.

He thought of the people he knew that were on the school's debate team and in Mock U.N. and Mock Congress before saying, "No. I don't debate. At least not about...I don't know..."

"Books?" she asked.

"Books or...anything," he said. "Well, I would debate music but... never mind."

"Well, I appreciate you saying thank you. I'm Analisa but I go by Anna."

"I'm Cal," he said. "And I go by Cal because I don't like Calvin."

"Oh, like the comic strip," she said with a slight giggle. "*Calvin and Hobbes.*"

"Yeah, just like *Calvin and Hobbs*," he said in a deadpan-like tone.

He'd had people joke about *Calvin and Hobbes* before. Like a hundred times before.

"Anyway, nice to meet you," he said. "And I hope I didn't piss you off back there in class."

"You did a little but it's fine," she said. "You made some good points but I still think I'm right."

Cal didn't care enough to continue debating it with her. Within 30 seconds he'd summed up the type of person she was, placing her in one of the various social circles of his imagination. He figured she was not the kind of person who would ever admit to losing an argument even if she was losing or had flat out lost.

"Well, okay then," he said. "Nice to meet you, Anna. And I guess I'm late in saying it...but welcome to Crestview."

He gave her a little wave as he walked away to his next class.

"Thank you," she called after him.

--

Anna had not spent much of her high school existence thinking about boys, or at least not as much as so many of her friends back in Kenosha always seemed to be thinking about them. She liked them, found herself attracted to certain ones, but by early in the 11th grade she

14

was unimpressed by the vast majority of them at her high school. It got to a point where no matter how good a guy looked on the basketball court or around the school hallways or even if he demonstrated some level of intellect there would inevitably be something that would disappoint her. It ranged from immature remarks at best and, at worst, unwanted efforts to go farther than kissing or touching on a date. Even when she was with Kyle, a boy in Kenosha she dated for close to a year, their relationship paralleled situations she had seen in too many movies and TV shows. He wanted to have sex, she said she wasn't ready, and it became a constant back and forth. By age 17 and entering her senior year she'd concluded that boys in general were not worth her time or energy. It felt especially true at Crestview, her new school. So it surprised her that two hours after meeting this boy, Cal, she was still thinking about him. Was it because he was the first boy she'd really talked to at this new school? She thought that might be it. But the bigger piece came when she realized he was the same boy she had spied on several days before from the other side of her backyard fence. Cal was the younger of the two boys she'd observed playing basketball.

In the middle of the Gatsby argument in English class she started disliking him a lot, which seemed incredibly irrational because she knew he wasn't being mean or rude. But she did think he was wrong about Daisy Buchanan and she was frustrated that he didn't seem to be grasping her points of argument. She was still a little upset on her way out of class and when he was walking toward her she expected him to say something snarky or cruel but he didn't. If anything he seemed apologetic. It was disarming and she had to give him credit for surprising her because she didn't think any boy could.

She sat at lunch with Tracy Hunt, a girl who had been assigned to her as a guide or "Welcome to Crestview" buddy on her first day. Tracy was very friendly, though at first Anna couldn't tell if it was genuine or just part of her assignment to show a new person around. But they seemed to have things in common and Tracy kept talking to her even after that first day, inviting Anna to sit with her and her other friends at lunch. Tracy didn't strike Anna as being super popular but she was definitely social and outgoing. She said hello to people constantly in the hallways and at the rows of lockers. She knew her way around, too, which made sense given that she was part of whatever welcoming crew the school had at the ready for new students.

"So do you hate it here yet?" Tracy asked from across the cafeteria table.

"No," Anna said. "It's just different. In small ways."

"Like what?"

"Well, it's October and some people are still in shorts," she explained. "In Kenosha we're usually getting ready for snow if we haven't had it already."

"Oh, yeah," Tracy said. "Some of the guys here just wear shorts year-round, even in January when it's freezing out. I guess it's a California thing."

"But a lot of things are similar, too," Anna added. "I mean, it's clear you all have cliques and certain circles...marching band folks, computer clubs... and cheerleaders and jocks."

"Definitely," Tracy said. "We have the whole menu."

Anna had spent days wondering where and how she was going to fit in at Crestview. At times she wondered if she even wanted to fit in at all. In some areas she was very outgoing and involved, especially with academic activities and basketball. But socially she knew she was a little shy. In Kenosha she had always considered herself "just popular enough" and never felt inspired to try to be more so. She'd concluded such efforts would never work anyway. She'd seen various friends try to change the way they look or talk, where they would hang out or who they'd hang out with, only to wind up disappointed when whatever their aim was missed the mark. For Anna, the biggest goal of high school, from her freshman year right up to the earliest days of her senior year, was to do well in her classes. Good grades would mean a great college and a great college would hopefully mean a good and meaningful future. She sometimes envied friends and classmates that seemed content in the present because she was always thinking about, and even sometimes obsessed with, the future and what would come after four years of high school. Adulthood had always seemed enticing and as it got closer, at least in the legal sense, it had not lost its appeal. Things like "Live in the now" or "Carpe diem" -- a term that in her opinion had gotten grossly overused and cliche after everyone saw *Dead Poets Society* -- didn't seem terribly practical when so many Monday morning stories in the hallways had to do with getting crazy drunk over the weekend. Ore they were full of rumors about who was dating who or who was or wasn't having sex. She felt like she had outgrown that and prided herself for never having embraced it much in the first place.

The lone exception was sports. She loved playing high school sports and watching them, too. Her biggest fear heading to a new school, aside from making sure all her AP credits and classes would still be in place, was worrying there might not be Girls basketball or volleyball. At 5' 8" Anna didn't consider herself tall because someone else was always taller but as her basketball coach in Kenosha had said to her many times, "You're still taller than average. And you see the game better than anyone." She'd led her team in assists the prior year and was very relieved when she learned Crestview had a full slate of Girls teams, though Tracy told her they were hardly championship caliber.

"I think the basketball team made district a few years ago but the girls track team wins constantly," she'd explained. "But football is the thing here. Even though the team usually sucks. Everyone goes to the games, mostly just to see friends and then hang out after."

Kyle, her ex-boyfriend back in Kenosha, was a football player, a basketball player, and a baseball player. A three-sport varsity athlete and very good at two out of the three. Part of her attraction to him was how good he'd looked playing basketball. But as they got to know each she found she was paying just as much attention to his shooting percentage and his stats in a game as she was with how his hair looked or what he was wearing. In the end, when she had decided to break up with him, she had written in her journal that no amount of his sports prowess could overcome his immaturity and hormones.

She still loved watching guys play sports but as she glanced across the cafeteria at a group of male Crestview students in their varsity jackets she doubted she'd ever want to date one again. She found it both off putting and comforting to see that even the body language of guys like that wasn't much different in California than it had been in Wisconsin.

---

Reed Bennett was far and away the most inquisitive and observant person Cal had ever met. He could find himself in a

17

conversation with Reed about any given person at their school and Reed would know multiple things about them: Where they lived, what their parents did for a living, who they were dating, where they might be going to college, and then some. It was more than Cal would ever know and as often more than he would ever *want* to know. But he thought of Reed as a great friend to have, especially if someone had been talking about him behind his back or if he wanted to know if some girl had even an inkling of interest in him. If Reed relayed a piece of information it was almost always accurate.

"So that new girl is apparently from Wisconsin," Reed reported as they were eating lunch.

They were sitting on the floor in an open space near the lockers as they always did at lunch time when Reed presented his newfound information out of nowhere.

"Do you mean the new girl in English class?" Cal asked.

"Yeah, the one who got all pissed at you."

"I don't think she was pissed," he said. "I went and talked to her. She was fine about it. A little weird, too."

"She also lives in your neighborhood," Reed reported.

Cal had long since stopped asking his friend how he knew such things. Reed just knew. Cal secretly appreciated such information but still liked to rib his friend over his curious nature.

"Does she have pets?" he asked. "Siblings? What kind of car does she drive, Sherlock?"

Given his knack for investigation and information gathering Cal found it fitting that Reed was active with the school paper and had every intention of majoring in Journalism. Reed had a variety of universities and colleges on his list, with his dream school a small college in Portland, Oregon named Lewis & Clark that Cal had never heard of until Reed mentioned it the previous year.

Talk of would-be colleges and majors and where everyone was planning to apply had begun to dominate the October conversations among seniors and Cal was a bit envious of Reed's master plans and overall ability to map things out. At the same time he thought Reed was way too much of a planner. He would elaborately plan out how he would ask someone on a date and then if they said yes he'd have a minute-by-minute breakdown for how said date would roll out. By Reed's own admission such plans never played out as he hoped. But when it came to college and the future, though he'd never admit it out loud, Cal knew Reed's approach was good and better than his own. His closest friend was throwing multiple darts at the board and they both knew at least one was going to stick eventually.

Cal had taken the SAT and done better than average, at least according to his guidance counselor, Mrs. Sheller. At his mother's insistence Cal took the test a second time and scored ten points lower than the first. After his scores came back Mrs. Sheller explained, "This score, coupled with your GPA gives you options. Probably not UC-level options but any state colleges here or out of state will likely accept you."

Mrs. Sheller was blunt and honest with him, more so than most teachers and other adults, and Cal liked that.

"Cal, you're a classic case of being smarter than your GPA," she said. "You got 1010 on your SAT and you might be able to get it to 1100 or higher if you really studied up and took it a third time. But that GPA is still a 3.1 and you can't get it to where UC's will give you a look. It's too late in the game."

"Can you put that in writing for my Mom so she'll get off my back?" he asked.

"Oh, Cal. You are the most challenging kind of student I get," she said. "I don't know what it is about kids like you but I always find it frustrating when you excel in so many areas... AP English, your excellent writing, your participation in theater, even some sports... but those C's in science and math? That's your Achilles heel."

"Someday I am coming back here with proof that I didn't need calculus or zoology," he said with a smile.

"I've had many past students say the same thing," Mrs. Sheller reminded him.

"And what happened to them?" he asked.

"The truth? I helped most of them get into college, they majored in some kind of liberal arts subject, got their bachelors and never needed math or science beyond the minimum requirement. But it's my job up until this point to try and get you to think otherwise," she said with a wink.

"So you're saying I'm right?" he asked, excited at the prospect of any teacher or counselor telling him he was.

19

"You're not right but you'll probably be fine. But I still hope you'll aim for more than 'fine'. I think you've got it in you," she said.

Even before his start-of-year October check-in with Mrs. Sheller, Cal knew elite and UC schools were not going to be a part of his future. It was something he'd known for a while because he'd seen what it took to get into Berkeley, UCLA, Davis, or Santa Barbara or Santa Cruz because those were the types of schools his older brother, Tyler, had applied to 3 years before. Tyler ended up making the waiting list for Berkeley, got acceptance from many other schools, and ultimately opted for UC Santa Barbara. Once there Tyler had some "struggles adjusting", as their parents had called it. Cal described it as "Developing a minor drinking problem". Tyler later transferred to UC Davis. His brother had cast a bit of a shadow at Crestview and it took Cal some time to get out of it. Cal ran track, just as his brother had, but he wasn't great at it. Tyler had been. He led the team in contributing points his Senior year and was named team MVP. Tyler was an excellent student in almost every subject, with English being the only subject Cal ever surpassed him in. His parents were proud of him when he made AP for his final year, something Tyler hadn't even tried to achieve because, as he'd put it, "I don't do flowery creative writing and poetry."

Tyler had also never taken a Drama class and Cal wasn't even sure if his brother had known where the Crestview Theater was, let alone if he'd ever stepped foot in it. But Cal was in Advanced Drama, something his mother was thrilled about and his father thought was "something you're passionate about and that's good to have, too".

Cal knew getting out of an older sibling's shadow or legacy was not an especially unique experience, but even as he got out of that shadow he could still see it lingering. That was how he'd described it the previous year in a poem he'd written for the literary issue of the school paper under the title "Opposite Side of the Son".

*There is no ticket here for that ride you took*
*But paths of glory have a dirt road by their side*
*Your shoes are spotless, I've got holes in mine*
*You'll bask in sunshine while they tell you're the one*
*But it's cool and dry here where I'm standing*
*On the other side of the son*

Cal had several fellow younger brothers and sisters of Crestview alumni tell him they really liked it. The full poem had made his mother cry.

"Do you really feel that kind of pressure from us to try to be more like Ty?" she'd asked after reading it.

"Just a little," he'd said. "But I'm over it. It was easier to let it go after the failed suicide attempt."

It was a joke and not a funny one, but by 17 that was where his sense of humor had arrived. The quickest way out of any uncomfortable situation, conversation, confrontation, or challenging moment with a friend, teacher or his parents was to find a way to laugh or get another person to do the same.

"You're not funny," his mother chided about his sometimes-dark sense of humor.

"I'm a little funny," he said.

And he was confident he was.

"So do you really think Daisy Buchanan wasn't a product of the time in history Fitzgerald was trying to capture in Gatsby?"

That was how she greeted him, asking the question from the other side of his locker door. He wasn't even sure who it was when he heard her and hadn't seen her approach.

"I'm sorry, what?" he asked, closing the locker, and seeing this new girl, Anna, standing there. It was before the first bell of the morning had even rung.

"I was just curious," she said.

He noticed that she still had her coat and backpack on, which seemed to indicate that her first priority after getting to school was not to put her things away but to continue their debate over The Great Gatsby.

"I think Daisy was selfish," he said, opting to return to the subject for the sake of talking with her. "And I'm not sure if that's unique to the 1920's. But honestly I only read the book once and then I rented the movie so maybe I just didn't like what's-her-face's portrayal of her."

"Mia Farrow," she informed him.

"Yeah, her."

21

"Interesting," she said.

He was beginning to wonder why she was talking to him at all. It was early, pre-first period and Cal, who had begun drinking coffee regularly since the year before, felt like he was still a cup short for any kind of debate at all, let alone with some strange girl he didn't know.

"I'm sorry," she said. "It's just that yesterday's class discussion sort of stuck with me and I guess I associated that with you and then I came in and saw you as I was walking to my locker so…"

"I get it," he said. "You needed to finish making your point."

"I guess so," she said.

"That's cool. I get like that, too," he said, adding, "But not usually about books."

His mind flashed to the debates he'd had over music with other members of the school's Mixtape Club, a group he'd co-founded where members made mixes once every two or three weeks, randomly exchanged them with other members, took them home and listened to them, and then talked about their mixes at the next meeting. They'd tell each other what songs they liked, what songs they hated, how the mix flowed from song to song. Even as a co-founder he had a love/hate relationship with the entire membership, as heated debates often emerged over what bands were the best or what styles and genres of music ruled or sucked or were overrated.

"So… how do you like it here?" he asked Anna, hoping he could talk to her about anything other than *The Great Gatsby*.

She shrugged her shoulders.

"It's different but also the same. It's louder here," she said, gesturing toward the sea of students around them who were all at once retrieving and putting things away in their lockers. Crestview was a bit different when it came to lockers. Instead of having them spread out throughout various hallways they existed in a series of rows near the school entrance. This made for a cacophony of conversations, laughter, and metal clanging of locker doors opening and closing.

"My brother says it's a fire hazard waiting for a lawsuit," he said about the area they were standing in.

"Does he go here?" she asked.

"He used to. He graduated in '88."

"Oh. My little sister is at Diablo Middle. She'll be here next year."

22

"Cool," he said, closing his locker. "I'm heading to class. Where's your first period?"

She pointed toward the west end of the school.

"I've got Chemistry," he said, gesturing toward the north.

"I guess I'll see you in English then," she said.

She started to walk away but he called to her before she was out of earshot.

"You know, you're probably right... about Daisy," he said. "Sometimes I just argue or disagree because it seems like what Ms. Cook wants us to do, ya know?"

"So what do you actually think about it? About Daisy?" she asked.

He tried to come up with some kind of intellectual response but after about 3 seconds he gave up.

"I got nothing," he said. "So I guess I probably don't think about it."

She rolled her eyes and let out a long sigh. "I'll see you in class."

--

Anna always felt stupid and immature in asking anyone what they knew about another person in any kind of gossipy or second-hand way. And yet she knew she had done it many times, to find out if someone said something about her or if it would let her know more information about whatever or whoever she might be curious about. So it was with a sense of shame that she asked Tracy about Cal. She and Tracy had their first period class together. In the few minutes before it started, fresh off what she felt been had akin to an ambush at his locker, she hoped she might learn a bit more about Cal from the one friend she'd made so far.

"So there's this guy in my English class that..."

She wasn't quite sure how to describe it.

"A guy that I got into a conversation with," she decided. "His name is Cal. I don't know his last name."

"Sorensen," Tracy said. "Cal Sorensen."

"Do you know him?" Anna asked.

"Sure. What about him?"

"He lives near me," she explained. She added what she knew was a small lie. "I saw him walking around the neighborhood and then recognized him in English and we talked and..."

23

"Do you like him or something?" Tracy asked.

Anna was thrown off by the bluntness of the question. Her new friend certainly got to the point, even though Anna didn't think it was the point at all. She hadn't even given that idea much thought.

"I don't even really know him," she explained. "But I was just wondering if you knew anything about him. Like, as someone new here should I avoid him? Is he a jerk? I guess I just wanted to get a sense of who's who if that makes sense."

Tracy seemed a little puzzled by the explanation but answered just the same.

"I don't really know Cal all that well but we have some friends in common. I know his best friend Reed pretty well because we've been in school together since forever. I know Cal's really into music and I've heard he's a good writer. He and Reed are both in theater. I think he does track or at least used to. He's not a jerk or anything. I mean, he's always been nice to me."

"Is he...not that it matters...but is he popular?" Anna asked.

She didn't know Tracy very well but Anna sensed she had a mental index of nearly everyone at Crestview.

"I wouldn't say popular. But not unpopular. Just kind of in the middle. Why are you so curious?" Tracy asked in a playful tone and raised her eyebrows.

"It's not like that," Anna said.

"Sure it isn't," Tracy teased.

"I've been here a week. I can barely remember my locker combination some days! So it's really not like that."

She wanted to drive home the point because she didn't want anything circulating around. She'd known rumors before and could imagine how even a tiny one, like a new girl liking someone, could circulate fast. Things like that happened at her school in Kenosha all the time and there was nothing to suggest it would be any different at Crestview.

Anna thought the conversation was over, and she was beginning to regret even having it all when less than a minute later, just as class was getting ready to start, Tracy shared another bit of information.

"I just remembered. A girl I know, Lizzie... she went to Prom with Cal last year," Tracy said. "I remember her saying he's really sweet and funny but also a little weird. And he made her a mixtape. I remember because she said she wound up liking his taste in music more than she liked him."

--

If Reed Bennett was his friend that planned too much, Doug Fowler was the one who planned too little, if at all. A year or so younger than Cal and two grades behind him, they'd met the year before when Cal became Doug's English tutor.

"I should warn you before we start that I'm Lexick Diss," was the first thing Doug ever said to him. He was sitting across from Cal at a library table

"You're what?" Cal had asked him.

"I'm Dyslexic. It's a joke," Doug said.

Over the course of a few months Cal helped him compose several essays and book summaries that he was behind on in his class. By year's end they'd managed to get his grade all the way up to a B. Along the way they discovered they liked a lot of the same music. Cal liked that Doug was just as eclectic in his tastes as he was. They would constantly go back and forth about a song they heard on the radio or a video they saw on MTV. Doug was the only other person Cal knew who would make a point of watching both *Headbanger's Ball*, which played hard rock and heavy metal videos, and Sunday night's *120 Minutes*, which showcased a lot of bands labeled "alternative". Doug had opened him up to bands like Soundgarden, Jane's Addiction, Alice in Chains and the San Francisco band Primus, which Doug called his "absolute all-time favorite". Cal never had to twist Doug's arm to take a 45-minute drive into Berkeley to go Rasputin Records or Amoeba Music and buy up anything that seemed interesting.

Eventually the formal tutoring became "helping out a friend". With the gaps in age and grade it wasn't too long before Cal would openly tell Doug, "You're like the younger brother I never had but also never wanted." Cal knew Doug had some problems, some of which he'd even admit to out loud or talk about in an honest moment. Doug also did many things Cal was either afraid to do, like smoking weed or taking LSD, or unable to do, with the clearest example being attracting girls without really trying at all, later having sex with them, seemingly on a regular basis, and having no discretion about it whatsoever. Even though he was the younger of the two, Doug oozed a level of confidence that Cal envied, though he never admitted it.

Doug also carried with him a level or recklessness. On the smaller side that included things throwing up in Cal's car after drinking too much. On the much larger side, Doug had got his former girlfriend, Emma, pregnant. She later had an abortion, never spoke to Doug again, and became very active with her church and a controversial student club at Crestview, known as Friends of Faith. Cal was the only friend Doug confided in about the abortion. To most people it just looked like he and Emma broke up and that she was so hurt over it that she found religion. Her activity in Friends of Faith resulted in many of Doug's other friends saying things like, "You're the guy that winds up making girls find Jesus." Cal never cracked such jokes. But he wasn't afraid to call Doug out, often asking things like, "What are you gonna do next year when I'm not here to stop you from being the worst version of yourself?"

"Dude, you're going to be the one calling me from whatever fucking college you wind up at saying, 'Doug, I met this girl and I don't know what I'm doing'. And then I'll have to come visit you and you'll tell some college chick that I am visiting from Sacramento University and --"

"It's Sacramento State, jackass," Cal corrected.

"Whatever," Doug continued. "I know I need you like the good angel on my shoulder but, dude, you know you need me, too. You know it!"

It was hard to argue and it sometimes felt a bit pathetic or shameful to Cal. But when a Friday night came and Doug knew where a party was or called him and said, "Dude, there is a show at the Omni and the last time this band played a bunch of guys from Primus and Faith No More showed up to jam. We *have* to go!" all the embarrassment of being less cool or less smooth than his younger friend was swept aside.

Cal was at the Friday night football game with Doug when he found himself once again face-to-face with this new girl, Anna. She was in line at the concession stand with Tracy Hunt and a few other girls.

"We meet again," he said, greeting her.

She smiled and he was glad that she seemed happy to see him. He tilted his head toward the scoreboard.

"I assume someone already told you our team sucks?" he asked.

"Tracy told me," she said. "This has been hard to watch."

Hearing her name, Tracy jumped in.

"Hey, Cal," she said.

Doug gave Cal a light kick in the leg.

"Oh...Anna...this is Doug Fowler. Doug, Anna. She just moved her."

"Welcome. I moved here last year," Doug said. "From Oakland. You?"

"Kenosha, Wisconsin," she said.

Cal could see his friend trying to place it on a map.

"It's near the middle, dude," he said.

Doug replied with his common retort of, "Fuck you."

For Cal, seeing someone outside of school was always preferable to seeing them *at* school. He'd theorized that everyone, himself included, had a slightly different personality outside the hallways and classrooms of Crestview. Even at a school function like a football game people were a little different. He was curious to see if that was true with Anna.

"Did you go to football games back in Kenosha?" he asked her.

"Usually. Unless it was single digits out," she said. "Watching a game when it's freezing outside can be fun but also *not* very fun. It's considerably warmer here."

They got to the front of the concessions line and as Anna, Tracy, and their group were ordering Doug leaned into him.

"Do you want me to go find some other place to be?" Doug asked, keeping his voice down.

It was another reason he liked Doug. For all his struggles with academics, Doug always seemed to just get it on the social side, and wasn't shy about telling others to get lost if he wanted to try and talk to a girl at a party or in any other setting.

Cal hadn't even really thought of Anna that way or asked himself if he was interested in her or if maybe she was interested in him. For starters, they were both seniors and Cal hadn't tried to date anyone in his same grade since his freshman year. It just seemed easier to impress someone a year or two years behind him in school. Anna also seemed too smart for him. He didn't know her very well but it was easy to see she took school seriously. He'd learned to add up these factors quickly, like how old or how smart someone was, before he'd consider if he liked

27

them or imagined trying to ask them out. Anna didn't check any of his "pre-liking" boxes. But there was no getting around that she was pretty, and looked similar to every other girl he'd ever taken an interest in. She wasn't overdone with her hair or makeup; her light brown hair wasn't any more or less done up for a Friday night then it was at school. She was the kind of pretty or attractive that Cal associated with being down to earth, not too popular but not a weirdo or outcast, and, just as importantly, the kind of person that might like him back.

"I could catch up with you in a bit, I guess," he told Doug, hoping that his friend's absence might make it easier to talk to Anna.

"Don't fuck it up," Doug whispered. "And if you do…send her my way. Older girls always like me."

It would have been easier to laugh at or to just kick Doug for saying it if it wasn't true.

---

Anna was amused at how suddenly Cal's friend Doug had disappeared or wandered off to hang out with other friends on their way back from the concession stand. It was an exaggerated count but Anna figured it was at least the hundredth time she'd seen boys make such a move, all the while acting like they weren't doing it on purpose. Girls did it too, of course, but as freshman year turned to sophomore year and right on up to her final year she privately hoped such childish tactics or efforts would end. But there she was, new city, new school, and witnessing the same old playbook from the opposite sex.

But Cal *was* nice. She'd been trying to figure him out a bit and finally admitted it, writing in her journal at home that she at least wanted to know more about him. She traced it back to the spying over the fence and what little she'd learned of him since that day. She wrote, *I guess it's like the lost duck who sees another duck and just wants to follow it. This Cal guy was the first Crestview guy I really interacted with so maybe that's why I'm so curious?*

She knew he was a younger brother and she thought his older brother seemed like a bit of a jerk. So there was a level of invented sympathy and she was aware it was just that: Invented. But there it was just the same. And she'd observed that even if he was a little rough around the edges, dressing mostly in jeans and t-shirts, with his sandy brownish-blonde hair less kept than most, he was attractive. She thought he could be better looking if he upped his wardrobe with a collar or maybe some Dockers and did something a little different with that hair. She was usually more drawn to preppy guys and athletes but those types had always let her down. If nothing else, Cal didn't look like those types and she wondered if maybe that would make him different on the inside.

Cal sat beside her at the football game and they small talked amid the cheering and the chant-alongs from the cheerleaders. He got her up to speed on some of Crestview's unique cheers and was chatty without being flirtatious, which made her wonder if he was just bad at it or if he wasn't trying at all. She reminded herself a few times to stop overthinking, a habit she was constantly trying to break. She had managed to calm her brain down to even-paced thoughts instead of racing ones just before he asked her if she wanted to go walk the track at halftime.

She looked down at the field before answering and noticed many people doing the same. In Kenosha halftime was often a race for something warm to drink, so at least California was a little different in that regard.

"Sure," she said, turning to Tracy. "We're gonna take a walk, do you want anything from the snack bar?"

"Nope, I'm good," Tracy said. She raised her eyebrows suspiciously. Anna managed to not visibly blush, but it still made her feel self-conscious.

Once they were down at the track she opened the conversation with what felt like an obvious topic.

"So… AP English," she said. "Do you like it?"

"Yeah," he said. "I had Ms. Cook sophomore year so it's kinda cool to be back with her."

"Do you have other AP classes?"

"No," he said. "To tell you the truth I kind of surprised myself a bit when I tested into the class. You probably don't know everybody else in our class yet but pretty much everybody in there is AP everything. Chem, French, Spanish, math…I'm the only underachiever."

She stopped walking and pulled a bit at his arm.

"I'm afraid I can't be your friend," she said.

He looked hurt by the comment.

29

"I'm AP Chem, AP French, and AP Trig and I don't talk to underachievers."

He gave her a more serious look before slowly saying, "You don't talk to…"

She laughed, proud of herself for the joke.

"I'm kidding. Not about AP stuff. I am *in* those classes but I wouldn't call anyone who gets an AP class of any kind an underachiever," she said. "And you just said you took a test to get in. An underachiever doesn't even take the test."

"I suppose that's true," he said.

She could visibly see the relief come over him, which in turn made her own nerves settle down.

"So is English your favorite class?" she asked.

"One of them. I like my theater class a lot, too. And history is pretty good," he said. "Do you have Mr. J… Johnston?"

She shook her head.

"I have history with him and I also take Psychology from him," he explained.

"Oh, I wanted to take that but it was full!"

"It's fun," he said. "I thought it was going to be a bit more figuring ourselves out but we're learning about Freud and Jung and all these different theories for the first quarter. I guess we get into Mommy and Daddy issues later."

She laughed.

"How about you?" he asked. "What classes do you like?"

"So far I like our English class. And the French teacher is lively. You guys require three years of P.E. so I'm doing that because I only had two years back home."

She stopped herself.

"I mean back in Kenosha," she said. "I'm trying not to say 'home' so much. It just makes me miss it."

"I get it," he said. "I can't imagine being in your shoes… new school and as a senior…"

"It's been a little tough. I look around and I see all these well-defined groups of people who have been friends for years. I mean, everybody's been super nice… Tracy is fast becoming a good friend. But everything reminds me of my friends in Kenosha and it hurts."

"That makes sense."

"How long have you lived here?" she asked.

"Since 5th grade. But before that we moved like every 2 to 3 years because of my Dad's work. So I know how the new school thing feels...at least a little. But obviously it would be harder at our age."

"It is," she said. "But I just keep reminding myself that next year is going to be different no matter what, ya know? With college. Nothing lasts forever and high school was going to end either here or there. So I try to keep that in mind."

"Good approach," he said.

"Are you planning to go to college?" she asked.

"Yeah," he said.

She detected a hint of worry in his voice.

"I mean, I've got a few schools I'm going to apply to," he explained. "You?"

"A handful. University of Wisconsin, for sure. Northwestern is very high on my list," she said. "And then my parents want me to strongly consider some UC schools. Which ones are you looking at?"

"Sacramento State," he replied. "My parents want me to look there because my brother is at Davis and I guess they like the idea of two birds with one stone on visits or something. I might apply to Chico State, too."

He didn't sound excited. At least not as enthused as she would get when she talked about the prospects of the next year and continuing to college. She'd been dreaming of it since midway through junior high and it had only intensified in the years since, especially after she decided very early in 9th grade that she didn't like high school all that much.

"Anywhere else?" she asked.

He hesitated before answering.

"Have you ever heard of Southern Oregon State?" he asked.

"No," she admitted.

"No one has. I checked it out late last year when my theater class got to go to Ashland. It's this cool little city in Oregon. We saw these Shakespeare plays up there and toured the school and ...I don't know...I liked it. So I'm going to apply there, too."

"So a theater major?" she asked.

"No," he said quickly. "I'm not good enough at it. I like it but I know my limits, ya know what I mean?"

"Plus, it's hard to be an actor," she said. "So what are you going to study?"

"Sac has a good communications department. So does Southern Oregon, and they have a good English and writing thing, too," he said. "Mrs. Sheller has sent a few students there before and…"

"Mrs. Sheller is…?" she asked

"My guidance counselor. She told me that about once every 2 or 3 years she has a student that she thinks would be just perfect for Southern and--"

"And she thinks you're perfect for that school?" she asked.

"Yeah."

"That's awesome. Especially to have someone in your corner like that," she said.

The game was set to resume and as the teams took the field they headed back toward the bleachers.

"I'm actually going to go find Doug," he told her. "But…um…would you want to…get together sometime?"

"Like another walk?" she asked.

She knew what he was trying to ask but was trying to avoid it because she wasn't sure how she wanted to answer.

"Or maybe a movie or something?" he suggested.

"Are you asking me out?" she asked.

"If you put it that way then yes," he said.

She took a step closer to him along the stairs.

"I have an idea," she said. "I don't know if you know this, but I live in your neighborhood. And I liked this… our little walk. I haven't met that many people here and I like talking with you. You're really easy to talk to. How about we do that again sometime?"

"That'd be great," he said.

She wasn't sure if it would or wouldn't be, but she was glad to avoid the word 'date', at least for the moment.

# Chapter Two - November 1990

## *"Things She Said"*

At her insistence, Cal Sorenson promised he would not define, or at least try not to define, whatever it was they were. Not to himself, not to her, not to his friends or her friends, but to instead just let things be. She had tried to explain it to him after the end of their first long walk around Bell Ridge, the subdivision they both lived in.

"You said to me earlier the worst words in the English language for a guy are 'I just wanna be friends', right?" she asked.

He had said that during their walk while explaining his history of dates and brief relationships with the opposed sex.

"So, the opposite of that or the way to avoid the worst thing I can say to you would be to say we're something more than friends. But I don't know if I want that. And it's not about you because I *do* like you but I have to think there is something else in the middle of liking you as 'just a friend' or 'Okay, let's go out and be boyfriend and girlfriend'. Something that is not so black and white."

"I know I'm still getting to know you," he replied, "but I somehow doubt I am the first person to ever tell you that you think things through way too much."

"I think everyone our age thinks things through too *little*," she fired back. "Just look at what you've told me so far about some of the girls you've liked or dated and how that went. And I've seen it happen with so many of my friends, too. You meet a boy, you like him, he likes you, you go out for however long and then when it ends you either never talk again or you're mortal enemies."

"Is that what happened with the guy in Kenosha? Kyle, the boyfriend you told me about," he asked.

Cal was a bit intimidated by her story of her ex-boyfriend. This Kyle person sounded like a jock, and if that was her type he feared he'd never be to her liking.

"Kyle wasn't my enemy," she explained. "But, yes, he said some really hurtful things to people about me and it was all because I didn't want to be the kind of girlfriend he wanted."

"What kind of girlfriend did he want?" he asked.

He could see the question had made her uncomfortable, but she answered anyway.

"I didn't want to have sex," she said with a sigh. "I know it's like an 'After School Special' or a movie plot seen a zillion times, but I wasn't ready. I'm not ready. And in the end I felt like I hadn't even been a person to him. I was just someone he expected that if he was boyfriend-girlfriend with for a certain amount of time then we'd get to a point where we had sex. And when I told him there was never going to be that time he got really mean about it."

"And that's why you don't like to date people?" he asked.

"There's a lot of reasons I don't want to date people but that's one of them," she said. "I mean, be honest...isn't sex the end goal? To get a girl to go prom and then get a room and…"

Cal desperately wanted to lie. He wanted to tell her that not all guys were like that, but he knew *he* was like that. Maybe not the hotel room on Prom Night part but he did hope to have sex, sooner rather than later. He wasn't waiting for marriage and ideally he wouldn't even be waiting for college. But having rarely gotten to the steady girlfriend level with anyone, the idea of sex, while ever present, still seemed far off.

"It's not the *only* goal," was the best he could tell her.

"See? I'm right!" she exclaimed. "So let's say we start going out and then we wind up in that place and then what? I can tell you. You get frustrated because I won't change my mind and then somewhere down the line we both have all these bad feelings about each other. It's just a no-win situation and I hate that."

"So, you can't win at dating or win in having a boyfriend so you don't even try?" he asked.

"Basically, yes," she said.

"But then how am I ever gonna make you a mixtape?" he asked.

She laughed because she had confided in him what Tracy had told her about a mixtape he'd given Lizzie, a girl he'd gone out with for a few months the previous school year. It was embarrassing to hear it relayed from one girl via another but at least Anna had told him she thought it was more sweet than stupid.

"Can I ask you something about that?" she inquired. "About this, I don't know... reputation?... that you have for making mixtapes for girls?"

"I don't make them just for girls," he defended. He'd told her about the Mixtape Club he'd helped start. Within the club, a guy could, at least in theory, pull one of Cal's mixes from the grab bag, even though he always hoped they'd end up in the hands of a girl.

"Fair enough," she conceded. "But let me just see if I have this right in my head. You meet someone, you like them, you ask her out, she says yes, you go out for a bit and then at some point you make her a mixtape, right?"

He had to admit the pattern she described was not far off and it had been repeated more than once. Hearing someone else describe it, especially so quickly, was beginning to make him feel like a fool.

"I don't like this thread of conversation," he said, doing his best to laugh it away.

"It's a nice thing to do, Cal," she said, touching his shoulder.

He already knew he liked her beyond friendship but small gestures like that just reinforced it.

"But," she continued, "I guess what I really want to know is if it has ever really worked out?"

"I don't currently have a girlfriend so obviously not," he said.

"Okay. But let's say it did. Let's say you and I go out on dates and you make me some mixtape full of songs I fall madly in love with and right along with them I fall madly in love with you."

To Cal that sounded like a brilliant idea.

"And then we graduate," she continued. "We walk across the stage in our caps and gowns and maybe we spend a summer still being a couple. But then you go off to your school, I go off to mine and..."

He could see the point but didn't want to accept it.

"You skipped a lot of really good things in the middle of all that," he said.

"I did?"

"Yes. Like seeing a funny movie or going to a concert or, God forbid, Ball," he explained, adding with a smile, "But no hotel room."

35

"I like the movie part. And the concert part. Depending on the group," she said.

"And...and... I would probably make you more than one mixtape if we went out that long. Just sayin'."

She giggled. "Oh really?"

"I would! I mean, if nothing else it's Christmas next month and I make wicked good holiday mixes," he said.

"Ooh. I want one of those no matter what," she said

"Sorry, I only make them for girls I date," he teased.

"You mean girls that you give tapes to that eventually dump you, right?" she teased

"Ouch. That stings."

They walked back to her house and before going inside she turned to him.

"Here's what I want," she said. "I want us to agree to not have this kind of conversation over and over. Because I can see that happening, can't you?"

"I can," he admitted.

"And you've made it pretty clearly that you like me. And I am going to do something I never do or admit to myself. And that is to tell you I like you, too. As much as anyone I have met since I got here. I really like getting to know you. So, can we agree on that?"

"You mean not dating but still admitting we like each other and hanging out?" he asked.

"Yeah. I know that's hard because people see two people together and they gossip."

"They do," he said. "Especially at Crestview."

He didn't mind being the subject of gossip. There were times he'd craved it. But there was something about Anna and her early ability to call him out, to see every trick he thought he had, and get him to admit truths out loud he would previously only tell himself in private or write down in a notebook that he kept to himself.

"That's the thing though, Anna. Sooner or later Doug asks me about you or Tracy asks you about me and why we were sitting next to each other or we run into people at a movie and they just assume something, whether it's true or not."

"I know that," she said. "But I feel like after 3 years and counting of high school I'm really just over caring what other people talk about."

He knew he wasn't that person, so he didn't even try to agree.

"If anyone asks I guess I'll just say, 'None of your business'," he said

"Or maybe say nothing to them at all?" she suggested with a wide smile.

"I am not good at that. At all."

"Well, work on it," she said.

He went back home after their walk. He was laying on his bed listening to music and trying to not think about Anna and what she'd said to him when his mother knocked on his door.

"There's someone downstairs for you," she said, adding in a whisper, "Some girl."

He hated his mother in those moments.

"Why are you whispering, Mom?" he whispered back at her.

He went downstairs to find Anna standing in the entryway of the house. She motioned for him to come outside to the front porch.

"I thought of something," she said.

"What?" he asked. "What did you think of?"

"My Dad gives me and my sister rides to school on his way to work and it's a pain in the butt because Diablo is close to his work but Crestview is in a total opposite direction. So, they have been asking me for weeks if I could see if anyone in the neighborhood would carpool or give me a ride to school. And I know you have your own car..."

"Right," he said, gesturing toward the used Toyota pickup in the driveway his parents had given him for his 16th birthday.

"So, I thought you could give me a ride to school, and we can keep having these talks and get to know each other," she said. "And then if anyone asks anything about why we're 'together' so much we just say we're neighbors and you give me a ride. That's not unusual around here, is it?"

It wasn't. And he liked her idea. A lot.

"You are very smart," he said.

"I thought it was a very clever idea but I also really don't like being dropped off by my Dad."

"So I'll pick you up Monday morning at 7:30?" he asked.

"Yes. That would be perfect."

"Great, he said. "It's a date."

He stuck his tongue out at her.

She raised a fist and shook it at him playfully.

"You walked into that one, Anna," he said. "I'll see you on Monday."

--

What had seemed like a perfect solution to quell gossip and get to know a boy she had confessed to the pages of her journal she found "intriguing" turned out to be only half perfect. Spending 20 minutes or so each morning with him, longer if they stopped at this bagel shop he introduced her to, was definitely a good way to talk with him. She was learning things about him and him about her, at least when he turned the stereo down.

"I'm sorry," he explained on one of the first morning rides. "I'm used to this little commute time being when I just put some music on for the ride. Like a before school ritual."

She understood it and even liked the way he lit up a bit when he talked about music, most of which she'd never even heard of: Mother Love Bone, The Church, the Dogs D'Amour, and others. A lot of it was heavier or just stranger rock music than she would ever listen to on her own but she tried to have an open mind when he'd say, "Tell me what you think of this."

She learned quickly that he was a big fan of clever lyrics and wordplay.

*Hey babe, let the devil in*
*You're lookin' real good but maybe too thin*
*Oh, why take a look at the sky*
*There's a guy up there, yeah, he's just about to die*
*And as he falls*
*He falls from grace*
*There's a billion-dollar silence then somebody takes his place*

"They sound drunk," she said about that particular song.

"I read in a magazine they were pretty drunk when they made it," he explained.

She rolled her eyes.

He asked her early on what kind of music she liked and she was hesitant to even answer for fear of what he would think. He was obviously far more knowledgeable about bands, songs, and albums. But she had promised herself going into this new school and approaching 18 years old that she was done trying to be anyone other than herself. And that included the movies, TV, or music she liked or didn't like.

"I mostly like stuff I hear on the radio," she said. "My parents really don't like MTV, but I see some stuff on there, too. Kinda the usual pop stuff. Billy Joel, Richard Marx, Bon Jovi, Gloria Estefan..."

He didn't say anything in reply.

"You hate all that stuff, don't you?" she asked.

"Just the last one," he confessed. "I can't deal with Gloria Estefan. The rest are fine."

"Huh. You seem too much of a rock guy to like Billy Joel or Richard Marx," she observed.

"I love Billy. And Elton John and piano based stuff like that. But Richard Marx? I'm not crazy about him. I had a bad experience with Richard Marx," he said.

"*With* him?" she asked.

"Well, I don't mean with him literally. I took a date to see him at the Pavilion last summer."

"Of course you did," she said, rolling her eyes again. "And how was that?"

She was pretty sure she already knew the answer.

"It wasn't particularly good."

"Was the concert her idea?" she asked.

"More like my idea because she said she liked his music a lot and I liked her...so there ya go," he said.

"You're hopeless," she said.

"I just wanted to do something nice for her or do something she liked," he argued. "Is that a bad thing?"

"Oh, it's nice but..."

"But what?" he asked

"Have you ever thought that somewhere out there is a girl that also likes... I don't know..." She grabbed one of the cassette cases near his car stereo and looked at it for the name of the band. "Maybe a girl that likes Death Angel."

"That's Doug's tape, by the way. I'm not really that into them," he said.

"Well, let's pretend you were. And you met some girl who likes Death Angel. Wouldn't it be more fun to go see them in concert knowing you both liked them?"

"I'm actually kinda terrified of girls who like bands like that," he said. "I don't know if you've heard them but they're kinda like Metallica or Megadeth."

"So *you* like bands like that but if a girl likes them you're scared of her?"

"Yeah."

"And then I have to explain to you why I don't date. Do you realize how illogical that it is?" she asked.

"It's not illogical," he said. "It is not even about the music. I am happy to talk music with someone. I just don't like metal chicks because they usually smoke and get high and drunk."

"But you told me the other day you and Doug get drunk!" she said.

"But I don't smoke and I don't get high. Like ever."

She actually liked that about him a lot. She didn't know if it was a rare quality in California, but it certainly would have been in Wisconsin.

"Okay, so this band," she said, still holding the Death Angel tape. "They're a bad example but I think you get what I mean."

"I do. Like if Bon Jovi rolled through town maybe we would go together?"

She ignored his subtle hint at a date. He'd been pretty good with the little promise they'd made but every so often he'd slip up. And she knew she had done the same a time or two.

"I have only been to one concert ever," she said, "And it was super loud! I couldn't hear the next day."

"Who'd you see?" he asked.

"INXS. In Chicago. Aside from the volume Michael Hutchence was *so* hot."

"*Kick* is a truly great good album," he added.

"But you understand what I mean, right?" she asked, trying to get back to her original point. "You should like someone you have things in common with and not to try to force yourself to enjoy Richard Marx just to impress a girl any more than I should try to appease someone by doing something I don't want to."

"That makes sense," he said.

She liked to challenge him. Or, as her mother liked to remind her, she liked to challenge *everyone*. But she enjoyed that Cal would ask questions right back that made her think beyond easy answers. On their third day of riding together to school, when he introduced her to the Phil-a-Bagel shop, he randomly asked her about coffee after she didn't order one, opting instead for orange juice.

"Do you not drink coffee at all or do just not drink coffee daily or very often?" he asked.

"I tried it a few years ago because I was getting up so early," she explained. "I had Zero Period... I think Crestview school calls it 'A Period'? I was up super early both sophomore and junior year and my Mom had me try some coffee. And it was okay. But a part of me just looks at it like something my parents do. Like it's not for me yet. And the last time I had some I got ridiculously jittery. I get rather anxious anyway if you haven't noticed yet."

"I've noticed," he said, rather dryly. "So what else are things that are 'for your parents' or something they do that you don't want to do?"

It was a tough question but she liked it. He was good at coming up with challenging questions. Some strange ones, too, but she didn't mind. His quirkiness was part of the appeal, and a strange attraction that sometimes was hard for her to ignore.

"I don't want to do something that seems like it puts people against each other," she said. "I mean, for a living. My Dad is a liability attorney and I don't know if you know what that is but a lot of it is defending a company that may have hurt someone or a group of people, either by accident or on purpose, and it gets pretty contentious."

"What else?" he asked.

"I wouldn't want to uproot my family from a good life just for a lot of money," she said. "I really liked my life back home in Kenosha."

She thought about her friends back home, not catching herself in referring to it as "home" and wondered what they might be up to. Every time that would happen, usually in private, it would make her sad and sometimes make her cry. Sitting in the front seat of his car she fought it off as best she could but some tears rolled out anyway. And he noticed.

"I'm sorry if I said something to upset you," he said.

"It's not your fault," she said, embarrassed. "I just miss my friends."

"I'm sure they miss you, too," he said.

"I guess."

"What do you mean you guess? Of course they must miss you! You're a really cool person. I feel awful that you're crying but I am also kinda glad you moved here. In a selfish way, of course," he said.

"That's nice of you to say," she said quietly, wiping a tear with her jacket sleeve. "I guess I always figure they still have each other so they might notice I'm gone. They might miss me a little but then it's like the way a circle might lose a section, the rest of it just closes in and reconnects. The circle is a little smaller but it's still a circle. And I'm out here. With no circle."

They'd reached the school parking lot and she was still crying.

"Can we sit here a few minutes until I can pull it together?" she asked.

She watched as he looked out the window and observed people walking by. People who knew him waved and he gave little waves back.

"Sure. We can stay in here," he said. "But, umm...people walking by and seeing us talking and you're crying... they may not think we're dating but they might think we just broke up."

She laughed, which she needed and appreciated.

"I'm just saying... it's not a good look for us, Anna. I'm going to be this asshole that made you cry. People are gonna talk. You're ruining my nice guy rep!"

She knew he was joking around but with an element of truth. Tracy had already asked a few questions about Cal and even her mother wanted to know at least a little about this boy she was getting rides to school with.

She took a deep breath to compose herself before reaching for her backpack to get out.

"Do I look like I've been crying?" she asked, still dabbing her eyes.

"A little," he replied. "If anyone asks, tell them I played a really sad song for you and it got you right in the sweet spot.

"What song?" she asked. "I'm not good at lying so if I'm going to do it I need some specifics."

42

He looked up and thought about it. She got a mental image of a jukebox inside his head and the imagery of it made her smile.

"'Joey' by Concrete Blonde," he finally said.

"I've never even heard of it," she said, again wondering how he had time to discover all the music he seemed to know.

"Trust me. It's super sad. This woman is singing about being in love with a hopeless alcoholic and it's kinda gut wrenching."

"Sounds like a real Top 40 hit," she joked.

"In a just world it would be," he said. "But not too many people know that song so you can just say that and they won't know you're lying. Or at least they won't question it. Or they'll think you've been hanging out with me too much. Or all of that."

She repeated the song and the name of the group in her head for memory.

She walked into school and found Tracy and some other friends in the locker rows. No one noticed her slightly puffy eyes from her parking lot cry or asked a single thing about them.

---

Under almost any other circumstances Reed would have spent their 6th period drama class peppering Cal about what was going on with Anna. It had come up more than once since he'd met her and it was part of a long-standing dynamic Cal had grown used to with Reed. Reed didn't go to parties on the weekends, so he'd often ask Cal about some party he might have gone to. Despite a less than stellar track record Cal had still managed to go on more dates than Reed, so Reed would ask a lot of questions about that, too. At times he felt like Reed was trying to live through him vicariously. But by Senior year he'd figured out Reed truly felt uneasy or intimidated about certain things, especially parties or gatherings where some of the more popular kids would be. He once explained to Cal that a fair number of what he called "the jocks" went as far back as elementary school with him. And a few used to relentlessly tease and bully him. explained to Call that a fair number of what he called "the jocks" went as far back as elementary school with him and a few used to relentlessly tease and bully him. Cal considered himself 'casual friends' with those same guys, having earned at least some sort of social

43

credit with them for the one year of JV football he'd played as part of a fruitless effort to try and raise his own popularity. From their behavior on the field and especially in the locker room Cal could easily imagine a younger version of them being vicious or cruel, so when Reed shared his experiences he believed every word. But overall, he thought, most of those guys had matured or were generally nice, just with different interests and different inside jokes.

"I know I should let it go," Reed explained, "but I don't know if I will ever feel comfortable around some of them. Or forgive a few of them."

Cal had tried to help him get over it in the best way he could think of: Taking him along to a big party. But within 5 minutes Reed became so uncomfortable he eventually retreated to the car to listen to music. After that Cal never tried again and just accepted that on most weekends he and Reed would part to different circles of friends that didn't have a lot of crossover. They'd never really talked about the dynamic and Cal just assumed they were both cool with it. Or, as he once said to Reed, "I won't judge you and some of the other guys for still playing *Dungeons and Dragons* on a Friday night if you don't give me any shit for going to a school dance or some party and getting my heart broken because some girl turned me down."

After the morning crying-in-the-car episode with Anna, Cal was grateful that her name wasn't likely to come up for at least one afternoon. Like Reed and everyone else in Advanced Drama he knew that particular day was when the cast list was going to be posted for *Twelve Angry Jurors*, a mixed cast adaptation of the play *Twelve Angry Men* that they'd be producing for the Fall Play. As seniors, it would be their last drama production and come Spring they'd be doing their last comedy. It had been a tense round of auditions because while 12 parts was a big cast there would be, by their teacher Mr. Deroy's decree, 6 female roles and 6 male roles. Cal wanted a part, any part, but he knew Reed wanted one of the two larger roles; either the "lone juror" protagonist that is the sole 'Not Guilty' vote at the start of the story, or the antagonist holdout, bigoted juror that eventually comes around. The other 10 parts all had plenty of lines and there were some strong supporting roles but the two lead roles were obvious.

Mr. Deroy's students often joked that their beloved teacher and director could have been a professional card player given how few hints he ever gave about what he was looking for in casting. In three years of class and in getting three parts along the way Cal had never once been able to guess in advance the role he was ultimately chosen for. Neither had most of his classmates. So when the cast list went up and Reed saw that he had, in fact, gotten the role of the antagonist it was all he wanted to talk about. Cal was cast as Juror #1, the foreman, which was a modest role but he was happy he'd get to be in it. Everyone in class was always a little jealous of those that got larger roles and Cal was no exception. He was envious of his friend but happy for him just the same. Reed had wanted it more.

"You get to play the bad guy," Cal said. "The racist, mean asshole bad guy."

It was hard to picture because on the surface it didn't seem to fit Reed very well at all. He was all of 5' 7", not terribly muscular or athletic, and it was hard to imagine him as being domineering or as imposing as the script seemed to call for.

Cal turned to Reed and said, "I'll bet you $5 Mr. Deroy asks you to read up on Napoleon or go watch some movie with a villain who's short."

He also chuckled a bit when he saw who was playing the "good" juror: Natalie O'Ryan, a junior who without question was a very good actress but also a had a reputation for knowing she was that good and for being "a bit of a bitch"; a phrase Cal himself had used more than once to describe her. If nothing else being in the play would be fun just from watching Reed trying to be horrible and Natalie trying to be noble.

With the cast now revealed and his new script in hand, Cal looked around his drama class, observing the familiar ritual where everyone did the delicate balance of congratulating those who got parts or being happy they had landed a part, all while not being too celebratory and trying to be considerate of those who might be disappointed. He felt particularly bad for some of his fellow seniors who weren't cast because in the months ahead there was only going to be one more shot at it; one more chance to get the kind of role they always wanted. He was thinking about that when he congratulated Natalie. He felt jealous of her, far more jealous than he was of Reed, even though he knew he could never play either role. But Natalie was a year behind them. She'd get to keep doing these things, the auditions, and the long rehearsals on weeknights and right into weekends. She'd still get to see the sets come together and do the group outings to Goodwill and Salvation Army to find costumes and props on a shoestring budget, all while goofing off and trying on things that had nothing to do with the play they were producing. Wallpaper pants from the 70's, feather boas from God knows where, the ugliest of ugly shoes. He knew the jealous feelings were irrational because Natalie or any of the other juniors and sophomores weren't going to get any more time than he'd had. It was all perfectly fair and he knew that but it didn't stop him from feeling like it was slipping away.

As that dose of reality was hitting him he turned his attention back to Reed.

"Playing an angry racist is not going to help your love life," Cal joked.

"But he does ultimately vote 'not guilty' and sees he was wrong, right?" Reed said.

"Sure. After threatening to kill a fellow juror and referring to the defendant as 'one of those people'," Cal said.

"Oh God, there's that."

"On the bright side it's a lead!" Cal reminded him. "I'm super pissed at you because I know you'd be pissed at me but I'm also happy for you, man. I know it's what you wanted."

Want and what he wanted had been on Cal's mind entirely too much in recent days. When it wasn't centered on things like "Anna as a girlfriend" it was around the oncoming train of college applications and essays and the growing tension at home from his parents. They were telling him things like "You can go to any school you get into" and "We want you to make your own decision", all while playing up Sacramento State. It made sense why they were doing it. His brother Tyler was at Davis, his father had done his Masters at Sacramento way back when, and his mother had ultimately graduated from there after transferring from Humboldt decades before. Sacramento was an hour and a half away, far enough to still be "going away to school" but nearby and safe. He knew some of his classmates were planning to go there assuming they got in, so there would be familiar faces around. But every time he thought about college Ashland and Southern Oregon State would find its way into his thinking. Southern Oregon was a good 5 to 6 hours away, he didn't know a single person with that school on their application list, and the idea of going there came with fluctuations between excitement of going someplace far away and the worry that it might be too far, that he might be too alone if chose that place. He had known from Mrs. Sheller's warnings and even from Ty's recollections that the entire process -- applying, waiting for acceptance or rejection, and deciding where to go -- would be stressful. But Cal had imagined it would also be thrilling, to know and to plan for this big, exciting future and next steps and all these things his parents and teachers and class assemblies had been selling him for years. It wasn't feeling that way. It was more scary than inviting.

It was only early November but with all the talk of college and the future it was hard to see something like his last fall play as anything other than the beginning of a series of ends. The 'last times' for things like that were piling up one after the other and it was beginning to hit him, sometimes quite hard. He knew he didn't want to pursue theater in college but saying goodbye to it in high school began to feel very real. Even the thrill of getting a part in *Twelve Angry Jurors* was bittersweet. He started thinking about the Thornton Wilder comedy they'd done the Spring before and the Chekhov play they'd done the year before that and how the last night of the Spring Comedy run, despite the laughs on stage, was always full of tears behind the scenes. It was the traditional last hurrah for seniors. He'd seen it happen, had cried with the soon-to-be-graduates he'd gotten to know so well, that felt like family, all the while knowing that someday it'd be him and Reed and others in their shoes. Mr. Deroy would always say that graduating seniors became "ghosts" within the Crestview Theater. He would get sentimental about it.

"You are surrounded by ghosts in here," he'd say, motioning around the school theater and the backstage area. "Past students who literally helped build parts of the stage you're standing on. People who worked as hard as you are working, finding their best voice and talent. Some of them work in other theaters now or have written plays or screenplays or appeared on TV or in movies. You're a part of something here and you will still be part of it even after you graduate."

Cal sat in one of the theater seats, with his feet propped up on the back of one in front of him, highlighting his lines in the *Twelve Angry Jurors* script. His mind wandered and he imagined himself as an actual ghost, floating around the theater. It was the place he always felt most comfortable in at Crestview. No matter how bad any given day could be, whether it was a low grade or some girl rejecting him, for three years straight there was always his 6th period. He could count on the end of the day usually being better than anything that came before it.

He flipped through the script with his highlighter, making notes with a pencil at various points. As he often did in any class he jotted down random words or phrases, sometimes the lyrics of songs he knew or quotes from a movie or TV show. And sometimes he'd scribble down his own original thoughts or a poem. On the inside cover of his new script he wrote:

> *If this is the last part then this is the best part.*
> *I don't know the next one, can't think that far.*
> *Whatever comes next is sure to break my heart.*

---

It was very rare for Anna to find herself in trouble or on the wrong side of her parents. She'd never been grounded, had never had privileges like using the car revoked, and her parents usually said "Yes" more than "No" when she wanted to go out with friends, so long as they knew where she was going and what time she was expected home. Her curfew had been 11pm during her Junior year and with Senior year they bumped it up to 11:30, and she even managed to negotiate it up to midnight. Even then her curfew always came with the caveat that if she was going to be late she needed to call and "you'd better have a good reason, like a flat tire or you're getting someone else home safe."

When it came to boys and dating they'd been a little stricter, insisting on meeting any would-be suitor before she could leave the house and, unlike hanging out with friends, they wanted an itinerary. A movie would come with questions of "What movie and what time is it showing and where?" Going bowling or ice skating meant, "What rink or alley?" Before Kyle there had only been two other boys who had to come into her house and met her parents to receive the greenlight for her to go out. With Kyle they not only approved but after a few months of dating her father even confessed that he liked Kyle.

"My preference would still be to lock you in your room on the weekends and then hide the room but your mother tells me that these days we don't do that sort of thing," he joked.

Kyle won her father over one afternoon when, without even so much as a request or an ask, he stepped in to assist with putting up Christmas lights. They considered Kyle polite, smart, knew he was a good athlete, and treated their daughter with respect. Anna knew at least some of what her parents believed about him was true. They didn't see him when he got frustrated with her not wanting to do more than kiss and touch. They didn't see the argument at a party that was the catalyst for breaking up; when he got drunk and called her a "prudish bitch" in front of a dozen people. When she told her parents she and Kyle broke up her father said, "I am both relieved and disappointed. I always worry about you with boys because I was one, but Kyle seems like a good young man."

She wanted to disagree when he said it, to tell him or her Mom the truth, but that would mean telling them things they didn't know or wouldn't want to know. The want and need to keep such things private had clashed more than once in moments where she was upset, especially after their breakup. At times she wanted to burst into tears and have one or both of her parents hold her and remind her no one should ever talk to her that way. But that level of honesty didn't really come to light. Instead it was being respectful of her parents enough to meet curfew, greet them if they were awake, and then taking whatever she was feeling to her bedroom and letting it out in her journal or maybe on the phone with her best friend, Eileen.

Ultimately there was not much Anna could do to upset her parents. She had excellent grades, did most of what was asked of her in terms of chores and responsibilities around the house, never argued or tried to resist when they went to church on Sundays, and only occasionally got scolded for saying something critical or mean to her younger sister. When she'd reached 13 she began babysitting for neighbors, at 15 she got a summer job at a Sizzler, and later became a junior counselor for summer day camps. Even Anna herself would say her parents should be proud of her and they were. But the move to California had raised the friction level, with Anna feeling like no one else in her family was experiencing the kind of upheaval she was.

She was doing homework when her father called for her to come downstairs. She knew his various tones of voice; cheery or at least specific if it was a call to come down for dinner or to help with something. Sometimes a request would sound more like a question if he needed clarification about something. By 17 and having seen enough movies with lawyers in them she had concluded these different tones and approaches to conversations were her Dad in what she dubbed "attorney mode". His tone that day was angry, so she rushed downstairs.

"I was doing bills and I wanted to know why…." he paused for effect, "there is a huge bill for a late-night long-distance call to Kenosha?"

Anna, despite rarely needing to try, had learned she was not a good liar. More accurately, she knew when there was no way to make an excuse that her parents would believe. The phone call in question fell into that category.

She took a deep breath.

"I'm sorry. A few weeks ago I was really homesick and I couldn't sleep so I called Eileen and I know we talked too long," she said.

"Yes, you did. Over an hour, Analisa."

When her father was upset or disappointed it was always Analisa instead of Anna.

"I'm sorry," she said.

"Have we not let you or your sister make some short calls to friends *when you ask*?"

"You have," she said.

Her father let out a long sigh.

"Calls like that are not cheap, Anna."

"I'll pay you guys back," she offered.

"That isn't the point and you know it," he said.

She was trying to be apologetic and accountable but in her mind she was thinking how stupid it was for him to be so upset about the money part because, after all, the entire move had been about his job with a bigger firm, which meant a lot more money, the bigger new house they were in, and the "'better life and better opportunities" they had mentioned a thousand times. There had been many explanations for why they were moving her entire life 2000 miles.

"I am sorry," she said again.

"If you wanted to call Eileen all you had to do was ask. There are times of day when it's way cheaper to make such calls," he explained

"I know. You've explained that before," she said.

"So why call at...." he looked down at the bill, "10pm? Not to mention it being so late in Kenosha?"

She had known all that when she made the call but Eileen, like some of her other friends, had her own phone line so the late hour hadn't even entered Anna's thinking.

"It was dumb and irresponsible," she said, continuing with her strategy to be accountable and apologetic. "I can pay you back or not make any more calls if that helps."

"I just need you to be responsible," he said. "You're going to need to do more and more of that next year and beyond. Trust me on that."

She nodded and he gave her a look that indicated she could leave and go back to her room.

The full story she didn't tell him about that call and that night made her feel childish and a bit ashamed. It was in early October, after the first few weeks in her new school, and on that particular Saturday night the height of her teenage excitement had been popping *Steel Magnolias* into the VCR and watching it with Jackie for the dozenth time while her parents were out to dinner with one of her Dad's new colleagues. She didn't hate Crestview or anything and felt like she was making some new friends but on the Friday heading into that weekend Tracy and some others had referenced a party they were going to, and even though parties were not Anna's favorite thing she still hoped someone in the group might ask her if she wanted to come along. When no one did she began to question if her new friendship with Tracy or anyone else was real or if the various invitations to games or some other outings had just been an initial courtesy or kindness. Did these new people really like her? Questions like that ran through her head that Saturday night as she sat and watched the movie, cried at the parts that always made her cry, and thought of what her friends in Kenosha might be doing, knowing that whatever it was she would be doing it right along with them if she were there. She tried to stop thinking about it, to focus on the movie, and after that by reading a book in her room. She even double checked her schoolwork, which was not typical for a Saturday night, but she was all caught up. By 10 she was in her room crying. And when she thought about it being midnight in Kenosha and knowing Eileen, her best friend, had an 11:30 curfew, it would likely mean she was home. So she called. Eileen was just getting ready to go to sleep but was so happy to hear her voice that she stayed up and talked. A conversation that had ended with, "I love you, my friend. And it's going to be okay. Next year we'll be at Northwestern or UW and it'll all be okay."

It was exactly what Anna had needed.

In the minutes after her father confronted her with the bill, she grew angry all over again, frustrated with him at a level she wasn't used to because they had always been a pretty close father-daughter pair. But ever since the move she'd been upset in ways she wasn't used to, over and over, fluctuating back and forth between feeling justified for her anger and then feeling childish or selfish for it. But as she grabbed her journal to write about the events of the day, including his being upset over the phone bill, she surprised herself by whispering, "Fuck him", and from there her pen moved quickly across the page.

*I have tried and tried and even when things are good I don't feel like I belong here. The people here are nice enough but why would they really want to bring someone new into their lives? If I were them I wouldn't be eager to spend that kind of time and energy with a new friend. It's hard enough knowing we're all going to be going our separate ways from people we've been friends with for years! And it's not their fault. I think about Tracy and how if we had more time we could probably be as close as I am with Eileen but then what? Same thing with Cal. I hate that I met him NOW! Where was this strange, sweet guy in Kenosha? If we'd moved here a year ago I'd have said yes when he asked me out. I'd have been curious instead of scared. Most of the time I wish I could just fast forward and skip over all of it. It's so much easier to just think about where I'll be in a year because no matter what I'm going to get in somewhere, right?*

*So I think that's what I need to remember: Stay focused on college. Get my applications in and make my essays the best they can be. Hopefully once I get that done and then get my acceptances (please no rejections!) I can make a decision. Then maybe, just maybe, this won't all feel so empty.*

--

Cal's family had lived in their Bell Ridge house since moving to Concord in the 5th grade. The half basketball court had been in the side yard since the very first day. He had taken countless shots, played hundreds of games against Tyler and even his older sister, Rachel, a few times, along with dozens of friends. It had been the center of birthday parties when he was in grade school, a major source of competition in middle school whenever his mother would insist he and his friends get off Nintendo and play outside, and it had been host for a memorable "Drunk Dunk" contest when Cal had thrown a high school party while his parents were away for their anniversary. In all of that he had never stopped to really assess his own basketball skills or care all that much about it. That was until he found himself in a game of H.O.R.S.E. against Anna.

"I've secretly been wanting to play ever since I looked over that fence last month," she confessed.

She had told him the story of spying on him and his brother. It had become a recurring joke as they'd gotten to know each other.

As she took a shot she said, "Can I ask you something?"

It was something she said a lot before asking a question, a trait Cal had noticed but had not commented on. He was sure she wasn't conscious she was doing it and he didn't want to make fun of her. And it was also cute.

"You can ask me whatever I might want to answer," he said back.

"How can you have this hoop in your yard," she began, then taking her shot and sinking it, "and still absolutely *suck* at basketball?"

She stuck her tongue out at him.

"I don't know. Lack of height?" he offered.

She shook her head.

"You're about 5' 10". Granted, that's not tall but it's not short and it's no excuse," she said. "Just look at Spud Webb."

He had no idea who she was talking about, as sports in his home were tied to his 49er's fanatic mother and his Dodger fan father. Cal casually liked both football and baseball, was the only hockey fan in his family, and never really got into the NBA.

"Maybe a lack of caring?" he offered next.

"I guess it's that," she said. "Too bad. Guys look sexy in basketball shorts."

He hated it when she would say things like that. It was flirty and teasing, all in the face of the promise he'd made her to just let things be, to not inquire with her about what was ultimately going on between them. They were riding to school together every morning, sometimes they drove home together, they'd sat together at two more football games, he'd introduced her to Tower Records, and they had rented movies together. He'd met her parents and they seemed to like him just fine, and she'd met his folks a few times, too.

His mother had begun to ask him about her, adding comments like, "I think she is a just lovely young woman" or questions like, "So are you two a couple"?

He had no answer to that, even if he'd wanted to share such information with her, which he didn't. Nor could he give answers to people like Reed or Doug, who asked him the same question regularly.

"Are you trying to tell me I might have a better shot with you if I played basketball?" he asked.

He figured since she had flirted at least a little with her basketball shorts comment it was fair to throw a question like that at her.

"First of all," she said, taking another shot at the net, "You clearly have *no* shot when it comes to basketball…"

Again, she stuck her tongue out at him, amused by her own joke.

"And second," she continued, "it's not about anything you do or don't do or who you are or aren't. I've actually been thinking about this. And I've concluded it's about timing."

"Because we're seniors?"

"Yes. And also because you're the first guy I've really met here," she said.

That felt like at least a small opening to promote himself.

"Every other guy at our school sucks, Anna. I'm as good as it gets."

"Well, if that's true then I'm going to be a nun," she shot back quickly.

They both laughed and she sat down with her back against the side of the house.

"It's not that I would want to… I don't know… play the field," she said, "Or see who else is out there or whatever you want to call it. I just…and this is going to sound terrible… but I don't want to get attached to anyone here because I think I might want to go to school in Chicago or even back in Wisconsin at Madison. If you and I become a thing then it could start to influence my decisions. Like maybe I apply to Davis because I know you might be in Sacramento or something like that."

He was shocked by the admission. Nothing about Anna had led him to believe she would ever make him or anyone else that big a priority in her life, particularly in connection to college, which he knew was very important to her.

"I can't imagine you doing that," he said. "I've known people who've done that… picked a school because it was close to their boyfriend or girlfriend. My friend T.J.…. he graduated last year and went to Pepperdine because his girlfriend was at USC. He did it even though he'd always talked about going to school back east."

"And what happened to him?" she asked.

"When I saw him at the homecoming game last month he said they broke up. She met someone in her dorm like the 2nd week of school," he explained.

"See?! That's why high school relationships are dumb," she said.

Everything about her arguments were logical and yet none of them cooled his desire to be more than friends with her. Everything between them was so easy and relaxed. He'd never found talking to a girl so simple and natural, or at the very least not someone he was attracted to. It was like hanging out with Reed or Doug, though with less respective neurosis and swearing. He had other female friends, even some he had been attracted to at one point or another and a few he'd even been on dates with. But with those girls the friendships had been something he'd come to accept after something else failed. With Anna nothing felt fully defined.

He tried to come up with a counter argument for her declaration that any kind of romance between them would be foolish but he knew he was dancing on a thin line in talking about it at all. He'd made a promise to not have that conversation.

His mother called from around the corner of the house, informing them she was getting dinner started and inquired if Anna would like to stay and join them, which would be a first.

Anna looked at him for some kind of stamp of approval.

"That'd be cool," he said before calling to his mother to say 'Yes'.

55

They stood back up to play one more game. It occurred to him that no girl, not anyone he'd dated or even someone that was just a friend, had ever come over for dinner. Studying, listening to music, or playing Nintendo in his room? A few girls had done some or all those things. Anna had done all of them, too, and he'd known her less than 2 months. In every other way she felt like a girlfriend but the exceptions were obvious. He'd held her hand exactly one time, while she was crying in the front seat of his car. Nothing else like that had happened between the two of them. Not even close. As he thought about that he began to wish she wasn't staying for dinner after all, not because it wouldn't be fun or something he'd enjoy, because it would be. But it was also the kind of thing he always hoped would come with having a lasting girlfriend. Anna wasn't that person and it was beginning to sink in that no matter how much he wished she was, it wasn't going to happen. And despite all her perfectly good reasons and logic he couldn't help feeling she wasn't telling him the whole truth; that she was sparing his feelings and that one of her reasons had to be because she just didn't like him "that way". He'd heard many variations of the "I like you but I just don't like you that way" speech in the past and he couldn't shake that he was eventually going to hear Anna's version of it

# Chapter Three - December 1990

## *"Somebody's Falling"*

The disagreement was spirited and even though the subject at hand seemed a bit trivial, Anna loved arguing with him. She would regularly think back to the first time she talked with Cal, stemming from *The Great Gatsby* discussion in class. In the short time since she'd come to love their back and forth over TV shows and music or, as they exited the theater to go home, a movie they had just seen together. He thought it was hilarious. She laughed a lot, too, but still thought the film was way too over the top.

"First of all, his parents were unrealistically dumb," she said. "Are you trying to tell me every last person they knew within a few miles of their house was out of town?"

"They said the phones were down on their street," he said, reminding her of part of the movie's explanation.

"Okay, fine. But I can tell you as someone from the Midwest, winter storms do not knock out every phone line in a 10-mile radius," she said. "They could have called someone and said, 'Hey, we screwed up and left Kevin behind. Can you please go check on him and let him stay with you until we can get back?'"

"I think you're taking it all a little too seriously," he said. "It's a comedy."

"I know. And I laughed a lot. You heard me. But I just can't get over stuff like that. These people have a huge house and all this money and they're too stupid to just stop and think it through for 5 minutes?" she asked.

"Anna, if they do that then there's no movie. There's no crooks and the kid setting them on fire and all that."

"Which is another thing! Those guys aren't getting up over and over from all that stuff," she argued. "They'd be in a coma or dead!"

She could see Cal roll his eyes as they were driving.

"Do you break down *Tom and Jerry* cartoons this way? Because if you do I fear you're really missing out on the fun," he said.

Anna knew one of her problems or flaws was that once she got her opinion entrenched she would just dig in deeper. He was right about *Home Alone* and she knew she was being too literal with her criticisms but even knowing that she didn't want to back down, mostly because she found it so much fun to debate it.

"First, you're comparing a cartoon to real people," she said. "Second, I'm willing to overlook that this Kevin kid would have to be an engineer or professional assassin to pull off what he did because that part was super funny. I just had a hard time getting over that we're supposed to believe these people with a big beautiful house that usually comes from being successful are so dense that they can't correctly count their kids or know how to call and send someone over to rescue him."

"You're assuming people with money are smarter than people who don't have money," he said. "That makes you a snob."

He laughed along with his assertion.

"Says the boy who lives in a nice house with his own basketball court and a hot tub in the backyard," she fired back. "You're not exactly poverty stricken, Cal."

She knew he was just giving her a hard time and had become more and more comfortable giving some back. Their conversation coming out of the movie was not much different than the ones they'd been having on the way to school five mornings a week. Everything was up for debate: Popularity and whether it makes life easier, whether college would be worth it or not, what kind of music was good and what kind wasn't. She was happy that at the very least they had gotten off discussing the pros and cons of dating.

"You live in the same neighborhood I do," he said. "If you're saying my family has money then so does yours. And I'm sure you've figured out by now that some people at Crestview have even *more* money."

She had. It took a few weeks to figure it all out but the more she'd heard some of her new classmates talk about vacations they'd been on, where they were heading for Christmas, or even what kind of graduation gifts they were looking forward to in June the more it sank in.

"My Dad is definitely making more now than he did in Kenosha," she said. "He doesn't pretend otherwise. I'm personally still waiting for *my* car."

She followed it with an obvious cough, signaling what they were driving in.

"Hey now," he said. "I didn't ask for this car. They asked me about it because they told me I'd have to help with the insurance and cover my gas and all that. And I paid for the stereo myself."

"Woo," she said. "No wonder you always make sure I lock the door."

"Tyler got his stereo stolen last year," he said. "I'm just protecting my investment."

"Your investment? I love that you think of your Kenwood tape deck that way," she said.

"And the speakers," he added.

She could see the smile curl up on his face.

"I think the biggest thing at Crestview is how many people there don't even recognize that their families are really well off," she said. "I know my family isn't hurting or anything close to that but I do think I can at least see the difference because more money is still kind of new to me, ya know?"

"I get ya," he said. "I've gotten used to whatever it is we have because it's always been there. I honestly didn't even figure out that the reason we moved 3 times in seven years was because my Dad kept taking promotions and being transferred and all of it was because of money."

"I think that's why this has been so weird for me," she said. "Obviously moving as a senior is not ideal for any reason but I never really thought of my Dad as being... ambitious? He's always worked hard but when he told us we were moving and why I thought it was...I don't know..."

"Unfair?" he asked.

"A little," she said, trying to find the right word. "This is going to sound awful but I also thought it was a little greedy. Kind of like 'Don't you think we have enough? Is it really so important to take this job in California?'"

"My father said to me a few weeks ago that the main thing with college is to get a degree in something where you can make a really good living," Cal said.

"Hmm. I can imagine my Dad saying the same thing," she replied. "And it's not that I don't want to do well because if I go into biology it's so I can do something in the medical field and doctors do pretty well for themselves. So maybe that *is* what it's about."

He was quiet, which was something she noticed would happen when he seemed to be daydreaming or truly thinking about something she'd said. Kyle had never been like that. Anna's mother had observed that Cal seemed like a "dreamer". She didn't necessarily say it as a compliment but Anna had noticed when he could get lost in thought. If Cal was looking straight ahead while he drove it wasn't just his concentrating on traffic.

"My Dad told me that...about the college and money thing...after I told him I wanted to write," he said. "He was asking me about what I'd want to do after college... like if I pursue the writing program in Oregon."

"And what'd you say?" she asked.

He shook his head and chuckled.

"I told him I want to write for a magazine or a newspaper. Or maybe biographies about musicians and bands. Album reviews or maybe movies or concerts, things like that."

"That is exactly what I can imagine you doing," she said.

"Me too," he said. "But my Dad was, like, 'You'll never make much money in that.'"

What he said made her sad. For all her recent frustrations with her parents, particularly her father, they had never discouraged her from things she wanted to do. If anything they pushed her. She had forgotten or never even asked herself which thing came first: Her parents championing her efforts to get into the hardest classes or her own ambitions to take on those classes. Her going to college was never a question. It was a given. It was also a goal and one they were supportive of for as long as she could remember. When she told them she wanted to pursue science with an eye toward medicine they said things like, "That'll be a lot of schooling but it'll be worth it" or "That's a competitive field and you'll have to work very hard" but there was never any doubt in their words.

"Does it matter to you?" she asked. "Whether you make money or not? Or is it just about enjoying what you're doing?"

"I guess I want both," he said. "I want to do what I like and I want to be able to make some money doing it. I just know I can't see myself doing what my Dad does. Long commute, big office building, suits and ties… all that."

"So your career path is about staying in jeans and t-shirts?" she asked, trying to lighten the mood a little.

"I don't know. Maybe a coat but no tie, like Kurt Loder on MTV or something," he said. "But if interviewing Madonna means I need to wear a suit then I'll wear a suit."

"Madonna? Is that the dream interview?" she asked, amused that he named that pop star of all pop stars.

"Not really. But I guess that's where my ambition would be. Like, if you're going to write about music then aim for the big names. Madonna, Prince, Bono. But it'd probably be more fun to write about bands that no one knows about yet. I don't know. I just want to be able to be excited about what I do."

"Hmmm," she said. "I'll say this for my Dad. He does love the law. He gets very excited when he's working. I like that about him. And I'm sure it makes me a big nerd but I like science and figuring out how things work or why they work. I know the money would be good in those fields but I really do like that stuff. And I know medicine can help people."

"I don't think you're a big nerd," he said.

"Thank you," she said.

"You're like a small to medium nerd," he added.

The familiar grin returned to his face after he said it and she felt like she had put it there. After he dropped her off at home she was still thinking of what he said about money and jobs and careers, and in particular the conversation he described with his Dad. She wrote down a few of her thoughts in her journal, including a small confession to herself:

*Sometimes, but just sometimes, I wish he would try to kiss me goodnight. I don't think he will and I'm sure by tomorrow I'll be glad he didn't. But tonight if he'd have tried I wouldn't have minded. I'd never tell him but sometimes that whole heart on his sleeve thing makes me wonder "What if?"*

--

For the second holiday season in a row Cal had taken a part time, after school job that he knew wouldn't last beyond the New Year. The year before it had been at a Toys R Us near the mall, where it was explained to him during the entire 2 hours' worth of training he received that the store and all of their stores did 80 percent of their annual business in a one month period.

"We double the size of our staff," the store manager explained. "And on the day after Thanksgiving and pretty much every weekend after, you're going to feel like you're in a war zone. Prepare for a retail battle!"

Cal had burst out with laughter when the guy said it, turning the heads of many other new employees in the room.

"Oh, just you wait, kid," the manager said, staring daggers at him. "Just. You. Wait."

It had turned out to be crazy and yet mind numbing, too, as his job mostly consisted of stocking toys in various aisles. When he wasn't doing that he was helping customers find an item. He eventually found his favorite place to be of help was in the video game section. He thought he should get a commission for the number of *Tetris* games he recommended to customers who asked, "What's a game you think my kid would like?"

"Everyone can play this game," he'd said. "Even adults. It's simple and it's addictive. You'll be trying to sleep and have all these shapes floating and turning and falling faster and faster in your head."

That was his Christmas work for 1989. For 1990 he found himself in the mall, working at Suncoast Motion Picture Company, a store that sold VHS tapes and all kinds of movie memorabilia like posters, shirts, and even replica Oscar awards. It was better than Toys R Us had been, the managers were pretty nice, and he got a 25 percent discount on movies and, more importantly to him, to the Sam Goody and Musicland stores in the same mall, as all three stores were owned by the same company. He'd spent a good chunk of his first paycheck on tapes he wanted and some blank cassettes for the Christmas mixes he planned to make for various friends.

On the first day of training he recognized Melody Thompson, a sophomore at his school and a regular at Mixtape Club. As they were listening to the store manager explain the kind of work they'd all be doing she gave him a quick wave from across the room and when they got a break they found their way to each other.

"I can already tell I'm gonna hate this job," she said.

"They'll fire you after Christmas," he said. "I think they actually have that here in print."

They'd both been given a three-sheet handout labeled as "Work Guidelines and Regulations."

"This is my first job ever," she said.

"Well, the good news is it won't be your last."

He didn't know Melody very well, beyond that most people called her "Mel" and that she seemed to wear a lot of dark clothing and a good portion of the time wore rock t-shirts displaying that she liked a lot of bands that began with the word "The": The Cure, The Smiths, The Smithereens, The Replacements, The Cult, The Alarm, and even The The.

"I just want to make a little money for the holidays," he explained to her. "My parents seem to expect me to pay for the presents I buy for them and my brother and sister."

"The nerve!" she said.

"Right?!"

"Fuck that," she said. "I'm keeping my money and just making my Mom something and even if it's weird she'll be happy because she always says making gifts is more thoughtful. Which is bullshit but I'm going to throw that back in her face."

"You should make her a mix," he suggested.

"Oh Jesus," she said, before adding, "No way."

"By the way," he said. "I never got a chance to tell you but I really liked your mix when I got it out of the grab bag a while back."

'The Grab Bag' was part of Mixtape Club. Once a month each member would create a 60-minute mixtape, putting only their name on it. No lists of song titles or artists allowed. Then they'd throw the mixes in a bag and each member would reach in and grab a random mix, take it home and listen, and then at the next meeting find the person who'd made it and talk with them about it. Earlier in the year he'd drawn a mix Melody made but she wasn't at the next meeting and he'd never had a chance to talk with her about it.

"Oh, right! I remember. I was really scared when I saw that you got mine," she said.

"Why would you be scared?"

"I thought you might not like it. You seem like more of a rock or metal guy and I'm just not all that into that stuff. Well, except a few guilty pleasures," she said.

"Such as?"

She put her hand up near her mouth, seemingly embarrassed by what she was about to say.

"'Uncle Tom's Cabin' by Warrant," she said, cringing.

"That's a pretty good song," he said. "I like songs that tell a story. Even if it is a bit dumb."

"Me too. But I still think that band should be shot for 'Cherry Pie'. That's a horrible song."

"It's a fun song," he argued.

"No. It's stupid as fuck," she said. "But 'Uncle Tom's Cabin' is good. I should hate it because, again, they're horrible in general, but I secretly like that song."

He thought back to her mix, recalling songs from it he'd enjoyed, particularly ones he's never heard before.

"Your mix had this one song...," He closed his eyes and tried to recall how it went. "It had this huge guitar hook and the singer's all 'Jealous!'... and then over and over with 'Something's wrong...Something's wrong with you...'"

"Oh, that's Gene Loves Jezebel! Great song," she said enthusiastically. "And it makes sense that you'd like it. It's a bit more rock and glam than their other stuff."

He thought of other songs from her tape and got more animated as he remembered certain ones he liked.

"You might be the only other person I know who likes The Replacements," he said. "I think you had two songs by them on there, right?"

Her eyes got wide when he said it. "Yeah, wow."

"You had 'I'll Be You' and...?"

"Swingin' Party," she said.

"Right. I'd never heard that song by them, though. Which album is it on?"

"It's called *Tim*," she said.

She looked surprised. "I would not have thought you'd be into them."

64

""I like everything," he said. "Especially good lyrics and that band has really good ones."

"Good to know," she said.

Their conversation ended as the training for Suncoast resumed but he kept glancing at her and he noticed her doing the same. It was exciting and a little bewildering to see someone he knew from around, that he had passed in the halls or sat across from in a circle at Mixtape Club many, many times, and then noticing something more about them. Melody was suddenly very cool and interesting. Before she was just some sophomore who wore certain shirts, dyed her hair black, and that he always seemed to think was a little angry at the world. He knew she was still all or most of those things, but he thought he might be wrong about the anger part because when they talked he found her sarcasm rather funny. He also liked the tiny ruby stud in her nose that he'd never noticed before. And for the rest of their training session she kept looking at him, which wasn't something that had never happened to him before with a member of the opposite sex, but this time he knew what it meant. Or at least he was pretty sure he knew.

--

Ever since she was old enough to grasp the idea of days and dates Anna was grateful that her December birthday was near the start of the month, with just under 3 weeks between that day and Christmas. Her best friend, Eileen, had a December 29th birthday and when they were growing up she would often voice her frustrations about receiving presents from friends and relatives with cards that read "Merry Christmas and Happy Birthday!"

"Hello?!" Eileen would say, "I am not Jesus and therefore Christmas is not my birthday! I am getting short-changed on the gifts and it sucks!"

With a December 6th birthday Anna could always count on her parents to keep the celebrations separate. Just the same, turning 18 without her Kenosha friends around to celebrate was hard and she woke on the morning of her birthday excited to be a legal adult but feeling a distinct void. Nevertheless, her Mom got up early before school and made Anna her favorite breakfast, waffles with strawberries, and even though she had only mentioned her birthday coming up to him once Cal got her a card and made her a mixtape. When he gave them to her she took it as a sign that her sometimes conflicted feelings about him, back and forth between friendship and more, were probably not that different from how he felt about her. She was confident he still liked her, too, and promised herself she would reevaluate her feelings and figure it all out just as soon as she got through her birthday festivities and her college applications and essays.

"I want to listen to this on the way to school," she said, clutching the cassette case of her new mix.

He ejected whatever was in his car stereo and put it in the tape he'd made her.

"I don't think I've ever been in the same room with someone I've made a mix for when they listened to it the first time," he observed.

"Is that weird?" she asked.

"No," he said, though she didn't believe him. If the roles were reversed she knew she'd be terrified that he might not like it.

The first thing she heard was a familiar male voice singing, "You say it's your birthday... it's my birthday too" followed by an equally familiar female voice saying, "Don't sing that, okay?" Then the song "Birthday" by The Beatles began.

"Was that talking part from *Sixteen Candles*?" she asked. "Right before this song started?"

"Yeah," he said.

"I love that movie!" she said

"*Everyone* loves that movie."

"How did you get it onto the tape?" she asked. "That's really cute."

"It's pretty easy. I taped the movie off HBO and I just wired the VCR into the auxiliary input on my stereo and taped it from there," he explained.

"You wired the what into the what-what-what?" she asked, laughing at how elementary he made it all sound.

"It's just a little trick. I like to drop stuff from movies or TV shows into my mixes. Little surprises or things people don't expect to hear."

"Are there more of them in this mix?" she asked excitedly.

"I can't tell you that," he said. "Magicians don't share their tricks."

"But you just told me how you did it," she said. "I could go home now and wire my VCR into the oxen...whatever or other."

66

"Auxiliary input," he said.

"You're a dork," she said. "I've seen many hints that you're a dork but this makes it definitive."

"Hey now," he said. "Was Anthony Michael Hall and Molly Ringwald *not* a nice touch before the Beatles song?"

"It's very clever," she said. "And I really do love that you made this for me. Thank you."

"You're welcome. And happy birthday," he said. "Now please go buy me a lottery ticket. You can do that kind of thing now."

She laughed and listened on. The next song was Fleetwood Mac. The third was someone she'd never heard of. All the songs and who performed them were in his handwriting on the cassette insert. It was fun to examine it a little. No one had ever made her a mixtape. She was about to tell him that but didn't because she knew saying it out loud would be another reminder that he had become a very unique person to her very quickly. She was once again having second thoughts about what she wanted with him or from him or whatever it was they were or weren't. At his kindest, at his sweetest, like with the card and the tape, she couldn't think of a single reason not to say something like, "Okay, I've changed my mind. Let's be more than friends."

When they pulled into the Crestview parking lot and she ejected the tape she was tempted to reach over and kiss him. She imagined it, telling herself that if something like that was going to happen it would be a great time for it.

Instead she reached over and hugged him.

"I woke up this morning and my first thought was 'It's my birthday and I miss my friends so much'," she said. "But you've made it better. So thank you."

"You're very welcome," he said.

She was listening to the mixtape later in the day, in the boombox in her bedroom while waiting for dinner to start, along with the usual traditions of cake, ice cream, and presents from her parents and sister. The songs he'd picked were mostly quite good, even the ones she didn't know, and when a song wasn't to her taste she wondered if he was trying to say something by choosing it. He had also, as he hinted, included little excerpts from movies, sprinkling the mix with dialog from *Pretty In Pink*, *Some Kind of Wonderful*, and even *Spaceballs*, which made her laugh when she recognized it. If it hadn't been for what came next it might have been the best present she got. But her parents wound up shocking her, which she didn't believe they were capable of doing because most of her birthday celebrations had become so routine. A pleasant routine that she loved but she had given up on any major surprises like a car on her 16th birthday or some other larger-than-normal gesture in any given year.

As she ate red velvet cake and vanilla ice cream her father put a large envelope in front of her.

"Before you open this," her mother began, "Your Dad and I just want you to know we know how hard the move has been on you and how unfair it has felt to have to finish high school in a new city and new school. So we hope this present is a good one."

She opened the envelope and the first thing she read was "United Airlines". It was a plane ticket.

"What did you do?" she asked, even as the answer was starting to sink in.

"We talked with Eileen's parents and they've said that you're welcome to fly out a few days after Christmas and stay until the 2nd and spend a few days and New Year's with your old friends," her mother explained. "One of the perks of being 18. You're not an unaccompanied minor and you don't need your parents to help you find your way around an airport."

Anna was stunned. Her eyes welled up and she covered them with her hands. She leapt up and hugged both of her parents tightly.

"I can't believe you did this!" she cried. "Thank you so much. Oh my God!"

Her mind raced with thoughts of seeing Eileen and other friends and getting to do some of the things she missed in Kenosha. Even just the usual things she had done countless times like ice skating or simply staying up late and talking with Eileen. It felt like going back home.

"You've earned it," her Dad said.

"You called Eileen's folks and all that?" she asked.

"Yes," her mother said proudly. "They're totally on board."

"And yes," her father added, reading her mind. "You can go upstairs and call Eileen but keep it short."

Anna immediately ran up to her room, dove onto her bed, and called her best friend.

Anna had to hand it to the Crestview High School Advanced Drama class: They were excellent, leaving any of the plays she'd seem at her school in Kenosha in the dust. The production of *Twelve Angry Jurors*, from the set that captured the look of a jury deliberation room to the costumes, and especially the acting were better than she ever expected. Tracy, who went with her to see it, had told her how good their theater department was, citing the awards many drama students at Crestview had won at competitions and the reputation Mr. Deroy had for being an amazing, inspiring teacher.

The lead characters in the play, in particular Cal's friend Reed, were especially impressive. Cal, for his part, had told her that his character wasn't really all that important but she still thought he did a good job along with everyone else. She told him so when the entire cast was lined up outside the school theater to greet friends and parents.

"I am really blown away," she said, giving him a hug.

He was still in costume, with makeup still present on his face, some gray coloring sprayed on to his usually sandy blonde hair, decked out in dress shirt and pants, with a loosened tie and jacket.

She turned to Reed standing next to him.

"And *you*," she said. "Can I just say you were so convincing that I totally hated you?! I mean, your character. Not you, of course. But I wanted to *kill* your character."

"Thank you," Reed said.

"I really didn't know a high school play could be this good," she said.

"Were they that bad in Kenosha?" Cal asked.

"Not bad, like, awful bad, but you guys clearly put more into it. Maybe it's a west coast, closer to Hollywood thing?" she speculated.

Being in theater had never appealed to her at all. Just the thought of being on stage like Cal and Reed had done was terrifying, which made her further admire their ability to do it. She was about to tell both of them that when she was interrupted by another person approaching Cal.

"That was so cool!" the girl shouted.

She looked familiar to Anna, in that she'd likely passed her in the halls but they had never met.

"Thanks," Cal said, accepting a hug from the girl.

"I was wondering if you were gonna get stabbed in that one scene," the girl joked.

She was referring to a moment at the play's climax where Reed's character charges at a fellow juror with a switchblade, a piece of evidence from the case, and yells, "I'll kill her, I swear I'll kill her!" Cal's character got in between them to break things up.

"I thought of letting him actually stab Natalie many times during rehearsals," Cal joked.

"And I *wanted* to stab Natalie many times during rehearsals," Reed added, joining in the laughter.

Anna wondered who this girl hugging Cal was and decided the best way to find out was to just say hello.

"Hi, we haven't met," she said, turning to the girl and offering her hand. "I'm Anna."

"Oh, hey, I'm Mel," the girl said.

"Short for Melanie?" Anna asked

"Melody," she said.

"That's so pretty," Anna said.

"I guess," Melody said, shrugging her shoulders and then quickly turning her attention back toward Cal, telling him, "Thanks for getting me the free ticket."

"No problem," he said. "I'm just glad you came."

Anna started to watch Melody closely, particularly the way she was looking at Cal. She thought it looked like an obvious crush but with the person harboring it trying to hide it. Anna didn't think she was doing a very effective job, as anyone with a set of eyes could spot it. It was enough to make Anna want to roll hers, particularly that Cal seemed to know it, too, but it wasn't bothering him one iota

"Well, my mom is picking me up," Melody said to him. "But I didn't want to take off without saying good job and thanks and all that."

"Thanks for coming over," he said, adding, "I'll see you on…are you working Sunday?"

Melody nodded.

"Cool. Then I'll see you Sunday."

At least the brief exchange offered her some clues. She knew Cal had been working at the mall and obviously Mel or Melody or whatever she chose to call herself was working there, too. He'd made no mention of her at all. Not in the car rides to school or when they went to a movie the week before. She figured maybe there was nothing to tell. But then why did she thank him for a ticket to the play?

As she walked from the theater toward the parking lot with Tracy she started to feel angry. Then stupid. And then inquisitive.

"Do you know that girl at all? Mel or Melody?" she asked.

"Not really. I mean I've seen her around," Tracy said.

"She likes Cal," Anna said flatly.

"Duh," Tracy said. "Freshman and sophomore girls aren't even subtle about such things."

"I guess not," Anna added.

Tracy stopped walking and turned to her.

"Oh, this is funny," Tracy said. "Anna, are you jealous? It would be kind of hilarious if you were."

"Hilarious?" she asked.

"Yes, *hilarious*. Because it's always seemed pretty obvious that Cal really likes you."

Anna couldn't deny that. But he'd been very good of late in not reminding her of it or having conversations around it. As she retraced the past few weeks she realized that change or difference paralleled when he told her he had gotten a job at the mall. Which meant right when he started working with Melody. Multiple light bulbs were popping on in her head.

"I am so stupid," she said, not even intending to say it out loud.

"Why are you stupid?" Tracy asked.

"Because I didn't notice. It's so classically guy-like of him, really," she said. "Boys have the attention span of a moth. If the light goes dim they just go fly over to the next bright thing."

"Are you the dim light in this story?" Tracy asked, chuckling with her question.

"I don't know. I don't care," Anna said, knowing the second part was a lie.

"Well, I wouldn't worry," Tracy said. "Like you've told me before...going out with Cal or anybody would be a bad idea, right?

She had said that exact thing to Tracy as part of her answers to the several times Tracy had asked about Cal. After she had given the same explanation enough times Tracy eventually stopped asking.

"I did say that," Anna said. "It would be a bad idea. And I was right."

--

Doug had needled Cal for weeks about what Cal insisted was an "undefined" relationship with Anna.

"Yeah, okay," Doug said to him. "It's undefined. It's also untouched, un-kissed, and un-fucked."

Doug didn't seem to like Anna that much, often reminding Cal that she was, in his opinion, "stuck up, too tightly wound, and not even really hot except in a librarian kind of way." So when Cal asked him what he knew about Melody Thompson, who was in Doug's class of sophomores, he was far more enthusiastic.

"I have a few classes with Mel," he said. "I've run into her at a few parties. A little bit of a goth chick...the black hair thing...but not over the top. I'd hit it."

Doug's assessment of the opposite sex always seemed to end with whether he'd have sex with a person or not if given the opportunity.

"Anything else?" Cal asked.

"I know she's like me in the no Dad around thing. Just her Mom."

When Cal heard his friend say 'no Dad' he wasn't quite sure what it meant, given what he knew about Doug.

"No Dad as in…" he began to ask.

"No Dad as in Mom and Dad split. Not no Dad as in *really* gone," Doug clarified.

Doug's father had committed suicide when Doug was 8. It was a topic Doug had written about in an essay Cal helped him with. They had exactly one conversation of any length about it during tutoring sessions and Cal never mentioned it unless Doug somehow referred to it.

"Why are you suddenly so interested in Mel?" Doug asked

"I work with her at Suncoast," Cal explained. "And I'm 99 percent sure she likes me."

Doug was less convinced.

"Just because she talks to you at work doesn't mean she likes you," he said. "You might just be the only person she knows there."

It was true but it didn't explain why she seemed to be finding him around the halls of Crestview more and more, or waving to him when she saw him, why she had come to *Twelve Angry Jurors* or why she had not missed either of the last two Mixtape Club meetings leading up to the holiday break.

"I don't think it's just because of that," Cal said.

Being confident that someone liked him was not a common feeling for him. With every other girl he'd liked there was always some guess work. He'd get a sense that maybe someone was interested in him only to seek out answers or inquire with a friend or a friend of a friend or, if he was very brave, to just ask the person out, only to find his instincts had been wrong. The guessing, the uncertainty, and the cycle of all of it was very familiar, so having it seem obvious that Melody liked him was a bit foreign.

"I can ask her," Doug suggested. "I know her well enough and I'm sure she is aware that you and I are tight so…"

Cal was tempted to take Doug up on the offer because it was an easy way to get an answer. But those kinds of past inquiries had never changed the result. If the answer was "No" it made him feel like an idiot for ever thinking there was something there in the first place. And the handfuls of "Yes, she likes you" answers, while resulting in some dates, still ultimately ended the same. He figured maybe that was inevitable but with his growing interest in Melody he felt an urge to approach things differently and see if maybe it would change anything that might follow.

"I think I'll just ask her myself," he said.

"Like walk up to her and say, 'Do you like me?'" Doug asked.

"I probably wouldn't put it quite like that."

"You *definitely* shouldn't put it like that," Doug said. "Like, nothing in the fucking realm of that."

"I think I got this," Cal said, trying to sound more assured than he was.

"You never have this," Doug joked. "*Never.*"

It would have been funnier if it hadn't felt so humiliatingly true. Just the same, Cal promised himself he'd figure out Melody in a different way than in his past.

At the start of his Sunday afternoon shift at Suncoast the store manager, Keith, pulled Cal aside. Keith was cheerier than usual, especially given how busy the store was.

"Boy, have I got a job for you," he said, motioning for Cal to follow him to the back of the store past the 'Employees Only' curtain. When they got there he pointed Cal toward pieces of a costume that were laid out on the floor.

"Congratulations," Keith said. "You're going to be Michelangelo for the afternoon."

The costume pieces were like the kind he'd seen people wearing as characters at Disneyland or Six Flags. The one on the floor was of Michelangelo, one of the popular Teenage Mutant Ninja Turtles.

"I'm going to be what?" Cal asked.

"I want you to put on the costume and then you and Mel are going to walk up and down the mall and hand out flyers with coupons for the store to shoppers," Keith explained. "And greet kids and all that shit."

"You've got to be kidding me," Cal said.

"Nope. It's a promotional thing and I need someone to do it and you told me once you've done theater so all you have to do is walk around, wave, and don't say anything except, like, 'Cowabunga' or 'Turtle power' or 'Pizza power' or whatever the fuck they say."

"Can I say I don't want to do this?" Cal asked.

"What do you think?" Keith asked, shaking his head.

Cal grew a bit worried as he looked over the pieces of the costume. They were far more elaborate than a Halloween outfit or even various costumes he'd worn for theater. It was more akin to a suit of armor, with each leg covering like open and close cast. The middle section went over his head, with the weight of the front and back on his shoulders via straps. It reminded him of the one season of football he'd attempted. It was immediately uncomfortable and he could only walk at a slow pace. The head was massive, sliding on like a fully encompassing helmet. Cal was able to see out of what to people on the outside was the Ninja Turtle's mouth.

"I hate this!" he cried from inside the costume, hearing his own words echo around him.

"You look great!" Keith said, also laughing hysterically. "I'm going to go get Mel and she'll go with you to hand out the flyers."

He stood in the costume, instantly sweating from the internal heat. It made him think of the single time he'd ever been in a sauna.

When Melody came through the curtain and saw him she immediately burst into laughter.

"Holy shit! This is the best day ever!" she cracked, clapping her hands, and squealing with happiness.

She led him out of the store into the mall fairway. With the limited vision he had, complete with sweat that had started dripping into his eyes, he could see holiday shoppers staring in dismay, some laughing, some bewildered as to why a Mutant Ninja Turtle and a teenage escort were walking through the mall. Eventually people started approaching them, especially those with children. One mother came up to them with a little girl that Cal guessed was maybe 2 or 3 years old. She immediately started crying. Her reaction made sense to Cal because he'd have done the same thing at her age.

"Oh, don't cry," Melody said, leaning down and trying to comfort the girl. "Mikey is a friendly turtle. I promise."

Melody was clearly enjoying the experience, which made the increasingly intolerable heat from within the costume a little more bearable.

He did his best to wave at people as they walked down the mall. He even smiled from inside the costume before remembering the Ninja Turtle head had a scowling smile already on it. His theater-learned skills of trying to be in character were not really going to matter for this adventure.

"Are you doing okay in there?" Melody asked.

"No. I'm in Teenage Mutant Ninja Hell!" he replied.

"I'm sorry," she said, still giggling about all of it. "But this is still the best thing ever!"

Again, her enthusiasm helped. He'd learned pretty fast that Melody had a different kind of sense of humor than many other girls he knew. It was more sarcastic, darker, and she was more inclined to swear or see something off-color as humorous.

When they got near the Santa Claus Station at the far end of the mall Cal started to turn around.

"Where are you going?" she asked.

"Keith told us not to disrupt the Santa House," he whispered through the costume.

"Oh, hell no," Melody said. "We are totally going to steal Santa's thunder. I'm taking you to sit on his lap and have your ninja picture taken with him."

"No," he said sternly. "We are *not* doing that!"

She pulled him toward the Santa House and despite his protest he followed her.

As more and more shoppers and especially kids noticed Michelangelo the Ninja Turtle the more they gathered around him. Most just wanted to come up and high five him, some little kids hugged up against the costume, which was made of firm material so he couldn't really feel much beyond a light pressing against him. But then he felt a hard push.

"What the hell?!" he cried. The area of the mall they were in was loud and he didn't think anyone heard him.

"Please don't do that!" Melody said to someone. Cal couldn't see who it was. The view from inside had almost no peripheral vision.

"Come on, fight Turtle!" he heard a boy shout.

This time he saw it. A boy of maybe 9 or 10 had kicked the stomach area of the costume. It didn't hurt but it threw Cal off balance. And given that he couldn't bend in the knees in the slightest he nearly fell over.

"Don't do that, boys!" he heard Melody say again. And just as he was registering that she had used the plural of 'boy' he felt multiple kicks and punches to the front and the back of the costume.

"Can some of the parents please get your kids to stop?!" Melody shouted.

Cal could hear parents and other shoppers laughing at the spectacle. None of them appeared interested in intervening.

"How about we just get out of here?!" he shouted from inside.

More kicks and punches were thrown as Melody tried to guide him away.

"Jesus Christ!" she shouted. "Get your damn kids off my turtle!"

Sweat began salting his eyes to the point where everything he saw was blurry. One kid kicked him in the groin very close to his crotch. Cal tried to turn things around by playing along.

76

"Cowabunga!" he yelled.

The group of 3 or 4 boys that had been mugging him cheered, followed by a few more punches and kicks, and then eventually Cal saw some mothers and fathers coming over and pulling them back.

"You all better come to the store!" Melody scolded them. "You owe Michelangelo an apology so come buy something at Suncoast!"

"Get me back to the store, please!" he cried.

"Bye, kids! We're going back to the sewer!" Melody shouted. She then turned toward the Santa Station and cried, "Santa! All these kids were bad! They beat up a defenseless turtle! Lumps of coal! Lumps of coal for all of them I tell you!"

"We are so gonna get fired," Cal whispered to himself.

They made their way back down the other side of the mall, stopping a few more times to greet kids. On their second and third attempts at interaction with shoppers Melody had started stepping in between him and any oncoming children.

"You need to be gentle with Mikey," she instructed them. "He just got back from a big adventure and had to fight off a band of bratty thugs."

Finally they got back to the store. Cal could feel the sweat breaking through his Suncoast polo shirt and thought maybe it was even coming through his Dockers. His hair was matted down.

"I need to get out of this thing before I pass out," he said.

She took him back into the Employees Only area and helped him get the masked helmet off.

"That was fucking hilarious," she said.

"Yeah, for you," he said. "I got beat up by a vicious gang of kids who haven't even hit puberty yet."

She then helped him lift the shell part of the costume up over his head.

"You're fun," she said, smiling.

"So are you," he said.

He didn't even think about how sweaty or gross he was. He just looked quickly to see if anyone else was in the back of the store and when it was clear no one else was around he leaned down and kissed her.

She put a hand on his cheek while they kissed, and with his eyes open he could see she had closed hers.

"Yeah," she said, pulling back, blushing a little, and making her way through the curtain but not before adding, "Wow. Okay. So, yeah...Cowabunga, dude."

As he stood there with the ninja leg casings still around his thighs and calves, he thought it might have been the coolest thing any girl had ever said to him after a first kiss.

--

Anna had never flown without her parents before. She thought about that and how grown up it felt to be doing so as she found her seat on the plane leaving Oakland for Chicago. Her parents and sister had dropped her off at the gate and she knew Eileen and her family would be waiting for her at the one in Chicago, followed by the hour-long drive back to Kenosha.

"The Wilsons know your arrival time but if you can't find them just find a payphone and call their house," her Mom said. Her parents had given her a calling card for just such an emergency.

She waved to them as she walked down the boarding tunnel and let the excitement take over. It had felt so much longer than 4 months since she had last seen Eileen and her other friends.

She wound up seated next to a nice older lady who was very conversational, asking things like "How were your holidays?" and "Where are you traveling to?"

"Oh, visiting old friends is so wonderful," the woman commented after Anna told her where she was headed and why. "You must really love them if you're willing to endure the Midwest winter to see them."

The East Bay area of California, while certainly not sunny or warm for December, was entirely too overcast and boring for Anna. Her entire life had consisted of cold and icy winters, for good and for bad, with everything from sled hills to ice skating to nearly wrecking the car when her father was teaching her how to drive on snow and ice. She missed all of it so much, but in the name of things like maturity and trying to be strong or, as her parents advised, "making the best of it", she had done all she could to suppress her homesickness. She had tried so hard that the many nights on her bed crying about it had made her feel weak or like she'd failed. Ever since her parents had surprised her with the plane tickets the sadness had lifted and there hadn't been any tears, just excitement and anticipation. But even when she imagined the visit and all the people she wanted to see and things she wanted to do she knew it wasn't going to be a very long stay. As she sat in her seat awaiting departure she was all too aware she'd be in another seat just like it in a few days to fly back. It was going to be heartbreaking, perhaps as bad or worse than back in September when the moving van was pulling away and her family had gone to the airport for the flight out west.

As the plane taxied around the runway she tried to silence those thoughts, to not think about January 2nd, when she'd fly home, and instead just focus on the moment, to enjoy her first trip of any kind without her Mom, Dad, or Jackie. She thought about how the type of flight she was on might become very familiar. If she got into Northwestern or UW she'd be on flights just like it, probably returning to school after a holiday break during her first year of college. Such visions of the future excited her for the most part, coupled with doses of anxiety and worry. But it didn't feel like some crazy wish. Those things were very real possibilities and they weren't that far away. Over the holiday break from school she had been filling out college applications and working on various essays to go with them. Northwestern, Wisconsin, UCLA, and USC applications were all in the works; the latter two to appease both her competitive nature and her parents, who kept reminding her that California schools would be considerably less expensive.

Once the plane was up she got out her Walkman and listened to the birthday mixtape Cal had given her. She had listened to it start to finish several times. There were some songs on it she really liked, the ones she was pretty sure he'd picked to try to say something to her that he wasn't saying in conversation. A Crowded House song on it that she'd never heard really caught her attention. She knew the group's music a little bit from radio and MTV but Cal had placed a song by them called "Never Be The Same" and she loved it right from the first time she heard it. She loved finding a connection to lyrics in it like *"But we might still survive and rise up through the maze. If you could change your life and never be the same."* The first time she played the mix and heard the song she hit rewind and listened again. Then again. She wasn't sure why he'd chosen it. For Anna, it was unusual for any song to resonate and stick with her

79

in the way books and occasionally a movie would. She had explained that once to Cal.

"I like the way you take songs into your heart and soul a bit and let them become a part of you," she told him. "For me songs are usually more in the background. I don't pay that much attention to what they're saying."

But she had taken "Never Be The Same" to heart. It made her think about the future ahead, about not missing chances, and to not let her life become like her parents. A line that went *"How long must I wait for you to release me? I pay for each mistake while you suffer in silence"* made her think of her Dad and how much he would work, as much as 60 or 70 hours a week if he was on a major case. As she got older she felt like she and her sister and even her mother were paying for it. Months before, back in Kenosha, she'd overheard her Mom raise some concerns and doubts about the new job and moving so far away and what that would mean for all four of them. Her father had countered with arguments about the opportunity and how much better their lives could be. She thought her Mom should have argued more and that her father had been selfish. Those kinds of thoughts and critiques used to make her feel guilty and disloyal to them, flying in the face of what she'd heard at church all her life about respecting her parents and all they did for her. But the move to California had changed that. Their lives in Kenosha had not been wealthy or as well-to-do as some of her friends but they had a good house, they went camping in the summer and vacationed in Chicago and St. Louis and other interesting places. They had two cars. Those were all things that made her feel fortunate and that she would express gratitude for in prayer, be it at service or at the dinner table. As she got older she had heard more and more of her friends be critical of their parents, which Anna attributed to being teenagers. She applauded herself for having the maturity to see those kinds of critiques and gripes as normal. Even when she would dream of college she had always thought the one downside to going away would be how much she would miss her family. But such concerns about that had started to diminish considerably in the past 6 months.

As her flight approached Chicago she thought more and more of the trip she was on and how all that was to come in the days ahead was like a preview of the kind of 'escape' mentioned in the Crowded House song that had resonated with her so strongly. Her life and the decisions with it would become more and more her own. That pending reality had previously come with equal parts excitement and fear, but of late it leaned more toward the former, with added feelings of impatience. On the flight she scribbled in her journal: *Next year is not coming soon enough. Sometimes I wish I could hit the fast forward button on my life.*

--

The four of them -- Cal, Doug, Melody, and Melody's friend, Heidi -- were sitting on the back deck at Doug's house on Friday night after leaving a party that had been broken up far earlier than such festivities usually would. An hour before they had been in the backyard of a classmate they didn't personally know, who was throwing a pre-New Year's bash. Cal and Doug met up with Melody and Heidi and the plan was to see if the party was any good and then maybe go to Denny's or Lyon's afterward and hang out.

The script for what would happen and what to do when a party got broken up had become routine for Cal and Doug and, they assumed, most anyone that went to parties regularly. Whether the gathering was 10 people or 100 or some number usually in between, whether it was inside a house or in someone's backyard or a combination of both, all parties would inevitably get broken up. This was just understood by everyone, from revelers to the hosts. The best hope among all attending was that it wouldn't happen before a keg ran out and that whoever was throwing said party wouldn't get in too much trouble in the aftermath. At some point in the night someone would hear or more likely see a police car on the street or in the driveway and that was that. Even if the police came inside a house, which Cal had only experienced once in over three years, they couldn't talk to or round up every kid at once. So at the first sight of authorities everyone made for the exit. In another unwritten code or rule, it was perfectly acceptable to ask a fellow partygoer you may not even know if you could jump in their car to make a complete and fast getaway.

"Dude, can I get a ride?" was a question Cal had been asked more than once by someone running alongside him away from a party being broken up.

Cal had a pickup truck, complete with a camper shell, and he usually had extra room. It was not out of the ordinary to find people he barely knew jumping in the back to escape squad cars and flashing lights. From there it was often a "Where do you live?" or "Where do you want to be dropped off?" And sometimes someone who had jumped in the truck bed would say, "Hey, I know where another party is. Do you want to go check it out?"

It wasn't even 9 o'clock when someone at the party Cal, Doug, Melody and Heidi met up at yelled, "Cops!" and that was the end. The four of them were all in the backyard, trying to stay warm by standing near a barbeque grill that someone had thrown twigs, sticks, and what looked like landscaping markers into and lit on fire.

"Let's go!" Doug yelled, already running toward the gate leading to the side yard. The other three followed and from behind a row of bushes they could see that there was indeed a police car, but it was in the opposite direction of where Cal had parked.

It was Doug who suggested they go to his house to hang out, as his mother, a neonatal nurse at an area hospital, was working until at least midnight. When they got there Doug suggested they congregate on the backyard patio. Cal knew the reason why. And if there was any doubt it was answered within seconds when Doug pulled out his pipe, lighter, and weed. He lit up, took a toke, and then motioned it toward Heidi. She shook her head. Doug knew enough to not offer it to Cal so he passed it toward Melody, who took a toke.

Cal was a little surprised by Melody's indulgence. They hadn't talked about whether either of them got high. They hadn't even really been on a date. Since what they had come to call "The Teenage Mutant Ninja Kiss" a few weeks before they'd talked on the phone, seen each other at Suncoast, and he'd started giving her rides home after work. They had gotten in a routine of making out in his car, listening to music, talking, and then making out again. The party was the first time they'd seen each other since they were both let go from Suncoast a few days before. There hadn't been any real conversations between them about what all the making out and hanging out together meant. Usually Cal would have brought it up with someone after a date or two, as he was always eager to take on the title of "Boyfriend" if someone wanted him to, and even more so to have someone else become his girlfriend. But Melody didn't seem to want or need such a conversation and in his ongoing efforts to try and take a different approach with her he was happy to just let things play out.

Melody passed the marijuana pipe toward Cal and he shook his head.

"He doesn't get high," Doug announced.

"Really?!" she asked, sounding rather surprised.

"Not my thing," he said, not wanting to say more than that.

"Not tonight or not ever?" she asked.

"Not ever," he said. "Something about things on fire that close to my face has always just kinda freaked me out. I know it's stupid but…"

It wasn't even remotely true except that he genuinely did not like the smell of cigarettes. He had other reasons, too, but didn't want to talk about it.

Melody nodded and then looked at him a bit curiously.

"So wait," she said. "All these shows you have been to and told me about… Metallica, Motley Crue, Ozzy, Poison, Def Leppard... I thought it was a rule that everyone got high at those shows. I think you'd *want* to be high to get over how bad so much of that music is!"

She was teasing his music tastes, which had become part of their rapport and, he'd concluded, also part of their mutual attraction. Debating songs and bands with her had been a major turn-on for him and he figured it was the same for her.

He had a half-truth go-to explanation for why he didn't get high or drink at shows.

"I don't like to get wasted at concerts," he said. "With very few exceptions every ticket I've ever bought has been with money from summer or seasonal jobs and if I'm going to pay to see a band I'd like to remember what they played the next day, ya know?"

"I get that," Melody said, all the while taking another hit.

"Me too," Heidi said.

Cal barely knew Heidi but was glad to have some backup.

"Plus, when you hang out with this jackass," Cal said, kicking a leg toward Doug sitting across from him, "Somebody has to stay semi-responsible."

Doug didn't protest the remark. Cal had told Doug his bigger reasons about not wanting to get high. As they sat around bouncing from topic to topic he appreciated his friend keeping past conversations out

83

of the current one. Cal knew Doug had things he didn't like to talk about with most people and he liked that Doug seemed to understand other people had their off-limits topics, too.

Doug and Heidi eventually went inside to watch a movie, leaving Cal with Melody. Before he could say anything she got up from her chair and sat on his lap, putting her arms around him, pulling him into a kiss. She then squeezed him tightly.

"You're sweet," he whispered to her, enjoying the show of affection.

"I'm also cold," she said.

He kissed her again, detecting only the slightest hint of marijuana smell from her mouth.

"I hope it doesn't bother you that I get high," she said.

"It doesn't. I hang out with Doug for God's sake. He gets baked all the time."

"Yeah, but you don't make out with Doug. You're not dating..."

She stopped herself.

"Dating Doug?" he asked. "I am definitely *not* dating Doug. I babysit Doug and I talk him off the cliff when he's on one of..."

He stopped himself before he revealed anything more. It wasn't for her to hear about.

"I didn't mean to say we're dating or anything or that... I don't know," she said.

He put a finger over her lips.

"I like you, Melody. A lot," he told her.

They kissed again. He wasn't lying about how he felt. He liked so many things about her, enough to look over the pot thing which he usually saw as a potential dealbreaker. As much as anything he liked that she didn't make him nervous or leave him confused about whether she liked him back. She was the first girl he instinctively knew the answers about. She liked him and had made it obvious. And as that had become apparent he was more and more attracted to her. He liked that one of her favorite things to do was put on music in her room and let herself get lost in it. He liked her dark hair and the pixie cut she'd gotten a week or so before. She did occasionally say things that seemed a little immature, she could get upset or pouty sometimes, and he wasn't crazy about the pot smoking she had just revealed. But all those things felt very minor because everything else with her was easier than it had ever been with any other girl.

The only hesitation he felt about Melody was when he thought of the future. He was graduating in 6 months and he had two full years left after he finished at Crestview. That felt entirely too long, and he thought about bringing it up with her right after the first time they'd fooled around in his car but he didn't. He thought, 'If she is worried about it then let her bring it up' and he was proud of himself for just letting go and being happy. In the same way she hadn't left him guessing about whether she liked him he wasn't having the all too familiar sense of dread about when or if those feelings would change.

As they sat in the December cold, cuddled together in Doug's backyard, she said, "Heidi did ask me earlier if we're a couple."

"And what'd you say?" he asked.

"That we hadn't talked about it."

"What did you want the answer to be?" he asked.

She turned and looked at him more squarely.

"I told her that you're so fucking nice and sweet that I was shocked you like me."

"I do. Like you…"

"I guess I'm just used to most guys being jerks," she said. "Maybe it's because you're a little older or whatever but you say nice things to me and…."

"Guys don't say nice things to you?"

"Nope. Well, they do and then they don't," she added. "You know what I mean? Like, 'Oh, Mel you're so cool and, wow, yeah, I like that band, too and let's go out'. And then later it's 'Leave me alone, bitch' or 'Sorry, your tits aren't big enough, I'm gonna go chase this blonde skank over here.'"

He felt bad that anyone had said anything like that to her. He knew some guys did talk to girls that way and it always baffled him that those same guys had girlfriends at all, while he always hoped for one.

"That's not me, Melody," he said. "I would never talk to you that way."

"I know. But I've been kind of waiting for you to turn into an asshole."

"Oh, I'm sure I can be an asshole sometimes. But I wouldn't want to be. Not to you."

She kissed him, then hugged him tight again.

"You can tell Heidi we're a couple, if you want," he said, doing his best to sound less invested in the idea than he truly was.

"I'd like that," she whispered.

They got up to go inside. Her hand was on the sliding glass door handle before she turned to him again.

"Oh, and I love that you never call me Mel," she said. "You've always said Melody. Usually the only time I hear that is when my mother is super pissed at me."

"My mother does that with me. When she's pissed at me I'm Calvin," he said. "But don't ever call me that. Like, ever."

"Oh, I totally am now," she said, with a smile he loved more and more each time he witnessed it. "I'm calling you that all the time now."

--

The visit to Kenosha had been everything Anna hoped it would be, with very few exceptions and even those were minor. A few friends she had hoped to see were out of town with their parents, still visiting relatives or on some kind of post-Christmas vacation. But most of her closest friends were there and Eileen had made a long list of things they were going to do, just as Anna suspected she might. It had all served as a reminder of so many things she missed and had taken for granted, from small things like ice skating on a pond to more meaningful things, like long conversations with people she'd known since kindergarten.

When they went ice skating, as she made her way across the surface, she thought of the people she'd met in California and wondered if any of them could do what she was doing at that moment. Tracy had told her she'd never even been on ice skates and Cal said he'd only done it once. She couldn't remember a time in her life when she hadn't known how to skate. Her father had told her many times that the first time he put her on the ice was before she was even 3 years old. She glided around the pond and it felt so wonderfully familiar. The only thing that threw her off at first was the cold against her face. She hadn't been outside in temperatures that cold since the previous winter.

"I think my body has gotten a little acclimated to California," she told Eileen.

Eileen and some other friends had asked her a lot of questions about her "new life out West", wondering if people their age in California were different from the friends she'd left behind.

"This will sound really dumb but they are literally sunnier," Anna explained. "Cheerier. Not even nicer, per se, but I think the better weather just makes them have a little more energy all around. But I think people here are tougher. Out there they complain when it drops below 50 degrees or even if it rains hard."

She had to dispel myths of surfers or people that talked like Bill or Ted from the movies or looked like Luke Perry or Jason Priestley from *Beverly Hills, 90210* or every other California cliche people had.

"I think the whole beach culture is a southern California thing, not a San Francisco bay area thing," she explained. "My friend Tracy told me she used to live in Orange County and that sunshine and sand was definitely more of a regular activity in L.A. and San Diego."

Eileen's boyfriend, Jonathan, asked, "Are there are a lot of fags and lesbos at your school?"

Anna never liked Jonathan all that much and liked his question even less. She hadn't met anyone at her school that was gay, at least to the best of her knowledge. It was another San Francisco area cliche or stereotype that even she'd probably believed at one point. But the way he asked the question upset her.

"I don't think it matters," she answered. "It hasn't ever come up with anyone I've met."

She had long talks into the night with Eileen every night of her visit, discussing their college plans, where they were planning to apply or had already applied, the nervousness and anticipation that went with doing so, and trying to imagine what their lives would look like in a year. Even before the visit Anna had mentioned the California schools she'd applied to and that she was scheduled to tour both USC and UCLA in a few weeks with her parents. She was doing it to appease them, she told herself, but she had to admit that both were excellent schools, especially UCLA. Before the move it had never been on her radar. Like Anna, Eileen had Northwestern high on her list, followed by Marquette and then UW. They both agreed the only hesitation with UW was that it might be too familiar, as they'd been to Madison so many times over the years.

"Lately I am torn between Northwestern and UW," Eileen said. "Northwestern is just crazy expensive. I'm gonna really have to work my ass off this summer to help out if I go there."

"My folks are worried about that, too," Anna said. "That's why they're kind of in favor of USC or UCLA. And the UW thing...it's so weird. Before the move I really didn't have it very high up. Definitely more of a backup because of what you said. We've been going to Badger games since we were kids. But now, at least for me, it would feel kind of like going away and coming home all at the same time. So I'm thinking about it."

For as long as Anna could remember she and Eileen had kept their plans and dreams closely tied together. They'd been talking about it since 7th grade when they each naively thought their junior high grades could hurt their college chances. They were very competitive, not remotely shy about turning around in their seats to flash their test scores, with rarely more than a point or two's worth of separation between them. They were, by their own admission, overachievers and proud of it. But Eileen made it look easy, and Anna wasn't afraid to say how envious she was of that. Anna had done the clubs and the extracurriculars she thought would pay dividends on her record to show to colleges, even when it meant taking on too much and stressing herself out to where she felt physically sick or could be so anxious she couldn't sleep. Eileen did similar things, taking high level courses and joining clubs but was also a cheerleader, sang in the school choir, and had a boyfriend she would hang out with all the time, even the night before the SATs. And, of course, when the scores came back she was just 10 points below Anna. It had hardly felt like a victory considering Eileen had taken a one-day prep seminar on a Saturday and Anna had taken night classes at the community college to prepare. But she loved her best friend and she knew Eileen felt the same about her.

Their long talks continued at the New Year's Eve Party they attended at Drew Swensen's house. Drew was one of Jonathan's best friends and while rowdy parties were never Anna's favorite she knew it was both New Year's and the last New Year's of her high school life, so she did her best to endure the loud music, the drinking games, the whooping and hollering and the drunken, slurred greetings from old classmates.

"Wait, wait," one boy, Ryan, said to her, slurring his words and with a full plastic cup of beer in his hands, "Didn't you go away or something?"

"Yes," she said, feeling like she was talking to 2nd grader. "I moved to California but I am visiting Eileen. Happy New Year, Ryan."

He opened his arms and before she could dodge it he gave her a massive hug.

"Happy Fuckin' `91! Woo hoo!" he shouted.

Anna turned to Eileen.

"Are you really going to miss any of this?" she asked

Eileen shrugged.

They found a semi quiet spot upstairs and sat in a pair of beanbags, with Eileen drinking a beer and Anna pretending to, taking very tiny sips, and disliking each one.

"You really need to just love it for what it is, ya know?" Eileen said, taking in their surroundings. She was always trying to get Anna to loosen up a little.

"Be a little more here and now," she continued. "I mean...really...you, me...we...we've worked really hard! And for all the worry about getting in here or getting in there are you really *that* worried?"

"Yes," Anna said. "It's not done until I get the acceptance letters."

Eileen rolled her eyes.

"Analisa Williams," Eileen said, taking a long drink of her beer before continuing, "I want you to please and I mean *please* just say 'I am going to get into Northwestern because I am that friggin' brilliant and awesome'. Please just say it."

Anna shook her head.

"You are killing me," Eileen said. "Before you guys moved I had been promising myself that this year, our *last* year, was when I was going to finally get you to enjoy the last days of it. To drink a little, screw up a little, find a new boyfriend... all that. Don't you want to just enjoy at least *some* of this?"

Anna looked around the house they were in. There were empty plastic cups and a few stained paper plates near their feet that other party guests had just left on the carpet.

"I've never liked this stuff," Anna said. "I've tolerated stuff like this because I love you."

"I know," Eileen conceded.

"It's not that I don't want to have fun but you know me," Anna said. "I am future focused and stuff like this, stuff like going out with Kyle. None of it lasts."

Eileen looked at her with a sad face.

"You and I will be fine because we've been friends since forever but you know what I mean," Anna said in a reassuring tone. "I just can't embrace this temporary thing. Especially out in California. That makes it even worse. It's why it's been so tough to really connect with people. I feel like 'What's the point?'"

"The point is there is no point," Eileen said.

In Anna's view, her friend was getting ever more philosophical as she drank.

"So what if it doesn't last?" Eileen asked. "So what if it's not part of this future you have planned? You already know what you want for your future when it comes to the important stuff like what college and what to study. The rest is just the fun stuff. Do you really think I think about a future with Jonathan? Because I *know* Jonathan's future. He's going to go to UW, drink too much, probably marry a fraternity girl and end up overweight and having an ulcer like his Dad."

Anna felt bad for laughing, even though she knew it was spot on.

"But for right now?" Eileen continued. "For right now he's funny and he's hot and because of me he isn't going to college as a virgin and because of him I'm not going to fall for the first dorm RA that suckers me in by listening to Tracy Chapman records and swearing he's a feminist."

Anna giggled again, confident that despite Eileen's assertions an RA at the college of her choosing probably could impress her if he liked Tracy Chapman or Indigo Girls or some of the other women-with-guitars that Eileen liked.

"It's okay to be a little present tense, Anna. If not now then when? I wouldn't look at the new school in California as a reason why you can't be spontaneous or have fun. I'd look at it as a reason to be a little more carefree. You've earned it!"

She had to admit that her friend had a point. Eileen had argued such points before and even when her arguments were valid and logical Anna had only sporadically followed such advice. Every time she'd tried to be a little more "in the now" she'd eventually return her focus to what she thought was more important: The future.

"I guess I'm also a little afraid to get attached to people out there or let my guard down. That's what happened with Cal. I started to and then I pulled back."

She had told Eileen a fair amount about Cal because, as she knew would happen, Eileen had asked if any guys at her new school had caught her interest.

"Well...it's not too late," Eileen said. "It's going to be a New Year just minutes from now. I say if you like this Cal guy you need to grab hold and just be with him. And if you both wind up broken hearted then that's what happens. And it's fine."

"It's really not," Anna said. "I don't want my heart broken and I don't want to break Cal's. God knows he's good enough at doing it to himself."

"Yeah, from what you've told me it sounds like he is the fall hard type," Eileen said.

"He is," she said.

"But that doesn't have to be your problem," Eileen said.

"But it would be. I'd never forgive myself if I wound up hurting him," she explained.

"So instead of a story someday about how you moved to California your senior year and didn't know a soul but you met this really nice guy and felt this great connection and even though you knew it was probably doomed you decided to let it be what it is and it was great while it lasted. Instead of *that* you get to say 'Years ago I met this really nice guy and I let him go because I didn't want to mess up my future which was already impossible to mess up'."

Eileen was on a roll, which Anna knew was propelled by the beer in her bloodstream.

"I've been watching too many romantic comedies and I've had too much to drink, huh?" Eileen asked.

Anna put up her thumb and index finger to signal 'A little bit'.

"I think you need to jump this guy. There. That's my grand advice," Eileen said.

From the stereo downstairs someone -- Anna suspected it was Jonathan -- had put on the 80's song "Come On Eileen".

"Hot damn, they are playing my song!" Eileen shouted.

It was not the first time Eileen had laid claim to it as her anthem. Anna watched as her friend took another swig of beer till her cup was empty.

"Come on! We gotta dance and I gotta go find Jonathan and kiss him at midnight."

"That's sweet," Anna said, wondering for a moment where Cal might be out in California.

"I guess it's sweet," Eileen agreed, adding," I'm going to break up with him before summer, though. I figure we'll both need some time to get over it and it'd be nice if by the time we left for our different schools he didn't hate me, you know?"

Anna threw her arms up and said, "*Now* who's thinking about the future?!"

# Chapter Four - January 1991

## *"Tears Don't Lie"*

On the flight back to California Anna wrote down a series of New Year's goals. She'd done similar lists in the first week of each new year since about age 12, but 1991 felt bigger. She was, after all, now an adult and the goals she jotted down felt even more massive:

*Get into at least 3 or more of the schools you've applied to*
*Make a decision on which school you want to attend*
*Make sure whatever decisions you make are yours and FOR YOU*
*Make the Crestview Girls Basketball Team*
*Stop overthinking!!*

She'd written down #5 in past years and when she finished writing it yet again she knew it might be the hardest item on the list. Despite her nervousness and anxieties she was still confident she had the grades and scores to get into her chosen schools. Even her guidance counselor at Crestview, who didn't really know Anna very well, had concurred when they met before the holiday break. Getting into a good school seemed very likely and she was starting to realize that choosing the school she wanted was going to be tougher than she'd initially thought. She'd read more of the UCLA catalogues on the flight out and back and the more she read the more she was impressed. It was a very prestigious school. It had a much bigger national reputation than Wisconsin for sure and was on par with or higher than Northwestern. Tucked in between the many, many pictures of sunshine and beautiful people in the UCLA and USC catalogues were also the kinds of courses she'd be taking if she pursued the fields she was leaning toward: Biology, Medicine or maybe Secondary Education. For Anna, the classes were the most exciting part.

Making the basketball team was more of a curiosity than a goal. She wouldn't be crushed if she didn't make it but was interested in seeing what kind of game the girls at Crestview had in comparison to her team back in Kenosha. If nothing else it she thought she might make some additional friends and, as Eileen had reminded her, so what if they weren't lasting, lifelong friends?

Eileen's New Year's Eve pep talk had gotten to her, which led her to think more about what *wasn't* on her goals list for the new year: Talking to Cal and admitting that she liked him. She had a strong suspicion he had moved on, not that there was ever really anything between them to move on from. When she'd reached out to him a few times during the holiday break from school he'd been less available than usual, saying "I have to work and I'm closing the store" or "I'm actually going to go visit my sister that night but maybe on the other side of Christmas?" When she'd reminded him of her trip to Wisconsin he said, "Oh, duh. Well, right after you get back then. Have a fantastic time and bring me back something!" And she had. In her bag was a University of Wisconsin Badger Hockey t-shirt, as he'd told her once that hockey was the only sport he followed closely.

She had no idea how she'd approach him about it. She'd never in her life said to a boy, "I like you and I was wondering if you felt the same?" or anything akin to it. Just the thought of saying something like that made her so nervous that she changed her mind at least 3 or 4 times during the flight from Chicago. She tried to think of how'd she say it. She looked out the window of the plane and then back down at a blank page in a notebook. She scribbled down "*While I was on my trip I realized I should have just said 'Yes' when she asked me out that first time.*"

That wasn't bad, she thought. She also wrote "*I know for a while there you liked me and I don't know how you feel about it now but I was kind of hoping you might still feel that way?*" She immediately crossed that idea out. "*This might seem weird or maybe too late but would you want to go out? And I mean really go out.*" She crossed that out too, thinking to herself, "Gee, Anna, why don't you just give him a note asking him to a movie with a box for Yes, a box for No, and a box for Maybe!"

She tried "*I overthink everything and I know I do that and I overthought you and now I don't want to think about anything except how much I like spending time with you.*" It reminded her of something he might say, which she thought was a good thing because then he'd understand it. She circled the idea with her pen.

"Don't chicken out," Eileen had warned her. It came after Anna told her she wanted to tell Cal how she felt once she got back to California.

"The worse he can say is 'No'," Eileen reminded her.

"Or he could say he is going out with this little gothy sophomore who is clearly into him," she'd added.

"How gothy?" Eileen asked. "Like pale vampire goth?"

"No," Anna explained. "More like dark hair, dark clothes but still really cute in a weird sort of way."

"I hate her already," Eileen said.

"You don't even know her. I don't know her," Anna said.

"Well, I'm gonna hate her *for* you because I want you to get what you want," Eileen added.

Getting what she wanted had always been important to Anna, more so than she wanted to admit. Good grades, high test scores, winning a basketball game. But she'd never felt competitive about a boy, not even Kyle because things with him had just kind of happened. She hadn't pursued him and to the best of her knowledge there hadn't been anyone jealous when they became a couple. He'd asked her to go bowling, she said yes, they had a good time, kissed goodnight, went to a movie a week later, kissed some more, and then without even a real conversation they were a couple around school. She felt a little foolish because she knew if she had just said 'Yes' when Cal had approached her in the same way that she wouldn't be writing down ways to try and tell him that now, 3 months later, she wanted to say just that: "Yes".

--

The first week back after the holiday break consisted of two kinds of conversations among Seniors at Crestview: The first was "How was your break?" with subsequent questions of "Did you go anywhere?", "Did you get anything good for Christmas?" and "Did you hear so and so broke up over break?" or "Did you hear so and so got together?" The second set was more general and academic: "How are your applications coming?" and "Where are you applying to?" By lunch on the first day back Cal had engaged in both topics, letting friends know that he was applying to Sacramento, Chico as a backup, and, as he often put it, "A school up in Oregon that most people haven't even heard of." He mentioned Southern Oregon nonchalantly, both because he didn't want to answer questions about it and because he liked the idea of that college being his alone, like a secret. He told Reed, "I know everyone else can look it up but so far as I know I'm the only person even applying there. Part of the appeal is I get to be completely new to people there. No one will know what I was like here unless I tell them."

He knew Reed understood, since Reed had his own secret or lesser known school on his list with Lewis and Clark. Cal had never heard of it until Reed mentioned it a time or two. Reed told him he was just as eager to see if college really was a chance to restart; to put whatever teenage caste system label had been put on him in the past. By junior year Cal had accepted and would even describe himself as being a "B+ Crowd" kid, with the plus meaning he was never ostracized from more popular cliques. If he saw someone of higher social status at a party or around school he was never shy about saying hello or engaging in conversation. He knew it was a different story for Reed.

"The dice were cast on me before high school even started," Reed explained. "I can't reinvent myself even if I wanted to because there are some assholes here that would never let me.".

When Reed told him that back in sophomore year Cal hadn't really believed it and for his own sake didn't want to believe it. But in the 2 years since he'd learned Reed was mostly right. He'd seen classmates come back from a summer with some kind of drastic change; a weight loss, a different look, different hair, different attitude, and then try to add different friends only to find that they weren't welcome. He once equated such a dynamic to concerts, telling Reed, "A sold out show is a sold-out show. It doesn't matter how cool you look at the door. You're only getting in if you know someone."

"Or if you're willing to screw someone in the band," Reed said, continuing the metaphor. "And I'm not doing that."

Cal was sitting with Reed at lunch on the first day back from break, hearing about his family's trip up to Seattle over the holidays when Melody sat down next to him.

"Hey," she said, leaning in close to him and then reaching for his hand.

"Hey there," he said, wrapping his fingers around hers. "Reed, you remember Melody, right?"

96

Reed greeted her with a simple, "How's it going?"

"So this," Cal said, waving his free hand back and forth between himself and Melody, "This is what happened with me over the holiday."

"He likes me," Melody said with a smile. "Even though I told him Poison sucks."

Reed laughed. Cal and Reed had seen Poison at the Cow Palace the previous Spring and had tickets to see them again the next month.

"They're really fun to see live," Reed said to her.

"Yeah, but I just can't deal with girls who flash their boobs for bands," she said.

"That's just in videos," Cal said, before turning to Reed. "Though remember there was that one girl at that one show…"

Melody slapped his arm lightly.

"It's just lame," she said. "I haven't been to many concerts but you'd probably have to pay me to see a band like that."

"Well, then I guess you wouldn't want to come with me to see Love/Hate this weekend then," he said.

"I don't even know who they are," she said. "You like way too many bands, Cal."

"This is absolutely true," Reed said in agreement. "Glad I'm not the only one whose noticed."

Cal couldn't put up a reasonable argument.

"Whatever," he said, continuing to try and describe to Melody what the band in question was all about. "Love/Hate are sort of like Guns 'n Roses with a little 60's psychedelic vibe going. Lots of songs about drugs and booze and crazy L.A. stuff. I was going to ask you to come with me to Oakland to see them but since you're not into 'those bands'…"

"I'll go," she said, pulling at his arm. "But I'm not flashing my boobs for 'em."

"But they make you do it at the door," Cal said seriously.

Reed shook his head.

"They absolutely do not make you do that at the door, Melody," Reed said.

"What time is the show?" she asked. "Or when does it end? I'd have to check it with my Mom."

"I would guess it'll be over by 11. We could be back by midnight."

"Ooh," she said. "That might be a tough one but I'll figure it out. She doesn't like me out past 11 or so unless I'm spending the night somewhere. It's lame, but she's a bitch so…"

Cal had started to pick up on a few things about his new girlfriend. She had mentioned a few times that she saw her father less than she wanted but generally got along with him. Life at home was just her and her Mom. Cal got the impression they argued a lot, that Melody liked to rebel a bit, and that her mom had a particular concern about Melody when it came to boys. The more he got to know her the more he recognized the person Melody reminded him of most was his older sister. Rachel was 6 years older than Cal and had never finished high school, in part because she was constantly getting into trouble by cutting classes, skipping entire days, running off with her boyfriend who later became her husband and then, the previous summer, her ex-husband. She'd left home at 17 and except for a one week stay during the divorce had not lived there since. She had come over for Christmas day, with a new boyfriend who seemed, if nothing else, nicer than Derek, her ex-husband.

Cal noticed Melody had a similar toughness and attitude that he could remember Rachel having at the same age of 16. He was just 10 at the time but had vivid memories of the arguments from downstairs between his sister and their parents, with a lot of shouting, a lot of slammed doors, a lot of his mother crying and equal shares of his father yelling. Amid all the arguments he'd once gone into Tyler's room and asked, "What do we do?" Tyler answered quickly with "We don't do anything. We stay out of it." So whenever Rachel and their parents got into over her latest F in a class or not coming home or the pot they smelled from her bedroom Cal just stayed in his own room until it was over.

Cal also reminded himself that Melody was nothing like Rachel at all. She had revealed the occasional pot smoking but didn't smoke cigarettes, she was right there at school with him, and so far as he knew she didn't cut classes or find herself in detention regularly. She had some edginess to her that Cal wasn't used to, especially compared to other girls he'd gone out with. But he told himself repeatedly that difference was the entire point and part of the attraction. He also got the impression that her attraction to him was similar; he was different than other guys she'd been out with. She'd said at least a dozen times since they'd made their relationship 'official' that he was the nicest guy she'd ever known, never starting an argument or making fun of her or telling her she was wrong or dumb for liking a certain movie, TV show, or band.

"I know the Cure isn't really your thing," she told him one night when she'd brought a tape of their album *Disintegration* to listen to in his car, "But I like that you'll just sit here and listen to it with me and not laugh at me when I sing along. I feel like I can be myself with you."

She was affectionate and didn't seem to mind showing it in front of others, which was also new to him. Even the way she'd just casually come up at lunch, sat next to him, and made it clear to anyone watching that they were a couple was unlike anything he'd experienced before. He'd heard Doug complain before about girls he'd been out with being "too clingy" or "getting too attached" and then breaking up with them because of it. And though Cal never said a word out loud about it, he'd been jealous that Doug had anyone like that in his life. Someone being that way with him was what Cal had always hoped for. He didn't expect such a person to be quite like Melody but when it was he was so happy to have it that the various tiny things about her that gave him pause were easy to brush away.

--

Anna would later write in her journal *"The bravery I had built up to talk to Cal about going out on a date together turned out to be like a soap bubble. You blow it up as big as you can and for a few magic seconds you get to watch it rise in the air and then fall before it pops."*

At first she'd planned to talk to him on the first day back to school. She thought their daily car ride would be as good a time as any. But she quickly dismissed the idea, figuring it needed to be a longer talk and they wouldn't have enough time, especially after catching up on their holidays, with him wanting to hear about her trip to Kenosha and then letting him share whatever he'd done over the break. She'd concluded it would be best to wait and approach him after school. She'd call him or maybe even just walk the few blocks to his house and see if he was up for a walk and talk like they'd done so many times since becoming friends.

By 1pm on Monday she knew it wasn't going to happen. Before even seeing him from afar with her at lunch she had heard from Tracy during the mid-morning break that Cal was going out with Melody.

"I saw him with her at the movies last week. It was kinda gross," Tracy said. "Lot of kissing and just--"

Anna cut her off. "I don't need to know that."

She hadn't told anyone, not Tracy or Eileen, that she planned to talk to Cal and tell him how she felt. She'd come to learn that Tracy was a bit of a gossip and mentioned the news about Cal and Melody without any real prompting.

"I would have thought he'd have told you about Melody this morning," Tracy said.

"Nope. We just talked about what we did on break and then how nervous we are about applications. He didn't mention her at all."

"Well, for what it's worth I doubt it'll last," Tracy commented. "A Senior starting to date a sophomore is just a recipe for a breakup."

"Who knows?" Anna said, doing her best to not show her disappointment.

"It's like *Sixteen Candles*," Tracy added. "It's always bothered me that people think, 'Aww, he kisses her sitting on the table over the cake and they live happily after'."

"What's wrong with that ending?" Anna asked. She'd seen the move in question countless times and always liked the ending just fine.

"It's bullshit," Tracy continued. "Samantha is a sophomore, Jake is a senior, he's too hot for her anyway, and in the sequel he'd be off to college and breaking up with her before he goes to some frat party for Halloween."

Tracy's knowledge of all things John Hughes had been one of the first things Anna had liked about her. She could both recite and dismantle the stories and plots of just about any of the most popular movies that seemingly their entire class had grown up watching.

"Thank you. I needed that." Anna said, laughing at the visual of Tracy's imagined *Seventeen Candles* plot. "So what would have happened to Long Duck Dong?"

Tracy started in on a wild tale of Long Duck Dong ultimately transferring to Samantha's school and becoming part of a new, invented story. As she described it Anna concluded the whole idea of anything romantic with Cal had ended for the best. He had found someone he liked, she had found out about it before potentially humiliating herself, and they were still good friends, which was her original instinct and, as she reminded herself, the right one. But she didn't like Melody. She didn't know her at all and it felt a little silly to think that way but she could hear Eileen in her head telling her what to do.

"Oh, just hate the little bitch for a while," is what Eileen would say if she were at Crestview.

Anna decided that was fair and was pleased she was ready to follow her best friend's advice, even without her really giving it.

--

Cal sat across the desk from Mrs. Shellers, watching as she looked over his application and essay for Southern Oregon State College. She quietly made remarks like "That looks good" and "Oh, good you noted that your drama class is by audition only". When she finished reading she said, "I could nitpick but the fact of the matter is you're a very good writer and you actually did something that a lot of my students don't do in these essays: You showed a sense of humor. That whole thing about the person you are at school versus how you feel inside and the hope that college will bring it out. Your metaphor for it was very clever."

In his essay Cal wrote *I really love music and I love some of the most popular songs that everyone likes. They're catchy, they have a verse-chorus-verse structure that is easy to memorize or get stuck in your head and they become the ones thousands of people sing along to in unison. But the songs I admire, the songs that move me the most, are the ones I always find hidden on an album; the song that doesn't get made into a single or a video because it's longer or it isn't catchy enough. But it says something deeper when you really listen to it. That's how I've felt a lot of the time in high school, both in class and socially. I know what pleases the crowd, what pleases teachers, and it never seems too hard to find what strikes a familiar and pleasing chord. But I know those more challenging, poetic, risky, less mainstream words, thoughts, and ideas are inside me and I want to find a way to show more of that to the world. I am hoping that is what college will give me the opportunity to do and I believe Southern Oregon State would be the place I could do it.*

It was the section he was most nervous about but also the proudest of. He was glad Mrs. Shellers had noticed it.

101

"I really want you to get into this school," she said, writing something down in her notebook. "So, before you send all that off give me until Monday because I want to write you a letter of recommendation."

Cal wasn't sure what to think of that. He asked "Do you think I need one?"

"They never hurt and they're not required but I think someone vouching for your unique qualities will be a nice addition. I am 95 percent confident you'll get accepted but I want to get to 99," she explained.

"Wow. Thank you," he said. "I don't want that to be too much trouble, though."

"I usually only have to write them if someone is appealing their rejection but from time to time I like to write one up front. But I do want to know...Are you serious about this school? Is it your first choice?" she asked.

Cal had been wrestling with that question for what felt like forever but it only dated back to the prior Spring. It was the most expensive of his three schools, the farthest away, and would be devoid of any familiar faces. He knew several people applying to Sacramento and a few to Chico. It felt ridiculous to have that be a factor but he couldn't escape it. He'd been having an internal tug-of-war between what he thought was the bold and brave thing in going to Oregon, or a choice that would come with more comfort, like seeing some familiar faces more often and being closer to home.

"It's kind of a tie, to tell you the truth," he said. "It's like we've talked about. Southern is way less students, way smaller town, and so much farther away. And I wouldn't know a soul. Where with Sac I'd know a few people and home wouldn't be too far but still far enough, you know?"

Mrs. Shellers nodded.

"I do know," she said. "This happens all the time. It's not an easy decision. But it's *your* future and I will tell you the same thing I tell everyone. Don't do it for your parents. Don't stay close to home because your best friend or your girlfriend is doing the same thing. Because I know you may not believe it but you probably haven't had your last best friend or girlfriend yet, Cal."

"Yeah," he said, but was completely unconvinced.

He left her office agreeing to pick up her letter on Monday, all the while thinking about what she'd said about friends and girlfriends. He wasn't terribly worried about Reed because so long as he got in he was going to go to Lewis and Clark in Portland. They'd stay in touch. Cal thought it would be a blast to go visit his friend up the I-5 north. Doug, on the other hand, had two years left and Cal worried more about going his separate ways from him than he did about anyone else. Cal knew they were both aware of the part of their friendship that was like a big brother and little brother. He could point to specific nights, specific parties, and some moments in hanging out where things might have been different for Doug if he wasn't around. It was always Cal that got his hot-tempered friend to calm down and not get in a fight. It was Cal who would take a cup of beer out of Doug's hand and say, "Enough." Cal had pulled him out of parties when he was crazy drunk, picking fights or making fun of some other guy's girlfriend. He would then have Doug spend the night at his house so that Doug's Mom wouldn't know about any of it. He knew there was no choice he could make for college that would keep him around to look after Doug and he felt guilty about it.

Then there was Melody, who rarely let two days go by without mentioning things like "Next year" or "When you're gone" or "I hope you're not going to go too far away because just thinking about it makes me sad." Even her mere mention of there being a next year as a couple was completely new to him. If she was saying it that meant she was imagining it and he didn't want to lose that. But he didn't want to be naive either. He'd known girls whose older boyfriends had left for college and got their hearts shattered. Cal had literally been the shoulder some of them cried on when it did. He was also the guy who would tell a girl whose boyfriend was off at college that said boyfriend would eventually break her heart and that is why she should be preemptive and go out with *him* instead. That approach and argument had never once worked but he'd tried it multiple times.

Tyler visited home for the Martin Luther King holiday weekend and Cal found himself in a rare moment of asking his older brother for advice.

"I don't remember if you were dating anyone when you left for Santa Barbara but just out of curiosity were you?" he asked Tyler.

Tyler chuckled.

"Oh my God, it's January and you're already worried about leaving your little girlfriend behind." Tyler said "That's adorable, Cal."

"Fuck you," felt like the appropriate response. *And how the hell does Ty even know about Melody anyway?*, he thought.

"I dated a girl over the summer that I was working with but it was casual from the start because I was going south and she was going north and we decided to just be a summer thing," Tyler explained. "But, yeah, things like going away and having a girlfriend or boyfriend back home that has a year or two left of high school? That never works."

He had to give his brother credit. He almost seemed like he was trying to be helpful. Tyler added, "Well, Tim Hayes married Becca but that's because she got pregnant but I wouldn't exactly call that a success story."

Cal had seen Tim Hayes, a guy who had graduated the same year as Tyler, around town a few times. He thought he'd seen him working at the new Blockbuster video store right near the Phil-a-Bagel.

Tyler continued with, "But you may want to hold on to this chick, Cal, because remember how when you were a freshman at Crestview and all the girls in your grade went out with sophomores and juniors and even a few seniors that went cradle robbing?"

"Sure, I remember."

Cal remembered it all too well. It was painful at the time in his young love life.

"Well...same thing in college," Tyler explained. "You get in the dorm and if the girl doesn't have a boyfriend off at another school or back home then she gets swept off her feet by some older guy that knows his way around campus. They find that very comforting."

"So that was your approach, too? Prey on the vulnerable college freshmen girls?" he asked.

"Pretty much. Next year if you meet some girl in the dorm and she tells you some guy helped her put her dorm bed up on cinder blocks to make more space that's code for they probably slept together. Or he was trying to."

"Seriously?" Cal asked.

"That's just an example," Tyler said. "But, hey, college is cool and you'll have fun. And in your second year you'll be the guy welcoming in the new coeds. So it all goes in a cycle."

It was a surprisingly nice or at least semi-supportive thing for Tyler to say. He had done that with greater frequency in recent months, including when he'd come over from Davis for Christmas. He'd even said to Cal that he was working on being a "kinder, gentler person" at the suggestion of his girlfriend, Katherine, who he had also brought around to the house over the break.

"Are you still thinking about Sac State for school?" Tyler asked.

"A little," Cal said. "I'm considering that school in Oregon, too."

"You know Mom and Dad aren't as high on that one, right?" Tyler asked.

He knew it all too well. Anytime they mentioned colleges they'd say Sacramento first and if they mentioned Southern Oregon at all it was later in the conversation, often as "that nice little school in Oregon."

"Where do you think I should go?" Cal asked.

He couldn't believe he was asking Tyler for such advice but he seemed to have caught his brother in one of these new kinder, gentler moments.

"I honestly don't care where you go," he answered.

That was the Tyler he knew.

"But," his brother continued, "For me personally? If you went to Sac I'd be a 30-minute drive away if you really needed something but I wouldn't factor that in because I'm already looking at grad schools and some out of state jobs. I won't be there forever. Plus…"

Tyler stopped.

"Plus what?" Cal asked.

"You're not me. And truly, I don't mean that to be a dick. You write, you do plays, you're way more right brain and creative. People I've known who are like you tend to do better at smaller schools. Not always but a lot of the time."

Tyler dug into his pocket. A second later he was holding a quarter.

"Here, let me show you something I saw in a psych class," Tyler said. "I'm going to flip a coin. Heads is Sacramento, tails is Oregon."

Tyler flipped the coin into the air. It landed on his palm, he flipped it over to his wrist and covered it with his hands, teasing the reveal

"Quick...what do you *want* it to be?" Tyler asked him.

"What?"

"The whole time I was flipping the coin a part of you was rooting for one or the other, and you know it," Tyler explained. "Deep down you already know."

"I wanted it to be Oregon," Cal admitted.

Tyler put away his quarter.

"Then go," he said. "It's not that far. A friend of mine has been up near there for skiing and Katherine's parents went to the Shakespeare thing and said it was amazing. It sounds like a cool little city. I might even visit. And Mom and Dad will get over it."

Cal was shocked by what his brother was saying.

"If you're being this nice is because of Katherine you better never break up with her," he said.

"I'll do my best," Tyler promised.

--

After abandoning the conversation she'd planned to have with Cal about her shift in feelings toward him, Anna worried she wasn't being a very good friend at all. She hadn't so much as asked him about Melody. He'd made passing references to her on the drives to school but she sensed he was just as uneasy talking to her about it as she was with bringing it up. But one morning she decided it was time for that to stop.

"So," she said, as they pulled away from her driveway on their way to Crestview. "I was thinking about this last night and I've got the impression that you might not be talking to me about Melody for some reason."

"What reason would that be?" he asked.

She could hear a hint of nervousness in his voice.

"I don't know. Maybe it's weird because I'm a girl or because you don't want to confide in me or something?" she suggested

"It's not because you're a girl," he said. "It's just I've had a lot of people lately talking with me about her."

106

"What are they saying?" she asked.

He sighed before answering.

"Things like it's not a good idea and 'What about next year?' and 'Aren't you going to end up hurting this poor girl?' Stuff like that."

"Whose saying all that?" she asked.

"Everyone," he said. "My mother, my brother, Reed. Even my guidance counselor hinted at it."

"Your guidance counselor? How would she know who you're dating?"

"She didn't say it specifically," he explained. "But she mentioned something about not letting where friends are going to school or some relationship you have right now be part of your decision about what college to go to.".

"That's good advice, actually," she said.

"I suppose. Doesn't make it any less annoying."

"But have you thought about that? Like if this lasts what next year looks like?"

"A little," he said. "But it's not even a thing yet. There's a chance I don't get in anywhere, right? And then I'm living at home and going to Diablo Valley like so many other people will and then it doesn't matter."

"That's true," she said, adding, "And you two might not even last that long."

She regretted the words the moment they came out of her mouth. She immediately braced herself for him to be defensive. And he was.

"Thanks for the vote of confidence," he said.

"I didn't mean it like that. It's just you've told me that in the past when you've dated someone it never lasts," she said.

Once again she felt like she had done the verbal equal of a bad pass on the basketball court.

"So it's doomed anyway and I should spare myself or her or both of us the pain? Is that what you're telling me?" he asked.

He was getting upset and she searched for a subject change.

"It's really none of my business," she offered.

"Oh, Anna," he said. "We go to Crestview. Everything is everybody's business. You haven't figured that out yet?"

107

"It's not unique to Crestview," she said. "People gossip and it's annoying. I'm sorry I brought it up."

"I just want one person to say, 'Hey, Cal, I'm really glad you met someone that really seems to like you.' Because let me tell you...that hasn't happened very often."

She immediately thought of her own feelings and what she had hoped to tell him just a few weeks before.

"I don't think that's true at all," she said.

The front seat of the truck felt smaller than usual. She thought of just grabbing a cassette from below the stereo where he always had a couple ready to go. Just grabbing one and pretending to be interested in it or asking about whatever album it was could break the tension.

"You don't know that about me," he said, staying on the subject. "You've known me for 3, 4 months? So let me tell you. It's always been me in pursuit. Me trying to tell someone how I feel. It gets exhausting. So, yeah, I'm kinda happy that I met someone and she just liked me right from the start without some kind of sales pitch or whatever."

She was quiet, letting his words linger and hoping that whatever she'd said to upset him would subside. The entire conversation had been a bad idea. But after several moments she found herself wanting to add something for her own sake.

"For what it's worth," she said. "You never had to sell yourself to me. I liked you from the start."

And she knew she had. She'd reflected on it, as far back as seeing him over the back fence of the new house. Before they'd even met her instincts were that he seemed like a nice person and she'd been drawn to him.

"As a friend," he said quietly.

"Yes," she said. It felt diminishing, like what she was or what she had wanted at the time wasn't enough. So she said as much. "I'm sorry if that hasn't been good enough."

"It's fine," he said.

"Great," she said quietly. "I was really aiming for 'fine.'"

He let out a long sigh.

"What do you want me to say?" he asked. "We met, I liked you, I asked you out, we had half a dozen conversations about it and I accepted that you just wanted to be friends. And then I moved on. That's what people do, Anna."

"I know. I've seen people do it. Again, whatever you think is unique about this school or this city or this state? It isn't. I've seen this all before with friends and guys and everything."

"Well then why do you seem to be…I don't want to say 'jealous' because that's arrogant but…pissed?" he asked. "It's like you're pissed off about me and Melody."

"Disappointed," she said, just as they had reached the school parking lot.

He parked the truck and turned the car off.

"Out of curiosity, how exactly have I been so disappointing?" he asked.

"Because I thought you were different," she said. "You're different in so many other ways… how you talk, how you think, how nice you are…most of the time. And I just thought you saw things the same way I did about getting involved with someone this year."

"Well there you go. I'm not different. I'm the same. I'm like anybody else," he said. "When I tell someone how I feel and I get rejected I get hurt and then I make the best of it and then I move on. But I'm not going to apologize for meeting Melody, especially to you."

"Especially to *me?*" she asked. "That seems a little uncalled for."

He let out a groan. "Did you or did you not say to me at one point, 'Why don't you meet someone who likes music the way you do or wants to go to concerts like you do'? Well, guess what? I did. Melody likes those things."

She had said those things but she didn't like having them thrown back in her face. When she said that they were having a general conversation about finding things in common with people. It had been a nice back and forth, and moments like that had been what she liked about him in the first place. It was those kinds of exchanges she'd told Eileen about in explaining why Cal was special.

"I'm happy for you," she said. "This isn't me attacking you or saying something about Melody. I would be worried about any friend getting involved with anyone when they knew they're not going to be around in a year. Maybe I'm worried about Melody."

"You don't know Melody," he said. "And I doubt you're so concerned about her."

"It doesn't matter. I assume she's a nice person because I don't think you'd go out with her if she wasn't. But you're the older person. The more mature person. The one who *leaves* has it easier. The one that gets left behind gets hurt."

He shook his head.

"Really? Did it work that way for you? Because it seems like you left Kenosha and--"

"I was *taken* from Kenosha. I didn't leave. I didn't have a choice. My family moved! And thank you for throwing that hurt right back in my face."

He went quiet. Anna sensed that if they kept up the arguing she was going to cry, and it would be yet another moment where she had cried in front of him. When she thought about it she became all too aware that she had done that more with Cal then she had anyone else in her entire high school existence. She had cried that one morning in the car, once or twice on a walk when she mentioned how homesick she was, and once while watching a movie with him.

"Anna," he said, calmer than before. "You don't need to worry about me, okay? I will figure it out. If Melody and I keep going strong, that's my thing. If it blows up in my face, then that's my problem, too. So I promise I won't come to you and cry or whatever if it doesn't work out, okay?"

She felt the tear welp up in her right eye.

"I'd *want* you to come to me if something went wrong," she said. "Or if something goes good or if something is weird or anything. Because I care about you. A lot. I'm sorry that I'm not good at saying it or saying it in the way you need to hear it but I really do. When I was visiting home I talked about you... this amazing friend I'd made. I told my best friend ever that you were the closest thing I'd found to her out here. How meeting you has made this move that I never wanted, that I spent so much time being sad about, suddenly okay. Better than okay."

She waited for him to say something, watching as other students walked by the car, a few peering into what clearly must have looked like an intense conversation.

He stayed quiet.

110

"I'm sorry that you don't value that kind of friendship the way I do." she said. "That maybe it isn't as important to you as if we'd gone out or started being a couple. Because for me, what you've been is what I needed. And I know that sounds selfish but it has made me appreciate you more than I would if we'd become something else."

"I get it," he said.

"Do you?"

"Maybe," he said. "But I've heard things like this before, Anna. I could recite it. 'You're such a nice guy, Cal.' 'I really want to find a guy *like* you, Cal. But not you.' It's nice and it's meant to not hurt my feelings or keep me around or whatever but I've heard it."

"That's not what I'm saying at all," she said, feeling upset all over again.

"You're just saying a nicer version of it," he said. "A remix."

She grabbed her backpack and opened the car door.

"You're right. I'm just giving you the same thing you've heard before," she said. "But maybe there's a reason you hear that from people, Cal."

"And why's that?" he asked

"Because as nice as you are, as thoughtful as you can be...and I've seen it and I like that part of you *so* much. But there is a side of you that is *so* typical. And I've seen that before, too. And I don't think I want to see it anymore."

She got out, closed the door somewhere between normal and slamming it and walked away, trying not to cry, but also fighting the urge to go back and shout at him. But her first period class was looming and she knew she needed to pull herself together. She told herself there was nothing about him worth being late to class for.

# Chapter Five - February 1991

## *"Opportunity"*

If he was being 100 percent honest Cal would admit the end goal or greatest hope for himself or any other guy he knew when dating someone was to eventually have sex. He thought it was especially true for anyone like himself that had never had sex before. It was not an admission he ever made among friends, not even with Doug, who would often boast, brag, gloat or share the various sexual escapades he'd had by age 16. There were times he thought Doug might be lying about all the sex he claimed he'd had, but when he saw the genuine fear and look of terror in Doug's eyes when he confided that he'd gotten his then-girlfriend Emma pregnant, Cal began to err on the side of believing him. Cal figured that Doug knew he'd never had sex but they also never talked about it. Doug didn't taunt him over it. Cal had concluded it was an unspoken understanding: "You don't give me hell about being a virgin and I never say a word about Emma to you and what a dumb ass you are for ever getting her pregnant."

After just a month and half of dating the physical side of his relationship with Melody had already escalated beyond anything with anyone before her. It was easy to find time alone with her, as Melody's mom worked till 6 or 6:30 most evenings. That gave them a window of about 2 to 3 hours after school on any given day. By February they had spent a lot of time in her bedroom, kissing, touching, laughing, listening to music, tickling each other, and various other things Cal both had and had not done with other girls.

They were laying on her bed, both shirtless, listening to music on her stereo that he loved and had eagerly shared with her. It had turned out to be a good album to make out to, at least according to Melody.

"Thank you for not trying to do...too much," she said, lying next to him with her legs over his.

Her comment caught him off guard because he thought they'd already done quite a bit. She had touched him more than any other girl had, had more readily taken her clothes off down to just her underwear, all of which was new to him.

"I'm not in a huge rush or anything," he said, lying at least a little because he absolutely wanted to go farther. But he was also happy to have reached a new height of sexual activity with someone.

"It'll happen, though," she said, kissing his cheek.

He tried to contain his surprise and the excitement of what she said. His next thought was, "When?", but he didn't want to appear like he was in a hurry.

"It's really fine," he said as casually as he could muster.

"Thank you," she said. "It's just... I kinda regret the way I lost my... ya know. Because then he cheated and was such an asshole and I can't, like, get it back."

Again he found himself trying not to show shock or respond verbally but it had surprised him just the same. Melody, 2 years his junior, had had sex. He wondered "With who and how often?"

"I'm sorry it was a bad experience," was all he could come up with. Again, he tried to play it cool.

"Me too," she said. "I hate that that's how I'm gonna remember losing my virginity."

They were quiet, listening to the music, and he thought he'd gotten away from the subject, relieved that he could let him his head swim around in it later.

"How many people have you had sex with?" she asked him.

She said it rather nonchalantly, assumingly, and he felt his body tense up, hoping she wouldn't literally feel it as she was cuddling him on the bed.

"Um, just one person," he said, lying. He hoped she wouldn't go fishing for specifics.

"Who? Anyone I know?" she asked immediately.

He wanted out of the room, which he never thought he'd find himself wanting considering he was in a girl's bedroom, on a girl's bed, with a girl's arms spread out over his bare chest and her bare breasts pressing against his rib cage.

"I don't think it's my place to share that," he said, ready to use some level of maturity and respect as his defense if she pushed the subject.

"You really are a good person," she said softly. "Aaron...the guy I had sex with...he told fucking everyone he knows we did it."

"I'm sorry," he said.

His mental rolodex of everyone at Crestview named Aaron began spinning through his mind. He knew two guys named Aaron and knew it wasn't either of them. One was a junior in his drama class who he was almost certain couldn't have been the Aaron in question given that that Aaron, while never saying he was, at least *seemed* to be gay.

"We could hunt him down," Cal suggested. "I could hold him, you kick him in the balls. We could do that anytime. Just point him out."

She laughed and Cal impressed himself with his conversational approach to finding out who Aaron was.

"He moved to Chicago," she said. "He's living with his Dad."

Cal felt at least a little relief, glad that he wouldn't accidentally pass some guy named Aaron in the halls who, as it turned out, had deflowered his girlfriend, then cheated on her, and left her not wanting to have sex at all.

She shifted her body, straddling his waist and touched his stomach.

"Talking about it totally makes me want to do it," she said, closing her eyes. "Because I can feel you."

He knew that was true. And no girl had ever said anything like that to him.

She leaned down and kissed his mouth.

"We can wait," he whispered.

"I don't want to," she said in his ear. "Do you have a...condom?"

He did. It was in his wallet and had been for a while. That caused him a moment of panic as there had been a safe sex assembly at school a few months before that had included a speaker who warned that storing a condom in a wallet could result in said condom already being broken before it was used. But he opted to use the one he had anyway and as he opened it he was relieved that, so far as he could tell, it had not broken or disintegrated in storage.

It all happened so quickly. He was self-conscious through all of it, worried that at any moment she would stop and say something like, "I thought you said you've done this before" or telling him that he was doing it wrong. That never happened and while he had no basis for comparison he felt like in terms of what was supposed to happen he had done everything right. But it was over relatively fast and he couldn't tell if she'd noticed. It went so rapidly, from excitement as it sunk in that he was going to have sex, to then taking the rest of his clothes off, getting the condom on, and then actually *having* sex, that he soon found himself in the awkward place of having to get the condom off.

"You can put in my wastebasket over there," she pointed. "I'll take it out to the dumpster later but please bury it if you can because I don't want Mom to…"

"Right," he said, not wanting his younger girlfriend to further break down the steps for disposing of a used condom. It was just a reminder that she had done it before and that this Aaron guy she had mentioned probably placed a used condom in the same wastebasket.

He wanted to ask her if it was good, if it had felt good, if he'd done it right, if it was too fast or if they should maybe do it again. There were a lot of things he wanted to say to her but amid his own sense of relief, disbelief, and excitement he couldn't find the words.

As he laid down next to her, both still naked, she had her own thing to say.

"I love you, Cal," she whispered.

He hadn't thought about those words or if he felt them. He had said them to someone before, his former girlfriend Lizzie, and that had come with its own fears and trepidation. He had not imagined someone else might say it to him first so he replied with what seemed like the right thing to say, especially to someone who he'd just lost his virginity with.

"I love you, too," he said.

After he left her house he wanted to shout the news of the day from the top of his lungs, not at or to anyone but more of a cry of relief: "I'm not going to die a virgin! I'm not going to go to college as a virgin! I did it!"

Instead he drove home, still in a bit of shock and disbelief that it had happened and rather spontaneously at that. Sure, he and Melody had talked about it and he was beginning to believe it might happen but he'd always believed there would be more build up to it or at least some kind of planning. Instead it had shifted so quickly from "Thank you for not rushing it" to "We don't need to wait" and within minutes it was over. He cursed himself for having believed too many movies and TV shows

116

that had placed entire plots or multi-episode story arcs into characters trying to have sex or deciding to have sex and how to make the first time perfect. Usually in those shows and films it was the eager, horny boy who would do it anywhere at any time vs. the chaste girl who wanted the right room, the right mood, the right song in the background. He wondered if Melody had wanted those things at some point, knowing full well that his first time had not been her first time. Maybe girls didn't really want that or maybe just Melody didn't? As quick as it had happened though, Cal was glad they'd been listening to music he really liked when it did. On his drive home from her house he promised himself he'd never forget the song "Bedspring Kiss" by Jellyfish. It was playing from her boombox the moment he lost his virginity.

--

Anna's family had attended an Episcopal church in Kenosha for as long as she could remember. Most Sunday mornings in her life had included having breakfast with her family and then going to a service. There had been a few exceptions as she got older, like if her father had to work on a case then he might stay home. When her high school basketball team was playing in weekend tournaments her parents would bypass church to come watch her play. If someone in her family was sick they would generally all stay home, and as her academic life got more and more intense she could get away with saying she had to work on a big paper or project, and her parents would abide because they knew she wasn't making it up. If they missed church it was for a reason. Generally, though, it was a family ritual, and the only changes to it had been ones she liked, like not eating much before they went and instead getting donuts or some other snack on the way home or an outing like going to a movie as a family right after. Going to church with her parents and sister was among a handful of things she knew she was going to genuinely miss when she got to college.

When they found a new church to attend in Concord the experience was different for obvious reasons. They didn't know any of the other parishioners and the pastor was new to them, some of the hymns were selected differently, and they had to find a new donut shop

117

for after church before Anna ultimately suggested they go to Phil-A-Bagel instead

"I've stopped there with Cal," she told her parents. "Californians do bagels differently than they did back home. They have strawberry ones, blueberry ones, raspberry ones…" It had been an instant hit with her parents and sister.

By February they had stopped being the "new family from Kenosha" among their fellow churchgoers. Her parents had gotten to know some other families, which Anna knew was important to them. Her sister Jackie had met some friends there, too. While Anna recognized some other Crestview students in the pews, she decided not to make too many new connections. So while her parents would socialize with other couples after services and Jackie would race off to go talk to a friend, Anna found it more relaxing to sit on a bench in the lobby of the church and either take some time to reflect on the service itself or, because it was Sunday, begin making her mental to-do list for the week ahead. She was thinking about her upcoming mid-year final exams, how prepared she felt for them, and how they at least symbolically marked the midpoint of her final year of high school when her thoughts were interrupted by a stranger.

"Hi," a voice said.

She looked up and saw a boy around her age. He was, without question, one of the most handsome young men she had ever seen. She tended to feel shallow or immature whenever that was the first thing she noticed about someone but with him it was hard to miss.

"Hello," she said, a bit flustered in the moment.

"I'm Owen Myers," he said, offering his hand, then gesturing toward the other side of the room. "I was over there talking with my parents and apparently *your* parents and they mentioned you were over here so I wanted to come introduce myself."

She instantly recognized the last name, as her parents had been to dinner at the Myers and had hosted them a month or so before. If this Owen Myers person standing in front of her had been at that dinner she knew she would have recognized and remembered him.

"I'm Analisa," she said, shaking his hand and standing up. "Or Anna, as most people say. Very nice to meet you."

"How did you like the service?" he asked, motioning to the bench as an invitation to sit down. She obliged.

"It was nice," she said. "I like Pastor Nelson. He has a good sense of humor, and I like the way he uses it."

"Me too," Owen said. "We've come here for years and he's been here for most of them."

Why then, she wondered, had she not seen his blondish-brown hair, blue eyes, and tanned skin face before then?

"I miss coming here," he said. "I go to Stanford but I'm home visiting this weekend and it's nice to be able to come today before I head back."

His explanation shifted her mind to how old he might be, as it was difficult to tell. She guessed he was anywhere from a year to three years older than her.

"How long have you been at Stanford?" she asked, impressed that he was at such a big deal of a school.

"It's my first year," he said. "I graduated from Crestview last year. Your parents mentioned you're graduating there in a few months?"

"I am," she said.

"You like it?"

"I do," she said. "I don't know if my parents mentioned it but we moved here this year so doing my senior year at a new school has been a little weird."

"That would be hard. I'm sorry you're having to go through that," he said.

They sat together for several minutes, talking about his time at Crestview. It sounded like he had been rather popular, which didn't surprise her one iota. He was incredibly good looking, as well as very polite and conversational. As he talked about life at Stanford she added "intelligent", "driven", and "interesting" to her first impressions of him. He told her he was hoping to get a degree in civil engineering but had also taken an interest in technology and computers. That wasn't unusual among many people their age but the things he talked made it sound more fascinating than she typically found the subject.

"Not to get too nerdy about it," he explained, "but how people use their personal computers is about to change dramatically. Like, did you ever see the movie *War Games*?"

She nodded that she had, though it had been many years before. It was, as she recalled, about a teenager who uses his computer to break into a government computer he thinks is a video game company and then inadvertently almost starts World War III.

"So you remember how he uses his modem to connect to other computers and all that?" Owen asked.

"Sure," she said.

"I am taking a course on computer technology and the short version of it is that by the time you and I are done with college we're all going to be connecting our computers to a wider network, with information you normally go to the library for. People will be communicating person to person more on their computers than they do by mail or even by phone. A lot of people already do it but it's expected to grow in leaps and bounds in the near future. And I find it interesting, so that might be a field to consider," he explained.

He had goals, he was taking college seriously, he used words like "future" a lot, all things that Anna found so many of her peers at school didn't talk about or talk about enough. And she was talking to him at church, and church was an important part of her life. It wasn't something she'd readily shared with many people at Crestview but back in Kenosha everyone knew she and her family went most Sundays and she didn't mind being labeled as "religious". It was a point of pride she had only revealed to a handful of her new friends.

They talked for a few more minutes as parishioners continued to make their way out of the lobby and toward the parking lot. She wished their conversation could continue because Owen Myers was very impressive. After her argument with Cal, the only boy in Concord she'd been attracted to, it felt nice to feel an unexpected onset of butterflies in her stomach.

He stood up and surprised her by gently taking her hand to help her up. *Dear God*, she thought, *my knees are going to buckle now*. But she held it together and braced herself to say goodbye to this beautiful person she would likely never see again.

"It's been really nice to meet you," he said.

"You too."

They started walking over to where their parents were still talking when he stopped.

"Analisa, I hope it wouldn't be too forward to ask if I could give you a call?" he said

"A call?" she asked, as though the concept of a telephone and telephone call was new to her. She immediately felt ridiculous for asking.

"I've really enjoyed talking to you and I thought maybe we could keep talking sometime," he explained. "If you'd rather not I completely understand. It's just nice to meet someone new and interesting."

"I would like that," she said.

She quickly went over to the first table she saw with any kind of paper or something to write with, finally finding a stack of flyers for an upcoming church event and a pen nearby. Her hand was shaking a little but she jotted down her name and phone number, folded the flyer, and handed it to him.

"Great," he said. "I'll give you a call tomorrow night if that works for you."

She smiled and nodded.

He'd even been specific about when he'd call, taking away the kind of agony she hated, waiting around to see *if* a guy would call and *when*. He was so definitive when he said it, like a promise, and one she knew he would keep.

As she reunited with her parents and Jackie she had embraced an emotion she knew was a bit childish and thought she was done feeling: She was smitten and giddy from meeting someone. Even if nothing came from it this lovely person had taken an interest in her, wanted to call her, and get to know her. She felt so light that as they walked out of the church she looked up and thought, *Thank you, Jesus,* giggling out loud and hoping her parents wouldn't notice or, if they did, ask why she was so happy.

--

They rode the BART train into Oakland just as they had many times before. To see Ozzy Osbourne, or Motley Crue, or Metallica, and several other concerts dating all the way back to the first one they'd gone to during freshman year. Back then, when they were just 14, their parents had agreed it would be okay for them to go without parents or older siblings as long as they knew the BART route and transfer stations. That

121

show had been David Lee Roth, with Poison as an opening act, so it felt appropriate to both Cal and Reed that what might possibly be their last Coliseum show together had Poison as the headliner, with the band Warrant opening the show.

"It's kinda symbolic, really," Reed said as they sat on the train. "When we saw Poison they were opening and just starting to get bigger and we were freshman. Now we're seniors and they're headliners. Get what I mean?"

Cal understood it, had even thought something similar himself but still said to Reed, "You're a dork, you know that?"

Cal felt a little guilty leaving Melody behind on a Friday night to go to a show with his friend. When they talked about it she'd expressed some frustration that struck him as being a bit of unjustified jealousy.

"Reed and I bought tickets back in late November. I didn't even really know you then," he explained. "And I'd get a third ticket but you've said you hate both bands. Like, *a lot*."

"I know, but I'd still go," she said, pouting her mouth a bit. "And make fun of those ridiculous bands."

Even if that had been the case, with her poking fun at the over the top songs and live theatrics that, for better or worse, Cal felt were part of his personal soundtrack, he still wished she had come. Ever since they'd started having sex he hated the thought of leaving her behind or not including her in anything he did socially that she might enjoy. By being the first girl he'd ever been sexual with it felt like she had given him something, and that in turn made him feel like he owed her. At one point he considered just giving his ticket to Reed, suggesting he go find a girl or another friend to take to the show. But he knew Reed would need more time than that to wrangle someone into going and he would be letting down his longest running friend. Plus, since meeting Melody he hadn't spent as much time with Reed or other friends.

"I'm going to see this show with Reed and then how about you pick a show coming up that you're into, and even if I don't like the band we'll go?" he suggested to her.

He thought it was a nice idea and even though she pretended to still be upset about missing the Poison show he could tell she liked it, too.

"And I'll get you a Warrant t-shirt from this show," he joked.

"Oh, please do… like with a picture of a girl with her legs spread and a stupid fucking Cherry Pie over her crotch," she said, referencing the band's biggest hit song, with sarcasm dripping from her mouth. Cal stifled a laugh as he couldn't rule out Warrant literally having a t-shirt just like the one Melody imagined.

He hadn't told anyone except Doug that he and Melody had been having sex, in large part because his broader circle of friends were not, so far he knew, having sex or even dating anyone for that matter. Over the previous three years most of his friends hadn't even dated as much as he had or had his level of luck with the opposite sex. And that was even with his own level of luck feeling limited. Until Doug had come along no one in his social life had made him feel like he was a loser or socially inept because he was a virgin. Conversations around who was having it simply didn't happen with his other friends because the unspoken assumption was none of them were.

It was only when Reed asked him about Melody on their way to the concert that he confided it, even as he stumbled with how to put it.

"We've been... she is...We've been having a lot sex, actually," he said, giving a forced laugh to try and make it sound as casual as any other topic. Even as he said it, "a lot" seemed a bit of a stretch, as it had happened 3 more times in 10 days. He had been keeping an accurate count.

"Well, okay then," Reed said, sounding a bit uncomfortable with the topic.

"You asked," Cal said.

"I asked you how things are with your little girlfriend," Reed reminded him. "As in, are you still happy dating her? I didn't need to know the intimate details."

"I'm sorry," he said. "Things are good. Obviously. I really like her."

'I really like her' felt like such a funny thing to say given the growing volume of times he'd said "I love you" to Melody. He'd learned it was something she liked to hear and a few times had even said she *needed* to hear it. The more he got to know her the more he noticed some things about her that gave him variations of worry and pause. It was something he wanted to talk about with someone but he didn't know who. Doug was too immature and too much of a big mouth for such a conversation. And he hadn't talked much with Anna since their

123

argument in his car weeks before. When he went to pick her up the next morning she came out and told him she'd found a different ride to school and wouldn't need to ride with him anymore. And even if they were talking he knew it wouldn't be a conversation he could have with her. The thought of talking with any girl about the girl he was having sex with was terrifying. He knew Reed was smarter and more mature than he was, at least when it came to school or making important decisions. But when it came to girls Cal considered himself the more experienced and wiser one. He figured Reed wouldn't be able to ease his mind of the minor worries he was having about Melody. With no one in his closest circles to talk to he was keeping it to himself.

For a few hours on that Friday night Cal managed to put those thoughts aside, first taking in Warrant's set, singing along with thousands of others in attendance. It was a familiar experience, one he'd always loved, but that night it felt almost too similar, mirroring past shows by similar bands. The song styles, the pace of the set, and interaction with the crowd were not especially unique. Nor was the band on stage.

"How the fuck's everyone doing in Oakland, C-A tooooniiight?!" the leader singer of Warrant called out. He continued with other shout outs of, "Check you fuckers out! I love all of you!" and "For this next one I want you to scream the hair off your nuts!"

They were followed by the headliner, Poison. He and Reed stood and cheered through the various concert staples that came with their live show, like sparking and lifting the flame of cigarette lighters they had only brought with them for the very purpose of holding them up during "Every Rose Has Its Thorn" and other ballads, doing call and response between songs with the onstage banter of their lead singer. There were also the extended guitar and drum solos, then the last song, followed by the lights going black only for the band to return for two more songs, concluding with one last grand flash of pyro, popping confetti, and "Goodnight! We love you, Oakland!"

As with so many shows before his ears were ringing on the way out. It would die down to a muffled buzzing by the time they got home and it would be gone by the next morning.

Reed was a bigger fan of the band than he was and thought the show was excellent. Cal commented that their set and even what they said on stage was almost word for word the same as the last time they saw them.

124

"I wish they'd mix it up a bit," Cal said. "They always open with 'Look What the Cat Dragged In', they always close with 'Talk Dirty To Me'. I feel like some of these bands are getting a bit predictable."

"I still like it," Reed said. "I like knowing they're going to play the songs I want to hear. I like knowing when I get a ticket I'm going to see lasers and explosions and all that. It's like a very loud circus! Who cares if it's familiar if it's fun?"

As they walked across the sky bridge from the arena to the BART station Cal wondered if he'd get out to another show with his friend before graduation. Would they be able to squeeze something in over the summer amid their summer jobs and getting ready to leave for college? He was confident they could, but even if that night wasn't going to be the last show they saw together he still felt a wave of sadness or finality come over him.

"Do shows like this come to Portland?" he asked as they took their seats on BART.

"I would think so. They have an NBA team so there is obviously an arena," Reed said.

"Good to know. If I go to Southern I'll definitely visit.

"If?" Reed asked.

"I gotta get in first," he reminded him.

Cal knew one thing for sure: Ashland didn't have arenas. He'd asked on the campus tour if bands ever rolled through town and the answer from the student giving the tour wasn't inspiring.

"On campus? Very rarely," he'd said. "Sometimes bands roll through Medford, which is about 20 minutes from here. But usually just country acts and over the hill classic rock bands. Not much worth seeing."

Ashland was small. Going to a college of around 4000 students in a town of less than 20 thousand would be very different. Growing up and living in the suburbs, Cal had grown used to hundreds of thousands of people in his city and the others around it, all feeding into San Francisco. He knew there would be some culture shock if he went to school in Oregon and the idea both appealed to and terrified him. He knew it shouldn't matter but going to shows had been such a regular part of his years in high school that he questioned how he'd do without them. But sitting next to Reed on the train got him to thinking that maybe it wasn't the shows he'd miss but the people he went to them with. Maybe he'd been putting too much stock into the idea of going someplace so unfamiliar and with no one he knew within hundreds of miles.

He turned to Reed and asked, "Are you gonna miss this? Hanging out and going to shows? You're the only other person I know who is looking at a school where so far as I know no one else from our class is planning to go."

"That's why I wanna go," Reed said. "It's a big reason I want to go. The thing is... what stops you from being as psyched about Southern as I am about Lewis and Clark is the same thing that makes my decision really easy."

"What do you mean?" Cal asked.

"You're going to miss Crestview. At least a little. I won't," Reed said. "Don't get me wrong. You're my friend and I do love going to these shows because way back when you *made* me go to these shows. And now I love it. I'll miss Concord, I'll miss Blondies and Rasputin's and all the other haunts. But I can live without it. I can live without so many things about Crestview. The cliques, the who's cool and who isn't, the secret handshakes...all of it."

It was true what Reed said about concerts. As freshmen Cal had to convince him that going to see David Lee Roth would not mean being crushed among a throng of fans on the arena floor, doing drugs, or being ridiculed by metal fans for having short hair and not dressing the part in head to toe denim or leather.

"I'll miss you and I'll miss Keith and Adam and everyone else," Reed continued. "But for me getting out of that school and waving goodbye to most of our classmates? That's easy. That can't come soon enough."

"Oh come on," Cal argued. "You're not gonna miss theater?! We've had a blast. You were the lead in December. And by the way, some of the guys you've told me were assholes to you in elementary and middle school came up to you after the shows and told you 'good job' and shook your hand and stuff. I know because I was there."

"I know," Reed said. "But it doesn't make up for all the other shit."

"Really? I know you've said they were jerks but we've all grown up and matured at least a little bit, right?"

"Some have. But you didn't know me then. We weren't friends yet. Did I ever tell that back in 7th grade Clark Baylor said he'd beat me up if I even showed up to the school dance?"

· "I don't remember that story," Cal said.

"It was the first dance of junior high and I wasn't even planning to go anyway but he still had to be an asshole," Reed said.

Cal couldn't make much of an argument, as Clark Baylor, now in 12th grade with them, was *still* an asshole. He remembered when Clark made varsity football as a sophomore, which was quite an accomplishment. But he still felt the need to bully and ridicule everyone on the JV and freshman teams, including Cal. Cal played one year of football and while Clark wasn't the only reason he didn't play the next year he definitely was among them. As he sat on the train next to Reed, Cal's mind flashed back to those locker room taunts. He could only imagine how much worse it was a few years before that in junior high.

"For what it's worth, Clark is a dick. Even his friends...after he's left a party...will say he's a dick. If I got a dollar for every one of his friends that talks behind his back..."

"And that's the kind of shit that baffles me," Reed said. "I'm a nice person! You're a nice person and I'm willing to admit that even some of the guys who used to pick on me don't do it anymore and haven't for a long time. But guys like Clark are still popular, they go to parties, he has a girlfriend and--"

"Danielle's a super bitch," Cal interrupted, referring to Clark's girlfriend.

"But he has one! Because he's tall and he's a good athlete and he's confident. So guys like him get popularity and guys like you...no offense... are somewhere in the middle... and then I'm me. They get proms and pep rallies and because of assholes like Clark I've avoided that stuff like the plague."

Cal felt bad for him, wondering if he could have done more or tried to include Reed into more of his weekend life, where he was able to at least dip a toe into the social circles Reed seemed to feel excluded from. He'd tried a time or two but ultimately had reached a place where he was just happy in his own right to be welcome at a party. He was content in being able to have found a prom date the previous year. Cal didn't feel embraced by people like Clark Baylor but he wasn't ridiculed by them either.

"Well, I'd tell you to just go throw a punch at Clark and get it out of your system but we know how that'd turn out," Cal joked.

"Exactly," Reed said, but still smiling at the thought. "I know people like that aren't worth it but you still wish...I don't know..."

After they got back to the BART station in Concord they decided to drive to the closest Denny's for a late-night snack. While he was swirling a french fry in ketchup Cal got a dose of inspiration.

"You need to go to Ball," he said to Reed, referring to the Senior Ball a few months away.

"No, I don't," Reed said.

"Yes, you do."

"Why?" Reed asked.

"Because I hate the idea that in a few months this all gonna be over and you won't have gone to a single Homecoming Dance and you didn't go to Prom last year, you haven't come to many football games and I can't get your ass to a party even if I'm the one throwing it!"

Cal had thrown a party at his house the prior spring while his parents were out of town and had deliberately invited some of the less popular kids with a grand notion of throwing the most socially eclectic bash in Crestview history. The results had been a little mixed but some of their lunchtime friends had come and been in the same place as party scene regulars for at least one night. Reed had not been one of them.

"Ball seems like a waste of time and money," Reed said.

"Fuck the money," Cal said forcefully. "I know your Mom and she will pay for everything and probably even spring for a limo because she'd be thrilled if you go."

He knew Reed couldn't counter that one. Reed's Mom may have put even more pressure on Reed to get out more or find a girlfriend than Cal or any of his other friends ever had.

"Why? Why go just for the sake of going?" Reed asked again.

"Because it's gonna be fun. It's at the friggin' Mark Hopkins in the city. That is cool. I understand missing prom last year because we had it at the rec center but this is a fancy hotel with a ballroom and city lights and maybe roaming around the city after."

He could see Reed mulling it over.

"I really don't have the energy to go try and pursue someone, go on some dates, and then hopefully have them say yes to going to Ball," Reed lamented.

"Bonk! Wrong answer!" Cal exclaimed. "You don't have to go find a girlfriend or start dating someone. It can be someone you're just friends with. Hell, ask someone in drama class. But go! Find a date. We'll go as a group."

"Have you asked Mel?" Reed asked.

"No, but I am guessing she'll say yes given that we're... I told you...never mind," he said, remembering to leave out the details.

"Why is it so important to you that I go?" Reed asked

"Because it should be important to *you*."

"It's not, though," Reed said, but then backtracked with, "I'd *like* to go but I was ready to not go, you know what I mean?"

"I do. Obviously it would be great for me if you found someone because it's fun to go in a group," he said. "But I was also thinking about all that stuff you said back on the train... about feeling like certain things aren't for you, like only certain people get to do this or that? I think it's time to say, 'Fuck that', because it's not just for them or at least it shouldn't be. It's the Senior Ball...that means Seniors. That means you, that means me."

Reed smirked before finally saying, "I'll think about it."

"I'm not going to leave you alone about this," Cal said, smiling before sipping from his soda glass.

"I know," Reed said. "It's why I am only gonna *kinda* miss you next year."

--

Anna had spent a little over 36 hours wondering why in the world Owen Myers, a stunningly good looking and very intelligent guy, had asked for her number. She gave herself plenty of credit for being a good conversationalist and even though he had Stanford attached to his name she was confident in her own intelligence, even if she was a year behind him. Her doubts were more about her physical self. She always thought she was too tall, pretty but not a head turner, admittedly a little shy, and a few boys in Kenosha had used terms like "stuck up", "bookish", and "goody goody" to describe her.

As she anticipated Owen's promised phone call she was curious about his motivations. Was he just polite or maybe the type of person who wanted to finish conversations? She doubted the latter as they hadn't really left any topic of conversation lingering or unfinished. Was it really that hard for a college freshman to meet a girl on campus? Did he have to pursue a high school girl? She hoped that wasn't the case and quickly dismissed it because, again, Owen was very handsome and kind. She couldn't imagine him struggling to attract people. So maybe he was shy, like she could be, and when he'd suddenly found someone easy to talk to he didn't want to lose that? Of all her theories and questions that was the one she most hoped was true.

It turned out it was a little of that, as he admitted as much during their first phone call, but he'd also told her he thought she was quite beautiful.

"I mostly went over to talk to you because our parents were talking about work and the fallout from Desert Storm and I didn't agree with what they were saying so I really wanted to get out of it," he'd explained. "And then your Mom had quickly mentioned your name and then pointed to where you were sitting and I thought you were beautiful so I was kind of scared to go say hi. But I did. And then I really liked talking to you."

As their phone conversation continued she felt more relaxed, all the while finding him more and more interesting. It reached a level of embarrassment, as she hadn't felt that way about talking on the phone with a boy since way back in junior high when it had happened for the first time. Owen talked about life at Stanford, how it had been a big adjustment in the Fall term but now, midway through the year, he was finding it much easier. He talked about his classes and then later his dorm and his first roommate, who had been a terrible mismatch.

"Make sure you do whatever survey they send you for roommate matching because I really didn't do a thorough job on mine," he advised. "And I got paired with a messy, kind of wild guy who was coming in really late and sleeping till noon and all that. I finally had to request a room change because I wasn't getting in any sleep!"

She told him about the schools she'd applied to and the budding anxiety that kept growing as she waited for her acceptance or rejection letters to arrive in the mail.

"That is the worst," he said. "I got my Berkeley rejection pretty quick, which definitely hurt my ego. But Stanford came through a few weeks later. I'm sure yours are going to work out."

He seemed particularly excited when she mentioned UCLA as one of the schools she'd applied to. He told her he had some friends going there who all raved about what a great campus it was, from classes to dorm life, athletics, and the never-ending number of things to do near Los Angeles. He also mentioned he'd visited there a few times already during the academic year.

They talked about their church, their faith, and she was struck by how important it was to both of them, but that neither considered themselves to be as conservative or moralistic as their parents.

"I had some friends in Kenosha that are *very* Christian," she explained. "And their parents were so strict about it that even movies like *Star Wars* were off limits. I'm very glad my parents aren't like that even though they worry about certain music and violence and sex in movies."

His parents, he said, were much the same.

"Have you heard that one song by R.E.M.? The new one, 'Losing My Religion'?" he asked.

She hadn't heard it. The shift in subject to music briefly made her think of Cal. She imagined if she was still riding to school with him she probably would have heard it by now.

"I go to this discussion group on faith and secularism on campus," he continued. "And we talked about that song the other day. I personally love it. But it was interesting because one person there thought it was literally about losing faith when, really, if you pay attention to the words it's just metaphorical. Like losing faith in a person. And I love stuff like that. I don't remember having conversations like that at Crestview. Not to sound... I don't know...superior...but it's kind of nice to be surrounded by a higher percentage of really smart people than there was in high school."

He made it sound so interesting, so intellectual, even when talking about a pop song. It was the kind of thing she also looked forward to in college.

Two days after their conversation she was with her Mom and Jackie at the mall and found herself wandering into Musicland and getting the cassette single of the R.E.M. song he mentioned, thinking about Owen the entire time.

They talked again a few days later and at the end of the conversation he asked her out.

"I'm going to be coming up next weekend for my little sister's birthday," he said. "It's on Saturday. Would you want to go out to dinner the night before?"

"I would love to," she said.

She had butterflies when she got off the phone and wasn't even shy about sharing the news with her parents. She would have to tell them anyway, as they had a rule going all the way back to freshman year that all dates needed to be approved, all boys had to come to the door and be met. Where she was going, what she'd be doing, and when she'd be back were prerequisites for being able to leave the house. On her 18th birthday she had joked with them about it.

"I'm an adult so do I still have to clear all things guys with you?" she asked.

"Yes. Because you're an adult living in our house, you're still my baby, and I still don't trust anyone with a...what you learned about in health class," her Dad joked.

She knew how much they liked the Myers family and had mentioned they were happy she'd met Owen. She figured asking their permission to go out with him would be relatively easy. She brought it up over dinner.

"Owen Myers asked me out on a date for next Friday," she said. "I am assuming that's it okay?"

Her father looked over to her mother.

"Owen seems like a good young man," her father said. "Smart, too."

Her mother agreed.

"Wait," Jackie chimed in. "That guy from church?"

Anna nodded.

"That movie star good looking guy asked *you* out?"

"Thank you for acting so shocked, Jacks."

"He was really fine," Jackie said.

"Jackie," her mother scolded.

"She's in 8th grade, Mom," Anna said. "She's going to notice guys that look like Owen."

"Oh heavens, everyone notices boys that look like Owen," her Mom said, laughing and letting go of the harsher tone.

"I can't believe I'm saying this," Jackie said, "But I'm actually going to want to hear about your date when you get back."

"Can I go out with him?" Anna asked again.

"Yes," her father said. "All the rules apply beforehand, though."

"Understood," she said. "Now can we all *not* talk about Owen?"

"Yes," her parents said in unison.

The hard part from there was waiting nearly a week for the date to happen. She again felt a little foolish for the giddy excitement and anticipation of seeing him. It was a feeling she had dismissed to the past, to crushes from years before that in hindsight made her laugh at herself for ever letting her mind or heart be so occupied about a call or a date or what might happen next.

She was upstairs when he arrived at her house. She called down to her mother that she needed another minute to get ready. It wasn't true. She'd been ready at least 20 minutes but she didn't want to seem overeager. She dressed casually for the night because he'd suggested as much on the phone.

"I thought maybe we'd just grab Skip's," he said. "Have you been there?"

She hadn't. He told her it was the best pizza anywhere near Concord, located in the next small city over, and there was bowling or a movie theater nearby if they wanted to do something after.

Owen greeted her parents with handshakes and a level of manners she knew Kyle or any other past date wouldn't have been able to pull off even if given specific instructions from her in advance. He looked nicer than most boys, too, even in what he had called "casual" clothes: Dark gray Dockers, a navy-blue Polo shirt, a light jacket for the February chill. The night before their date she'd described him over the phone to Eileen as "Jackson in *Steel Magnolias* level good looking", which had left Eileen nearly hysterical and jealous. Just looking at him made Anna feel a bit shallow. But there she was, eyeing him as she walked down the stairs, praying she wouldn't trip over her own two feet.

When they got outside he politely opened the passenger side door of his car, a gesture she'd never had anyone do for her. The interior of his Nissan Sentra was clean, another first, and he didn't even start the car until she had clicked her seatbelt. She thought if anything he might be too tidy, too kind, too smart, too easy to talk to.

As excited as she was she was still trying to figure out why he'd asked in the first place. As her sister had rudely pointed out, there had to be some girls at Stanford that would love to receive his attention and were probably more attractive than she felt she was. She tried to push such questions and self-doubt to the back of her mind as they made their way to dinner.

After they ordered their pizza Owen managed to make a conversation that was literally about pizza engaging and fun.

"Is pizza in Kenosha different from pizza here?" he asked her.

"Different? Like, how?" she asked, a bit thrown off by the subject.

"I was lucky enough to visit New York a few years ago," he said. "And the pizza there is completely different. I made the mistake of asking for mushrooms on mine and the guy behind the counter, who I kid you not actually had a name tag that said 'Mario', laughed at me and said, 'You must be from out west, kid. We don't do mushrooms on a slice here.'"

She giggled at Owen's attempt at a New York accent and her own visual of anyone named Mario. The name made her think of a little man in overalls running around a video game smashing turtles and dodging fireballs.

"I've never been to New York," she said, "But I have been to Chicago a few times and the deep-dish pizza there is incredible."

That led them to a longer conversation about what cities or states they had been to and where they hadn't and, in Owen's case, what countries he'd visited

"I went to London last summer, right after graduation," he said. "And a few years ago our family went up to Vancouver, BC."

"I haven't been anywhere," she said. "Never been out of the country and the move out here was the first time I've been to California."

"So no Disneyland? No Universal Studios or Six Flags?" he asked.

"Not yet."

She had been to several states he hadn't been to but she quickly got the impression that in addition to being well-traveled Owen's family was wealthier than hers. Her father was making considerably more money since the move to California but prior to that their family vacations had usually been by car. It sounded like Owen's family were constantly on planes whereas the move out west was only her second time on a flight to anywhere. When Owen rattled off London and Canada, a family trip to Hawaii, the Grand Canyon, and New York he made it sound rather casual. She wondered if he knew how lucky he was.

It was a warmer than average night for February so they opted to go to a miniature golf course that wasn't too far away from the pizza place. As they tried to hit golf balls over ramps, past rotating windmills and other obstacles they talked and shared stories. She liked how easily their conversations flowed. He made Stanford and college in general sound like a wonderful change. But he also asked a lot of questions, getting her to talk more than she normally would, be it on a first date or in any other setting.

"What do you hope to do after college?"

"Have you ever had a book you read change your life?"

She loved that one.

And he wasn't shy about asking how she felt about dating in general.

"Honestly," she said, "Back in Kenosha I had one boyfriend and it lasted about a year. When I moved here I thought 'What's the point?' It's going to be hard enough just to make new friends, get adjusted to a new school, apply for college, bite my nails off waiting for acceptance and rejection letters and so on…"

"But you said 'Yes' when I asked," he said.

"I did," she said, blushing a little. "I guess you caught me at a good time. The applications are out so I'm not stressed out about that part and, no offense to your former high school, but the guys at Crestview have not been terribly impressive."

She felt a little bad saying it, realizing he probably still had friends there and thinking of Cal in particular. A few weeks before she had been very angry with him, then it shifted to what she considered disappointment. But she also wished they were friends and that she hadn't let things get so mixed up. They had barely spoken since and she missed talking to him.

"I think if you'd met me a year ago you might not have been too impressed with me," Owen said, quickly adding, "Not to imply you are now or anything."

"I'm impressed," she said. "I really enjoy this. You haven't suggested we hit some kegger or told repeated dirty jokes or shared your Pauly Shore impersonation or other ridiculous things I've heard around school."

"I have to confess, though," he said. "Not too long ago I was really good at being your typical jock type. I was probably more like some of those things you just mentioned."

She had a hard time imagining him behaving the way so many of her peers did. She kept having to remind herself he was only a year older than her because he seemed leaps and bounds more mature.

"What changed?" she asked. "What made you not act that way?"

"I got away," he said. "I got to start over and be more of myself."

"You weren't yourself at Crestview?"

"Not as much as I wanted to be," he said. "It was like... I had this group of friends, mostly athletes, and we'd all been tight ever since we figured out we were good at sports. That was my circle and it came together before we even got to high school, really. But by the time Senior year rolled around we were all still together for football and baseball but some of them were party guys and others still thought it was fun to pick on freshmen or things like that. And I...this sounds bad...but I kind of started to hate some of them."

To Anna, 'hate' seemed like a very strong word.

Owen sat along a brick bench near the snack area. She sat next to him, the closest she had been to him all evening.

"What did you do?" she asked. "About your friends?"

"I just kept hanging out with them," he said with a shrug. "Because that's all I knew how to do. They'd say stupid things or crack gross jokes and I'd laugh and when they'd pick on someone or do something I didn't like I wouldn't take part... but I didn't speak up either. I was just going through the motions. Not being very true to myself."

"That must have been hard," she said.

"It wasn't all bad. I mean, I still care a lot about some of those guys. But this last summer and into the fall, when we all started leaving for our different schools, I was kind of relieved to see that circle break or shrink a bit."

"And do you like the people you've met at Stanford?" she asked.

136

"Definitely," he said, the tone of his voice much more positive. "I've been able to find people I can be more authentic with. And then, I also met someone like you."

He reached over for her hand and she took it. She wondered if he was going to try and kiss her, bracing herself for the moment, quickly deciding if he did that she would kiss him back, even though there were people around them playing mini-golf and getting snacks. She didn't like kissing in public. It had driven Kyle crazy because he would try to kiss her at movies or even at school and sometimes she'd just go along with it to avoid an argument.

Owen didn't try to kiss her. He just held her hand and asked her some more questions. About church, about her favorite books and movies, about winters in Kenosha and a variety of other things. When they finished up playing he drove her home, walked her to her porch, and it was then that they shared a soft kiss goodnight.

She went inside still thinking about him, about kissing him, and eager to write in her journal about the best date she'd ever been on.

# Chapter Six - March 1991

## *"Come Back Down"*

It was a tradition Cal had been looking forward to, along with several other Senior year traditions at Crestview that had already come and gone and others still ahead.

In late September, just a few weeks after school had started, there was the Senior Picnic. The location changed from year to year. Sometimes it was just a trip to the Walnut Festival grounds, where Seniors could spend the day playing touch football or swimming at the pool. His brother Tyler's class had been the first and last class to have their picnic at a nearby waterslide park. The class of 1988 broke too many park rules about how many people could go down a slide at once or how long they could stay in the pool at the bottom and, of course, the rules about stopping in the middle of the slide. Two students had wound up in the ER and three years later teachers and staff still talked about it. Cal's class of Seniors wound up the Putt `n Play, which had been a total blast with mini-golf, go-karts, and batting cages, among other things.

In late January there had been the Senior Banquet, which was a mix of awards for some academic achievements and a talent show, where various students or groups of them performed comedy, singing, and skits. Clark Baylor had attempted standup comedy but it was mostly him going person by person through the audience and making fun of them. Cal and three others in his drama class had dressed as The Village People for a lip sync. It was a Crestview Senior Banquet Tradition. Every class for years going years back had done "YMCA". Cal was proud of himself for mixing it up at least a little, as he'd managed to find a medley of "YMCA", "Macho Man", and "In the Navy" on a random cassette at a record shop.

"Senior Cut Day" wasn't as grand a tradition, nor was it directly supported or sponsored by the school, it's teachers, or principals. At best, teachers looked the other way on the first Monday of March in any given year when the Senior class would collectively skip school and, ideally, find groups of friends to go do something fun with for the day.

139

It dated back over 20 years and had gained even more popularity after the movie *Ferris Bueller's Day Off* had become a huge hit a few years before. The goal for any class of Seniors was to see what percentage of the total class would take part, document it in the school paper, and see how they compared to previous years. Tyler's class had the 3rd highest participation rate in school history at 84 percent. Cal wasn't sure his class could top that, as he could think of at least a dozen students that either weren't willing to jeopardize their perfect attendance records or, as he learned with Reed, didn't want to potentially get in trouble. On the morning of Cut Day, Cal drove to school because Reed had agreed to meet up with him in the parking lot and then go from there to Berkeley for the day. It had been a plan set well in advance and it had taken a lot of coaxing to get Reed to agree to go. But before he'd even finished parking he saw Reed standing in the lot and he could tell from the look on his friend's face that he was bowing out.

"I just don't see the point," Reed said a few minutes later.

"The point is there is no point. It's tradition. It's also fun," Cal argued. "It's not going to be the determining factor of whether you get into college because you already sent them your life story. And it's because they can't punish everyone or throw everyone in detention. It's one day!"

Cal made one more sales pitch but Reed wasn't budging. He shouldn't have been surprised but it was frustrating just the same, in large part because he had no backup plan. Everyone else he knew was either cutting with another group or not cutting at all and Cal found himself resigned to being in the latter group. As he walked into the school and locker area he was still mulling over whether to just bail on his own. That was when he saw Anna standing by her locker. She was seemingly lost in thought. He doubted if the look of concern on her face was whether to cut school or not, as he figured she would fall into the not-cutting minority. They'd started saying hi to each other in the halls again and in recent weeks he had thought about going over to her house to apologize, though he couldn't pinpoint exactly what he'd be apologizing for.

He slowly walked toward her locker. She was still staring off, looking out the large glass windows near the school's main entrance. Once he was close enough for her to hear him he asked, "Are you contemplating a run for it?"

She seemed a little startled and surprised he was talking to her.

140

"If you're thinking of cutting you don't have to sneak out. No one's going to detain you at the driveway," he joked.

"It's not that. I mean, I know today is Cut Day but I wasn't gonna," she stopped, giving him a look that she knew what he knew.

"You look... confused?" he asked.

She shook her head.

"Sad?" he offered.

She shook her head again.

"Stressed out? Waiting for that all important large or small envelope and pinning all your hopes and dreams to the mailbox?" he asked.

She frowned.

"Sort of," she confessed.

A few of their classmates had started getting their acceptance and rejection letters for college, mostly students who had applied early or had been a part of an early answer program that a few colleges and universities offered.

"You're going to get into your schools," he said. "Maybe not all of them but I'd be willing to bet my music collection you get into over half of them."

Her eyes grew wide.

"That's a bold bet," she said. "Especially from you."

"You showed me your transcripts. You showed me your essays," he reminded her. "If you of all people don't get in somewhere we're all screwed."

"Thank you," she said. "But I'm not as confident as I was a few days ago."

"Why?"

"It's dumb," she said. "I'm just being anxious and scared."

He put his back up against the locker next to hers and waited for her to continue.

"Okay... so here's what happened," she began. "It turns out my best friend, Eileen... I've told you about her..."

He nodded.

"Anyway, it turns out that she, as kind of an act of solidarity or what-if or just because we're competitive as can be...she applied to UCLA, even though she would probably never attend even if she got accepted.

She told me on the phone that it was so I couldn't hold my future acceptance letter over her head."

"You and this Eileen chick really need to get some therapy," he said, trying to keep things light.

Cal had been feeling rather carefree about college, especially after a few people he knew with lower SATs and a lower GPA than he held had gotten into state schools comparable to Sacramento.

"Let me finish," she said. "The thing is she told me this story because yesterday her letter came from UCLA. Her *rejection* letter."

Cal didn't see the problem. He shrugged at her news.

"Eileen and I have nearly identical school records," she explained. "Nearly identical SATs. If they rejected her, they could reject me. Easily."

The picture became a little clearer to him and he could hear the worry in her voice. He tried his best to imagine he was like her or any of his other classmates aiming high in their college hopes. He had his own moments of worry about acceptances or rejections to come. But seeing friends and classmates, one by one, growing more and more on edge as they waited for their answer, he knew his anxiety was not on their level. They really wanted it badly. Anna wanted it that badly. As hard as he'd worked at times in his high school life he knew he hadn't worked the way she or others had. He had no idea how it felt to be an overachiever.

"If she applied just for the hell of it I doubt she worked as hard as you did on the essay," he offered. "And you said *almost* identical transcripts and tests. Like how close are talking here?"

"I've taken maybe one more AP class than her. And I've done debate and more academic-based clubs. She's a cheerleader and she sings. But my SAT is only 10 points higher."

"And you did three drafts of your essay," he said. "You showed me two of them."

She was biting her fingernail and still periodically looking away from him.

"I feel like I'm going to throw up," she said. "You know, like how you feel sick to your stomach before a big test?"

He chuckled.

"What are you laughing at?" she asked.

"Anna, I've never felt like that about a test. Ever. I took the SAT twice, once with a mild hangover and once on a good night's sleep like you're supposed to and I did better with the hangover."

She shook her head and finally laughed. "How in the world did you become the one close friend I have here?"

"You stalked me from your backyard," he reminded her.

"It wasn't stalking."

"Okay," he said. "And, hey, you just said 'friend'. You even said *close* friend."

"I did," she said quietly.

He thought back to the argument they'd had weeks before and how little they had talked since. Whatever reasons he'd had to be angry with her had vanished.

"I'm sorry," he said. "About that morning."

"I am too," she said.

She reached over and hugged him.

"So," he said. "You're stressed out. And my Cut Day partner in crime bailed on me. And it's a nice day out."

She shook her head.

"My parents would freak!" she said.

He thought she might say that. And he was ready.

"Have I ever told you what month my brother was born in?" he asked.

She shook her head.

"He's a February birthday. He just turned 21. So when he did Cut Day he was 18. And he wrote his own note for why he was absent because it turns out you can do that. He told me that's why Cut Day is in March, so that a larger number of us will be 18."

"I couldn't do that," she said.

"Can't or won't? Come on, my birthday isn't until May. I'm just taking the unexcused absence. You can write whatever you need to excuse yourself. If you really think about it it's *you* that should cut and I should stay."

She shook her head again but smiled.

"Yeah...so *you* go to Berkeley," he said. "And get me the new Replacements album at Amoeba and I'll go to your classes and take notes. How about that?"

143

She giggled and he could see she was at least considering it. He peered in at her face, leaning in toward her cheek.

"Anna, your cheek is a little swollen. I think somewhere in your teeth or your gums you've got a toothache or a cavity. You should go get it looked at. Because, like, if you had a dentist appointment today you'd have an excuse to..."

"I've never had a cavity in my life," she said proudly.

"Of course you haven't," he said. "I'm sure you brush and floss three times a day. But maybe you have a... a fever? A severe headache?"

"I have anxiety. Legitimate. It's been diagnosed. A few years ago," she said.

"Excellent. So you're having a panic attack. You need a day. If you can't do it today when 75 percent of Seniors didn't even show up, then when can you?"

"You make a lousy Ferris Bueller," she said.

"Matthew Broderick was about 25 when he did that part. Did you know that?" he asked.

"How do you know that? *Why* do you know that? Your knowledge of things like that just blows me away!"

He shrugged but didn't want to relent.

"Come with me to Berkeley," he said. "And I'll explain on the way how I know such important things about Matthew Broderick and stupid movies."

He tilted his head at the big clock at the far end of the lockers. It was getting close to first period.

She slowly began to nod her head.

"If I get in trouble for this I'm going to kill you," she said.

--

Anna couldn't believe she was cutting school. At the first red light they reached on the drive away from Crestview she came very close to asking him to turn around and take her back. She thought the same thing when they got out to the main boulevard leading them to the freeway.

"And you sure no one pays the price for this?" she asked him.

"The price?" he said, laughing at her. "This is Cut Day, Anna, not war with Iraq."

144

She finally settled down, rationalizing why it was okay to leave school and take part in this tradition others had told her about that she'd quickly dismissed as juvenile and not for her. When Tracy said it was about Class of 1991 solidarity it just served to remind her that no matter how hard she tried Anna didn't feel like a full-fledged member of their class. So as they made their way toward Berkeley she decided it wasn't about taking part in a tradition or trying to be a rebel against teachers and principals. This was about Cal, and how he'd noticed her by her locker, could sense something was wrong with her, and even after their falling out had still come over to check on her. It reminded her of why she liked him so much in the first place. And she figured taking part in Cut Day would also give her a story to share with Owen or maybe with Eileen the next time they talked.

She hadn't mentioned Owen to anyone except Eileen, not to Tracy or any other Crestview friends. They'd only been on one date, even if it had been an excellent one, so there wasn't all that much to tell. They'd talked several times since, with him always calling first so that her parents wouldn't get upset with a long-distance bill. She also didn't feel like sharing anything about it, especially since Owen still knew several students at Crestview. They'd gone back and forth on the phone one night with him asking if she knew some of his friends that were in her class, and her asking him about the handful of people she'd gotten to know. Owen said he knew Tracy a little, that she always seemed very nice, adding, "I wish I had gotten to know more people like her instead of some of the crowd I told you about." She mentioned Cal, too, and Owen recalled a few things, saying, "I saw him at a few parties. Nice enough guy but we never really talked." She didn't mention to Owen that just weeks before meeting him she was going to see how Cal felt about going on a date. And by that morning in the car on the way to Berkeley it didn't seem to matter anymore. Cal had Melody and while she didn't feel she had anything similar with Owen just yet, she was still uncharacteristically hopeful.

She wasn't sure whether to ask Cal about Melody. She still saw them around school together and they seemed happy; more affectionate than she would ever want to be but not as bad as other couples at Crestview or back in Kenosha.

"Thank you for this," she said as they drove, feeling better about both the pending letter from UCLA and the fact that she was cutting school for the first time in her life. "I think you're right. I do think I needed a day. And it looked like a huge swath of our class skipped today anyway."

"I've been waiting for this," he said. "Which is stupid. I've cut a class here or there before but usually because some assignment was due and I didn't have it done. But never an entire day."

She had no experience with such things but was curious.

"How did you get the absences excused?" she asked.

He seemed hesitant to answer but finally did.

"I went to my Mom and told her that I needed her to say I had a dentist or a doctor appointment. I'd tell her I didn't finish something I should have. Just a few times but she wrote the note."

"Was she angry?"

"A little. But she told me once she'd rather it because I was behind on work then because I didn't want to go to class or I was failing or whatever. My sister would do that. A lot. At first it was cutting a class. Then a few of them. And then skipping entire days."

Anna had noticed that he would often talk about his big brother but hadn't mentioned his older sister nearly as often.

"Can I ask you about Rachel?" she asked gently.

"What about her?"

"I don't know if you know this but every time you mention her… and you don't do it often…but you get kind of quiet. Which is weird because you're… *you*. Usually so chatty and upbeat and full of energy. Not quiet at all."

She watched him as he drove, his eyes focused on the road and getting on the interchange.

He finally said simply and still rather quietly, "Rachel's great."

"Cal," she said. "You can talk to me. About anything, and if you want to tell me it's none of my business I understand that, especially since we haven't talked in a bit. But I've just noticed that you always seem a little uneasy about her."

She watched his side profile, wondering if he was going to stay on the subject or take the opt out that she'd given him.

"Rachel went through a lot," he said. "And she was tough for my folks and I guess they were a little tough for her, if that makes sense."

"It does."

"And that was also a bit tough for me, and I guess for Tyler, too," he continued. "It's like…I guess some people hear their parents argue or shout at each other all the time. My parents never do that, or at least not very often. But for a good two, three years, the fights between them and my sister were just epic. And loud."

"How old is Rachel again?" she asked. She knew he'd told her at some point but had forgotten the specific number.

"We're six years apart," he said. "So at the height of all the drama I was, like, 11…12."

"What would you do when they argued?' she asked. She tried to put herself in her shoes or even Rachel's but she'd never really gotten into shouting arguments with her parents.

"I just hid in my room. Ty would leave because he was 14, 15…he could run off with his friends a little easier than I could. I like to joke with him sometimes that it was while all that was happening that I started to like playing music a bit loudly in my room. Def Leppard was really good for that, by the way."

She watched as he smiled at the music part of it. But it was also another part of him she'd noticed: Anytime he was uncomfortable he'd try to say something silly or light. She hoped her questions about Rachel hadn't upset him or brought up bad memories.

"It's funny you ask about her as we're headed to Berkeley," he said.

"Why's that?" she asked.

"The first time I ever went into the part of Berkeley we're going to today, Telegraph and near the campus, was a few years ago. My sophomore year. My parents were visiting my brother at UCSB so they had Rachel and her then husband come stay at the house to keep an eye on me. And that Saturday they wanted to go into Berkeley because my sister likes it and so did her husband. I'd never been but I was just starting to really like record stores and music shops and they showed me Amoeba and Rasputin's, which you'll see are just huge and amazing. And we walked up and down the street where people sell stuff….a lot of weirdos and colorful hippy types."

"It sounds fun. And right up your alley," she said, wondering for her own sake if Berkeley would be to *her* liking.

"It was fun," he said, but with no real enthusiasm behind it.

She watched his expression turn again from a smile to what looked like sadness.

"What happened?"

"Nothing bad. I mean, I didn't get hurt or anything like that. We spent the day hanging out and then, Derek, her ex, thought we should grab some dinner and we did and he was a bit of a drinker and had several. And then before we went back to the car Rachel and Derek and Terry, their friend that was with us, stopped at a park and lit up because they wanted to get high. And my sister passed it to me. I told her I didn't or at least *hadn't* ever smoked weed. And she said I should start. And she was laughing about how if she hadn't had pot she would have never survived living in our parent's house and stuff."

Anna thought it sounded awful. She could tell from the way he talked about it, the noticeable frustration in his voice, that it bothered him.

"That was the first time anyone had even *offered* me pot," he said. "Which is crazy because I knew it was around. People at Crestview smoke a lot of weed but among my friends it had never been a thing. And it's not a huge deal but my sister was beyond just pot at that point, ya know? Coke, acid...and I didn't want anything to do with it."

"I'm sorry," she said.

"Eh. It was over two year ago. And if it hadn't been her it would have been someone else, right?" he asked.

"I guess," she said.

"It just kind of sucked because right up until then it had been an amazing day. Rachel showed me all these albums I should buy because before then I'd never really dug into older stuff, like The Stones or Zeppelin except what gets played on radio. She bought me a Def Leppard poster because she was the one who gave me *Pyromania* for my birthday when I was 10. My sister is kinda the whole reason I ever got into music, really. But then they smoked out and Derek was clearly buzzed from drinking. So when we got to the car they said I should drive."

"How old were you?" she asked, trying to do the math.

"I was 15. I had my permit and had been out driving with my Dad a few times but that was it. So my first big driving lesson on the freeway was at night, with a car full of high and drunk assholes."

He laughed a little but it seemed forced.

"You've told me before you don't smoke pot. Is that why?" she asked.

"Yeah," he said. "I guess so."

She decided to leave the topic alone, even though she was still curious. He'd told her the day was supposed to be about fun and she decided at that moment to try her best to stop worrying about the absence from school or what might or might not be in the mailbox that day or the next. Cal was always so present and in the moment, and she liked that about him, even though she'd given up hope of ever being like that herself. But for at least one day she wanted to try.

--

Cal did his best to push the thoughts of his sister and the things he'd told Anna about out of his head, especially the trip into Berkeley. It was a story he'd never shared with anyone until then, not with a friend, and certainly not with his parents. And he'd never talked with Rachel about it. He'd reached a place where he didn't think it was that big of a deal or much of a story to tell. He doubted he was the first kid to ever have an older brother or sister try and get them high. Just the same, he'd never been able to go into Berkeley, where the smell of pot around Telegraph and Ashby was common, or to concerts, where he'd also frequently catch the scent, without thinking of that afternoon. Even as he'd gotten a little older and saw friends who smoked pot or used others drugs and *didn't* drop out of school or lash out like Rachel used to he'd never been able to disconnect the idea that her use was part of her problems with school and, just as important to him, with their parents.

There wasn't so much as a hint of pot smell in the air as he walked with Anna along Telegraph Avenue. But it also wasn't even 10 A.M. yet. It was a Monday and Cal knew the streets and shops wouldn't be as busy as they were on weekends, which was when he'd typically come into the city with friends and sometimes by himself. But as they made their way toward the UC campus they still saw a few tables being set up on the sidewalk by various merchants.

"Wait till later," he told her. "There will be all kinds of necklaces, beads, oils, earrings... maybe some people playing music. It's kind of a

149

street fair any given day, especially on Saturdays in the spring and summer."

At her insistence, and since very few of the shops were open yet, they decided to walk on to the UC Berkeley campus.

"Ya know, I've come in here so many times but I've never walked onto this campus, just around the edge of it," he said.

"Really?! It'd be the first place I'd want to see," she said. "When you first mentioned Berkeley to me months ago I thought about what the campus must be like."

They walked through part of the campus and watched as dozens of students made their way from dorms to classes or vice versa, while other students were just hanging out and talking. There were a few tables and booths set up near one building, with signs for Greenpeace, "Save the People's Park", and various other causes. One student approached them, asking them to sign a petition to legalize marijuana. Cal was used to being approached along Telegraph on past visits, as there always seemed to be a signature gatherer of some variety on any given Saturday. He told Anna about a few protest marches he'd seen, too, and one he'd taken part in against the U.S. war in Iraq.

"I like this," she said, looking around the campus. "All this activity and engagement. Even if I don't agree with some of this. It's nice to see people care about something. In a few months this will be us."

Cal tried to imagine what kind of person he would be once he got to whichever school he might got to, if he'd really be all that much different than he was in that moment.

"You'll be that girl over there," he said to Anna, pointing to a female student who was sitting at a table with a cup of coffee and buried in a book.

"And you'll be one of those guys over there," she said, pointing out two students passing a hacky sack between their bare feet, both wearing shorts and having kicked off their Birkenstocks.

"I don't wear Birks," he said defensively.

"But you'll be the guy taking a break having fun on a nice sunny day and I'll be the girl who is afraid to stop studying," she said.

"You took a break today," he reminded her. "There's hope for you. And you'll also be the one totally rocking it in your classes and then getting a good job and doing something important. I'll probably end up with an English degree I can use for future employment working in a record store or fetching coffee for some radio DJ."

"I'm kind of shocked you don't already work in a record store," she commented.

"I'm not cool enough," he said. "At least not for Tower Records. I applied. They never called back."

"Maybe you can work at one in Ashland?" she said. "Do they some record stores there?"

He nodded.

"I saw one on the drama class trip when we were walking downtown but I couldn't go inside because we had to stick together with the group," he said.

"That must have been torture for you, Cal," she said, bumping his shoulder with hers.

She seemed in awe of the campus and her enthusiasm for it was somewhat contagious. He thought about his campus tour a few months before at Sacramento and the one he'd taken the previous spring at Southern Oregon. The Oregon campus was considerably smaller, even more so in comparison to Berkeley. But the city of Ashland itself had reminded him of Berkeley, like a tinier version of it.

"I can't believe you've never just wandered on to this campus," she said.

"I guess I've always figured there is no way in hell I'd ever be attending here," he said. "It'd be like I'm an imposter because I'm not smart enough to get in."

"A *lot* of people aren't smart enough to get in here," she reminded him. "I didn't even bother to try."

They made their way to the campus's main library after Anna said she simply had to look inside to get a sense of its size and scope.

"You do realize the point of Cut Day is to *not* be in a library or at a school, right?" he asked. "You're killing the spirit of this thing!"

But he had to admit the library was impressive. Even just the ground floor was bigger than any library he'd ever stepped foot in.

"This makes me so excited," she whispered. "I know that seems nerdy but I really love libraries and huge bookstores."

"I get it," he whispered. "This is like your version of me in a record store."

151

"Exactly," she said.

After the library they made their way back off campus, toward the various shops and eateries along Telegraph, with Cal pointing out a few places he'd been to or had grabbed food at. He pointed toward the UC Theater.

"I've been in there a few times," he said.

"What do you see?" she asked.

"Oh, I've only been in there for *The Rocky Horror Picture Show*. They do midnight showings every Saturday with this wild live cast and people who come to the movie dress up like characters from it. Some of us from drama class went last spring and I dragged Doug and some other friends in last summer."

He tried to explain to her both the movie and the crazy cult following that had built around it since it came out in the 70's, with audience participation and shouting lines at the screen, the wild array of costumes people wore to the theater, and the razzing that first time attendees, aptly dubbed "virgins", were put through.

"That does not sound like my thing. At all," she said.

"Are you telling me you don't want someone dressed as a Sweet Transvestite from Transylvania to come sit on your lap and sing songs from a really bad movie to you?"

She shook her head.

"How on Earth do your parents let you do that?" she asked. "I don't mean about the movie so much but coming into this theater for a midnight movie and getting home at 2 in the morning? Or 3?"

It was a fair question, and Cal had only recently come up with a theory for why his parents had grown so lax in the last two years of his high school life.

"I think they just got tired of waiting up," he said. "I'm the baby in the family. The last of three and my sister...I mean...she blazed the trail. Like a pioneer of teen rebellion. There is nothing I have done, nothing I can ever do that could top some of her stuff. And then Ty... Ty was so slick and smart with getting away with things, at least most of the time. But I can remember them still worrying if he was late or staying up to make sure he got home safe, and he always did. So with me? I don't think they have the energy left. That or that they've just stopped worrying altogether."

152

"My parents worry about me all the time," she said. "I think maybe that's why I'm so excited for next year. I don't even know what I'll do with the freedom. Probably nothing too crazy but it'll be nice to know I can do that if I want."

Cal thought for a moment about some of the antics he'd gotten into that his parents didn't know about, mostly parties with a lot of alcohol and pot. He thought for a moment about Melody, and how neither his Mom or Dad had tried to caution him about having sex or not having sex with her. He wondered if they even suspected it was happening.

"So tell me," he said to Anna, "What is the craziest thing you've done in the last almost 4 years of your life?"

"Honestly," she said, "Today might be it. I've never even cut a class, let alone skipped a day. Oh, and we tee-peed the house of a girl on the South Kenosha basketball team last year. That was fun! I felt bad afterward but she really is a terrible person."

"So taking part today in what is pretty much a school sanctioned day of playing hooky and some minor league vandalism? That's it?"

"I'm afraid so," she said. "I'm just not that kind of person. Sometimes I wish I was but..."

He knew she wasn't. And he hoped she didn't think he was teasing her or trying to get her to be wilder or more rebellious. Cal didn't think of himself as being either of those things, as he could rattle off the names of several people he knew that were far more likely to skip school on any given day, drink more at a party, or take a pill someone told them would make them feel good or be an escape from reality. For him, it had always felt like enough to be somewhere right between completely careful and reserved, like Anna or Reed, and completely out of control, like Doug could be sometimes, and Rachel, who had been like that a great deal of the time.

"Do you worry about Jackie next year, when she starts Crestview?" he asked.

He hadn't really gotten to know Anna's younger sister very well, beyond her name and age. From the outside she looked like a younger, shorter version of Anna. Darker hair and Cal got the impression, based solely on appearance, that Jackie might be less reserved.

153

"Oh, I worry about Jacks sometimes," she said. "And my parents worry about her *all* the time. I think they've calmed their worries about me a bit, at least for now. I guess because they're confident I'll be okay. But Jacks... she just...I feel guilty sometimes because I know I've made really good grades and that's hard to match or beat and I worry that she knows that and doesn't want to even try. Like she's already decided she's going to go in a whole other direction."

Her words made him think of Tyler. The way she described Jackie was very much like how he'd felt at times, as a little brother realizing there was no way to mirror his older sibling.

"Tyler was a great student. And I knew, like freshman year I knew, I didn't have that in me," he said. "But he was also kind of an asshole so I figured 'Don't be that. Don't be that and it'll be enough.'"

"Well, I certainly hope my sister doesn't try to be me," she said. "But I also hope she doesn't think I'm...what you said."

"You're not," he said. "You are the farthest thing from that. I'm sure your sister will do her own thing because as a younger brother or sibling or whatever it's kind of an instinct. But if she is like you? That wouldn't be bad at all. She'd be smart...and get into UCLA."

"I haven't gotten in," she said sternly. "But thank you for saying all that. And the vote of confidence."

As they wandered in and out of a few shops in route to the far end of Telegraph where his two favorite records stores were located, he remembered why he'd been attracted to Anna in the first place. It wasn't the way she looked, though he'd always thought she looked nice and was far prettier than she gave herself credit for. And it wasn't that she'd approached him first, even though it had been welcome and had made getting to know her much easier. It was all the ways she was different. He knew part of the difference was because she'd come to Crestview from far away. But as they eyeballed jewelry and trinkets on the street and went in and out of a candle shop, a magic shop, and a small art gallery, it struck him that what made Anna so appealing was that when he was with her he never had to try to find the right thing to say or think too much about what he should do. With other people he always felt like he had to. With her he didn't have to try to be funny or come off as smarter or more studious than he was. It didn't matter what he said because if it was the wrong thing she would let him know. He'd learned that from their argument in January. He thought of when he'd first met her, and how she had made him feel chosen. Like she had picked him to talk to instead of anyone else. For the longest time he wondered "Why me?" And he'd never quite gotten to the bottom of it. He still had no answer. But there in Berkeley, watching her as she took in her surroundings, he found himself with a whole new set of questions, the biggest among them "Why was it so hard to look at her and not still be attracted to her?" That feeling came with a massive wave of guilt, leading him to wonder why he felt that way at all, especially because of everything he had with Melody. He tried to dismiss the attraction as just being happy that he and Anna were talking again, back to being friends, but he couldn't dodge those feelings returning. Maybe they weren't the exact same as when he'd first met her and all the ways he'd felt so many times in weeks and months past but it was close. Close enough to make him wonder if Anna knew or what she would think if she did.

"Do you want to grab something to eat before we wander into your records stores?" she asked. "Because I have a sneaking suspicion you'll go into those stores the way I go into bookstores and time will just disappear."

"That sounds good," he said. "And there's a killer Chinese noodles place right around the block from here."

He put his guilt ridden thoughts away for the moment, all the while wondering if maybe it would be good to just say something to her about all of it over lunch; to put it out in the open and admit it. But he quickly put the idea away, knowing he'd never be able to find an easy way to say, "So I love my girlfriend... but every time I look at you I see more than just a friend..."

--

They were in the middle of having lunch when Anna worked up the nerve to ask Cal about how things were going with Melody. It was a nerve wracking set of questions to ask, as the last time they'd talked about her it led to Anna getting out of his car in anger, finding her way to a bathroom in the school, and crying for reasons she couldn't quite sort out at the time. She later concluded that what upset her the most wasn't that he'd found a girl he liked, because she had actually suggested

155

he try to find someone else. It wasn't fair to blame him for that. Her greater frustration was with herself. She'd been ready put her heart on her sleeve and when it turned out to be all for naught she felt stupid. And Anna hated to feel stupid about anything. She knew she had missed her window to tell him how she felt and just like with his meeting someone else, that wasn't his fault either. She told herself she wasn't jealous of Melody because that would be pointless. But she did let herself have a few moments of spite and even a little ego, confident that if she'd expressed interest in Cal from the get-go then he'd never have taken up with Melody at all.

She sat across the table from Cal, with both doing their best to navigate chopsticks and noodles. She thought to herself if they couldn't talk about certain topics, such as his girlfriend, then what kind of friendship was it? If the subject of Melody was going to cause a rift again then she'd just have to live with it and so would he. She figured the very worst that could happen would be that he'd get so angry he'd get up and leave, she'd be stranded in Berkeley, forced to call her parents for rescue and then explain why she wasn't in school, all of which would be horrible. But Cal wouldn't do that and she knew it. The worst that could happen would be an awkward ride home and that was a risk she was willing to take.

"So...I am just going to ask and I really don't want it to lead to us arguing but... how's Melody?" she asked, opting to just be up front and not dance around it.

"She's really good," he said, pausing a moment before continuing. She thought maybe he was measuring whether he wanted to discuss the subject. But he continued. "It's been about 3 months now and she doesn't seem tired of me yet."

"I'm glad," she said. "I just want you to know that if you ever need a girl's perspective on things I'm here. As long as it's not weird to talk about."

"It's not weird," he said. "Well, maybe a little. But I'm glad you mentioned her. I need to remember to grab her something while we're here. Like an album or a poster."

"Or maybe something pretty," she suggested.

"Melody isn't all that girly," he said with a smile. "I'm sure you've noticed."

Anna had noticed, of course. In her view, Melody was an attractive girl that would be prettier, even adorable, if she changed things up. As it was she tended to dress in black jeans or sometimes stretch pants, the occasional dark skirt over that. It was easy for anyone at Crestview to know she liked The Cure because she appeared to have at least 2 or 3 different shirts of the group.

"Maybe you should get her a necklace or a pendant or even some of the earrings people are selling out there along the street," she suggested. "I'm sure she'd like that. Not that she wouldn't like something from the record store but, Cal, you can make her a mixtape of songs anytime. I'd get her something that says 'Hey, I went to Berkeley and I saw this thing and thought of you'. Trust me."

He seemed open to the idea and that made her happy. She wanted to let him know she was on his side even if she still worried that he was dating the wrong person or that it would end in heartbreak sooner rather than later. But she didn't want to be negative or try to take him off his cloud. He seemed happy about things. Which then made her want to share her own happy news.

"I was wondering," she began, "Do you know a guy that graduated last year named Owen Myers?"

He seemed a little surprised to hear the name but nodded. "Yeah, I knew him a little. Good athlete. Really popular. But nice. Why do you ask?"

"His family goes to my church and I met him a few weeks back," she said.

A smile crossed his face, like he already knew. If there was one thing she had to hand to Cal it was that his antenna for such things was finely tuned. His grade point average may have been wanting but he didn't miss a beat on things like that.

"I think I talked to him once at a party about music," he said. "I wouldn't say we were friends or anything but, yeah, Owen always seemed like a good guy. How well do you know him?"

She put her hands over her eyes like she wanted to hide.

"A little. I've been getting to know him," she confessed.

Again he gave her a knowing look.

"Anna, do you have a boyfriend I don't know about?" he asked playfully.

157

"He's not my boyfriend. We've been on one date. And another is planned."

"Hmmm," he said.

"Hmm what?"

"Hmmm...I can see it. Owen is...how do I put it? He seems like...your type."

"I don't think I have a type," she said.

"Sure you do. You told me about the guy back in Kenosha and you even showed me his picture. He was tall, a basketball player, right?"

She nodded.

"And Owen played football...baseball too if I remember. Really smart, which makes sense because you're also really smart. I'm not surprised you like him."

"Thanks. I'm still trying to figure out why he likes *me*," she said.

"Because you're you," he said quickly. "You're also smart. You're thoughtful. You're the most honest person I've ever met and you're...umm..."

"I'm what?" she asked.

"Challenging."

It was not the adjective she'd been expecting. She thought he was going to say 'Pretty' or maybe even 'Driven'.

"I'm *challenging*?" she asked. "Is that a nice word for 'difficult'?"

"No," he said. "I just mean you really think things through and that makes it hard for someone on the outside to figure out what you're thinking because it seems like your brain is always in motion."

She had to marvel sometimes at just how well Cal seemed to get things about her that even she hadn't quite put a finger on.

"I've always been an overthinker," she said. "Always."

"That's not a bad thing," he said. "I mean, I don't think enough. If I did maybe I'd be like my brother...better grades, better college. I mean, probably not attending up the street from here but better than I've done."

"I think you've balanced it, though. It always seems to me like you've had fun. You're going to have more high school stories to tell than I ever will. Just that *Rocky Horror* thing you told me about alone is something."

"It's not going to get me anywhere, though," he said. "Stuff like that and way too many hours and time and energy trying to find a girlfriend for 3 years. I probably should have put some of that into my books, don't ya think?"

"Yeah, but you still found Melody in all that," she reminded him.

"That's the funny part. I wasn't even really trying with her. It just happened."

She was reminded of Owen. She'd thought similar things in how she'd met him, just sitting alone at the end of a church service. It was not the kind of place she expected to meet someone she liked that way.

"So I guess both of us should learn not to try so hard or think too much or maybe find a better balance between the two?" she asked.

"Yeah, maybe," he said, but not sounding very convinced.

She had just been rattling off ideas and thoughts when she said it but the very notion of it, of balancing things, stuck with her. It was a small epiphany, the kind she usually felt when she solved a problem in a class or figuring out a science formula or a calculation.

She stopped him as they were walking out of the restaurant, putting her hand between his chest and shoulder.

"I figured something out," she said.

"Figured what out?" he asked.

"Why I've liked you right from the start," she said.

"You didn't know that until right this moment?" he asked, chuckling at the idea.

"I did but I didn't," she said. She was still trying to piece it all together and try to convey to him why it was important to her. "But now I know for sure."

"Lay it on me," he said.

"It's because you make me think. Or more like *how* you make me think. I know we just talked about how I *always* think and think too much. But you make me think *differently*. And I really appreciate that."

She hugged him, which seemed to catch him off guard, but she felt his arms around her returning the gesture, and was proud of herself for getting it out, telling him that, and not keeping it to herself. She had done that with him before; not telling him how she felt about him, and as they walked to their next destination in Berkeley she promised herself she would never do that again.

--

159

Cal thought he'd handled the news about Anna dating Owen Myers rather well, especially in not showing her his surprise, and then acting like it wasn't that big of a deal. When he heard her say Owen's name it had felt like a *very* big deal. He downplayed it while talking to her, all the while thinking "Of course I know Owen Myers! *Everyone* at Crestview knew Owen Meyers!"

The entire time she was talking to him about her thinking too much and him not thinking enough, he was only half listening. His mind had started rifling through his memory banks for every Owen Myers moment he'd ever witnessed. He was trying to recall if he'd been at a certain party or what they'd talked about specifically the one time he knew for certain they'd conversed. He didn't say it out loud and had no intention of doing so but he was also jealous. He had, after all, been interested in Anna and had made it rather obvious to her. He thought he was at peace with nothing coming from that attraction but he couldn't help feeling like maybe if he'd been more of the Owen Meyers type that things might have gone differently. Cal always felt like he was losing the girl, whoever she may be, to guys like Owen; the more genetically gifted, the more naturally athletic, the more confident. He'd decided it was part of a teenage hierarchy, where guys like himself would ultimately lose out to their more beautiful peers, relegated to being the male friend that would be there to talk to when hearts were broken in their path. Reed had once called it "Duckie Syndrome", named after a character in the movie *Pretty In Pink*. Duckie was in love with his best female friend and in the end had to concede she was better off with the beautiful, popular guy that also liked her. Cal could relate, though he hoped he might be a bit more like Lloyd Dobbler in *Say Anything*, or even John Cusack's more hopeless character in *Better Off Dead*, which was one of Cal's favorite movies. All those films had guys like him in it, and they all had the good-looking jerk, villainous characters that looked like Owen Myers. But as he took in the news from Anna he had to accept that no matter how hard he tried to think of something or remember anything wicked about Owen Myers it didn't change what was true: Owen was a nice guy. Cal had always thought that about him and he had never seen or heard anything remotely bad about him.

Whatever mess of thoughts that were still racing through his head about Owen and Anna, and why he was feeling jealous even

160

though he not only had a girlfriend but a girlfriend who was having sex with him, were swept away the moment they got inside Amoeba Music.

"This might very well be the place I'll miss most next year," he said to her as they walked into the store. "I'm sure record stores in Ashland or Sac are great but this place…"

Amoeba Music wasn't the biggest shop he'd ever been in; Rasputin Records across the street was twice as big, with three floors and more selections of t-shirts, posters, and other music-related items. But Amoeba was cheaper. It had a bargain section with cassettes that ran a dollar or two and some even as cheap as 50 cents. Even as the store had made changes in the prior year or two, giving more floor space to CDs as they were getting evermore popular, there were still plenty to choose from for Cal. Everything was broken down by genre, too: Rock, punk, country, folk, rap, and soundtracks, among others. He'd lost count of the hours he'd spent there.

"Wow, you weren't kidding," Anna said as they browsed the racks of cassettes. "Some of these tapes are really cheap."

She'd grabbed a Duran Duran cassette.

"Tapes are getting even cheaper and there's more of them. I think a lot of people are buying CDs of stuff they already have on cassette and then selling off the tapes."

"That seems a little wasteful," she said.

"I don't know," he said. "I've been fighting the temptation to get a CD player because, one, CDs are crazy expensive and, two, I know I'd want CD copies of a lot of music I already own."

"So you're a holdout?" she asked.

"For now," he said, grabbing a cassette by a band called Mindfunk. Anna peered over his shoulder at it.

"Who the heck are Mindfunk?"

"A new band. I read a review of their album in Circus magazine and it's 2 dollars so…"

"You haven't even heard them?" she asked.

"Nope," he said.

"But you're getting it anyway?"

"Probably," he said. "Based on what I read I'm sure at least some of it is good."

161

"Do you always buy music you've never actually *heard* before?" she asked.

"Not always. But if I read an article about something and then I see it really cheap I usually grab it. Or if someone I trust from Mixtape Club or someone like Doug says, 'Hey, you should check this out' I keep my eyes open."

"No wonder you have so much music," she said. "But it makes sense. Like if Eileen or someone I trust tells me to read a certain book."

His broad taste and open mind and a willingness to take suggestions from others had led to his owning over a hundred different cassettes.

"I know it's ridiculous and sometimes I wind up selling something right back. But I like to hear new stuff, ya know? And to be curious. Doug and I have this game we play when we've come here, where we each pick something $1 or less based on just the band's name."

"How does that work?" she asked.

"Well, sometimes it's, like, the band's name is cool so we guess maybe the music is too. Or the band has a really weird name or something."

"Have you ever found anything good?" she asked.

"Sometimes," he said. "I've definitely picked up some total crap but you'd be surprised how many bands with strange names actually turn out to be pretty good."

"Like who?" she asked.

"The last time I was here with Doug I stumbled on a really good album by a band called Toad the Wet Sprocket," he said, thinking of their music and reminding himself to keep an eye out for other albums by them he didn't have.

"That is a really dumb name," she said.

"But a really good band. They sound kinda like R.E.M.," he said. "Doug stumbled onto a band called Psychefunkapus that he really loves. It cost him all of 50 cents."

"You two are nerds," she said.

He'd had that label thrown at him before. Or 'Geek'. He'd once resisted or tried to defend himself against it but there wasn't much point anymore.

162

"Everyone is nerdy about something," he said. "If it's not music it's books. If it's not books its movies. Have you met some of the guys at school that are making a movie for their Senior Project?"

"I heard about that," she said. "There was an article in the school paper."

"One of them, Nathan, actually came to me and asked if I'd watch a few scenes and see if I could suggest some music for the background of a scene and I did. And I had a moment where I thought, 'God, we are *all* geeks of different kinds'. Because he was on and on about angles and lighting and all these things I don't think about when I watch a movie. But there I was, like, 'Oh, you know what song would be bad ass right here...'"

"Nerds of a different feather flocking together," she chimed.

They scanned through the Movie Soundtrack section after she told him most of the tapes she owned were from movies she liked.

"That's how I find music most of the time," she explained, grabbing a tape off the shelf. "Like this one. I had this and I listened to it so much the cassette wore out and broke. I'm gonna replace it because I love it so much"

It was the soundtrack to *Dirty Dancing*. He'd heard several songs from it on the radio and seen videos on MTV and pretty much hated each one.

"I'm just gonna leave that alone," he said.

"What?" she asked. "Is *Dirty Dancing* not angry enough or sad enough or weird or wild and loud enough for you?"

"I've never actually seen the movie. Not all of it, anyway. But that song that Patrick Swayze sings..."

"'She's Like The Wind'?" she said enthusiastically.

"Yeah, that. That is horrible. Like crime against humanity level horrible."

"I like it!" she said, smacking his arm.

"To each their own," he said, very much enjoying the back and forth. It was like debates in Mixtape Club or when he and Doug would argue which song or which album by a band was best or when he'd give Reed hell of for citing Journey as his all-time favorite band.

He pulled a copy of the soundtrack to *Pump Up The Volume* off the shelf. It was a movie he'd seen the prior summer.

"Now *this* is a soundtrack," he said. "It's got all these cool new bands and the songs totally tie to the movie."

She took it from his hands and read off the songs and artists.

"Liquid Jesus... The Pixies...Cowboy Junkies...Bad Brains with Henry Rollins... I've never heard of any of these people!" she cried.

"Have you seen that movie?" he asked. "With Christian Slater? He's an underground DJ in high school and..."

"I remember seeing a preview for it but I never saw it."

"It was really good," he said.

"So is *Dirty Dancing*," she said, sticking her tongue out at him.

They continued browsing, looking at "New Arrivals" in the used section, then going through the "Rock" section, with Cal commenting on various albums and bands. He was as enthusiastic as always but he got the sense that Anna had reached her fill on music and they hadn't even been across the street to Rasputin's yet. He wanted to spend more time looking around, hunting for musical treasures like he'd done so many times. But as it became more and more apparent that nothing in Amoeba was even half as interesting to her he thought back to the UC Berkeley library from a few hours before, and how he'd enjoyed it but not in the same way she had.

"So," he said, "there is a bookstore right next to Rasputin's. I've only been in it once but it's pretty big. Why don't we go there next?"

"Will we have time?" she asked. "You said you wanted to go to Rasputin before we tried to beat the traffic home."

"I can go there anytime," he said. "Hell, I'll probably be back here before the end of the month. When is the next time *you're* going to be here, right?"

"That's true," she said.

"Let's check out of here and head over there next," he said.

He wandered through the bookstore with Anna, listening to her give mini-reviews of what, by his count, were dozens and dozens of books she'd read. At one point he saw what time it was on a clock on the wall and knew there was no way they'd make it to Rasputin's. Normally there was no way he'd go to Berkeley without hitting both of his favorite shops. He still felt some disappointment but it was quickly offset by how happy Anna looked as she pointed at various book titles and summarized their plots. The entire time he wrestled with two conflicting emotions that had bubbled up earlier in the day: Complete attraction to Anna and a horrible feeling of guilt that came with feeling that way. He promised himself that if they got back home early enough he'd go find Melody, with the hope that seeing her would make the strange feelings toward Anna go away.

--

Anna wound up with three books, a couple of used cassettes, and, at her insistence, one half of a matching pair of friendship bracelets she bought from a merchant table along Telegraph.

"I know it's dumb," she told Cal. "But I don't do things like today very often and it wouldn't have happened without you so I need you to at least *keep* this. You don't have to wear it. I just wanted to find something to mark the day."

She would later take her bracelet and tape it to a page in her journal where she wrote about Senior Cut Day adventures.

He seemed to like the gesture, putting it on right away. She also helped him find a colorful cloth bracelet for Melody.

"It has some yellow and red and orange in it," she said. "It'll really pop out on her wrist because of her..."

She stopped herself, not wanting to say something she thought he might find critical. But he finished it for her.

"Because of her often-black t-shirts and pants?" he asked.

"You said it," she said, throwing her hands up in innocence.

"We can't all be as snappy as Owen Myers," he said.

She knew he was just teasing and was glad for that. If he was light about it she figured that meant he wasn't jealous or uncomfortable. As they headed back to his car to make their way home she thought about whether she'd tell Owen about the day. She wondered if maybe she should have bought him something the way Cal had for Melody, but quickly dismissed the idea. They'd only been on one date, after all. Melody was Cal's girlfriend and though he hadn't said it blatantly, Anna got the impression they were likely having sex. If that was true then it was one more reason to have not dated Cal, because that would have eventually found her right in the same place she'd been with Kyle. Sex was something she'd decided to not even consider unless she was with

165

someone on "a path to something meaningful and lasting"; something she had written in her journal a few weeks before. She wasn't certain that Owen wouldn't eventually be another guy wanting more than she was willing to offer, but at least he seemed to be on the same page with her spiritually. If she was going to date at all he was the right kind of person.

When they got back on the road Cal was eager to listen to some of his new music purchases. He promised he'd take whatever they were listening to out of the tape deck if it wasn't to her liking. Months before, when she'd first started getting a ride to school with him, he would sometimes have on the most God-awful hard rock or heavy metal or whatever anyone wanted to call it. Some of it was very loud or so fast she couldn't comprehend the words being sung, and in some cases both. Other times the music was familiar -- Def Leppard, Bon Jovi, all very popular -- but even that seemed a bit much for first thing in the morning. He said it helped him wake up, which seemed terribly funny since he always seemed to have energy and topped it off by having coffee on the way. One morning she finally asked if they could maybe rock out less and talk more or, if he wanted, maybe try to broaden her musical horizons with something a little more melodic. He obliged and from then on there had been more of The Police, Depeche Mode, U2 and some other names she'd never heard of but generally liked. She had missed those moments during the weeks when they weren't talking or riding to school together.

"I want to hear one of these 50 cent or one dollar take-a-chance things you talked about. Did you get anything like that today?" she asked.

"I did. Even without Doug being here," he confessed.

"Let's hear it!" she demanded.

He obliged by pulling one of his cassettes out of the Amoeba Records bag. She looked at the case.

"The Brothers Figaro...Gypsy Beat," she said out loud as she read it. "Which is the album name and which is the band name?"

"The group is The Brothers Figaro. I haven't heard a thing from them but it's a weird name. And I like the song titles, and they're on Geffen..."

"Why does it matter that they're on Geffen?" she asked, trying to get inside his strange thinking.

"A lot of good bands are on Geffen," he said. "And it was a dollar so if it sucks I'll put Scotch tape over the top and use it as a blank tape".

"You can do that?" she asked.

He nodded.

"Wow… nerd," she said, laughing.

He pushed the cassette into the stereo and she listened to the music, immediately noticing it wasn't his usual fare with loud electric guitars. Instead it was acoustic and she thought she heard an accordion in the mix.

"I like it," she said.

When the vocals hit she listened closer than she usually would.

*She was lyin' down with another*
*Lookin' for an answer like before*
*Sayin', "Take me back, show me which way to go,*
*Show me how to get by in this world*

"I really like this," she commented. "Especially the lyrics."

"Me too," he said.

*We fell hard, we fell easy*
*We felt lost, sometimes crazy*
*I thought everybody knew of our fate in this world*
*The weight that keeps draggin' us down*

"It's so funny to me how your tastes seem to go back and forth between stuff like this," she said. "Music that's really sort of poetic and then that obnoxious stuff I had to beg you to not play anymore."

"I guess it just depends on my mood," he said.

"That makes sense. Still, I don't know many people that can go from some of the music you put on my birthday mix, like the Crowded House song I just love, love, love to death and that really fun, funky Terence Trent D'Arby song. And then to juvenile, obnoxious stuff like Warrant and Poison."

"It's not obnoxious," he defended. "It's just a bit… bombastic."

"It's also a little sexist," she said.

She could see him rolling his eyes after she said it.

"That is the most overused argument ever for criticizing hard rock and heavy metal," he argued.

167

She wasn't having it.

"So you're going to tell me that 'Cherry Pie' song where he equates a girl to a dessert, complete with a video where a slice of pie lands in her lap right over her…

She stopped herself.

"Oh, my God, you can't even say it," he laughed. "Come on, Anna, you can do it…"

"Over her crotch!" she said a bit louder. "You're going to tell me that isn't sexist or objectifying women?!"

"When did you see the video?" he asked. "I thought you said your parents don't let you watch MTV."

He wasn't wrong. Her parents had cable, which came with MTV, but they'd told both her and Jackie many times it was a channel they weren't allowed to watch.

"I sometimes watch it when they're not home," she confessed.

"Dear Lord, you're watching videos with scantily clad models, you're cutting school…I'm totally calling UCLA," he kidded.

"You are not funny," she said even though she thought it was.

"Look, I get that bands like that have a lot of songs about sex and partying and having someone pour some sugar on them or talk to dirty to them, and blah blah blah. But when you go to their shows over half the crowd is female. And they love it! So how can that be sexist?" he asked.

"I think some of those girls and women aren't thinking it through," she said. She knew he was at least partly right because even she liked some of the songs he referenced. "And obviously some of those bands have very attractive lead singers….at least some girls think so. I've never seen the appeal. Well, Jon Bon Jovi is hot."

"And their shows are fun," he said. "That's why I go. I'd like to think that's why girls go, too. They don't seem to mind what the songs are about because it's almost like an act. It's theater."

"So you don't take something like Def Leppard or Metallica seriously?" she asked.

"Well, Metallica have very serious songs," he said.

"I'll take your word for it," she said.

"But, yeah. If I just want to have fun I listen to something loud and dumb. If I want something where the singer is saying something I wish

I could say I listen to something like this," he explained, pointing at the cassette deck and the new music they were listening to.

"I will admit that ever since I've gotten to know you I notice what a song is about or might be about a lot more. I never used to do that," she said.

"That's cool," he said. "And cool of you to say."

It was true. Even when she didn't understand Cal's thinking or why he saw things a certain way or heard music the way he did she still wanted to relate. It made her curious if he ever thought similar things about her.

"So you've changed how I listen to music," she said. "How has knowing me changed you?"

He was quiet and she really wanted an answer.

"That is a really deep question, Anna," he said.

"I don't do shallow ones," she said unapologetically. She wasn't going to let him joke his way out of it either. "What I am saying is you and I are really different and yet I really like who you are. But if you wrote what each of us are like down on paper I don't think anyone would read it and imagine us being friends like this. Does that make sense?"

"Yeah," he said, taking a moment to try and answer. "I just think you're real. Like, all the time real. And I admire that."

"What do you mean by 'all the time'?" she asked

"I mean… I've seen you around other people, in a group of friends or in a class and I've seen you around your family a few times and even around mine... and you don't change who you are in any of that. And I *do* do that. I have a different face I put on for a group of friends at a party, and another in classes or with a teacher, and probably even with--"

She could see him hesitating, not wanting to complete the thought.

"Probably not even with?" she asked.

"I was gonna say Melody but I don't want you to think I'm not being myself with her. But it's like there are 5 or 6 different ways I am with people and I see other people do that, too, and I get it. But you? You're just you. And sometimes I wish I was like that. And you make me think. Even just a minute ago with the hard rock and sexist thing. You question me and you challenge me. That's why I like you. Why I like hanging out

169

with you. I know it was just a month or so and we're cool now but I really missed talking to you."

It was not the answer she expected and she still wasn't quite sure what he meant in all of it, but she liked it just the same.

"This has been a really good day," she said.

"I told you it'd be good," he said. "But, umm, when you're done writing yourself an absence excuse note for today, do you think you could forge one for me? Like pretend you're my Mom and say, 'Cal has an appointment with the mental hospital' or something?"

She had to hand it to him: He knew when to lighten the mood.

He dropped her off at her house with just enough time to make it look like she had gotten home from school at the usual time of day. For the last few minutes in the car she'd grown anxious all over again, positive that Crestview had called her parents or that somehow she'd get caught.

"You're going to be fine," he said. "And, hey...would you like to start riding to school with me again?"

"I found a different ride and it's really not--"

He cut her off.

"Anna, I've seen your Dad drop you off at school," he said. "We got in a fight, you didn't want to ride with me anymore and I get it. But if we're good now... I like the company."

"Pick me up tomorrow then," she said.

"Cool. Tomorrow we'll go to Pier 39 in the city or something," he said with a laugh.

"Um, no. My days of delinquency are over. But thank you again for today."

She walked from the curb to her house, opened the front door and her mother instantly ran to the entryway.

"Finally!" her mother cried.

Anna was convinced that her worst nightmare had come true. She was caught. The school really had called.

Her mother took her by the arm and led her to the kitchen. There on the table was an envelope with UCLA written on the top left corner.

"This came in the mail and obviously I am not going to open for you," her mother said.

Anna looked at it and smiled, as excitement and a sense of relief came over her. The envelope was a large one and she knew what that meant before she even opened it.

--

"I got you something. A little present," was how Cal started the conversation by her locker on Tuesday morning.

"What is it?" Melody asked him.

"Well, you know I skipped yesterday for Cut Day and while I was in Berkeley I saw this," he said, taking out the bracelet he'd bought for her, "And it made me think of you."

She looked it over and he could tell straight away that she liked it. She immediately put it around her wrist.

"Thank you," she said. "I do like it. A lot. How was the day?"

"It was fun," he said. "I walked around the UC campus and went into some shops I'd never been into. Stuff like that."

"Cool," she said. "Was Reed freaking out the whole time about being in trouble for cutting?"

He'd told over the weekend that the original plan was to cut school with Reed. For a split second he thought about just answering with a quick lie, but he didn't see the point in doing that.

"Actually, Reed bailed out, so Anna came with me," he explained.

Melody knew Anna was a friend of his, as early on in their budding relationship they'd talked about who they considered their closest friends. She had named Marie, Gina, and Caroline, the three girls she usually hung out with, and Cal had mentioned both Reed and Doug, and Anna.

"Straight A's, uptight Anna went with you?" she asked.

"Uh huh."

"How did that happen?" she asked. There was an air of suspicion in her voice.

"I came into the lockers for a few minutes yesterday after Reed chickened out, debating whether to go to class or not and then I ran into Anna," he detailed. "And somehow I convinced her to live a little and come with me."

Melody looked squarely at him and whatever smile or happiness the bracelet had inspired was gone.

"So you spent the whole day running around Berkeley with Anna? Just the two of you?" she asked.

"Yeah," he said, not quite sure what the problem was except that Melody clearly didn't like it. "Is that a problem?"

"I'm just..." she began, pausing to find the words. "It just sounds a little like a date."

"No," he said, stretching out the word for emphasis. "It was hanging out with a friend. I'd have done the same thing with Reed if he wasn't such a puss."

"Or you could have come found me and we could have gone?" she suggested.

"You'd have got detention or worse for that," he said.

"So," she said. "I've cut classes before."

"I know" he said, knowing she had but still trying to make a larger point. "But it was also *senior* cut day."

"Yes, thank for you for reminding me because I'm dumb," she said sharply.

He let out a long sigh.

"I'm sorry if you feel left out," he said. "That wasn't my intention or anything."

"It's just you and I haven't even been into Berkeley together and you always talk about how we should go," she said.

He had mentioned to her that it would be fun to do that some Saturday but they'd never set up a specific time to do so.

"We'll go," he said. "Hell, we can go this weekend if you want."

"You were just there," she said scathingly. "I don't want to be, like, some encore to your fun day out."

"It wouldn't be like that," he said. "I don't get why you're upset. When I told you I was going to go there with Reed you were fine. So you seem more pissed that I went with Anna than anything else."

"I just don't like her," she said quickly.

"You don't even know her," he said.

"I've seen the way she looks at us," Melody snapped back. "You don't see it but I do. And I think she likes you. And she doesn't like me."

172

In the three months of dating Melody he'd noticed that, one, she tended to think the worst of people and, two, she assumed people didn't like her instead of giving them the benefit of the doubt. Or, heaven forbid, finding out for sure before letting that influence her opinion. Given how happy he'd been to reunite with Anna and set things straight between them he found Melody's response to be like a raincloud.

He put his hands on her shoulders and looked at her intently.

"Melody, it wouldn't matter if she did like me. Because I'm with you. I love *you*, remember?"

She gave him a quick nod and then hugged him tight.

"I love you, too. And I do like my bracelet," she said in a playful, but still pouty voice. "Thank you."

He made his way to his first period class, relieved to avoid a small argument before it became a bigger one. But he couldn't escape a nagging thought, which was compiled with others that had come before. Melody, for as much as he liked her and would tell her he loved her, had shown some sides of herself he wasn't as enamored with. She'd become jealous more frequently or, he thought, maybe just envious of any experience that didn't include her, some of which were beyond his control. Like when he couldn't bring her to Reed's 18th birthday party a few weeks before because she wasn't invited. She obviously couldn't attend the Senior Banquet so she didn't get to see the Village People lip sync. She heard it was hilarious from those who saw it and was upset she hadn't, which left Cal frustrated, as there was nothing he could do to remedy the situation. He'd never been in such a position before, on the receiving end of someone's jealousy. He'd been on the other side more times than he was proud of, like trying to sort through the uneasy feeling of seeing someone he'd been on a few dates with talking or flirting with another guy. He'd also seen his jealousy become wholly justified, like early in his Junior year when Beth Farren told him he shouldn't be jealous of her talking with Isaac Lawson because Isaac wasn't interested in her. That turned out not to be true, as two days later Beth suggested they "see other people". The "other people" ultimately meant another person, who turned out to be Isaac. That experience made it even more frustrating to have Melody worry about Anna or anyone else because he knew he wouldn't do something like that. Had he had feelings for Anna before? He hoped Melody would never ask that because he'd have to lie.

But he told himself those feelings were gone, and it didn't matter anyway because now she was seeing Owen Myers. He felt he couldn't compete with that even if he wanted to.

His swirling thoughts around Melody, Anna, and various kinds of jealousy were interrupted by Reed, sitting down next to him just before class started.

"How were things here yesterday, you coward?" Cal asked.

Reed seemed to take the insult in stride.

"It was quiet. I think one class had like 7 people in it. But guess what?" he asked.

"Journey's reuniting and you're camping out for concert tickets?" Cal offered.

"That would be awesome but, no," Reed said. "I got into Lewis and Clark."

Cal was just as relieved as he was happy for his friend. His own minor anxieties and worries in anticipation of letters from Southern Oregon, Sacramento and Chico felt like nothing in comparison to how some of his friends and classmates were acting. Reed's impatience and worries over it ran second only to the literally shaking anxiety he'd seen from Anna the day before.

"Congratulations, dude," he said, going so far as to shake Reed's hand.

"Thanks. It was a huge weight lifted."

"I know," he said. "Believe me, you've made it very clear."

"Yeah, I know. But you know how I get sometimes," Reed said.

"Yes, I do. And with that behind you we can now focus on the much more difficult and possibly even more important task of getting you a Senior Ball date," Cal said.

"I think I have a line on that, actually," Reed said.

"With who?!"

Cal was surprised because usually Reed would talk with him or someone else before he'd ponder even the very idea of approaching a girl.

"I don't want to jinx it," Reed said.

"Well, let me know if there is anything I can do to help," Cal said. "Apparently this is my help my friends out week."

"What do you mean?" Reed asked.

174

"Just a thing with Anna from yesterday. I'll catch you up on it later," he said.

--

Anna felt a great sense of pride from her acceptance to UCLA. But her level of excitement about it was dwarfed by the joy it seemed to bring her parents. They were thrilled and made no secret what their preference would be in her choosing a college. Their enthusiasm was matched by Owen, who was ecstatic when she shared the news with him on the phone.

"So are you going to go there?" he asked.

She told him she hadn't decided and was still waiting to hear from the other schools she'd applied to. But if nothing else she knew she was going to get to go to a very good school no matter what.

"I've still got USC and Northwestern out there," she explained. "And Wisconsin, but I'm not too worried about that one. It was my backup and even if I get in I'd go to UCLA over that one."

She still felt her usual level of panic and anxiety from not knowing about the other schools but she also recognized that her hard work had paid off. Northwestern University was a question mark and she desperately wanted an answer as it was her other top choice. But even with that still pending, getting the acceptance from UCLA let her take a breath. It was the first time since even before her high school life began, as far back as middle and elementary school, with always wanting to get straight A's, that she felt like she could stop worrying or planning, at least for a moment. She didn't have to ask herself if she'd read enough, studied enough, or if she should try out some additional activity or club to make herself look that much more attractive to these academic forces that would decide her future. For a moment the ever-present question of "Are you going to be good enough?" had been answered in the affirmative.

For his part, Owen turned the good news into a very nice second date, insisting they go somewhere at least a little fancier to eat before their additional plans to go bowling.

"Not super formal," he said. "Just something where we don't order at a counter."

It was between the Monday afternoon when the UCLA letter came and her Friday date that the rest of the good news poured in, with Northwestern accepting her on Wednesday, and the Wisconsin acceptance letter arriving Thursday. USC, which wasn't quite as high on her list, was still out there somewhere and she explained to Owen at dinner the only reason she was still eager for it to arrive was ego.

"I'd just like to know I went four for four," she said. "I know that sounds bad but I still want that. My best friend got into all but one, which was UCLA, and I want bragging rights. Is that horrible of me?"

"It's not horrible," he told her. "You had goals and you wanted to hit each one. I totally get it. I'm just glad one of your top schools came in first. The Berkeley rejection that came for me last spring was soul crushing."

His comment about that particular school reminded her of Cut Day.

"Oh, by the way, I finally got to see the Berkeley campus and library this week," she said. She wasn't sure if she wanted to give him the details but she hadn't told many people that she had been one of the cutting seniors. In the few days since, she'd grown at least a little proud of doing so.

"I went there with a friend on Monday because it was Cut Day," she explained.

"Oh right," he said. "First Monday in March. A Crestview tradition."

"Did you do it last year?" she asked.

He put his head down to show a sense of shame.

"Sadly, I did not." he said. "I was part of the minority that was afraid of the consequences."

"I was almost one of those. But Cal talked me out of it."

Until that moment she hadn't consciously realized she was not mentioning Cal's name. But she quickly recalled how much of a relief it had been when Cal didn't seem upset that she was dating someone and, in turn, she figured Owen wouldn't be upset about the friend in question being a guy.

Owen was in the middle of wrapping spaghetti noodles around his fork and when he set it down she had a moment of panic, worrying that the otherwise near-perfect Owen might be jealous after all.

"That makes sense," Owen said. "I think I mentioned not knowing him very well but he seems like the Cut Day type."

She relaxed again.

"How'd he get you to do it?" he asked. "I only ask because I wouldn't think of *you* as a Cut Day kind of person."

She told him the fuller story of Eileen and her getting rejected by UCLA and then running into Cal while she felt like she was about to have a panic attack, and how he coaxed or dared her to go with him for the day.

"It sounds like you and Cal are pretty tight," he commented.

The tinge of panic returned but she opted again to just be honest.

"We are. Surprisingly. He's become one of my best friends here," she said, adding, "I hope that's not weird."

"Why would it be weird?" he asked.

"I guess because he's a guy?"

He put his fork down again, which she now concluded might just be something he did as a habit.

"Anna, it's fine. I had female friends at Crestview. I have a few in my dorm at Stanford. Good friends. It's nice. They tell me things my guy friends never would or never could."

Another moment of relief washed over her.

"In fact, I've told some of them about you," he added, smiling, and then returning to his food.

"Oh, have you?" she asked playfully.

"Of course. I think that's been one of the cooler things about college. You can stay up late in someone's room just hanging out and talking. It's like you get to know people a lot quicker when you live next door or just a flight down and you're around each other every day, all day."

She was more curious about what he was saying about these female friends at Stanford than his description of dorm life but she couldn't bring herself to just come out and ask him to tell her more about that.

"I've always been a little slow to make friends," she said. "So I'm glad to hear it's not too hard at college."

As she had from the day she met him she wondered why Owen, as good looking and personable as he was, was spending time with her when he clearly could make friends or find a girlfriend at school. But she

177

knew her inquisitive and sometimes overly suspicious nature were among the things that made it hard for her to get close to people. She was trying to let go of some of the worry and questions she would harbor about almost anything and just accept that he liked her because he liked her, not for some reason that he wasn't talking about or hiding somewhere.

They made their way to the bowling alley and despite it being noisy and harder to carry on conversation it was still a very good time. Her competitive nature took over and when they'd each won a game she insisted on a third to break the tie. In the end she wasn't entirely sure if he'd thrown the third game or if she just had the best game of her life. But either way she was victorious. It felt like an exclamation point victory in a week that had gone incredibly well.

She later wrote in her journal that her light and victorious mood was probably why she was not only fine with parking in a secluded area to make out but that it had been her idea. And she let things go farther than she ever normally would on a second date:

*Maybe it's because I've been so happy all this week or maybe it's just that I trust Owen more than I ever trusted Kyle. But it was really, really hard to not get carried away tonight! I know Owen will stop if I say stop and not take it as "Try again later" like Kyle always did. It was months and months before I let him touch me or put his hand up my shirt. I must admit that I am laughing at how mad he'd be if he knew Owen got that far after just a few weeks!*

--

All week long at school Cal's friends and classmates had been getting their various acceptance and rejection letters, with the corresponding sighs of relief and assurance or, if it went the other way, a newfound hopelessness. There had been celebrations in the locker rows or in the hallways if someone got admittance into a competitive school and some tears, even rage, when some didn't get into their first or even second choice.

Cal overheard Clark Baylor talking with a friend on the other side of a locker row, saying, "I think it's a little fucked up when I have the same

178

grades as Shawn and he got into Irvine and I didn't. I wonder if he knows it's because he's black."

Cal wanted to go around to the other side of the row and say something but, as had happened many times with Clark and others who would say things that made his blood boil, he stayed quiet. When hearing a few stories from Reed over the years about how awful Clark had been to him, Cal thought perhaps his friend was exaggerating. But on that late March morning he was reminded that if anything Clark was even worse. What made the remark about Shawn Fordham, a rather popular guy and from every interaction Cal had ever had with him, an equally nice guy to boot, was that Shawn and Clark were a part of a circle of friends seen together all the time. From the outside looking in one would think Clark and Shawn were close friends. It was little moments like that, overhearing comments or backstabbing or gossiping about who was doing what and where and with whom, that Cal knew he wasn't going to miss at all once his days at Crestview were over.

That Friday he got his answers from Sacramento and Chico on the same day, both congratulating him on being accepted as part of the Fall 1991 class of first year students. His parents were elated with the news and Cal was relieved but still anxious for a response from Southern Oregon. He took the two letters and information packets upstairs to his room. As he sat on his bed thumbing through the various flyers of information about housing and campus life he realized why he wasn't jumping up and down or feeling the same kind of excitement his friends had with their schools, or even the level of happiness his parents had shown. It was nice to know he would be able to go away to school if he wanted to and be able to say to friends and teachers that he'd gotten into a four-year college. But when he put the Sacramento and Chico information back in the large envelopes they'd arrived in he knew where he ultimately wanted to go. There wasn't a decision to be made. He just needed to know if it was going to be possible.

He was still thinking about his decision later that night when he and Melody went to the movies. They were both excited to see the much-hyped Oliver Stone movie *The Doors*, a big screen portrayal of the iconic 60's band. When the movie was over Melody was enthused, extolling the poetic genius of the late Jim Morrison, drooling at Val Kilmer's portrayal of him, and expressing interest in hearing more of their music.

"I know their biggest songs but I don't know the deeper stuff, like some of what was in the movie," she said. As they were driving away from the theater she asked, "Do you own any of their albums?"

"Yeah, I've got a handful. I went through a Doors phase a few years ago where I got really into them. I even bought a book of Morrison's poetry," he said.

He briefly thought back to two years before, when he was 15, and how obsessed he got with The Doors for a brief period. Even though it was just a couple of years it felt longer.

"Could you dub me off some of their stuff? And maybe loan me the book?" Melody asked.

"Sure," he said.

"I just love his words and the imagery and his creativity. He was beautiful. It's sad he died so young," she said.

"It is," he agreed. "But...honestly, I think he was a bit overrated."

It was a conclusion he'd reached after his deep dive into The Doors work. He still liked them and for a brief time had loved them immensely but it was short lived.

"Overrated!? Says the guy who listens to hair bands!" Melody said.

"It's not that The Doors and Morrison aren't good but, really, his lyrics are just these drug-induced rambles that only make sense if you want it to make sense. Not to mention...and the movie showed it... he was kind of an asshole. And the other 3 guys in the band were super talented musicians all waiting around for him to get his shit together."

"Well, I'm still curious to hear more of it," she said.

"That's cool," he said. "I just think a lot of people who love them just love all the drug culture and 60's nostalgia that comes with it. That whole 'weren't the 60's awesome?' and 'Woodstock was great!' thing. I just can't really get into a band I need to be high or tripping on something to enjoy. Same thing with The Grateful Dead."

"My Dad really likes the Dead," Melody commented.

"So do some of the people at Mixtape Club. Like really into them! I just don't get it," he said.

"Well, maybe if you got high you'd like it more," she suggested.

It was not the first time she'd said something to that effect. He'd told her very early on that he wasn't into it and at a few parties since then he'd turned away or just bite his tongue when she ran off into someone's backyard to get high.

"That's the thing, though. I just want the music itself to be the high," he said. "I feel like that should be enough."

"You do know you're going to be like the only guy who goes off to college and has never gotten high or taken mushrooms," she said.

He'd heard that criticism before, too. He'd heard it from Doug and some other friends each time he took a pass on pot or other drugs.

"Well, I guess my writing or my mind will never be as expansive as Jim Morrison," he said. "But I also won't be fat and dead in a bathtub before age 30."

"Jesus," she said. "You sound like a D.A.R.E. person."

D.A.R.E. was a program at school, where a group of students would sign a pledge not to partake in drugs and alcohol and then do anti-drug and alcohol presentations for middle school kids. Cal had never signed up, as he did like to drink, but he'd thought about it. Mrs. Shellers had told him it would look good on his college applications.

"Melody... trust me. Listen to a lot of The Doors. And then, while sober, listen to someone on an acid trip rambling on and on about how a plastic cup is trying to tell them about Greek mythology and that Marty McFly never really traveled back in time but instead dreamed the whole thing. And you might realize there isn't that much difference between that person and Jim Morrison."

"Maybe some of us just like to feel good," she said. "Or have fun. Or we just want to get out of our own head for a little. I'm sorry if you don't understand that."

He knew he'd hurt her feelings with his comment but the conversation was bothering him just the same. The truth was he didn't like her getting high, he didn't like how she acted when she was, and if it were up to him she'd stop.

"I just care about you," he said. "And I'm sure you know that all this month a bunch of us have been getting our acceptance and rejection letters and all that."

"I know," she said. Then she held his hand from the passenger seat. "I've been trying not to think about it because I know what it means."

181

He felt awful for bringing up college and reminding her that he was graduating and probably leaving in a few months. But he still wanted to finish his thought.

"I don't want to tell anyone what to do but the truth is the biggest potheads I know, the craziest and the wildest people in my class? They're not waiting around for their college acceptance letters. They're going to be going to DVC or lucky to graduate on time. And I guess I just don't think that's a coincidence."

If he was being one hundred percent honest he wouldn't have just mentioned his classmates, as they weren't the people he was thinking of. He was thinking of his sister. Rachel dropped out in the 11th grade. And though he had tried to block out such thoughts, he couldn't get past that Melody reminded him of Rachel. Not nearly as out of control or as ambivalent about school but still similar.

"You're my boyfriend. Please just be my fucking boyfriend," she pleaded. "Because sometimes you talk to me like a teacher or a big brother which is really messed up if you think about it."

He didn't know how to react to that because he knew she was right. The more time they'd spent together, the closer he got to her, the more it was easy to see she was less mature than he was. And that was a strange admission, as he never felt overly mature in his own right. Even the conversation around The Doors had tripped him up a little, as he remembered that his own Doors fanatic phase was in his sophomore year, when he was closer to Melody's age. Even though that was only 2 years earlier he felt like a different person.

"I'm sorry if it feels like I'm being preachy," he said. "I don't want to be like that. Not ever. Not with you. And especially not when we're naked."

She laughed just enough to lighten the mood in the front seat.

"Speaking of that," she said. "My Mom is on a date and I don't know when she'll be back so we probably shouldn't go do that."

He was disappointed but after several weeks of having sex and nearly getting caught by her mother a few times he also didn't want to risk it.

"You know," he said. "We could swing by my house. I could grab some Doors tapes and maybe we can drive up to High Point and listen to 'Moonlight Drive' and some other songs you may not know. And just look at stars or whatever."

"I could go for that," she said. "Or we could listen to them also and also climb into the back of your truck."

Within seconds after she suggested that his worries and doubts about Melody disappeared, at least for the rest of the night.

# Chapter Seven - April 1991

## *"Lost"*

The letter Call had been waiting for finally arrived late in the afternoon on the first Saturday in April. The acceptance packages he'd received from Sacramento State and Chico State had prepared him for what a larger envelope meant, so it was with thrills and relief that he opened the materials from Southern Oregon State College confirming he was in. He'd been readying himself for the moment, as his decision was already made. But he knew he had to tell his parents and to make sure they were telling him the truth when they'd said, "No matter where you decide to go, even if it's the more expensive option, we'll find a way." They had added that if he chose Oregon he might have to get a part-time job sooner rather than later, but Cal accepted that as being part of his choice.

He shared the acceptance letter with them and just as they had done with the other two schools they congratulated him and told him how proud they were. He didn't know if they were ready for what he planned to say next but he didn't care. He blurted it out.

"This is my school," he said firmly. "This is where I want to go. I know it's far away. I know it's not cheap, but I also know it's where I want to be."

"And you're positive about that?" his father asked.

"100 percent," Cal said.

He'd been preparing himself for the conversation, wanting to make sure they knew his commitment and to try and present himself maturely. He hoped he could draw from his years of theater experience to be convincing should they have any doubts.

His father seemed more worried about the money part than the distance, whereas his mother was the opposite.

"Oh, honey," she said. "That is a big, bold decision. I wanted to give you your space to decide but I'm not all that surprised. Your face lights up when you talk about that school in a way it doesn't when you've talked about Sac or Chico."

She hugged him tightly, his father shook his hand and Cal felt a little ridiculous for having had a litany of arguments at the ready that he wasn't going to need after all. Instead he found himself back in his room, looking over the Southern Oregon paperwork, and trying to practice how he would tell Melody about it. He'd hinted his preference to her but hadn't ever come right out and said, "If I get in that's where I want to go." He knew it was a conversation to have with her in person and he had plans to see her later that night. But even that felt too far away. He was on the verge of calling her and talking about it by phone when his parents called him back downstairs.

He thought maybe they had some kind of congratulatory gift for him now that everything was official. He couldn't remember if they'd done anything like that for Tyler but such a gesture wouldn't have been out of character for them. But when he got downstairs they were already sitting at the kitchen table and there wasn't any kind of present or envelope in sight. Instead they motioned for him to have a seat and began sharing with him some big news of their own. Within 20 minutes Cal was in tears, enraged, confused, and then back in his bedroom alone, taking in all that he'd just heard. He called Melody and cancelled their plans for the evening, making up a story about why. From there he went back to trying to figure out how in the world anything in his life would ever feel the same.

--

Anna was just getting ready for church and looking forward to the service in the hope it might give her some clarity about the future. She'd been accepted at all four of her schools but had eliminated USC and Wisconsin from consideration. She reasoned that if she was going to study and live in southern California then UCLA had more to offer. It had felt almost like a betrayal to her home state that she still loved so much when she came to the conclusion that college should be about new experiences and new surroundings and going to the University of Wisconsin would be too familiar. It wouldn't challenge her enough, and with the challenge of getting into college behind her she knew she needed new ones. So it had come down to UCLA and Northwestern, with dueling external forces dancing around her head in concert with her own anxieties and worries. Eileen had decided on Northwestern and on their last phone call her friend had laid on the pressure pretty thick.

"This is what we always talked about, since we were in grade school," Eileen argued.

It was true. Which school and what they each wanted to study had changed and evolved over time but for as long as she could remember she and Eileen had talked about going to college together. And it still made sense. They both were hoping to pursue biology and possibly medicine, both liked that Northwestern was just far enough away from Kenosha to feel like leaving home, and for Anna there was the strong appeal of getting back to the Midwest.

"It's ultimately your decision," her father had said to her a few days before. "But a winter in L.A. versus winters in Chicago? I'll take the sunshine any day."

Her parents were trying to be supportive but she couldn't call them impartial. They had come to like their new lives in California and had hinted strongly that her being closer to home -- even a home that had never felt like home to her -- would be easier on all of them. She thought they were making arguments out of both sides of their mouths and it was driving her crazy, saying things like, "UCLA would mean no out of state tuition fees. But you could also put your Aunt down as your home address or establish your own residency after a year or so, so we wouldn't say 'no' to Northwestern." They also noted breaks from school and summer vacation, with comments like, "It's a lot easier to get you home from L.A. than Chicago", as well as expressing concerns about what they would do in an emergency from so far away.

For her part, Anna thought she'd made good counter arguments, saying "I'm going to do work study no matter where I go and I can help pay for flights back. And Eileen has already said I can spend short breaks with her family, or even summer for that matter."

Then there was the prestige. The two universities were just about equal from everything she could gather, with the only difference being geography. People closer to the west would praise UCLA up and down. Having lived in the Midwest for nearly her entire life Anna had grown up with Northwestern being mentioned time and time again as one of the best colleges in the country. But when she looked through the catalogs and course offerings and the packets they'd each sent to her, each one describing the kinds of jobs and further education that their graduates went on to, it all looked the same. She concluded that she was going to get the education she wanted from either school, so it was more about where she wanted to be. And that was where she was struggling.

"Obviously, I am biased," Owen had told her over the phone. "I think it'd be awesome if you were at UCLA."

He'd added how much he liked her, how he hoped she felt the same, which she did. But Anna was not going to let Owen, not his kind nature or beautiful eyes and his polite ways, be a part of her decision. She had even gone as far as to write down what she wanted to tell him before talking about it over the phone.

"I hope you won't take this the wrong way because I like you a lot," she began.

He interrupted by saying, "Uh oh, this sounds like a breakup conversation."

That comment flustered her but she stuck to her script.

"No, it's not. But I need to say that I applied for all these colleges for a reason. And I applied to all of them before I met you, so I feel like I owe it to myself to make this big decision from that same place. From when I was just thinking about my future. Which was before I met this incredible, thoughtful, intelligent and interesting man."

She hoped the kind words would help but was mostly proud of herself for saying it at all.

He was quiet but she could still hear him on the other end of the line.

"I understand," he said. "And like I said...I'd love it if you were at UCLA because it's such a great school and I think you and I have... connected?"

"We have," she said. "I would never say otherwise."

"But I also know we've only known each other a few months..."

"Right," she said. "And I really appreciate you for understanding."

"Of course. And I won't try to influence your decision except to say the beaches in southern California are beautiful at sunset."

She laughed and tried to put the lovely thought of walking with him on a beach out of her head.

"Thank you for that image but goodnight, Owen," she told him.

There was a comfort that came with turning to her faith and to God for guidance with decisions like the one she was trying to make, or in moments when she'd felt lost or confused about something. There had been a lot of those when her parents had come to her less than a year before and said there was this massive opportunity for her father in California. They told her they had prayed for guidance and concluded that even though it would be understandably hard for her and Jackie that it was a move they needed to make. The news that she would be spending her final year of high school in a new place with no friends and no familiarity had made her so angry with her parents, so furious with two people she always felt lucky to feel close to. She heard so many stories from friends and classmates over the years about how much they hated their parents for doing this or that, or not understanding them, and so much other teenage conflict. She'd never been able to relate to it until the past year. All the frustration and resentment toward them that she couldn't find a way to turn off had finally subsided at least in part when she turned to God. When they got to Concord and she spent the first weeks at her new school talking only with Tracy, who didn't feel like a friend so much as someone who had been assigned to her, followed by nights curling up on her bed and crying, she had again turned to her faith. And that faith had told her there had to be a reason for all of it. The move, the new school, the disruption to her life. The best comfort she'd found came from believing there was something she needed to learn in all of it.

As she was finishing getting dressed for church she thought back to those weeks, and the thoughts of why things happen and if they happen as part of a larger plan. Was her father taking his new job in California part of some bigger divine design to get her to look at UCLA? She reasoned that if they had never left Wisconsin that college would never have been part of her plans. Or was the whole experience part of a journey designed to make her appreciate the life she'd had before and return to it, only this time as a college student, with less of the comforts of family nearby? She hoped some time at church might give her a sign or maybe the pastor would say something that would be like a compass. She just knew she needed something.

The doorbell rang from downstairs just as she was getting her shoes on. She shouted, "I'll get it!" toward her sister's room next door and her

189

parents down the hall. When she got to the door it was with some surprise to see Cal standing on her porch.

"Hey," she said. "What's up?"

"I was wondering if you had a minute to talk," he said.

She peered back inside the house and looked at the hallway clock.

"We're heading to church soon but I have a few minutes," she said, stepping out and closing the front door behind her. She motioned for him to have a seat on the bench near the front rail of the porch.

"What's going on?" she asked.

He took a deep breath and she immediately thought he'd either broken up with Melody and needed reassurance that he'd done the right thing. Or perhaps Melody had broken up with him and he needed a shoulder to cry on. Her immediate worst thoughts were that the breakup had have something to do with her, like Melody being jealous of their friendship, which he'd told her about a few times. She also worried that maybe he had redeveloped feelings for her beyond friendship.

"Well, first," he said, "I made my decision about school. I got my acceptance letter from Southern Oregon and I'm going."

"Cal, that is awesome! I didn't want to say anything but I was rooting for you to do that," she said.

"Thanks," he said. "But it turns out that's not all."

Worry came over her again, waiting for his next words, again imagining some terrible scenarios. Had he foolishly gotten Melody pregnant? He'd never even said they were having sex but she got the strong impression they were.

"It turns out my parents have been waiting for me to make a decision about college so they could tell me their news," he said. "And their news is that they're splitting up."

She put her hand on his, wanting to say something but unable to find the words, instead watching her friend do his best to hold back from crying, even as she could see tears well up in his eyes.

"I'm so sorry," she said quietly.

"Thanks," he said softly. "I just...um...I didn't see it coming. Like, at all. They don't argue or anything but it turns out they've been talking about it and waiting. For, like, over a year. Waiting for me to finish school, get through applying and choosing and then...boom. I told them where I wanted to go right after my letter came and they asked me if I was sure and I told them 'Yes' and they said they had been hoping I might choose Sac but that they wanted my decision to be mine and all the other bullshit they're supposed to say. And then less than an hour later they told me it was time to tell me they were getting a divorce. Apparently they've been getting ready for it for a long time without my even noticing."

She squeezed his hand tight, all the while in her own disbelief. She'd been over to his house several times and his parents seemed very happy.

"They're going to be selling the house," he continued. "And on top of all of that my Dad wants to move closer to the city because the commute sucks and my Mom is moving to Eureka, where some of my aunts and uncles live."

"I just don't get it," he said, no longer fighting off the tears. "I just don't know why they waited or why they're telling me this after I make this big decision, ya know? It's like they were sitting on it for months and months and when they finally got a chance they couldn't wait. Not even a day. Not even 24 hours to let me be happy about *my* decision."

From what he'd said so far she thought his parents had done him a kindness by trying to stay together through his graduation. But she was also reminded of her own anger, her own feelings that had included words like "betrayal' and "unfair" and "selfish" when her parents had told her about moving to California. More than anything she hated seeing Cal in tears.

"That's horrible timing," she agreed. "But they obviously stuck it out because they love you. I know that sounds like I'm defending them. But it at least seems like they get along well enough to think about you and getting you ready for next year."

She wasn't remotely sure if it made sense, even to herself, and hoped Cal would not take it as trying to sympathize with his parents or take their side. She was still rather shocked by the news herself.

"I just feel like they took away whatever happiness or relief I was supposed to get from choosing my school. I've been wrestling with it and thinking about how far away it is and how I wouldn't know anybody up there but I thought, 'Okay, but you'll see everyone when you visit home for Christmas and summer and all that'. But now? They're taking all that away. My Dad's gonna be over toward the city and my Mom...I mean...fuck... have you ever been to Eureka?"

She shook her head.

"Try to imagine living by the ocean...except it's hardly ever sunny or warm, you can't surf or boogie board or all the other stuff you do at a beach, the town is boring, and for most of the year it's just constantly gray and if it's not raining it's like it's about to rain. It's not a place. It's a fucking Smiths song."

She didn't get his music reference but was glad he was getting his anger out. She was envious, as whenever she got mad she would bottle it, rarely verbalizing her feelings. His anger and venting his frustration reminded her of when she had told Eileen the news of her family moving, and how Eileen had been there for her.

She leaned over and hugged him. Then she had an idea.

"I've got to go to church," she said. "But why don't you come with us?"

He immediately shook his head.

"Why not?" she asked.

"It's not really my thing," he said.

"When was the last time you went to church? Any church?" she asked.

He looked up and took a few seconds thinking about it.

"I went to an open house at Reed's temple last year," he said.

She put both hands over his hands.

"I want you to come with us. No one's going to try and save you or make you do anything you don't want to," she said. "But if nothing else it might take your mind off things. And...*and*... we get donuts or bagels after."

He chuckled, which gave her a huge sense of relief.

"I don't feel like I'm dressed for it," he said, pointing at her in her dress and nice shoes and then back at his own clothes.

She looked him over and stifled a laugh as she thought about him walking into church as-is.

"I think you'll be fine in the jeans and your Vans but the Bang Tango t-shirt needs to go," she said, standing up from the porch bench. "I'm going to see if my Dad has a button up you can wear over it, okay?"

192

He looked uneasy about the idea but told her thank you and that he would come along.

--

Cal had spent the 14 hours between his parents telling him their big news and arriving at Anna's house doing one of two things: Trying to sleep, which had proved very difficult, or wondering what he'd missed along the way that might have given him some clue that they were going to divorce. He'd never thought of his parents as unhappy together, but as a collage of thoughts raced around his head he couldn't remember seeing them particularly happy either. They were mostly just there. He thought of how his father left early each morning because his commute into the city was long and he didn't like the BART trains, then getting back late or even later depending on the traffic. His mother, who worked closer to home, wasn't all that different. She just spent more time in the morning making sure Cal was good to go for the day, and he almost always was. Their lives as a trio, with Tyler and Rachel all grown up and moved out, had been routine. On the weekends Cal would go out at night with his friends and his parents were usually both at home, either watching something on TV or reading. Occasionally they would go to the movies or maybe out to dinner. They were, in his mind, a bit boring. But that was no different than how he imagined other parents and he wouldn't have had it any other way.

They'd opened the conversation by telling him how proud they were about his getting into all his schools and choosing which school he wanted to attend on his own, even though they still had some misgivings and worries about Oregon. But from there it had turned into something else entirely. They gave him the standard talk he'd seen in a hundred movies and TV shows about how it wasn't his fault, about how they both loved him and his brother and sister more than anything in the world, and that nothing would ever change that. But they said several times that with him heading off to school and becoming an adult it was time for them to accept that they wanted different things from life.

"We don't hate each other," his father explained. "And one of the reasons we've been able to put this off and let you finish up school is because we both want each other to be happy."

His mother took it from there, explaining that they had a plan and were ready to begin exercising it. They were going to sell the house but promised that even if it sold quickly they wouldn't be moving out until after he graduated. His father was already looking at condos and apartments in Richmond and Daly City that would be considerably closer to the CalVest headquarters where he worked. His mother's plan was far bigger, and it shook Cal up more than the idea of his father living closer to San Francisco. She was planning to move back to Eureka, where she'd grown up and where Cal's uncle and aunt ran a property management company. His mother had worked for a property manager in Concord for years and was planning to buy a share of the Eureka business and be closer to family, including Cal's grandparents who lived just outside Eureka.

"I know it's a huge change," she told him. "But the good news is that Eureka is closer to Ashland than we are now and I'm going to make sure I have a big enough place so you can stay on breaks from school or over the summer if you want."

"And you can also come stay with me," his father added quickly. "If you prefer."

His head began swimming and with each new detail he shifted more from confusion to anger, eventually lashing out.

"I'm glad you both have plans for my summers and holidays. Really...thank you for planning my fucking life."

They ignored his profanity, which was something they normally wouldn't dismiss. Instead they said they understood he was upset but there would never be a good or perfect time to tell him such news.

"But with your college decision made and Spring and Summer being the best time to sell a house we just think it's important to get things moving," they explained.

He eventually made his way up to his room, still reeling, still thinking about what it all would mean. Piece by piece it came together in his mind and none of the pieces felt like good ones. His mother in Eureka meant the month off from Southern Oregon in December would mean spending a month with her and extended family. There were cousins but none that he felt especially close to. And he hated the city of Eureka. It was cold, there was nothing to do, no concerts, not even a decent mall or anything like what he was used to. And the thought of going to stay with his father was equally dreadful. Of his two parents he was far closer with his mother and he could only imagine what kind of place his father would live in. Sure, it would be closer to San Francisco and the surrounding cities were all familiar. But when he thought of college he also thought of the trips back home to Concord. As much as he and friends talked about getting out of the suburbs and going away to their schools big and small, romanticizing all of it, there was a comfort in knowing the place he'd grown up in would still be there, unchanged and as predictable as needed.

He'd witnessed Tyler coming back from school his first few years before he got an off-campus house at Davis with some friends and started living there full time. In those first few years he came back for nearly a month in December, with neither of their parents telling Tyler to get a job or anything like that. His brother would go catch up with old high school friends and it always looked like he was having a blast when he did. Over the last two years of high school Cal had frequently caught up with people who'd graduated a year or two ahead of him. He'd see them at a party or in a line at the movie theater, particularly during winter or summer break, and such reunions were always full of laughs and getting to hear about how college was going. He was looking forward to being that guy for Doug or other friends a year or two behind him. With the house being sold and his parents going in separate directions there weren't going to be any homecomings. He'd always known the summer ahead and his departure for school was going to be a series of goodbyes but attached to each one would be a "but I'll see you around when I'm home for a visit." He'd had past graduates say such things to him. He was planning to say it to Reed and especially Doug. It was when that part of it sunk in, that goodbyes would be long and indefinite, that he called Melody. He apologized for having to cancel on going to a party together that night. He lied and told her it was because his parents were forcing him to go to dinner with family friends visiting from out of town. He then put on some music, played it loudly, buried his head in a pillow and in between some muffled shouts he cried more than he could remember crying in years.

Cal had only asked his parents a few times why their family didn't go to church. The first time he brought it up was when he was in middle school. His mother explained that his father, who was one of 6 children to Cal's grandmother, had started working odd jobs by the time he was 12, including on Sundays. For her part, his mother said she and her two siblings had always been ordered to attend church, never getting any say in the matter, or ever being asked what they personally believed in.

"So your father has no real history with it and my history with it is having it force fed to me. So we decided we weren't going to push it on you, Tyler, or Rachel, but instead to let you find it on your own if you want."

She'd added that if Cal was ever interested in going to a certain church that she would be happy to go with him. He was in 7th grade at the time he'd asked and by then Sunday mornings had become a good time for watching wrestling on TV or catching up on homework and he never once inquired again. Later, in high school, he'd been invited by Reed to a few functions at his temple and went once or twice. A few of his other friends that were part of the Mormon church regularly invited Cal and others to open houses but he always politely declined. By the time he found himself on Anna's porch being invited to her church he'd come to question if there was a God at all. It was a notion even he would admit had come from such questions being asked in songs he'd heard or books and poems he'd read. He had friends that were Christian, Mormon, Jewish, and Muslim but in terms of what each church or brand of faith stood for he was admittedly either uninterested or not informed enough to really have an opinion.

"They call that agnostic," is what his brother told him after Cal had asked Tyler if he'd ever considered going to church or if he felt particularly religious.

As he buttoned up the blue dress shirt Anna's father had loaned him he felt nervous about going to church with her family. He thought of bailing out, telling her that he should probably just go home and either talk with his parents some more or maybe just get in his car and go to Tower Records or a movie to get his mind off things.

"I think it'll do you some good," Anna said. "Plus, you'll be with me and I won't have to worry about how you're doing."

When she brought the shirt down to him she quickly explained she hadn't told her parents exactly why he had come by or any of the information he had shared with her.

196

"I just told them you came over this morning to share your news about Oregon, so that's all they know. It's not my place to tell them and you don't need to either," she said. "Not unless you want to."

He didn't. By talking to Anna he had doubled the number of people he'd talked to about it outside of his parents. They'd mentioned talking about it with Tyler the previous weekend when they had visited him at UC Davis. They'd made him promise not to mention anything to Cal until they'd had a chance to tell him themselves. Cal counted back the calendar days and realized his older brother had known for 5 or 6 days before he did. He and Tyler didn't talk by phone very often and even though he knew Tyler had promised their parents he still felt like his brother should have broken that promise and told him. Instead, amid his tears and shouts, he called Tyler, catching him just before he was going out for the night.

After Cal had spent a few minutes on the phone ranting at him about the situation, Tyler responded rather calmly.

"I'm sorry I'm not there with you," Tyler said.

It was one of the few times Cal could remember him apologizing for anything.

"I really am sorry," Tyler said again. "I was surprised by it, too. Maybe not as much as you but still...I'm sorry you're there alone without me or Rach."

Cal sat in the backseat of the Williams' car and wondered if his parents had even talked to Rachel yet. He had thought about driving out to Fairfield to see her the night before, just to get out of the house and have something to do or a place to go but decided not to.

"Anna told us your good news about college," Mr. Williams said from the front seat. "Congratulations. We've never been to Oregon but I hear it's beautiful."

"It is," Cal said, trying to sound chipper and excited. He told himself to get into theater mode; to just play the role of the graduating classmate of their daughter.

They asked him if he'd picked a major and praised him for making his decision quickly, which he knew was a subtle jab at Anna sitting next to him. Cal hadn't spent much time with the Williams family, as it was usually Anna coming to his house to play basketball or the two of them going somewhere to hang out. He wasn't even sure if they liked him as a person. Anna had explained to him early on that his parents were rather conservative and, as she'd put it to him, "you just sort of scream '*not* conservative'." But they were very nice whenever he'd been around them and after the night before and all the anger with his parents he was happy to have the distraction of polite, generic questions.

The service itself had, in the end, given him the distraction that Anna promised it might. He couldn't say he was especially moved by Pastor Nelson or eager to return some other Sunday in the future but he appreciated that the guy had a sense of humor, which Cal hadn't really expected. Midway through the service it occurred to him that his strongest perceptions of ministers, pastors, or other church figures were right out of movies and TV shows. On the far worse end of the spectrum were the TV evangelists like Jim Baker and Jerry Falwell that he would sometimes see because their preaching always seemed to be on right before WWF shows he watched all the time from about age 9 to 12. Sitting in the pew next to Anna he almost laughed as his mind drifted to Hulk Hogan and his call out to his fans, the Hulkamaniacs, to "train, say your prayers, eat your vitamins, and believe in yourself." As he listened to Pastor Nelson talk about putting one's faith out into the world in the same way one might do a daily exercise routine, Cal thought there really wasn't that much difference between a church service and those old wrestling shows. There was a lot of call and response to the people in the church, some music, some cheering, and plenty of stories of good overcoming evil. All that was missing was body slams and a ring.

He felt very out of place when they got to the hymns and people reciting passages from the Bible, as he didn't know any of it. As they were getting ready to sing Anna whispered over to him, "Just move your lips without sound as though you were saying 'Watermelon' over and over." He did it a few times, felt a bit ridiculous in doing so, but was smiling the whole way, which was a welcome relief.

The Pastor closed by asking everyone to bow their heads and before he led a prayer to take a few moments and quietly speak to God for themselves, to seek comfort in His presence and to ask for His help with anything that was making their soul or spirit uneasy. If there was one part of the service that came close to getting through to Cal it was that. He did as instructed and quietly thought, *I've never been here. I don't know if you're real. But if you are then you know what is going on and why I'm so angry right now. I couldn't sleep last night. I'm tired and I'm hurt and I don't want to go home because I don't want to look at either of them. If you're real and you can help then please give me a sign.*

When the service finished they exited out to the lobby and Cal watched as Anna's sister Jackie ran off to a group of friends and her parents drifted toward other adults, leaving him with Anna.

"What did you think?" she asked.

"It was nice. I felt a little out of place, though. Like an imposter."

"You're not," she said. "But we should probably go take the weekly quiz now."

"What?" he asked curiously.

"We have to go answer questions about the service to make sure we learned the material," she said firmly.

He stammered for a moment before she began laughing as hard as he'd ever seen her laugh.

"Oh wow, that was good," she said, still laughing and her face turning red. "The look on your face... I am so proud of myself!"

She kept laughing and began clapping too.

"I do not like you right now," he said, all the while having to hand it to her for a good joke. He was as aware as he'd ever been that he liked her as much or more than anyone in the world.

"Now you know how I felt with you in a record store," she said. "Or when you know more about some movie or actor or something."

He wanted to tell her how much he appreciated her bringing him along to church, even if he hadn't suddenly found religion or magically felt better about his parents. The thoughts about them and all the changes that lie ahead were already moving from the back of his mind, where he'd temporarily been able to place them, right back to the forefront. And he knew he needed to share the news further, especially with Melody and other friends.

"You know....you're the first person I told," he said to Anna. "About my parents."

"Really? Nobody else knows? You didn't call Mel--"

"Tyler knows," he interrupted. "I don't know about my sister. I'll get around to telling everybody. I mean, it's big. Especially the moving part. They're moving. I'm moving! I'm sure I'll share it with everyone eventually but right now I feel....almost dizzy, if that makes any sense."

"It does. And your friends will help you," she said. "I'll help you. I'm always here if you need to talk. I don't know about the whole parents splitting up part of it, but I know a thing or two about unwanted moves."

"I know you do. That's one of the reasons I told you first," he said.

"And here I thought it was just because I live a block over," she said.

"That was the other reason," he said with a smile.

They walked back over to her parents and then drove back to Bell Ridge after a stop for donuts, as promised. He returned the shirt he'd borrowed, thanked her parents for welcoming him to their church, and then thanked Anna again for the invite.

"This is the church girl in me saying this but I hope you can find some peace today," she told him. "And don't be afraid to look up if you feel lost."

He promised he'd try and walked the block back to his house. He took a deep breath before going inside, making an immediate run up the stairs to his room. He debated calling Melody first, was on the verge of calling Reed before remembering he was away at Tahoe for the weekend with his parents, and he knew Doug wasn't the person to talk to just yet. He did his best to not think about it, to not imagine what life would be like in 3 or 4 months once the house he'd been living in since he was 10 was sold and his parents were off in their two different directions. For almost 3 years he'd been the last of the three Sorenson kids left living there and he'd always liked that. But that afternoon he wished either Tyler or Rachel were around. Tyler would tell him it sucks but to be strong, to not cry over it, because it wouldn't do any good. Rachel would tell him to put on some loud music and if their Mom or Dad told him to turn it down to say something back like, "What?! I'm sorry, I can't hear you over my metal music and your own selfish bullshit!" He could imagine her saying something exactly like that. The thought of it gave him a quick laugh to himself.

He picked up the receiver of the phone in his room and called his big sister for the first time in a long time.

--

Anna knew her parents would say "No" but she promised Owen she'd ask them anyway. On their most recent phone call he'd made what

200

she was sure he believed was a respectful, thought out, and ultimately sweet invitation for her to visit him for a weekend at Stanford.

"If you were interested I thought I could come up and get you on a Friday afternoon, we could drive down, stop for dinner on the way or something, and then I could show you around campus, we could go to a baseball or softball game Saturday, go to the church I attend down here on Sunday and then I can take you home. I think it would be really fun," he explained. He'd even added, "And just to be clear, my friend Angie's roommate goes home almost every weekend and she said you are welcome to stay in her room."

She appreciated the invitation and his mention of her not staying in his room was a reminder of why she was glad she'd gone against her instincts about dating anyone at all. He had been nothing but a perfect, respectful gentleman since the moment they met. Nevertheless, she knew the temptation to spend the night with him, even without sex, would be very strong. She also knew her parents were not naive. She'd gotten pretty good at knowing what things she could keep from them without any suspicion, like the times she'd gone to parties in Kenosha where there was drinking and where she had even had the occasional sip. They also had at least an inkling that Eileen, who they always said was like a third daughter to them, was far wilder than Anna but they didn't say it out loud. Even her close friendship with Cal, who they'd expressed a few concerns about given his penchant for band t-shirts and the occasional rips in his jeans, had been easy to address by telling them about his best qualities.

"He's in AP English, he tutors other students, and he's nice to every single person I've ever seen him talk to," she'd explained months before. "And I'd like to think you trust that I wouldn't be friends with him if he wasn't a really good guy."

They also really liked Owen, in large part because they liked his parents, who had been among the first new friends they'd made after the move. Even her curfew, which they used to enforce strictly, had been loosened up because "if you're out with Owen we know you're fine." But she was almost certain they would nix Owen's idea and invitation for her to visit very quickly. And they did.

"Absolutely not," her mother said. "I'm actually surprised you'd even ask."

Her father was a bit more understanding about it.

"I know you're in a hurry to get to the college thing and all the experiences that go with it," he said. "And heaven knows I am already worried about you being away next year because I was a student just like Owen once upon a time."

The mental image of her father at that age was one she instantly wanted to block out.

"I know it's a big ask," she said, making what she knew was a longshot argument, mostly for Owen's sake. "But I also think it'd be a good idea if you guys started to trust me. I would stay in his friend's room, check in with you or whatever you want but I think it would be good to see what 48 hours on a big college campus is like."

"And you will," her Dad said, with a knowing smile crossing his face. "You will know what it's like the first weekend this fall at whatever school you choose when you finally make up your mind."

Her indecision on UCLA vs. Northwestern had become an ongoing discussion around her house.

With the Stanford invitation from Owen sure to be shot down she'd prepared a back-up alternative she thought might even work.

"So I can't go for the weekend and I understand why," she said. "But would it be okay for me to borrow one of the cars on a Saturday morning, drive down and visit Owen for the day, and then drive back by whatever curfew you set?"

She watched as her mother looked over to her father, an exchange in body language between them she'd grown familiar with. They did it whenever they weren't sure if they were on the same page about something.

"What if we drove down with you?" her father asked.

She imagined her, her parents, and Owen walking around the Stanford campus like they were on a tour, not much different than when they'd traveled down to visit UCLA and USC. It would be like having two chaperones and it wasn't at all appealing.

"Or what if you just let me go alone and trust that I'll be responsible?" she asked.

"I'm worried about you driving back in the dark," her mother said quickly.

"Really? Because I've driven in the dark before… on ice in the middle of winter back home. Driving back from Stanford would be nothing."

They were quiet again and she saw an opening to make another point.

"And you've both been saying lately that you know you need to start letting go, to know that I'm going to be okay on my own and make smart decisions for myself, right?"

They *had* been saying such things and they couldn't deny it, and Anna knew it. She watched them exchanging looks, like some kind of telepathy between them, and felt like she was very close to getting her way.

"I think it's okay," her father said reluctantly. "As long as you agree to be back by 11, not your usual later curfew. I don't want you on the road that late, especially after a long day. Deal?"

Anna looked to her Mom for confirmation, even though she knew if her Dad was on board that it was probably settled.

"We're trusting you, Analisa," her mother said. "And we trust Owen. But don't blow it."

"I won't," she promised.

She left it at that, proud of herself for making her arguments and winning. It would also make Owen happy, even if he might be disappointed she couldn't visit for longer. And for her own sake, while not willing to admit as much to Owen or her parents, she was a bit relieved to just be going for the day instead of a full weekend. She was concrete in her principles but she also knew she could easily get caught up in the moment with Owen. Going to visit him for just an afternoon felt like the right thing and she gave herself her due for knowing it.

--

Cal didn't share the news about his parents pending divorce with any of his teachers, as it made no sense to them to talk about it. But his favorite teachers at Crestview were thrilled when he told them he'd made a decision on college. His History and Psychology teacher, Mr. Johnston, expressed his congratulations and noted to Cal that he had also gone to a smaller college.

"You'll see the difference," Mr. Johnston told him. "You'll get to know your professors and they'll get to know you. Big schools are overrated."

His drama teacher Mr. Deroy, who Cal had been with all four years of high school, was the person who had introduced him to Ashland and Southern Oregon State in the first place. Still, he was a bit hurt when Mr. Deroy didn't seem surprised or disappointed when he told him he wasn't planning to major in theater.

"That seems like a good choice," he said. "I mean, being a writer is hard and competitive but the theater is worse. Trust me. It's really hard to stand out."

Cal took it as a subtle explanation for why in four years of drama he'd never landed a lead or starring role.

His guidance counselor, Mrs. Sheller, was the happiest of anyone. He thanked her for the letter of recommendation, though he had no idea if it had been necessary or made any difference.

"I'm thrilled you got in," she said. "It's a unique school and you're a unique young man, Cal. They're going to be lucky to have you."

In any other week, following any other weekend, he would have reveled in it. So many of his soon-to-be graduating classmates were now relieved of worries and indecision that had dogged them for weeks. Conversations had shifted from where people had been accepted to where they were choosing to go and why. They were easy, light conversations, because he felt like he could tell anyone about his college of choice. The only frustration at all was the high volume of his friends that had never heard of Southern Oregon or even knew where it was on a map.

"I feel like I've had to say the phrase, 'It's about 30 minutes north of the border' a hundred times," he told Reed.

Reed was the first person he told about his parents divorcing. He knew he needed to talk with Melody about college and about his parents but figured that conversation would be much tougher. Reed was shocked because he'd been over to Cal's home dozens of times and never saw any sign of unhappiness either. It made Cal feel a little less foolish for not noticing himself.

"I feel like they were holding their breath," Cal explained. "They had this big secret and they kept it until the right time, whatever the hell that means. But just over the past few days now with the cat out of the bag they haven't been shy about having more arguments or saying something harsh about each other. It's like they finally said it out loud and now they're acting like two people who want a divorce. They're not faking it anymore."

"That sucks," Reed said, offering at least a bit of sympathy for the tough situation before changing the subject to other students at Crestview whose parents had split in the last four or five years.

"I am really *not* going to miss how much you know about people," Cal said, grateful for the lighter moments that always came from Reed. "Speaking of which, how is the quest for a Ball date coming?"

"I'm going to ask her soon," Reed told him. "I just want to make sure she'll say yes."

Cal wondered how anyone could ever be sure of such a thing but didn't say as much.

"Who is this 'her' anyway?" he asked.

It was not like either of them to keep someone they were interested in a mystery. Usually if Reed made even the slightest mention of someone he liked Cal would be quick to offer advice or assess his friend's chances with the person in question.

"You don't know her but I don't want to mention her name because I feel like that will jinx it," Reed explained.

"How the hell would that jinx it if I don't know her?" Cal asked.

"I don't know. I just know I've done okay on my own so far with no one telling me 'Hey, you should do this' or 'You should say that'. And she and I have talked a lot and we went out Saturday and--"

"You went out?" Cal asked.

It surprised him, as Reed never kept him in the dark if he had an upcoming date or was even so much as thinking of trying to get a date. The more he talked about this mystery girl the more out of the loop Cal felt.

"Yeah. She plays golf so we went and hit balls at the driving range," Reed said.

Cal racked his brain for any girls he knew of at Crestview that played golf, as there wasn't a golf team, golf club or anything like that at their school.

205

"Beware of girls who like hitting balls," was the only retort or joke Cal could come up with and he knew it wasn't even a good one. The sense of humor or quick wit he prided himself in having had felt a bit off with all that was happening at home.

Doug was the next recipient of Cal's dual pieces of big news.

"I know college is supposed to be a new chapter and how you're supposed to move on and not look back but, damn, I was looking forward to coming home and catching up with you," Cal told him. "Now I gotta probably spend at least half the holidays in Eureka."

Doug at least tried to be reassuring, telling him, "Hey, nothing's stopping me from coming up to visit you at school. I'm gonna, like, pretend I'm from another college and see how many Oregon girls I can get together with on a weekend."

Cal had no idea what life was going to be like on the Southern Oregon campus, as most of his notions of college living were from *Animal House*, *Real Genius*, and *Revenge of the Nerds*. And while he loved all those movies he doubted they were an accurate reflection of what he was in for. But it was still fun to imagine Doug running loose, pretending to be older than he was, and seeing if he could fool anyone. Cal had no doubt he probably could.

"The thing with your parents, though," Doug added. "I really am sorry. Obviously my thing is different but..."

Doug never seemed to finish his thoughts whenever he brought up his family and his father. Cal had noticed the vague phrasings like "my thing" or "what happened" that Doug would use. He never pushed him to talk about it and had never invited him to open up about it either.

Cal had read about clinical depression in his Psychology class and he remembered Doug saying that his father was depressed.

"He died from his sadness," was how Doug had described it the first of the very few view times he ever mentioned it.

It took a while longer for Cal to piece together that it was suicide and that Doug just had a different way of saying it.

As he talked about his parents divorcing and what he viewed as a major upheaval to his life and future plans, Cal recognized it was nothing compared to what Doug had been through. He felt guilty for thinking his problems even came close.

"So are Oregon girls like lumberjack's daughters or some shit like that?" Doug asked, shifting the topic.

"I have no idea," Cal said. "When I toured the campus last spring I actually saw a lot of tie dye and sundresses."

"Awesome," Doug said. "Hippy chicks are easy."

Cal knew the hardest person to tell was going to be Melody. He put it off only for as long as it might take for her to hear it from someone else first. He was driving her home from school when he simply blurted it out with very little build up or lead in.

"I've decided on Oregon for school," he said shortly after they'd exited the Crestview parking lot.

He waited for her reaction, fearing she would be upset or sad but hopeful that she might see it as he did: The braver, bolder choice to go farther away and somewhere he could picture himself being happy.

Her reply was short.

"Why?" was all she said.

It was not the kind of simple question he expected.

"Because it's where I think I wanna be," he said.

She was quiet and from the corner of his eye he could see her turn her head toward the window. He couldn't see if she was angry or perhaps crying. He felt awful for thinking it but he wanted her to be sad. He thought she *should* be sad. It would mean she was going to miss him and he wanted to be missed.

"How far away is it again?" she asked.

He'd mentioned to her a few times that the drive from Concord to Ashland, Oregon was several hours, 3 or 4 times farther than if he'd chosen Sacramento or Chico State.

"It's pretty far," he reminded her. "A good 5 to 6-hour drive."

She let out a long sigh.

"I'm sorry," he said. "But it's where I want to go. It's always been where I want to go. I was really only considering Sac because my parents wanted me to for some reason."

"I know," she said, "And you told me all along it was a possibility but I guess I also thought that you might stay closer to home because of...God, I feel like a selfish bitch for saying it...but because of *me*."

After she mentioned "home" he had to steel himself up to share his other news.

"I don't know how to tell you the other part. 'Home' isn't going to be home much longer. It turns out my parents are moving," he said, leaving out the reasons why. There would be no dodging the topic but from talking to just a few people about it he was in no rush to dive right back into it.

"What?! Where are they moving to?" she asked.

"To Eureka... and somewhere to be determined," he said.

Over the previous 5 days Cal had discovered telling the whole story out loud triggered an anger and sadness in him that he hadn't yet learned to control. It had taken him a few days just to get to the place where each time he thought about it he wouldn't cry or want to shout or punch his fist against a wall.

"They're divorcing," he finally said. "They stuck it out together long enough to get me to the finish line at Crestview. And now they're going to go their separate ways."

"Wow," she said. "That's kinda fucked up."

He'd been expecting her to say 'I'm so sorry about your parents' or some version of it but her assessment wasn't that different from similar thoughts he'd had. They'd framed it to him like staying together even when they knew they wanted to divorce was something done for him; a noble sacrifice so he'd be a happy teenager while they apparently were unhappy adults. But in his mind all it had done was put off the sadness and the pain to a later date, overshadowing what he'd always thought should be the time of his life.

"So who's going where?" Melody asked. "Your parents."

He explained "The Plan" his parents had laid out, adding that the exact move date was still to be decided. A realtor had already come to see the house and his Mom had told him to straighten his room up as a cleaning crew were coming later in the week.

"Their hope is it sells quickly and then everyone gets to move by the middle of summer or sooner," he explained.

"And where are you gonna go?" she asked.

He shrugged.

"I have no idea. My Mom says she'd love it if I came up to Eureka until school starts in Ashland. My father said I can come to wherever the hell he is going to live, somewhere near the city. And no matter what I'm gone in September and the closest thing to coming back here is going to probably mean Daly City or maybe Marin or something."

"When did they tell you this?" she asked.

"Saturday," he said. "That's why I cancelled on you and was avoiding the phone the rest of the weekend."

"You've known since Saturday and you're telling me this *now*?!" she asked.

"Yeah. I needed a few days to let it sink in."

She turned toward him as much as she could from the passenger side of his car.

"I would have told you something like that right away," she said.

"Well, I didn't," he said. "I'm sorry but it wasn't good news or something I was psyched to share. It wasn't, 'Guess what, Melody?! I got us concert tickets!'"

She gave another exacerbated breath.

"This is what I've been afraid of," she said. "I told myself, 'Mel, don't go out with him. He's a senior and he's going to leave and it's not worth it' but I did it anyway. I'm so fucking stupid."

He took a hand off the wheel and reached over for hers, but she pulled it away.

"It's hard for me, too, ya know," he said. "I've known I'm going somewhere for a long time. Before I ever met you. But you've been the best thing about this entire year and I kept thinking it'll be okay even if I went north because I love you. And there'd be Christmas and Spring break and…"

"And *months* in between those times. Where you're off living in a dorm with all these other girls and I'm here," she said. "You'd dump me by Thanksgiving. Probably Halloween."

"I wouldn't," he said.

He said it with as much conviction as he could, knowing that if he was in Melody's position he wouldn't believe it. He'd known too many friends and classmates who tried and then ultimately failed to keep a long-distance relationship with a college-bound boyfriend or girlfriend.

"I just wish you would have told me that your plan was always to go so far away. If it was Sacramento I could even drive over and visit or something but I don't even know where Ashland is on a map and it sounds like its super fucking far," she said.

209

"I know."

They'd reached her house. He parked next to the sidewalk and turned the engine off.

"How about we just not think about it?" he suggested. "It's April. I'm not going anywhere for months. I might even be here till September if the house doesn't sell right away."

"It doesn't change what happens in September," she said.

He searched for the right thing to say but knew there wasn't much he could offer.

"I didn't want to share any of this because I knew it was going to suck," he said. "It would have sucked if it was just about going to Oregon. But the stuff with my parents has been... a lot. I got totally blindsided. It's been less than a week and they're already trying to get me to commit on who I want to stay with and when."

"At least you have a choice," she said quietly.

"What do you mean?" he asked.

"You can go spend time with your Mom or spend time with your Dad," she said. "I know it sucks they're splitting but it's not like they don't want you. I only see my Dad every couple of weeks and staying with him is impossible because his place is so small."

Cal knew Melody's relationship or lack of it with her father was a sore spot. She'd talked about it with him a lot. But sitting in the car that afternoon he was more concerned about *his* Dad, *his* Mom, and the disruption they'd thrown into the life he thought he had well planned out.

"This isn't about who has it worse," he argued.

"People who have it good always say stuff like that," she said, opening the car door. "I'm going to go inside. Do you want to come in?"

Usually when she asked that it meant 'Let's go inside and fool around in my room' but he doubted that was what she had in mind this time.

He followed her inside, where she went straight to the kitchen, grabbed a Diet Coke, and threw him one before she sat on a stool near the breakfast bar.

"I feel like I am running straight into a wall," she said. "Like the hurt is coming and it's just how soon I get it."

"I don't want you to feel that way."

210

Cal's first thought was about not hurting her. His second was how to avoid doing it. The third, one he had not even entertained the idea of until it hit him, was to end things right then and there. She'd told him her fears and he knew that it was not only a legitimate fear but one that was likely to come to pass. But he was scared, too. Scared of what life was going to be like in a few months once the house was empty and he would have to choose which moving van he was going to put his things in and which parent he'd spend time with. He was already dubbing it his "Broken Summer". The last few days had felt like such a loss, with his biggest life decision ever having been swept away by his parents making decisions about their lives.

He knew it was very likely that Melody was right about everything she said. She probably shouldn't have gotten involved with a guy two years ahead of her, especially one that said he wasn't going to Diablo Valley College or sticking around Concord indefinitely. But in the moment, looking at her as she looked at him for some kind of answer or comfort, he could only come up with one thing to say.

"I love you," he said. "And I know we'll have a lot to talk about and we will. But it's been a brutal couple of days. So can we just talk about something else?"

"Like what?" she asked.

"Like…I know you've told me you don't like poufy dresses and all the cliche prom stuff but I hope that doesn't mean you won't come with me to Senior Ball next month?" he asked.

She took a sip of her soda and then gave him a playful eye roll.

"Can I wear a black dress?" she asked.

"I wouldn't expect anything less," he said.

He opened his arms and she somewhat begrudgingly walked over and fell into them. He hugged her tight.

"I really am sorry about your parents," she said, wrapping her arms around his waist. "And I do love you even though you're going to destroy me."

He wanted to tell her he wouldn't do that but all he could say was that he loved her, too. He said it again and again.

--

The day spent at Stanford with Owen was just about everything Anna expected it to be. At its simplest, it was a lovely Spring day with her boyfriend, though she'd never called him that out loud and would often stop herself from even thinking of him that way. They walked around the large campus she'd never visited before and she got to see so many of the kinds of things she was looking forward to at either UCLA or Northwestern. Which one was a decision she was still sorting through, literally talking to herself about it on the solo drive down to visit Owen.

He showed her the football stadium, some of his favorite places on campus, the student union, the library, and the church he had found for most of his Sunday mornings. He admitted that he had skipped services a few times when Saturday nights out with friends turned into early Sunday mornings. He was, as always, the welcoming and charming guy she'd gotten to know.

The only part of the visit that made her uncomfortable was when they wandered up to his dorm room. She had wondered if there were any rules about having someone of the opposite sex in his room but didn't ask for fear of coming off too prudish or naive. As they entered the building he explained that his dorm was co-ed by floor. While they were walking down the hallway to his room they passed another resident who was making his way out of the bathroom wrapped only in a towel and with a toothbrush hanging from his mouth. It was 1:30 in the afternoon.

"Shit, sorry," the guy said, taking out the toothbrush and adding, "How ya doing O?"

"I'm good," Owen said, squeezing Anna's hand as if to say he was sorry for the spectacle.

When he opened the door to his room she noticed quickly that he left it open, which she imagined was not any kind of dorm rule but him doing everything he could to make her comfortable. His side of the room was nearly spotless, which didn't surprise her but stood in humorous contrast to the other side, where the bed was unmade and his roommates' desk was considerably less organized.

"I actually straightened up his side a little," Owen confessed. "It was worse this morning. But I thought making his bed for him would be a bit much."

"I really hope I don't get roomed with a slob next year," she said. "I might die. Have I mentioned that messy rooms make me visibly anxious?"

He had asked her earlier in the day where she thought her future dorm room might be, UCLA or Northwestern, and she felt like an indecisive fool for not having a clear answer yet. Most of the people she knew, both at Crestview and friends back in Kenosha, had made their choices. Eileen had committed to Northwestern. Cal was Oregon bound. Tracy had opted to stay close to home and attend St. Mary's College, just about 30 minutes away from Concord.

"How different is each dorm? Do some have bigger rooms than this?" she asked.

She'd seen dorm rooms on various tours of other schools and it seemed like the only variation in size was small, very small, or so tiny she couldn't imagine two people sharing that little space.

"It depends. I know three guys that share a triple but they also have a bathroom attached to it, which is kind of nice," Owen explained.

She'd looked at the housing options at both her would-be schools but it seemed the only difference from one to another was different dorms or halls catering to certain majors or student athletes. UCLA had a "wellness dorm", where students signed a pledge for no smoking, drugs or alcohol within the building and she thought that might be a good option if she chose Los Angeles.

"Do you want to sit down?" Owen asked.

The only options appeared to be the chair at his desk or on his bed. She made her way to the chair.

"You seem… nervous?" he commented.

She nodded.

"I didn't bring you up here for anything like that or even kissing," he said. "Not that I wouldn't want to kiss you because… never mind."

In the time since she'd met him she'd grown fond of his occasional level of nervousness. He was like her in so many ways; organized, driven, a good student who took his classes seriously, and a planner. She'd never seen him do it but she imagined he jotted down "To Do" lists just like she did. But he was also like her in ways she didn't like. He, like her, always seemed afraid to speak his mind out of fear of upsetting someone. Like her, he was a good listener, but maybe too

213

good. He was eager to please, just as she was. But she worried that he was too willing to put other people ahead of his own needs and wants. Her own discomfort sitting in his room felt like an example.

"I just don't think I should be in here," she said. "I know it's stupid because like you said, I totally trust you and your intentions but--"

He stood up and reached for her hand.

"Anna, you don't have to explain anything. How about we just head to the ball game early?"

They'd planned to go to a Cardinals baseball game and then dinner before she would head home.

"I'm really sorry," she said.

"It's nothing to be sorry about. I just wanted you to see this mailbox size room I sleep in," he said. "You know, the full tour."

Again, he was almost too perfect.

She thought once more about the aspects of dorm and college life she might be naive to. As they exited his room she asked, "Does someone spending the night in someone's room happen a lot?"

"I wouldn't say it's uncommon," he said. "But it's not something I do, obviously."

She squeezed his hand, letting him know she knew that.

"But I've had a few buddies tell me they've woken up to find that their roommate has a visitor in the bed across the room," he said.

She shuddered at the thought, which was one reason she had already told Eileen that if she did choose Northwestern they could not be roommates. She knew she would worry if Eileen were gone overnight and though she liked to believe her best friend wouldn't bring a guy back to their room she couldn't entirely rule it out.

"I would be mortified," she said to Owen.

"I know you would," he said, squeezing her hand.

The baseball game was fun and entertaining, different from the minor league games she'd seen in Kenosha and the one Oakland A's game she'd recently gone to with her family.

"I thought only kids played with aluminum bats," she'd commented. "It just doesn't sound right to hear a ping instead of a crack of the bat."

They ran into some of his friends on the way to and from the game and she marveled at how many people he seemed to know for someone who had been there less than a year. Cal had told her how popular he

214

remembered Owen being at Crestview and it had clearly crossed over to his college life at Stanford. He introduced her to others as his "friend", as they'd never really talked about what they were officially. One of his friends asked her where she went to school.

"I'm actually just finishing up high school," she explained.

She felt ridiculous in saying it but there was no point in lying. She hoped it didn't make Owen feel self-conscious to have someone know or presume he was dating a high school girl.

"Where are you headed in the fall?" the same boy asked.

"I'm deciding between Northwestern and UCLA," she said.

The boy turned to Owen, saying, "Owen, she's going to be the enemy!"

They both laughed and she understood why. Owen had explained the football rivalry between the schools.

"Hey, I didn't meet her until after she applied," Owen joked. "I would have tried to steer her away from the dark side otherwise."

Anna liked everyone she met while they were out and about. She guessed that, at most, they were all maybe 1 to 2 years older than her. But they seemed so different, very settled in and comfortable on the large campus. It gave her hope that her own transitions in the year ahead would be positive ones.

It wasn't until dinner that she realized what had been nagging at her brain on and off throughout the day, even during her drive down from Concord. At first she thought it was getting her mind tangled in knots over Northwestern vs. UCLA. Then it was from being in his dorm room. But she and Owen had talked about it and he put her at ease. She finally pinpointed it as feeling like she had stepped out of a time machine, to one year in the future, and the kinds of experiences she hoped would be part of it. The problem was she hadn't gone through all the experiences along the way. It was like skipping September through to April. She was able to summarize it for herself while they were having dinner at a little sandwich shop near campus. And she knew she needed to share her epiphany with Owen.

"I really want to thank you for having me come down here," she said. "I know you were hoping for a whole weekend but I'm glad you were okay with just the day."

"Of course," he said. "It's been really cool to have you here and show you my world a bit."

She was once again struck by how Owen, whether he meant to or not, was excellent at nailing things right on the head.

"And I am so happy you invited me," she said. "But I kinda realized something today and it's a little hard for me to explain. But... like you just said...this is your world. And it's going to be for a few more years."

He looked a little confused by where she was going with her words. She'd never seen such a look from him and causing such an expression to cross his face made her feel awful. She paused for a moment, not wanting to say anything more, telling herself to just let the strange feelings pass. But she knew there weren't going to be many more chances to say what she needed to.

"I think what is bothering me is that I want all of this. Finding new places like this shop, getting lost around a big campus, and meeting new people. And I know I will. No matter where I go."

"Yes, you will," he said. "It's exciting. Believe me, I know."

"I know you do. And being with you, even before today, I've felt like I'm getting a sneak preview of all of that. But..." she said, trying to figure out how to best phrase what she needed to say. "It's also a bit like someone went and saw a movie before I did and then they told me a few things about it. Even if they don't ruin the ending...I don't get to see it all totally fresh. And I guess it just--"

"I feel like you're breaking up with me," he said quickly.

It was strange to hear him use the term "break up" because she'd never been confident there was something specific or defined to end or break between them. But she knew the words fit.

"I think I am," she said softly. "And it's not because of you. Owen, you are...I pinch myself when I think about all the wonderful things about you. But I do think we're in different places. I've been walking around here all day and I love seeing things through your eyes ...but I'm not ready to be in that place. It's like I'm close to that place...or the start of that place. But you're steps ahead of me. Does that make sense?"

He held both her hands across the table.

"It does. I'm disappointed. Because I really don't mind that you're a year behind me. And sure, I'm obviously rooting for you to pick UCLA because I'll be home this summer and I thought we'd spend time

216

together and if you went there in the fall we'd make it work. And if you went to Northwestern? I guess I'd...."

"That wouldn't work," she interrupted. "The Northwestern part. And I love that you can imagine that far ahead and with me. I should jump into that with both feet. But putting aside that I really am still trying to decide on which school to go to I know that wherever I go I want to experience everything on my own. I also want to make the right decision about where that is. And I feel like the closer you and I get the more I feel pulled to UCLA, which might be the best place for me anyway. But I need it to be because I want it for me."

He was quiet for a few moments but nodded his head a bit before he spoke.

"You are so friggin' smart," he said. "I'm always amazed at how level-headed you are and how you want to do what's right. Even when you're letting someone down easy."

She did something she rarely ever did with anyone. She reached across the table and kissed him on the cheek, showing public affection even if it was just a quick gesture.

"I can't change your mind?" he asked.

She laughed. "I'm pretty sure you could but I know you won't try. And that's why you're such a good person, Owen."

"Thank you," he said.

They finished up dinner and he walked her to her car, still pointing out parts of the campus, still the nicest guy she'd ever been out with. When they reached her car she gave him one more long hug.

"I would really like to stay friends," she said. "Especially this summer if you're around."

"Of course," he said. "And thank you again for coming down today."

"Please, I should thank you. I owe you. You bought dinner and the game and... "

She had a quick thought and turned to him.

"Would you be willing to come up and be a part of *my* world for a night?" she asked.

He gave her a puzzled look.

"If it wouldn't feel too weird to visit your past, I was wondering if you'd be my date for Senior Ball? I've been debating if I even want to go but apparently it's at some amazing hotel in the city and… if you were up for it I thought we could go…as friends."

"You don't have to clarify the friend thing," he said. "And I'd be honored. It'd be fun. Call me and we'll get it all squared away."

She got in the car and watched him in the rear view as she made her way out of the visitor's parking lot. It was not the way she expected the day to end but she was proud of herself for making what she was confident was the right, mature decision. Plus, she had a Ball date, which normally wouldn't be a priority but she knew Owen would be a great one. *He'll look amazing in a suit or tux*, she thought.

--

The long drive out to Fairfield to visit Rachel didn't bother Cal too much, as long drives rarely did. Ever since he'd gotten his driver's license and especially when he got a car of his own he'd come to love time alone behind the wheel. His car stereo, which he'd saved up for from his summer job, was excellent and he regularly rotated the cassettes in his carrying case so there was always something new or different to listen to. Whatever his mood was he usually had something at hand to be a soundtrack for it. On that Saturday he was tapping his thumbs on the steering wheel to The Pixies cassette *Doolittle*. It was given to him by Melody.

"You have to listen to this," she'd instructed him. "They are so much more than just that one song that was on the radio and MTV!"

She was trying to expand his already very broad music universe and he liked that because he was usually the one trying to do that for other people. As he listened to the tape song by song he thought his big sister would like The Pixies, too. Cal considered himself the most eclectic music fan of anyone at school and he knew his broad tastes had started with Rachel playing a crazy array of 45's and albums for him when they were younger. They'd sit on the floor of her bedroom and Cal, all of 5 or 6, would try to read the names of songs or bands written on the records, even as they spun round and round on her record player. As he drove to go see her he smiled as he thought of those days.

218

He'd called Rachel the weekend before, a day or so after his parents announced their divorce to him. It turned out they had not talked with Rachel about it yet, so Cal got to break the news.

"Whoa," Rachel said. "Nice of them to not bother telling me at all."

As upset as he was with his parents Cal wasn't surprised that they hadn't had the same conversation with Rachel. The previous few years had been icy between them, even with Rachel not living at home. But things between them had started to improve over the last few months, with Rachel coming to the house for Christmas and stopping by a few more times since. Anytime she visited it would put him a little on edge, as he was all too aware that things could grow tense between his sister and their parents with one comment or even just the wrong look cast from one person to the other. When there was a side to take in any conflict between Rachel and his Mom and Dad he usually sided with his parents, even if he thought they were being too harsh on her. He considered it self-preservation. He lived in their house and if an argument erupted between his parents and his sister he knew he would still be there when it was over. In the past Rachel would storm off and go home until the next time they tried to do dinner or when it was someone's birthday or any other reason to get their family together. It was a pattern, and Cal had only seen it get better in tiny steps.

He was glad that he called her, though. She was a friendly ear and, like always, seemed to take his side.

"I really wish I could come give you a hug, Cal," she said on the phone. "Because I know things are way different for you when it comes to Mom and Dad. And I know it hurts."

He told her how stupid he felt for not having seen it coming and how he must have missed some signs along the way.

"You probably missed something," she said in agreement. "But give yourself a break. You're 17. You're supposed to be too caught up in your own shit to notice anything that doesn't have to do with you, your friends, your hormones, your girlfriends, or whatever."

She told him to hang in there as best he could and then invited him to come visit her, noting that he hadn't seen the new apartment she was sharing with a friend.

"I haven't seen you in months," she noted. "And I haven't seen Ty since Christmas."

When he reached her apartment complex he parked his car in what he hoped was a visitor spot, as she had instructed him to do. The words painted to signal such a spot on the concrete were faded and chipped and all he could make out were a few letters. It was an older building, with some noticeable damage around various windows and back decks. The swimming pool surrounded by a chain link fence looked more akin to a pond than the clearer water he'd expect. No one was swimming even though it was a nice Spring day out.

Rachel gave him a big hug when she answered the door, followed by a quick introduction to her roommate, Steph, and an even quicker tour of the small apartment.

"It's not much but thank God it's cheap," she said.

Their plan was to go grab lunch and catch up with each other. Rachel took him to a nearby taqueria. The second they got inside she was waving to some of the workers behind the counter.

"Que pasa, nina," one guy said. "Quién es este tipo?"

"Mi hermano, Cal," she said.

"Frio, frio," the guy said with a big smile. He waved at Cal like he knew him.

Cal, despite two years of Spanish at Crestview, only picked up a few words of the exchange. And he had no idea his sister even knew a lick of Spanish.

"How do you know everyone here?" he asked as they made their way to a table.

"I waited tables here for a few months before I got my latest job," she explained.

"And the Spanish?" he asked

"I'm working on it. The guys who work here are really great. I told them I wanted to pick up some Spanish and they've helped me out. It's kinda cool. They're super nice."

Rachel had had so many jobs by age 23 that Cal had lost count, so he wasn't surprised that her time working at the very place they were now eating had been short. Nor was he surprised that she was still friendly with people working there. For all the conflict, arguments, shouting, and wild temper he'd seen her have with their parents over the years Rachel always seemed to get along with everyone else she'd ever met.

"So tell me more about this college," she said from across the table.

He detailed all the things he was excited about with Southern Oregon State, how small the school was and how much less populated the city of Ashland was compared to the places where they had always lived. He explained the courses he hoped to take and the paperwork he was still sorting through for dorm life, like roommate matching and food plans.

"That sounds amazing," she said. "Especially getting to be someplace new and easy to explore. I'm kinda jealous."

"I think I'd be more excited about it if it wasn't for Mom and Dad and all their stuff," he said.

"I know," she said. "But you can't control any of that. You know that, right?"

"What do you mean?"

"I mean there is nothing you can do except to make your own plans for you and not worry about them," she explained.

Her advice was right on par with how she'd always seemed to approach their parents. Cal and Tyler had usually tried in various degrees to please them and it made for a generally peaceful life at home. Rachel, in his view, had given up trying, if she ever had at all, and went her own way in a fashion neither of the Sorenson boys ever had. He used to think his sister's way was foolish and reckless or, as their parents sometimes called it, disrespectful. Lately he wasn't so sure.

"I just wish they would have told me sooner," he said.

He'd said that many times to people over the past week.

"Why?" she asked. "So you could have it hanging over your head while you try to get ready for college? Or maybe they tell you and you make a different choice about where to go or what to do?"

Cal could not believe his sister was taking the same position his parents had taken when he'd asked them why they didn't just level with him earlier. Especially when they told him they'd been planning to divorce for a year or even longer.

"You're saying the same stuff they said," he remarked.

"Well, once in a blue moon Mom and Dad are right. They were trying their best, just like always," she said.

Again, Cal was stunned by her words. The person sitting across from him was the same person who had broken every rule, broke every curfew, made elaborate escapes from her second floor bedroom when grounded, and by the time she was Cal's age had moved out and moved back in at least twice. He didn't want to say it to her but he thought maybe all the trouble she caused had contributed to their parents' problems.

"Who are you and what did you do with my big sister?" he asked, trying to keep things light and not get angry with her.

She threw her head back and let out a little laugh but then looked right back at him from across the table.

"Your big sister has had a tough couple of years in case you hadn't noticed."

He knew she had. He didn't know every detail of her divorce from a marriage that had lasted less than 2 years but her parents had hinted that Derek, her ex-husband, had hit her a few times. She'd come to stay at the house very briefly during the split but Cal had never asked her about what was happening with her husband. At the time he'd just gotten his driver's license, his parents had bought him a used car, and he was wrapped up in the expanded freedom that came with it.

"So now you're on Mom and Dad's side?" he asked.

"No. But I can *see* their side. And I think maybe you should try to," she said.

"Why would I do that?"

"Because you're growing up," she said. "And that actually freaks me out a bit because you're the baby. But one of the things I've been trying to do in the last year or so is remember Mom and Dad are people. They're not just 'Mom and Dad'. They have things they want that have nothing to do with you or me or Ty. And as much as I hate to admit it they've worked hard. And my guess is now they see you're growing up and leaving just like Ty and me and it's their time to get to do a little more for themselves."

"I think splitting up and moving away is more than 'a little'," he said defensively.

"Okay, so divorcing is big," she conceded. "But what do you want them to do? Stay together so you can have the happy homecoming for Christmas and maybe one or two more summers after this coming one? Look at Ty. He's all the way out the door and never coming back. Just like me. They've seen this movie before. You're going to go off to school

222

just like he did and you'll come back less and less because you're becoming a grown ass man. Which, again, I'm having a hard time with," she said. She playfully threw a paper straw wrapping at him.

She was making a good point, and he knew it, even if he didn't want to admit it. Tyler had done just what she'd described. He had recently turned 21, had started living in Davis full time the summer before, and had hinted he and his girlfriend, Katherine, might move in together in the summer before their final year of college.

"I guess I just wanted to be able to still see my friends sometimes," Cal said. "To be able to go away but still come back."

"Of course you do. You like your friends and home is safe and comfortable. You're human," she said before adding, "And you're a spoiled kid."

There was the sister he knew. She'd said that about both him and Tyler for years.

"I'm spoiled, too," she added quickly.

That admission was new.

"Like I was saying before," she continued, "They've worked to have a house and cars and give us a lot. Look at Dad and his fucking commute. That's like three hours a day in his Nissan, stuck in traffic across the bridge."

"He could take BART," Cal said with a smile.

Rachel laughed. Riding BART had been an ongoing suggestion to their father for years, with all three kids and their Mom begging him to just take the train and stop complaining about traffic jams and his sore back from sitting in the car.

"Right, because he doesn't like riding with poor people," Rachel said, echoing their father's reason for not taking the train. "The point is, they work hard, too hard, because they want all the big things for themselves and for us. And they gave us toys and clothes and stereos and cars. Has either one of them told you you're going to have to pay for your own college?"

He shook his head.

"They just told me that once I'm settled into classes and the college routine I'll need to get a part time job on campus or something," he explained. "They call it Work Study.".

"See? You've got it good. I know you've worked summers and you had your paper routes before that and you're definitely less spoiled than Ty... but you're still lucky, Cal."

Rachel's reasoning was not at all what he expected. He'd driven over for the day expecting to hear how awful their parents were, how their being so selfish as to divorce and move to their new cities was proof that she'd been right all along, from age 14 right up to her current 23. He was hoping for solidarity between them.

"What about you?" he asked. "Are you pissed that they didn't give as much to you as they've given to me or to Ty?"

She shook her head.

"I was. I used to be super pissed," she said. "But a while back I realized all those things...college, help with a car....I could have had all that. I had every chance you guys had. Don't get me wrong, I still think Mom and Dad were too protective and too restrictive about a lot of things with me. But even with all that they gave me second chances and third chances and I fucked up. I didn't want to work hard enough at school, I married an abusive asshole they had told me they were worried about, and I've had more shitty jobs than I like to think about. Even now I have a job I don't hate but it doesn't pay much. I'm 23 with a GED and whatever Mom and Dad had set aside in my name for school is gone. I blew it. Things with them are still a little raw sometimes but I don't blame them as much as I used to. Or at least I'm trying not to."

He'd never seen Rachel show much regret for anything. For the longest time it seemed like she entered every situation with an excuse or ready to point a finger before anyone could point one at her. He felt sorry for her now.

"I'm sorry, Rach," he said. "For not calling or trying to see you more. Especially with all the stuff with Derek."

"Don't worry about it," she said. "I had a lot going on. And I know what it's like to be 16, 17. I'm sure you've been up to your eyes with schoolwork and friends and... Mom mentioned you have some little girlfriend?"

He nodded and told her about Melody, how they met, and Rachel even coaxed it out of him that he and Melody were having sex.

"Be careful there," she cautioned. "I'm not saying don't, I'm just saying be really careful. Nothing is foolproof with condoms or the pill, okay?"

He assured her he was being cautious, not mentioning the panic he'd gone through a few weeks before when a condom broke. Melody had told him many times she was on birth control but when it happened he'd still spent a few days freaking out.

"What are you going to do about this Melody girl when you leave for school?" Rachel asked.

He gave a shrug. "We've kind of agreed to just not talk about it for now."

Rachel raised her eyebrows at him.

"You've both agreed or you talked her into not talking about it for now?" she asked.

"I talked her into it, I guess," he admitted.

"Cal," she said slowly. "You can't do that. You can't talk her into stuff like that. You can't keep this girlfriend when you know you're going to leave her behind."

"But she *knows* I'm leaving," he argued.

"But she doesn't know what that means. She can't," Rachel said. "She's 16 and she's probably in love or thinks she's in love with someone for the first time and I'll bet you a hundred bucks she's convinced herself it'll all be okay. Love will conquer all..."

"I love her, too, though," he said. "She's the longest and best girlfriend I've ever had."

"And she's the first one having bunny rabbit sex with you," Rachel said pointedly. "Congratulations. And I am sure you do love her because you're a sweet, good guy. You always have been."

"I thought I was spoiled or selfish," he countered.

"You *are* spoiled. But I never said selfish," she said. "Ty is selfish as hell. But he's getting better. But you? You're the poster boy of 'good guy', even when you try not to be. I had guy friends that were like you when I was your age and younger."

"You did?" he asked. He had a hard time imagining his sister hanging out with anyone like him, even when she was 17.

"Yes," she said. "And some of them asked me out and I even went out with a couple of them. And then I told them I didn't want to date

225

them because I didn't want to lose them as a friend. Something tells me you've probably heard that before."

"Too many times," he said, thinking of the number of girls who had given him some version of the 'I like you as a friend' speech. "And that's why I don't want to lose Melody. She is the first person that seems to not mind that I'm whatever it is you said… the poster boy of nice guys."

"But she won't be the last person to like that about you," Rachel said. "Trust me on this one. Girls Melody's age always want the bad boy or the rebel or the jock or whatever because it's flashy or sexy or dangerous. I think it says a lot about her that she likes you instead of some jerk."

"She said she'd met a lot of jerks," he said, recalling Melody's many details about guys that had treated her badly.

"I'm sure she has. It's scary to think how many I met by the time I was 16. And how many more I met after that. Not to mention the one I married," she said.

Up until that afternoon Cal had regularly thought of his older siblings as being two sides to a coin. Even if Tyler was mean to him, which he often was, or talked down to him, which he often did, he still believed his big brother was smart and knew what he was talking about. On the other side he'd come to view Rachel as the screw up, the one who'd made mistakes and driven their parents crazy. He'd always thought following her advice on anything would be foolish. He didn't like Tyler much but he figured if he had to choose whose path to follow he'd take Tyler's over Rachel's without a moment of hesitation. Suddenly Rachel, for the first time, was the one making sense even if he didn't want to believe it.

"I just don't want things to end with Melody," he said. "I feel like with the house for sale and graduation and then Mom and Dad moving that everything I'm used to having…everything that's good and normal… it's all ending. And Melody is the one thing I can hold on to if that makes sense."

"It does," she said. "But she's not a thing to hold on to like a house or your favorite places to hang out. She's a person and you're older than her and more mature than she is, whether you want to own that or not. You're also the one who is leaving and she is the one who gets left and it's easier to be you than it is to be her. Think about it. Best case: You go off to your new life but you have this girlfriend far away that you're trying

226

to hold on to and it's really tough and it makes it harder for you to give someone else a chance to get to know you. Worst case...and I hate to say this...but you head off to school and within a few weeks she's at some Crestview kegger, has one beer too many, and winds up making out with a bad boy because she's sad or lonely about her boyfriend who went off to college in Oregon."

"Ouch," he said. "I don't think she'd do that."

"But you can't say she wouldn't," Rachel said quickly.

As hard as it was to think about it or try to deny it, he couldn't dismiss the what-ifs that Rachel was laying out for him.

"So what do I do?" he asked.

"You be the bigger person and let her down easy," Rachel said. "Sooner than later."

He tried as hard as he could to muster up a logical argument, some kind of reason why his sister was wrong and how it would be okay to keep things going with Melody. But he had nothing.

"Can I do it after the Senior Ball?" he asked.

Rachel cast him a deathly stare from across the table.

"Sure, Cal, take her out for a night in a fancy dress and maybe a limo and some power ballad slow dance and then sex in your formal wear and *then* break up with her. I'm sure that won't eventually make her go screw the next asshole who treats her like shit because she's decided that she's not worth someone who will be honest with her."

Once again he had to concede his sister was right. He could easily picture Melody doing exactly what Rachel had said.

"Don't take this the wrong way but I like the sister that wanted me to go get high with her better than this one," he said.

He wasn't serious because that older version had, as Anna had put it to him, broken his younger heart.

"Oh, we can go get high," Rachel said with a smile. "If you want. But I don't think that's you."

"It's not," he said.

She gave him another smile.

"I know. You're you," she said. "Don't tell Ty this but you're my favorite. And I know I've given you a bit of hell today but I'm really proud of you. About Oregon and all the good stuff you have ahead of you. Even with Mom and Dad and all their drama you have so much to be excited for. I'm really jealous. But mostly I'm just super proud of you."

--

Anna knocked on the front door of Cal's house. It was not long after she'd gotten home from church and changed her clothes and she hadn't even called ahead to see if he was home. She was eager to hear how his visit with his sister had gone and, for her own purposes, wanted some reassurance that she had done the right thing in breaking things off with Owen.

Cal's mother greeted her at the door and then fetched Cal him from his room, where Anna could hear music blasting, even from downstairs in the entryway. He emerged in sweatpants and a t-shirt. If it hadn't been almost noon she'd have thought she came over too early, given that his hair was out of order and he didn't look particularly good. She wondered if he'd gone to some party and maybe drank too much the night before.

"Hey," he said.

"Hey yourself," she replied. "I was wondering if you'd be up for a walk or maybe even going somewhere and doing something."

He looked down at his clothes but held up a finger, signaling for her to give him a minute to change. He ran back up the stairs and reemerged a few minutes later in jeans and a different shirt and his hair covered with an Angels baseball cap.

"Late night?" she asked.

"Very," he said.

They made their way out the front door and down his cul-de-sac to walk around Bell Ridge, just as they had done so many times over the months since they'd met. She was going to miss it, especially knowing the house she'd just stepped out of now had a "For Sale" sign in front of it.

"How was Stanford?" he asked her.

"It was nice," she said. "How was your day with your sister?"

"Really good, actually. Better than what came after," he said.

She listened as he detailed the talk he'd had with Rachel and the unexpectedly good but painful advice she'd given him. For all that Anna had previously heard about Cal's big sister it sounded like she wasn't in

228

any way the messed up, troubled person she'd been sold as. Cal told her it was the best visit he'd had with Rachel for as long as he could remember. But then he said the day had gone south from there.

"So after what she said about Melody I decided to just go to her house and do it," he said. "To do the hard thing and break up with her."

"You went straight there?" Anna asked. "Right after visiting your sister?"

"Yep. I guess I just knew if I went home I'd talk myself out of it."

"And how did it go?" she asked.

"Not good," he said. "A lot of anger. A lot of crying."

"From both of you?" she asked.

His face appeared a little puffy and she guessed his conversation with Melody might be the reason for it instead of a party.

He nodded.

"Oh, Cal," she said. "I'm sorry. I really am."

"She was really sad," he said. "And then really mad. And then sad again. And then mad again. It was really hard and it took...hours. I've never really broken up with anyone in my life."

She stopped walking, turned, and looked at him.

"You told me you've broken up with people a bunch of times," she said.

"Let me rephrase that," he said. "I've never been the one breaking up with someone before. I've always been on the receiving end."

She understood it better, thinking back to her own break-up just a day before, where she had also been the catalyst. She also remembered all the way back to Kyle. Even though she had ended it he still broke her heart, mentioning in the process of splitting up that she wasn't fun, needed to relax more, and that he didn't want to be with someone that didn't want to go to the "next step". It was his toned-down way of saying he was letting her go because he'd finally realized she was never going to have sex with him and therefore she was of no use or value.

"Well, this is ironic," she said, proud of herself for properly using the word. She'd rarely found herself in a situation where she could say it and have it truly fit the moment.

"How so?" he asked.

"I broke up with Owen," she said.

His eyes grew wide with surprise.

229

"Why would you do something as dumb as that?"

"I'm just chalking it up to bad timing," she said.

It was how she'd put it in her journal. She'd written up the whole day and at the end she wrote about how she had no regrets about getting to know him because Owen was a wonderful guy but that some things have bad timing and there is nothing you can do about it. She also remembered that she'd made the same assessment about Cal many months before.

"How'd Owen take it?" he asked.

"He was a little disappointed but he also understood. He is a really, really good person," she said.

"He is," Cal agreed. "If I was a chick I'd totally want him."

She laughed.

"I'm serious," he said. "Someday you're going to be like, 'I could have been Mrs. Owen Myers'. Or more like, 'I could have been First Lady Analisa Myers' because, seriously, he's going to be, like, President in 40 years."

She laughed again, mostly because she couldn't rule it out. Owen was charming and she suspected he would stay that way for a very long time.

"Owen is going to be fine," she said. "And Melody will be too."

He bobbed his head side to side a little, like he wasn't sure.

"I hope she will be," he said. "When I left she was still pretty upset and trying to get me to change my mind."

"Did you think about it? Changing your mind?"

"Of course. I'm still not sure about it. I mean, she and I...we've been..." He stopped himself before saying, "We've been really close."

She had wondered about how close or what that really meant and finally decided to just call him on it.

"I appreciate your discretion, Cal. It says a lot about you. But I think I've broken your code words for having sex with Melody."

She was proud of herself for saying it. He didn't say anything to confirm it but gave her a slight nod, indicating she was right.

"Anyway," he continued, "It ended with her saying she didn't want to lose me even though I'm leaving and then I told her I couldn't do that because I'd know I was using her. And she said I *could* use her because I wouldn't be the first guy to do that."

"And what did you say to that?" she asked.

"I told her I wasn't going to be the *next* guy that used her," he said. "That she deserves better than that."

She again stopped walking and turned to him. "You told her that? That you weren't going to be that kind of person?"

"Yeah," he said. "And then I left and drove home and I eventually fell asleep and I've spent all morning resisting the urge to call her and get back together and hoping she doesn't call me."

She lightly touched his arm near his elbow.

"Your sister gave you good advice," she said. "And that thing you said, where Rachel told you you're a good guy even when you don't want to be? She's right about that, too."

For about two seconds she thought of kissing him. She felt spontaneous, wondering how he would react, and what it would be like to finally just do it, especially given how many times she had thought of it before and how many times she'd sensed he wanted to kiss her. Even with his face showing that he'd been crying about a different girl, and the fact he didn't look good in a ball cap at all, that he'd never be as handsome as someone like Owen, and he'd just broken up with someone he'd admitted to having sex with, all of which she was still sorting through, she thought of it. Not on the cheek but kissing him the way she imagined they might if she'd let herself just like him that way months before and not talked herself out of it. Before there was Melody and before there was Owen, back when they'd first met. But the seconds passed and her mind shifted quick to a reason not to: Just a day before they'd each had someone else to call boyfriend or girlfriend. And as fun as it would be to shock Cal by doing it, she quickly assessed it would just re-complicate the puzzle-like feelings she'd always had for him and, she imagined, him toward her.

She got her focus back to why she had come to his door in the first place. The first thing was to tell him about Owen. The second was to hear about his visit with his sister. The whole thing with Melody was not what she'd expected and it had thrown her but she was determined to get her reasons for coming to find him back on track.

"I want to be a good friend," she began, "And if you're sad about Melody I'm happy to talk about it but if we could maybe do that later I'd really like your help with something."

"Sure," he said. "Whatever you need."

"Good," she said. "Because I need to figure out where I'm going to school next year and I wanted to talk to you about it because much to my surprise you're the best person I know when it comes to getting me to step out of my own head and see things in a different way."

He seemed stunned by her assessment.

"Wow. I'm...I'm not sure what to say to that," he said.

"You don't have to know. Just be the Cal I know and trust. Because I'm not letting this day end until I've made up my mind."

He agreed to listen and they continued walking, deciding that a coffee and tea shop about a mile away would be as good a place as any to make their way to.

She gave him a quick summary of her pros and cons for each school, starting with the pros, including their equally strong science departments, their large campuses, and great reputations from coast to coast.

"They both have excellent graduate programs if I decide to get my Masters, which I probably will. And medical schools if I really want to be in school till I'm 30! And they both have strong teaching programs if I want to go in that direction," she explained.

"So that's where they're equal," he said. "Now give me some cons."

She explained that if it weren't for the out of state tuition fees Northwestern would be just as expensive as UCLA but since her parents would officially have been in California long enough UCLA would be the cheaper option, at least at first. She also pointed out that despite a very long drive, an even longer bus ride, or a short flight that UCLA was obviously closer to her family.

"I wouldn't have a car but I've read that there are tons of bulletin boards for carpooling and sharing rides up to this area because so many people from all over the state go there," she continued. "And even though my parents drive me nuts I do love them and it scares me to go so far away from them."

"Then stay in California," he said.

She tried her best to explain what was holding her back, verbalizing various notes she'd made in her journal over the past several weeks.

"The problem I keep coming back to is that my family is my family but no matter how hard I try to shake it the Midwest is home. I lived there my whole life until this year. And it's not that people out here aren't nice, wonderful people but there is just something about Wisconsin that I still miss."

"But you're not talking about Wisconsin," he reminded her. "Northwestern is in Chicago."

"Sure, it's a bigger area but it's like an hour from Kenosha. It's also just a similar mentality. I think you'd have to live in cold weather to really get it."

He reminded her he'd spent a few years living in New Jersey when he was in 3rd and 4th grade.

"Yeah, but at that age it's all sled hills and snowball fights," she said. "And it's not about being in the weather so much. It's the way it seems to shape people. The biggest thing I've noticed about Californians, no offense, is that you have a lot less humility. I think brutal winters and humid summers make people a bit more down to earth."

"Are you sure your humility isn't from religion?" he asked.

She was pleasantly surprised that he'd thought of that.

"My goodness, Cal," she said. "You just went all religious on me?!"

"What? I paid attention that morning. Humble before God and recognize that you may have control of your life but he has a plan. That was a cool thing for your pastor to say. I kinda liked it."

She was momentarily sidetracked by how happy it made her that Cal had taken something away from what he'd admitted was his first trip to church in a very long time.

"Do you believe that?" she asked. "That you're part of a plan and that some things are going to happen to you because God wants them to?"

"I don't know. I just remember thinking that maybe the next time I'm caught off guard by something to think of it as a twist in some bigger plan. I've been trying to view my parents' divorce that way. For them and for me."

She didn't feel the same urge to kiss him as she had a few minutes before but did think for a moment of reaching for and holding his hand. Instead she remarked, "I like how you surprise me sometimes. You always seem to remind me to give people the room to do that."

She snapped her attention back to her mission of the day and picking her school, which she wasn't feeling any closer to accomplishing.

"I have more roots near Northwestern. Aunts, uncles, cousins, and of course a lot of my friends. Eileen is my best friend and I know she really wants me to go with her to Northwestern."

"Hmm," he said.

"What?" she asked.

"I just remember when Ty went to UCSB for a year one of the reasons he chose it was because some of his friends were also going there. So many others were going to school at USC and a few at UCLA," he explained. "Did you know he had a partial track scholarship offer from the University of Oregon, long before I ever got an Oregon school on my radar? But he wanted to be near his friends. So he went south. And so did his grades. And maybe his liver, too."

"My liver will be fine, thank you very much," she said. "But I get what you're saying. And I know you have chosen a very solo route with Oregon. That's one of the reasons I value your opinion about this. And truly, Eileen is the only close friend I know going to Northwestern. And even though we're best friends I know that we're going to have different priorities with college."

They reached the coffee shop and got their respective drinks; coffee for him and decaf tea for her.

"I feel like my coffee habit has been partial preparation for college," he joked. "You should take it up."

"Have you never noticed my constant anxiety and worrisome nature? Do you really want to add caffeine to that?" she asked.

"Point taken," he said, handing her tea to her.

They sat down at an outside table, enjoying the sunshine of the Spring afternoon.

"The other thing is...I know college isn't the last stop, just the next one," she continued. "I wouldn't be in Chicago or L.A. forever. And they both have great reputations, though UCLA seems to be better known nationally."

"Then go with that," he said. "Isn't that what overachievers do? You aim for the top and you take the best of the best? The thing that will get you to the next big thing?"

She had to admit that was her usual pattern, saying, "Pretty much."

"There's nothing wrong with wanting that," he said. "It's like what you said on the way here... I get you to see things from a different point

234

of view. Well, you've reminded me that maybe...and just maybe...I could try harder. Aim a little higher. You've kind of inspired me."

"You're sweet," she said. "I take that as a very high compliment."

She took a few sips of her tea and tried to again refocus on her mental list.

"One of the things my sister said to me yesterday that really hit home was that you and I are lucky," he said. "Even with feeling like my parents are screwing with my plans, Rachel reminded me that they never said anything like, 'Hey Cal, we're getting divorced and that's really expensive so, sorry, you're going to have to go to DVC because it's cheap.' Don't get me wrong, I'm not happy with any of it but they're still letting me go where I want to go. And it sounds like your parents are letting you do the same."

She knew what he was saying was true. At least at its core.

"They've hinted a *lot* that they'd prefer UCLA. When I say 'Northwestern' they always say it'll be challenging but 'We trust your choices, Analisa'," she said, mocking their tone as she described their words.

"My parents wanted Sac for me. But they're on the Southern Oregon train now. I think the divorcing has made them feel a little guilty so they've been pretty cool about it. I'm going to try to use their guilt as best as I can till then."

She took a few more sips of tea before continuing.

"I remember you told me that when you went to Ashland the first time that you just felt like it was the place for you," she said. "What was it about it?"

"I just looked around," he said. "We were walking around the campus and you know how it is in a tour group... You feel like you're this high school kid and everybody knows it. But even with that I looked and I saw people that looked like me. Dressed like me. And then when we were in downtown Ashland it felt a little like a smaller, cleaner Berkeley. But still lots of colorful people and musicians playing down in the plaza. Cool shops and kind of laid back. It felt like me. I just hope I'm right."

"It sounds like you are," she said.

"It's funny," he said. "The way you talked about the reasons why you'd choose Northwestern versus why you'd stay west. Like, your family versus home and how they don't seem to be the same thing?"

He'd nailed it perfectly.

"I think it's the moves my parents are making that has me even more upset than the divorce itself," he continued. "I'll always be good with my Mom because I always have been with her. And maybe this makes my Dad's life less stressful and he'll be easier to be around. I'm more upset that home isn't going to be Concord anymore, even though I'm totally ready to leave this place behind. Way, way behind."

"You'll miss it," she said, thinking of when she left Wisconsin. "I still miss Kenosha. I cried so much for days and days when we moved. Did I ever tell you that the story about how the first day I went to Crestview was a Tuesday?"

He shook his head.

"I was supposed to go the day before but I woke up and I was crying and shaking. Really, really shaking. Full anxiety attack. So my Mom gave me a day and then I went the next day and I didn't talk to a soul except Tracy and some teachers because I had to. And even then I got home and I cried some more. And then again the next day."

"When did it get better?" he asked.

She was a little embarrassed to tell him but she didn't want to hide it.

"The day you made me angry," she said. "In class. I hadn't even made the connection you were the same guy I saw over the fence a few days before. But then you came up and talked to me. And that was the first time of many that you have completely surprised me. But what I mean to say is that I think I get how you can want to leave a place behind but still want it there if things don't work out where you're going. Is that close?"

"That's the whole thing," he said. "But I guess it means I need to make Ashland home and just make the best of Eureka. God, just saying that is making me die a little inside. But my Dad will still be near here, at least for a while. And like I said...we're both lucky. We have these people that are willing to let us go where we want even if they don't love our choices."

She sat in her chair and reflected on everything they'd been talking about. She felt the sunshine on her hair and down her neck and thought how that feeling of warmth could become very familiar on the UCLA campus. She imagined having to get all new warmer clothes for

Northwestern if she went there because her entire family had donated most of their winter coats and other items to the Salvation Army before they moved from Kenosha. She tried to recall as much of the Northwestern campus as possible from when she'd toured it her junior year, picturing herself buying her books and finding her classes. She tried to visualize moments sitting at a table just like the one she was at with Cal, with nameless faces that were new to her. They were laughing and having interesting conversations about their classes. Or maybe discussing a movie or a book or music? She glanced at Cal, containing a laugh as she thought of how much better equipped she might be for something like that just from knowing him. Or maybe she'd meet someone really into politics and excited for the upcoming election in 1992?

She looked across the table at Cal and realized he was the only friend she'd made at Crestview she'd even want to see on visits back home from college. And he wasn't likely to be around because his version of "back home" was about to be plural or a bit scattered.

She pictured her family and Christmas time and summers in California, the latter of which she hadn't even experienced yet. And then she put her paper cup down on the table.

"I'm going to Northwestern," she said.

"You're sure?" he asked.

"Yes. My family is family and they can be anywhere. But Northwestern... that's where I want home to be. It's where I'm from, where I want to grow."

He looked across at her, quiet but smiling. He pulled the cap off his head for a second, pushing his hair back and then put it right back on.

"Well," he said finally. "I owe you 5 bucks. I made a private bet in my head you were going to say UCLA. But, seriously... I'm glad to be wrong, Anna. But I'm going to miss you."

She reached a hand across the table and grabbed his hand, squeezing his palm and fingers.

"I'm going to miss you, too," she said, before adding, "But I finally decided."

She felt a tear well up in her right eye.

"Yes, you did," he said. "I don't know if I helped at all, though."

237

"You did," she said, wiping the tear away, as another formed in her left eye. "You reminded me of what I'll miss and what I'll lose and what I get to keep no matter what. And you reminded me how lucky I am in so many ways."

She let out a long, relieved breath and tried not to cry any further, from both the joy of the moment and a level of sadness she knew would come with it at another time.

# Chapter Eight - May 1991

## *"Emotions In Gear"*

Two things had kicked in among a large portion of the Senior class at Crestview High School: The first was the commonly known and widespread "Senioritis", where much of the soon-to-be graduating class were on cruise control. Those who were college bound had sent off their letters of intent and even those who had no idea what they were going to do after graduation were all doing the minimum work needed for the last 5 weeks of school. Only the handful that were still scrambling to raise their grades enough to make sure they graduated at all seemed even remotely stressed out. The second thing was Senior Ball. Even those who tried to act like they didn't care were at least a little excited. It was hard not to be. The tradition at Crestview was that Senior Ball was a much bigger deal than the previous year's Junior Prom. Prom was typically held at the local rec center or in the school gym just like any other dance but with fancier clothes for all. Ball was always held at a much more enticing or elegant location. Usually it was a high-rise hotel in San Francisco but a few previous graduating classes had seen their Ball held on a chartered boat liner cruising around the Bay or an outdoor venue of some kind. For Cal's class it was going to be the Mark Hopkins Hotel in the Nob Hill area of San Francisco. Some couples or groups of couples had convinced their parents to pay for rooms at the hotel for post-Ball parties. Others planned to find various things to do around the city after the formal dance. And then there were the handful renting limos to get to and from the event.

After his breakup with Melody, Cal had made what he thought was a logical turn for a Ball date. After their long walk and talking about her college decision, during which she'd told him she had broken things off with Owen Myers, he asked Anna to be his date.

"I have to say 'No'," she said, even though she sounded a little sad about it.

She explained that despite ending things she was remaining friends with Owen and had asked him to be her date.

239

"If I had known you were about to break up with Melody I definitely would have been happy to go," she explained. "But it would be rude to cancel on Owen now."

From there he considered trying to patch things up with Melody or seeing if she might still want to go as "just friends" before concluding it would be a terrible idea. In the few days since their break-up she had barely looked his way at school. Even if he could talk her into going he knew there was no way he could have her as his date and not want to kiss her or possibly much more than that. His one hesitation in breaking up had been because of sex. Even though he felt horrible for admitting it to himself he knew it was true. He'd spent hours wondering if he'd ever have sex again.

He resigned himself to the idea of not going to Ball at all. He could just skip it and he wouldn't be the first person to ever do so. Plenty of people in his class wouldn't be going. He didn't like the idea of being one of them but felt like he didn't have a whole lot of choice in the matter.

"I think I'm going to have to bail on the whole double date, limo share thing for Ball," he told Reed.

Reed had his date. It was right after Cal had told him about Melody that Reed revealed the secret identity of his Senior Ball companion: A girl he'd met at his temple named Heather, a junior at Creek Valley, a high school in neighboring Clayton. He told Cal all about her as they sat in the school theater seats during 6th period drama class.

"When I first asked her out it really was to just try to build up to Ball," Reed explained. "But now we're pretty much a couple. I have a girlfriend!"

Cal was happy for him and opted to bite his tongue about questions around Reed graduating and this Heather girl still having a year of high school left. Cal figured his friend was likely getting his fair share of "what if's and "yeah, but what about" type questions from other people. He'd been through similar things with Melody and didn't want to bring Reed down.

"I'm glad you met someone," he said. "I'm just sorry I'm a little down on young love right now. But you guys will have a blast at Ball."

Reed wasn't in agreement with his choice.

"So you're not going to go?" he asked. "You're just gonna bail out?"

"It's a little late in the game," Cal said. "Melody and I are history and I asked Anna but she's got a date so…"

Reed let out a long sigh.

"You were the one who told me I had to go find a Ball date. You said I *had* to experience this thing and be a part of it. All up and down about how it's not just for the cool kids," Reed said, echoing back some of the things Cal had indeed said to him months before.

"And it's true," Cal defended. "It's not just for popular people or A crowd or whatever you want to call it. And you just said you have more than a date. You found a girlfriend! And I hope I can meet her sometime. I just don't think it's gonna be on Ball night."

Cal couldn't understand why Reed was so upset with the situation but it was clear he was and he wasn't letting it go.

"Let's forget for a second that my folks ordered a limo and you said you'd get your parents to cover part of it," Reed said. "I'm just sort of baffled by how your enthusiasm for stuff like this is always about how things are going for *you*. When you go out with someone once or twice or whatever it's all 'Love is grand. Just try harder, Reed. There's someone out there for you!' Or because you've had those dates and I haven't you're full of advice for what I should do when I like someone. You start going out with Melody and you're sky high with confidence and you tell me to not let this year end without going to this stupid dance. But then you…by your choice, I might add…you end things with Melody and suddenly it's 'Screw the Ball'."

Cal sat up a bit in his chair.

"I didn't say 'Screw the Ball'. I said I broke up with Melody and I don't really have a backup and I don't feel like going solo with you and your date in a limo and, trust me, you shouldn't want that either. Why are you so pissed?"

After the few weeks Cal had been living, with the divorce news, the breakup with Melody, and making what he thought were the right decisions and choices, only to have those things wind up hurting him, he was not in the mood to argue.

Reed was quiet and Cal thought that was the end of the conversation. But Reed eventually popped off.

"I'm pissed because when it comes to girls you've always been a bit of a dick," Reed said.

"Oh, really?"

"Yeah. I'll be the first person to admit that when it comes to girls you've had better luck," Reed continued. "You've had more dates, you've clearly had sex...and I haven't. But every time you meet some girl and pursue her and it starts to go well you disappear. You don't want to hang out. You focus on that person and you clear your calendar for them. And then when it collapses... and it *always* collapses, you come back to me and the rest of the guys at lunch or you go party with Doug or whatever and then it starts all over again."

Cal knew there was a lot of truth in what Reed was saying, but it still hurt to have his various romantic failures thrown back in his face, especially since the latest one was of his own making. He also wondered why Reed was saying such things all the sudden, with their high school lives having just weeks left in it.

"I'm sorry if I've had more luck or I forget about you or other friends but--

Reed cut him off.

"You've had more luck because you've spent more time on it. Seriously, man. Have you ever wondered what your GPA would have been or your SAT if you hadn't put so much energy into the dream of a girlfriend and having everyone know you have one? Because you're smart, Cal. I would never say you aren't. You can write circles around me in Ms. Cook's class and you know more about music and bands than anyone I know. And that's cool. But if I'm upset it's because you always told me I need to loosen up, not worry so much about my grades, go out and try to meet someone, have more fun. And now I did... on my own, without your help....and you're acting like none of it's worth it."

Everything Reed said felt like sharp ribbons cutting through him, ripping apart the kind of person he thought he was, and painting him instead as an idiot that should have paid more attention in class and less attention to the opposite sex.

"Have you been saving this little speech for right when my life feels a little messed up?" Cal fired back. "Because breaking up with someone I care about? All because it felt like the right thing to do? That wasn't very much fun for me. It was like a nice cherry on top of my parents divorcing and moving and my summer all fucked up in the air. So could you please save the 'Cal, you're an asshole ' monolog until later?"

"You *are* an asshole sometimes," Reed said.

"Thanks," Cal said sarcastically. "And sometimes you're your own worst enemy with all your worries about what jocks and the cool kids think of you. Is that why you're pissed I'm bailing on Ball? Because you think you need a field trip buddy for it? Well, let me tell you what those guys think of you: They *don't*. They don't give a shit. They're going to have their dates and their inside jokes and then they're going to get a room or go to a party. They won't notice if you're there or not. They won't notice if *I'm* there or not there. Because they don't fucking care."

"Screw you," Reed said.

Reed stood up and began to walk away but Cal followed him. He grabbed him by the arm.

"You got your date. It sounds like you got more than that," Cal said. "And I'm happy for you. I am. And I'm sorry if I've made all this stuff seem like some kind of contest. I didn't mean for it to be. And I'm sorry if I've been a lousy friend. And I get what you're saying but I'm...I'm...

He was trying to finish his thought but couldn't find the words for it. Reed stood there, looking at him and waiting for him to finish.

"I'm embarrassed," Cal finally said. "And I'm probably jealous because, damn, you have a girlfriend and suddenly I don't. I had one and I chose to throw it all away. I'm like Roth leaving Van Halen when they were on top."

He laughed, hoping Reed wouldn't think he was laughing over the very notion of him having someone.

"You did have someone. It's not my fault you dumped her before Ball," Reed said, chuckling.

"Trust me, it was..." He was about to say 'really hard' or 'really dumb' but instead he finished by saying, "It was the right thing to do. And it sucks."

"I'm sorry I blew up at you," Reed said, extending his hand.

Cal shook it. "It's cool. But, damn, that was like a volcano. How long have you been holding all that in?"

Reed laughed again. "Since last Spring. When you were trying to get me to find a Prom date and I felt like a loser because I couldn't. And then hearing about it from you and other people."

"You've never been a loser," he said. "And I'm sorry if I ever made you feel that way."

243

"It's not like that," Reed said." And I know neither of us is perfect."

Cal nodded.

"If you really want me to go to Ball, I'll try to find someone to go with me," he said. "I'll ask the first person I think might want to go."

"It'd be fun. And I think you'd like Heather. She likes Journey. And REO Speedwagon," Reed said with a wide smile.

"Okay, forget it, I'm not going. She sounds awful," Cal joked.

They both laughed. They shook hands again and Cal pulled Reed in for a quick hug, something he'd never done with any of his male friends.

They each headed off to begin working on their end of year theater scenes for "A Night of Shakespeare", which they'd be performing in a few weeks as the last theater night of the year and their final performances ever at Crestview. Cal's assigned partner for a scene from *Taming of the Shrew* was Susan Otis, a junior. They'd done scenes together before and been in plays dating back to the previous year when she had joined the class. As they were getting started she glanced across the theater to where Reed had gone to work on the scene he was student directing for two sophomores.

"It looked like you and Reed were having a tussle," she said. "Sorry, I don't mean to be nosy. I just notice those kinds of things."

"Oh, it was a dumb argument about Senior Ball," Cal explained.

"Aww, he doesn't want to go with you? Or you don't want to go with him?" she asked playfully.

"Oh, if it were just that simple, Suse," he said.

Susan was always fun, rather witty, and Cal had always enjoyed a good back and forth between them. One of the things he loved most about his drama class was how close everyone became, especially the juniors and seniors who'd known each other for a year or more from all the work that went into school plays and other productions.

"I'm gonna miss your sense of humor," he said to Susan. "Even when you're not funny you're funny."

"I'm gonna miss all you guys, too," she said. "Don't let it go to your head but you and Reed and Kelly and Denise and all the rest...you guys have always been so cool and welcoming. The seniors last year were kind of their own circle, ya know?"

244

"Thanks," he said. "I'm sure you'll be great to the sophomores next year, too."

"By the way," she said. "I heard you committed to Southern Oregon for college."

"I did," he said.

"My parents took me to the Shakespeare Festival up there last summer," she said. "I toured the festival theaters and the school, too. It seems like a pretty cool campus."

"I'm counting on it," he said.

"I've put it on my list, actually. For next year," she said. "I don't know if it's my top choice but I think I'm going to apply. Who knows?"

One of the reasons Cal had liked Southern Oregon from the start was that hardly anyone from Crestview had ever gone there. The idea of a clean slate where no one would know him at all had been part of the appeal. But he didn't mind the idea of someone else from Drama arriving there after he did, especially if it was someone he liked.

"I'll be sure to let you know how it is up there," he said. "I'm sure I'll be back to visit at some point."

"That would be cool," she said, opening her script for them to go through their lines.

He looked at Susan and while he'd never been attracted to her he always liked her personality and usually upbeat demeanor. Even when play rehearsals would grow intense or the cast and crew would argue like siblings, complete with shouts of "I hate you!" she would find a way to get things back to being light and funny. She was always the first person to step up and force two other classmates to make peace.

He looked across at Susan and decided to take a wild swing.

"Hey, umm, before we get started with the read through...this is gonna be very out of left field but I was wondering if you might want to come to Senior Ball with me?" he asked.

She put her script down and looked at him like he'd asked her to rob a bank or something truly outlandish. He read her body language as being concerned or confused about why he was asking, as he had never even so much as flirted with her. They were good friends within the theater circle but not very much outside of it.

"As a friend," he added. "What I mean is…that…umm… oh, hell… the truth is I broke up with my girlfriend just days ago and I had promised Reed we were going to double and share the limo expense. And I just thought you and I might have a good time if we went. You know...laughing at everyone else's poor choices in dress colors and tuxedo styles."

She grinned at the idea, and he thought the way he framed it might be right up her alley, given her sense of humor.

"Well, when you put it *that* way," she said. "Sure. I would love to be your break glass in case of emergency, I just-broke-up-with-my-girlfriend, 'help me! help me! help me!' Ball date."

"Cool," he said with a laugh. "Thank you. You're a lifesaver, Suse. Truly. And I promise it'll be fun."

--

Anna already had the strong impression that Owen Myers had been a very popular guy when he attended Crestview High School. But she had no idea just how popular until they got into the ballroom of the Mark Hopkins Hotel for her Senior Ball. Within seconds some of her classmates who knew Owen when he went to school with them began approaching in mass, excited about the unexpected reunion.

"What the hell are you doing here, O?"

"Owen! I haven't seen you since last year! Oh my God!"

"It is so good to see you, man! How is Stanford?!"

Owen, ever consistent in his manners, always made sure whoever was saying hello to him knew that he was there with Anna. He explained that they were friends from church instead of offering a longer story about their brief dating history. She was a bit overwhelmed, conversing with some of her classmates more in about 30 minutes than she had in 8 months of attending Crestview. One girl, Angie, whispered in her ear, "I had no idea you were going out with Owen", sounding shocked when she said it. Anna took it as, "How did *you*, this girl no one knows, get this former all-star to be your date!?" No one said that, of course, but she had to admit it was fun to see the surprised looks of various people who all seemed to know and genuinely like Owen but had never taken the time to get to know her, or in many cases even say 'hello'.

Given that it was May and with graduation just weeks away she had lost the motivation to try and create stronger bonds with anyone at

Crestview. Shortly after she sent her commitment letter to Northwestern she'd concluded that she never felt like a full member of the Crestview 1991 graduating class. She found that admission to herself a little sad but was at peace with it. With Owen on her arm, though, she was at least getting a chance to attract some attention and to talk with some people she had previously only seen around school. It made her feel, at least for the night, a little more included.

Owen seemed to be enjoying it and, as she expected, he looked fantastic. Before they got to the dance he'd put her mind at ease by saying that with a little time and reflection since the day they'd spent at Stanford he'd concluded she was right to end things. She had also told him about her commitment to attend Northwestern, which seemed to further drive it home.

"You have your path and I have mine," he said. "And that's the way it should be. But I do hope our paths will cross once in a while, just like tonight."

On the drive into the city she hoped that maybe he'd do something at the dance itself to break the near-perfect level of kindness and respect he always showed. She wanted Prince Charming to at least display some flaws, like maybe running into some old girlfriend or not being able to take his eyes off someone else in the room since he was free to look. But he quickly dispelled any such notion with how attentive he was.

Anna hadn't gone to many school dances outside of the Junior Prom and Homecoming Dance with Kyle the year before in Kenosha. She was a little self-conscious on a dance floor unless it was a slower song, which was easy because it was, as Eileen once called it, "slow swaying hugging". But Owen, of course, seemed perfectly content to dance, and once again old friends of his seemed to flock to him on the dance floor. Anna danced, too, because it would be weird not to join in with her date, but it wasn't her favorite activity. Nevertheless, Owen smiled and never moved too far from her, encouraging her to do silly dance moves to certain songs and she had to marvel again at his confidence and charisma. She tried not to laugh when she remembered something Cal had said: She might have missed her chance to be a future First Lady, because Owen did indeed seem to pull people in.

They sat down for dinner with Tracy and her date, and a few other people Anna had come to consider friends. As they ate and talked around the table she noticed Cal and the date he'd told her was "a fellow drama nerd, but just a friend" at another table, along with Reed and his date, a girl Anna didn't know. Cal had mentioned she was from another school.

"Smart move by Reed," he'd told her. "It means this Heather girl likes him for real and doesn't care where he is on the social ladder."

Anna realized she'd looked over at their table a bit too long because Cal suddenly waved at her. She waved back and smiled, shaking her head with embarrassment because she knew Cal had noticed. *He caught me*, she thought, all the while feeling a little flattered, too. *If he saw me looking at him then he was looking this way at me*, she figured.

--

The theme for the Crestview High School Class of 1991 Senior Ball was "Right Here, Right Now", a Jesus Jones song that had been a massive hit. It won the class vote to be the night's theme by a wide margin. Cal had not been part of the majority vote. When the song was finally played at the Ball itself he was out dancing with Susan, Reed, and Heather and he commented loudly to Reed over the music that it was a terrible choice.

"It's a good song," he said. "But as a Ball theme? Seriously?! We might be the least original class of all time."

Reed nodded but seemed to be more focused on his new girlfriend and date, who Cal had only met for the first time that night. There had been introductions, corsages, and lots of pictures at Reed's house, as his parents seemed eager to commemorate the night. Cal had been through the Spring formal steps the year before with Junior prom. He was admittedly more excited that night because he went with Lizzie, a girl he'd been romantically interested in and on a few dates with. Susan had been a great sport all through the planning for Ball, the back and forth over what her dress color was going to be so he could match it with his tie and cummerbund, getting her dinner choice pre-ordered, and all the other prerequisites. But it was not going to be a night of close slow dances and kisses in the middle of them. He knew she didn't want that from him and he didn't want that from her. And in that way it put them both at ease. There was no spark but also no pressure. Susan was hilarious and easy to be with and that was more than enough for Cal.

During a break from dancing she turned to him and said, "As your friend I have to tell you that you should not dance at college next year if you can help it. You're a good actor and a great guy but you can't fake your way out of two left feet, my friend."

He knew this was true. He could not dance to save his life, which felt like a cruel joke given how much he loved music. His lack of dance moves was one reason he had offered up for why his musical taste shied away from the kind of stuff that got played at the Ball and other dances: MC Hammer, Vanilla Ice, C&C Music Factory, Madonna, Bell Biv Devoe, and other music he didn't mind but would never listen to on his own. Whenever he went to a dance he tended to find musical respite in the fact that when a slow song was played it was usually a big guitar power ballad. "Every Rose Has It's Thorn", "Never Say Goodbye", "I Remember You" and others by the hard rock bands he liked, who always seem to score big hits by slowing things down. DJ's never seemed to have the slow songs Cal loved by far lesser known bands but he was used to it. That night, though, he'd requested Journey's "Faithfully", just so he could see Reed's face when it got played. And it worked. His friend immediately took Heather by the hand when he recognized the song and off they went. Cal smiled as he watched them from their table, feeling like he had done something nice just by getting a song played.

Susan seemed content to just enjoy the night and watch other people and comment from time to time on their behaviors. And he had to admit she was good at it.

"I like to think of myself as kind of like Sir David Attenborough," she said, "Observing the teenage animal in its habitats. Mating rituals, picking fights with other animals, the foolish squirrel that knows it will never defeat the mountain lion."

At one point she tapped him on the arm and said, "You really should go ask her to dance before this night is over."

"Who?" he asked.

"The girl at that table. Your friend that came with the Greek God looking guy that graduated last year," she said.

He felt guilty because he knew he'd been looking periodically at Anna's table, as much to see Owen Myers and all the people who seemed to flock to him like the hometown hero had returned. But he couldn't miss how nice Anna looked and how, if he was honest, he wished she was his date, even if they had just come as friends. But ever since the breakup with Melody and what he thought was a rather special afternoon together, it had been a little harder to see Anna only in a light of friendship. He had no plans to try to change anything but it was a feeling he couldn't turn off.

"I don't want to intrude on her night," he said to Susan.

He didn't feel like he needed to offer Susan an apology for looking at another girl, because he knew she would tell him none was needed.

"Just so you know," Susan said. "She's been looking over here a lot, too. I wouldn't tell you to go over there if I hadn't noticed."

He looked at Susan the way he sometimes looked at Reed, who was always noticing things he didn't.

"I'm observant," she defended. "And when a girl comes to a dance with a guy that looks like *that* guy and...no offense to you because you are a wonderful guy, Cal...but she keeps looking over here at *you* I can't help but think she's hoping you'll come over and talk to her."

"I think she's just looking at you, Suse. And probably Heather because she doesn't go to our school. And it's because she's my best....one of my best friends. That's all it is," he explained.

Susan kicked him lightly from under the table. "Then go dance with your best friend, dummy."

"You think?"

"Yes! And if it causes a scene then Adonis over there with her is going to knock you on your ass and there will be two idiots in a fight at Ball... and that'll be fun to watch," she said with a full teeth smile.

"You are the weirdest date ever," he said, standing up to go do what she'd ordered him to do.

--

Anna grew a little nervous as she realized Cal wasn't just walking in the direction of her table but coming right to it. She'd been planning to go over to his table and say hi, meet his date, and maybe talk for a few

250

minutes. She just hadn't found the right moment yet. She dismissed her nerves quickly, though, confident he wasn't going to do or say anything all that different then she would have. The only real surprise was that he said hi to Owen first.

"Hey...we never really met or knew each other well," Cal said, offering a handshake to Owen. "I'm Cal."

"Hey Cal," Owen said, shaking his hand. "I thought the same thing when Anna mentioned that you guys were good friends. It's funny how you can cross paths with somebody dozens of times and never really talk. How are you doing?"

"I'm good, thanks," Cal said.

She liked seeing them talk, even if there was a slight awkwardness to it given the various feelings she'd had for both at different times. But they were also two very nice guys that she imagined would be friends if they ever got to know each other.

"Anna told me you picked a school in Oregon," Owen said. "Is it University of Oregon? The Ducks?"

"No, I didn't have the transcripts for that one," Cal explained with a light laugh. "It's Southern Oregon State. Much smaller school. But apparently they do have a football team. With uniforms and everything. I saw it in the course catalog."

His light humor was something Anna had gotten used to and she'd come to recognize when he would use it most often. If Cal was nervous he would crack small jokes or be a bit self-deprecating. If a situation was tense he'd look for whatever humor he could find in it. She wondered if he knew he did that. She didn't blame him for it, though, as she'd also come to admire it. And at that moment it seemed to be working.

"That's funny," Owen said quickly. "Uniforms and everything..."

"Anyway," Cal continued. "I wanted to say hi to you because I was hoping you wouldn't mind if I asked your date to dance."

Anna had to give him credit for his etiquette. That or he was trying to one up Owen but she didn't think that was the case.

Owen looked to her without saying anything but didn't seem at all upset by the idea.

"I don't mind at all if you want to," he said to her.

It was a bit embarrassing to be in the middle of what was the farthest thing from a rivalry or competition for her attention. For a moment she wished they *weren't* being so nice to one another, as it would have been at least a little old fashioned and romantic to see them each trying to win her over, like something out of an old black and white movie. But the entire short exchange also demonstrated why she liked them both so much.

She stood up and turned to Owen.

"Thank you," she said to her date, then turned to Cal. "And of course I'd like to dance with you."

Cal had told her before that he was not a very good dancer and that whenever he'd attend dances he would linger in the shadows of whatever gymnasium or other room the dance was being held in and, as he'd put it, "stand there...waiting for a slow song start." So she appreciated, with humor, his attempt to dance with her to an upbeat song.

"This really is quite the fancy ballroom," she said over the music, looking around at all the decorations the Ball committee had put up, from the large banner reading 'Right Here, Right Now '91' to some colorful silhouettes that some art students had created of couples dancing. There was another one of the San Francisco Bay, and another of the Golden Gate bridge at night. There was even an ice sculpture.

"Nights like this remind me that most everyone at Crestview has families with money," he said. "And some of them with a *lot* of money."

A slow song came on next and he put out a hand as an invitation. She moved closer to him and put her arms up around his neck, feeling his hands move around her waist but not too far around to her back. Close but not so close that they couldn't see each other's faces and talk.

"So how is your date?" she asked. It was easier to talk while slow dancing since she could say it closer to his ear.

"Suse is cool. I'm glad I asked her. It's made things easy for tonight. No pressure or whatever, if that makes sense."

It did. Aside from the fact that Owen was far more popular with everyone else in the room than she would ever be, she was glad he'd agreed to come. But dancing with Cal gave her a moment of wondering what would have happened if she hadn't asked Owen and been available when Cal asked. She knew she would have said yes.

"Suse actually told me to come dance with you," he said. "She made me do it. Not that anyone would ever have to make me want to dance with you."

252

"I'm glad you asked me," she said. "And you were even a gentleman with Owen. Super polite! I'm kind of proud of you."

She felt something for him, which was frustrating because she couldn't pinpoint exactly what it was or why she felt that way. Cal never quite said the right things, but always seemed to come very close. Even his mess ups came off as well intended. She had thought about all of it a few weeks before, when they'd stopped mid walk and the sun was at his back and he looked about as unattractive as she'd ever seen him. But that was also the closest she'd ever come to saying something or doing something that would cross the line beyond friendship to something more. And now there he was, formal dressed and looking rather handsome, just as most guys in the room did.

"You clean up pretty good," she commented. "I've never seen you really dressed up."

"And you look really beautiful," he said. "Green is your color."

As the song played on it hit her that she wasn't the only one having mixed feelings. She'd never been good at knowing if someone liked her that way and even though Cal had made it obvious when they first met, she thought he was over it. But something in the way he said 'You look really beautiful' told her otherwise.

"What are you guys doing when this is over?" she asked, trying to sweep the thoughts out of her head.

"I think we're just taking the limo back to Reed's and then I figure I'll take Suse back to her house and then go home and get out of this tux. You?"

"The same," she said. "I think Owen's dropping me off and then going to his parents. Kind of boring."

"I guess that's the downside of coming with a friend," he said. "No further post-Ball adventures."

"Wow, you're really a downer, Cal," she said. "You make it sound so sad and tragic."

She looked at him and saw just a hint of sadness in his expression.

"What's going on?" she asked.

"Tragic is having a good time with your date but knowing you'd have had a better time with the other girl you asked," he said. "The one you wish you were here with. The one you wouldn't just drop off. The one you'd want to keep being with. Because I always like being with you."

She knew he wasn't trying to upset her. He was just being honest. But it made her feel like she had let him down, which was unfair given all the timing of their respective break ups with Owen and Melody.

"I know we'd have had fun," she said. "Probably a lot of fun. And a part of me wishes we were here together even if that would have been...complicated."

"I know," he said. "But lately I feel like everything gets complicated no matter what you do. I've quit even trying to figure things out. I'm just kinda glad I'm here. Even if it's not exactly how I'd want it to be."

She thought about where she was at that exact moment. A year before she would never have imagined she'd be at a hotel in San Francisco going to a formal dance at a different school in a different state and dancing with a guy who had somehow gotten to her in ways she'd never have expected.

"I feel like time has run out to ever figure this out," she said, barely realizing she was saying it out loud.

"Figure what out?" he asked.

"What we are," she said, unable to keep her guard up and not really wanting to.

"If you ever get to the bottom of that let me know. I'd love to know what we are," he said.

She pulled him a little bit closer, knowing the song would be over soon.

"How about we just are what we are?" she asked.

"I can live with that," he said.

The song faded out and she figured she should get back to Owen. She gave Cal a quick hug.

"Thank you for the dance," she said.

She made her way back to her table, fighting off the temptation to look over her shoulder to see if he had walked toward Susan yet or if he might still be watching her as she walked away. She hoped he was looking at her, but she didn't want to know for sure.

# Chapter Nine - June 1991

## *"One More Round"*

Cal's 18th birthday had come and gone with little fanfare, with his parents keeping things low key, apologetic that they didn't feel comfortable letting him have a big party at the house with it still being on the market. Instead, he went out with Doug and drank more than he usually would at a party. As he had done for years with birthday money that his grandparents sent, he loaded up on some tapes at Tower and Rasputin's. Anna made him cupcakes and gave them to him in the car on the way to school.

There was some weirdness in the air between the two of them the week after Senior Ball, where he was pretty sure they had both admitted out loud to liking each other but had, without actually saying as much, agreed to do nothing about it. Each morning for about 5 days it was on the tip of his tongue to say something like, "So about that dance on Ball night…" but he never did. He hoped she might mention it but it never came up, and after about a week things were back to normal, though he'd given up on what "normal" was even supposed to feel like or mean with her.

For something that had so much build up and hype, not just for one high school year but seemingly for all of four of them, he found his graduation from high school and all the events surrounding it a bit of a blur. He chalked it up to his parents' divorce moving into high gear, the house having gotten an offer, then some back and forth over it before it was finally sold just before graduation week. The new owners were hoping to move in in mid-July, so his father quickly began looking at condos and townhouses closer into San Francisco and his Mom started finalizing her move to Eureka. Her brother, Cal's Uncle Steve, a property manager, had already set up a place for her. The wheels were in quick motion and while his parents had been trying to give him some space and more freedom than he already had they'd also been nagging him to begin packing his room and let them know where he intended to stay for various parts of the summer. He described to his friends the range of

255

emotions that came with the increasing reality of the situation as "schizo"; accepting and finding the silver linings in all of it one minute and then feeling complete rage mixed with sadness the next.

He found the graduation ceremony itself as not very original, a critique he chalked up to having seen several ceremonies before. He'd been to Tyler's graduation three years earlier and had gone to every ceremony each year after as he always seemed to know a person or two that was finishing up at Crestview. The difference this time was that he was one of the many in caps and gowns on the stage of the Concord Pavilion -- the same stage where he and Reed had seen everyone from Kiss to Billy Idol to Metallica.

"Some really great music has been played up here," Reed noted as they were finding their assigned seats for graduation.

Cal thought again of his nightmarish date seeing Richard Marx the previous summer before saying, "And it must be said, some really shitty music has been played up here, too."

Somewhere in the crowd with Reed's family was his girlfriend, Heather. Cal's parents had kept up their united front for his sake, sitting together for the ceremony even though they had been less and less able to stop themselves from arguing about divorce details, even when Cal was in earshot. Tyler came over with his girlfriend, Katherine, and Rachel had called him earlier in the day, apologizing profusely that she had to work and there was no getting out of it.

"Make sure Mom and Dad take a ton of pictures," she said. "I'm still freaking out that you're graduating and leaving the state soon!"

Crestview had a Grad Night tradition dating back to the mid 80's, at the height of the Mothers Against Drunk Driving (MADD) campaign, when the school and concerned parents decided a big all-night, school-sanctioned party would be a good idea for graduates instead of the various individual parties students would throw, which often came with free flowing beer, weed, and other drugs.

The Grad Night Party, according to Tyler, was a lot of fun and should not be missed.

"Every year the raffle prizes seem to get bigger and bigger so you should go," his brother instructed. "Play the casino games and load up on your tickets. You could win some pretty cool shit." So, at his Grad Night festivities Cal did just that. He got on a roll at a blackjack table, loaded up on some tickets, and somewhere around midnight he won a drawing for a Sony CD Player and a $25 Tower Records gift certificate.

"That might be the most perfect prize you could have ever won!" Anna said to him.

Cal couldn't disagree. He'd held out on CDs longer than a lot of his Mixtape Club peers and both Reed and Doug had gotten players, regularly reminding him how great they made the music sound.

All night long he and near everyone else in the 1991 graduating class enjoyed a mix of food, games, dancing, some teacher and staff skits, a local comedian the Grad Night Committee had hired to do a set, and rounds and rounds of signing yearbooks and saying goodbye, even though most everyone knew they would see whoever they wanted to see all summer long. The real goodbyes would happen in stages, depending on the start dates of the various colleges and universities people were heading to.

At around 4am he was ready for the Grad Night to end and though he could leave at any time his Mom had agreed to pick him up at 6 when it officially ended. There was a sleeping and nap tent for those without the endurance to stay up all night and Anna had gone into it about an hour before. Cal sat against a wall in the gymnasium, watching people play the rented arcade games and pinball machines, trying not to fall asleep. Reed eventually joined him.

"I just walked around, and I realized how few of these people I'm going to miss," Reed said.

Cal knew that was true for his friend. Reed clearly had a very different Crestview experience than he'd had.

"I'll miss you," Cal said. In his exhausted state the sadness about moving to either Eureka with his Mom or further into the city with his Dad had crept back in.

"Me too," Reed said. "But I'm glad we're both going to be in Oregon. You're more than welcome to come check out Lewis and Clark sometime."

"Same for you with Ashland. I think it's about a five-hour drive?" he asked.

"Yeah, about that many. Heather is already planning to fly up some time," Reed said.

Cal hoped that was true and that it would work out for Reed. Ever since their quick argument in the lead-up to Ball he'd promised himself he'd be a better, more supportive friend, even if he did have his doubts about the longevity of Reed's newfound relationship.

"I've only been to Portland once," Cal said. "And that was when I was pretty young. So, yeah, a journey through record stores some weekend would be cool. Let's make that happen."

"Definitely," Reed said.

Cal fell asleep in a sitting position and when he woke the overnight grad party was winding down to a close. He walked out of the Crestview gym, holding the box with his newly won CD player in it, and found his Mom in the parking lot. He was too tired to tell her how he'd won it. It didn't register with him until he woke in his bedroom at around 1pm that same day that high school, and all that had come with it, was truly over.

\--

Anna was hesitant to accept Cal's invitation to go with him to what he called Doug Fowler's "First Blowout of the Summer" party. But as he'd done with many other things -- Senior Cut Day, movies she might not otherwise watch, and certainly music she would never have heard -- her friend had a knack for getting her out of her bubble. She knew she had done the same for him, at least a few times, and had spent the first part of the summer trying to do more of it. She forced him to do a back-to-back "Chick Flick Night", renting both *When Harry Met Sally* and *Steel Magnolias*.

"If you can quote anything from *Steel Magnolias* to a girl in Oregon, believe me, you'll win points," she said.

She thought she had coaxed him into seeing Hall & Oates at a theater in Oakland, but he admitted on the BART ride in it that it wasn't arm twisting at all since he secretly liked them.

"Their songs were the first ones I ever liked on the radio when I was, like, six years old," he explained. "And I've loved them ever since. I just don't admit it."

"Why would you not admit it?" she asked.

"Something like that could have got me kicked out of Mixtape Club," he said with a laugh.

He had thanked her profusely for a graduation present she made him, a small journal where she had written some of her favorite literary quotes and even a few Bible passages she thought he might appreciate. He even mentioned a few of the passages the next time she saw him, which meant a lot to her.

She'd also taken a job as a lifeguard at the local swimming pool. Between that and an upcoming family vacation she knew her time with Cal was going to be limited. He had told her the move out date for his family was mid-July, which wasn't too far away. So, she decided the second half of summer could be spent with Tracy and a handful of other friends she wanted to stay in touch with before her own departure for Northwestern. She was making Cal a priority for the first half of the season. It was with that in mind that she found herself going to Doug Fowler's house for the party.

The way Cal had explained it, Doug's mother was going to Reno for the weekend and for the first time was not having Doug's older sister come stay with him. Doug was approaching 17 and his mother said she trusted him to be okay on his own for a few days.

"From everything you have ever told me about Doug that sounds like the most naive, stupid, irresponsible thing she could possibly do," Anna observed.

"Oh, it totally is," Cal agreed. "But he has an empty house and a pool and claims he has a party ball of beer and the rest is BYOB."

Anna had heard the term a few times before but couldn't remember what it stood for.

"Bring your own beer," he explained. "You really need to learn these things, Anna. I'm pretty sure they drink at Northwestern."

She got him to agree that if she hated the party they would leave and go catch a movie or she would just go home on her own. She had been to parties in Kenosha, mostly because Eileen liked to drink and be carefree and Anna always felt it was her job to keep an eye on her. But she had not experienced a party thrown by anyone from Crestview. She doubted it would be any different and other than Doug having a swimming pool and it not being humid outside everything looked and felt much the same. There was, she guessed, around 20 or 30 people there when they arrived, some swimming, others just hanging out by the pool. A few people had brought some pizzas, others chips, but mostly it was a lot of beer cans, a few people drinking wine coolers, and one guy who was in Doug's kitchen bragging about how he was going to mix Bacardi with a pina colada Slurpee.

"Do you hate it yet?" Cal asked her after they'd been there about 10 minutes.

"It's fine," she said, promising herself to give it a try in the name of new experiences and hanging out with her soon to be departing friend.

She recognized a few of her classmates that she'd barely ever talked to, and another, Cindy, that she'd spoken with for a few minutes at Senior Ball after she had come over to talk with Owen. She learned that night that Cindy had also been accepted to UCLA and was headed there in the fall. When she came over to talk to her at Doug's party Anna was surprised that Cindy remembered her at all.

"Hello again," Anna said, doing her best to be warm and friendly. She was all too aware of her own shyness, especially in settings that were not her usual scene. It was something she hoped to work on before getting to Northwestern. So, if nothing else Doug's party would give her a chance to try and be chattier.

Cal motioned to her that he was going to go into the house and Anna nodded as she began talking with Cindy.

"I never asked you at Ball," Cindy began, "because it was so loud, but I have to know… are you and Owen Myers…"

"We're just friends," she said, but decided to share a bit more. "But we did go out on a few dates. Just not the right timing for it to work out."

"I hear ya," Cindy said, looking in the direction of another familiar face, a boy, who was kicking a soccer ball with some other guys in Doug's yard. "My boyfriend Eric is going to UC Santa Cruz and we're trying to figure out how it's going to work, ya know? I think you told me on Ball night… but where are you headed in the fall?"

"Northwestern, in Chicago," she said.

"Damn, that's far. And where's Cal going?" Cindy asked.

"Southern Oregon State," she answered.

"Whoa, that's some serious distance! Are you guys going to try to make that work?" Cindy asked.

"Oh...Cal and I are just friends," she said, clarifying it with. "Good friends."

"Oh, I'm sorry," Cindy said. "I shouldn't have assumed. I just saw you come in with him and I've seen you with him a lot at school."

She wondered how many other people may have gotten that impression. Tracy had mentioned it once or twice, but mostly back in October when she had first gotten to know Cal. It hardly mattered anymore, but it was funny to think about it. She was not going to miss the high school rumor mill at all.

"I've always liked Cal," Cindy said. "I feel like I never really got a chance to get to know him. And that kinda sucks. But it's all over now, right?"

"It is indeed," Anna said.

Anna liked the conversation and asked Cindy what she planned to major in, if she'd gotten her housing applications done, and some other college related questions. When Cindy told her she was going to go catch up with Eric, Anna wasn't left feeling like she had bored her new acquaintance or had driven her off. It felt good. She thought that when Eileen would inevitably get her to go to some fraternity house or other setting she could be more open-minded and maybe meet some nice people. Maybe not everyone went to parties for the sole purpose of drinking too much.

When Cal returned he was a little flustered.

"What's wrong?" she asked.

"Two things,' he said. "First, Melody just got here. With some dude."

Anna felt a little bad for him but then she laughed. "The nerve of some people to move on and come to a party on a summer night with a date."

He ignored her lack of moral support.

"Yeah, whatever. She gave me a dirty look. The second thing is Doug is already a bit drunk."

She was a little puzzled by that one.

"Why is that a problem? I thought that was kind of the point in having a party," she said.

"Not when you're the host," he said.

"And why is that?" she asked, curious about his reasoning.

"When you're hosting a bunch of drunk idiots it's a good idea to not be one of them," he explained. "My freshman year...Ty was a senior...my parents were out of town...he throws this big party and he makes sure all the valuables and breakables are locked away in Rachel's old room. He literally drew maps of where stuff was sitting on various tables around the house so my parents wouldn't know a thing. I thought he was so smart like that. Anyway, then the party starts and midway through it my brother is plowed. Everyone was. Except me. Because I'm just a freshman and we've got this house full of people and my brother is passed out on his bed. Finally, I found his one semi-sober friend to break things up and send everyone home but by then it was a huge mess. So ever since I've always told people 'Don't drink a lot if you're the host.' I threw one big party last year and I didn't have a drop. Nothing got broken, nothing went bonkers, cleared everyone out and on Monday everyone told me it was one of the best parties ever."

It was hard for Anna to imagine herself in his shoes. Even the first part of his story, which would be her parents leaving her and Jackie alone for the weekend, was something they'd never have done. Then, even if they did, letting in dozens of classmates and loading them up with beer would never be something she could do. The hundreds of different things she could think of that could go wrong with something like that made her anxieties do cartwheels, and that was from just thinking about it.

"So, yeah, I told Doug not to drink a lot if he was going to do this and it's not even 9 and he's already pretty messed up," Cal detailed.

"So even with that and the Melody thing I guess leaving and going to a movie is out?" she asked.

She knew the answer.

"It is for me," he said. "I gotta keep an eye on this for Doug's sake. Sorry."

"I was kidding," she said. "I'll stay and help you with whatever it is we're supposed to help with."

He went on to explain that it was mostly just making sure no one was doing anything truly stupid that could land Doug in a lot of trouble.

"Like if somebody's stumbling drunk we should probably keep them away from the pool," he explained. "Or if they look like they're going to puke guide them to the bathroom. Or the bushes outside. Don't let anyone fight, don't let anyone break anything or steal anything."

She put her palm to her head and lightly punched his shoulder.

"I should have said 'No' to you," she said. "I say this to you with affection but how are you my friend?!"

"You really don't have to stay," he said. "I know you drove us but I can crash here and get a ride tomorrow."

A part of her wanted to take him up on the escape clause he'd thrown her way, but as she looked around and saw the number of people in the backyard growing larger in numbers, the music getting louder, and then seeing Doug whooping and hollering on the diving board of the swimming pool, she didn't want to leave. The mistake had been coming at all and she knew that, but she was increasingly worried about someone getting hurt.

"I'm with you," she said. "But never again, okay?"

"Definitely," he promised "From now until moving day it's going to be movies and bookstores and shooting hoops. It'll be out own little 'Our Town'."

For the next hour or so they circulated around Doug's yard and house, keeping an eye on various people, most of whom appeared to be in Doug's class of soon-to-be juniors, some other inbound seniors, and a fair amount of people she recognized from their just-graduated class. Most everyone, even those drinking, seemed to be fine. A lot of laughing, some people playing drinking games, and many in the backyard hanging around the pool or on the lawn. She watched with a mix of disgust and amusement when Cal had to evict a boyfriend and girlfriend who had ignored the "Off Limits" sign posted on the door of Doug's mother's bedroom. Mercifully, the only clothing that appeared to have been removed was a t-shirt on the guy and the girl was tucking her shirt back in.

Anna grew a little worried that Jackie, her soon-to-be freshman younger sister, might find her ways to parties like the one she was in the middle of. She hoped not. She made a mental note to try and give Jackie some kind of big sister-little sister talk about such things before leaving in the fall.

She noticed Melody at one point, walking down the hallway toward the bathroom. She didn't recognize the boy that was with her. Melody acknowledged her with a not-too-friendly glance. Anna could easily imagine that Melody would have the impression that she and Cal were at the party as a couple. And though she felt a little petty for thinking it, she wouldn't correct her if she asked. In hindsight, Anna could admit she was jealous but still believed nothing would have ever happened between Melody and Cal if she'd made her own move with him.

At around 10 they noticed a fair number of people making their way out of the house and heading home or off to find another party.

"The party ball of beer ran out," Cal explained. "When the free beer is gone that usually sends some packing."

She watched as Cal checked with people to see if they were with someone that was okay to drive.

"You good?" he asked one pair.

"Yeah, I had a drink like two hours ago," someone explained.

"Who's your ride?" he asked another.

"I walked."

She chuckled to herself at the sight of him being responsible amid what otherwise struck her as a sea of irresponsible behavior

"It's good that you check with people about that, to make sure they're not going to drive," she told him.

"Yeah, another lesson from Ty," he said. "He ran his car off the road one night about a year and a half ago. He and a buddy. No one got hurt and he somehow dodged a police report but they'd both been drinking. It was a wakeup call of sorts."

She wondered if Cal was even having fun. For her part she liked the observations from it all, seeing how ridiculous some would act when they had a few drinks in them. She thought it was amusing but also a little sad. She was helping Cal pick up some bottles scattered around the kitchen when she remarked, "Your sister kept you off drugs and you said you've learned these lessons from your brother. So why do you even drink at all?"

He chuckled before answering.

"Well, at first it was honestly because everyone else was doing it. Then it was what I've since heard is called 'liquid courage'? It made it easier to talk to girls. And it's fun. But, yeah, when I see other people get really drunk it makes me not want to get drunk."

She had another question she was going to ask him when they heard the shriek from the backyard. Then came two people charging toward the sliding glass door between the living room and the patio.

"Cal! Cal!" a boy motioned, waving his arm to come out back.

Cal darted quickly and Anna followed. When they got outside they saw two other boys in the pool, their shirts soaked through. In between them was Doug. They were pulling him toward the shallow end of the pool and helping him get out.

Cal and Anna rushed over to where the two guys had pulled Doug, trying to get him to a lounge chair near the pool. Anna got in between the two of them quickly, her lifeguard training instincts kicking in. Doug was on his back in the lounger, his eyes were open and he was conscious. She could instantly smell a lot of chlorine and a lot of alcohol.

"Doug," she said, repeating his name multiple times.

"Yeah," he mumbled quietly.

"Do you know where you are?" she asked.

"My house," he said, slurring his words.

He tried to sit up but she wouldn't let him.

"Stay still," she said.

She checked his forehead, seeing if maybe there was a bump or some other sign he'd hit it.

"What the hell happened?!" Cal asked the crowd that had surrounded them.

"He was on the diving board and laughing and then shouting up to the sky about something. He's been drinking a lot," she heard someone say.

Anna couldn't believe people just watched Doug do that, with no one attempting to get him down from the diving board or making him stop drinking. She and Cal had been running around keeping an eye on everyone and everything else and when they'd last seen Doug he was definitely drunk but not falling over. Cal had said, "I've seen him worse."

"He was downing Bacardi really hard a bit ago," another girl said.

Anna looked down again at Doug who was soaking wet from the spill. He was also shivering even though the night air was warm. She turned around toward Cal.

"I think we need to get him inside and get everyone out of here," she said.

She thought about adding that someone should call 9-1-1 but her instincts told her that wouldn't go over well with the crowd in attendance.

"Do you think you can get up?" she asked Doug.

"Oh fuck," were the last words Doug spoke before he sat up and proceeded to throw up in Anna's direction, with some of the vomit getting her shirt squarely on the way down.

"Oh, God," she groaned.

He turned further sideways in the chair and threw up again, then again, missing her this time.

"Okay, everyone," she heard Cal say. "Party's over. If you don't have a ride or you're drunk you can hang out till I can get Doug's keys and give you a lift."

The two guys who had dove into the pool helped her take Doug back inside. Cal led them to Doug's bedroom and they placed him on his bed. Doug crashed on to his mattress quickly and Cal turned him to his side, placing a garbage can near the edge of the bed. He stripped the wet t-shirt off Doug and threw it toward the dresser.

"I'm sorry," she heard Doug say.

She turned to Cal and said, "I'll sit here with him and you make sure everyone gets out of here, okay?"

Cal nodded and left the room. She sat on the bed next to Doug, keeping an eye on his chest to make sure he was breathing. An ever-growing part of her was furious, angry for the situation and for agreeing to come be part of it. But she also felt sorry for the boy lying sprawled on his bed. He'd stopped shivering when she put a blanket over him.

"Doug, are you with me?" she asked.

"Yeah, I'm just tired and...I think I puked on you," he said.

"You did," she said.

"I'm sorry," he said, groaning it more than saying it.

"It's okay," she said, looking down at her shirt and the disgusting stain that was now on it.

"I fucked up," he mumbled.

"It's okay," she said again.

She wasn't sure whether to try and keep him awake or let him sleep. She looked him over to make sure he wasn't cut or bleeding or showing any major bruises. She lifted the blanket, double checking his shirtless torso. She shook her head and nearly laughed as she thought about how she had always tried to avoid a scenario of being alone with a guy in his room, with his shirt off and yet there she was. She sat with him for about 20 minutes, listening to him sleep, thinking again about what a dumb rite of passage nights like that were. She had come along because she'd thought maybe there were some high school experiences she should have had but didn't. If this was one of them it wasn't one she needed.

She looked around Doug's room, taking in the band posters on his walls, glancing at his music collection, a combination of cassettes and CDs that was almost as vast as Cal's. She stood up and examined the small, framed pictures on his dresser. One was Doug and what she assumed were his mother and older sister. His sister was wearing a graduation cap and gown in the picture. The other one was a much younger version of Doug, still recognizable though. He had a plastic baseball bat and there was a man standing behind him helping him swing it. She guessed that must have been his father. Cal had mentioned that Doug's father had died when he was young.

Cal eventually made his way back to the room, placing Doug's keys on his dresser.

"How is he?" Cal asked

"He fell asleep," she said.

"He passed out," Cal said in a corrective tone.

"Not much difference," she said.

"Except the hangover tomorrow."

She stood up and looked at her watch. It wasn't even 11 yet but it felt a lot later.

"How did he get so drunk so fast?" she asked.

"He mixed beers with Bacardi," Cal explained. "And he always drinks fast once he gets going."

She looked again at her stained shirt.

"Ugh. Pardon my French but... shit!" she exclaimed. "There is no way my parents miss this one if they're up when I get home."

She started to worry about what would happen if she came in smelling of some combination of booze, chlorine, and vomit.

Cal opened one of Doug's drawers and pulled out a t-shirt, tossing it to her and then turning his back so she could change.

"Put that on and we'll wash your shirt before you head home. I'm going to stay the night and clean this place up," he said.

She took off her shirt and put on Doug's shirt that had a design of some kind on it and read 'Red Hot Chili Peppers' and 'Freaky Styley'. She laughed as she looked at it.

"This night just gets worse and worse," she said.

"It looks good on you," Cal said with a smile.

"I seriously doubt that."

He took her dirty shirt out of the bedroom and from the hallway she could hear him starting the washing machine. When he came back in he motioned for her to leave the room. He turned the light off but kept the door open.

"Is he safe to leave alone?" she asked.

"We'll check on him every 20 minutes or so, make sure he's on his side or stomach. But I think he's just out cold."

They made their way into the kitchen and she helped him put empty bottles and cans into trash bags, along with pizza boxes and other assorted food wrappers. She picked up a squished Twinkie and threw it into the bag.

"He can be so stupid," Cal said, shoveling more items into the bag.

She agreed but felt the need to add more.

"So are you," she said.

He gave her a hurt look.

"I'm sorry but I have to say it," she continued. "I get that nights like tonight have been part of your friendships with people and with Doug but it's all pretty stupid, especially what happened to him. What if he'd fallen and hit the concrete or no one had noticed him fall in and he sinks to the bottom?"

He pushed his hand back through his hair and nodded back at her.

"I tried to warn him," he said sheepishly. "About drinking when you're the host."

"I know," she said. "You told me. And I know you think that's good advice for your buddy. But I think you owe him more than that."

She sat down on the couch, shoving aside a wet towel.

"Right now I feel like I owe him a punch in the mouth when he wakes up," he said.

"Or you can come over here and I'll punch you in the mouth," she said calmly, too tired to be angry about it.

"Have I done something to piss you off?" he asked. "I'm sorry Doug threw up on you. But I didn't do it."

She shook her head and tapped the seat next to her on the couch for him to come sit down.

"I know Doug is your good friend," she said. "But you've also said to me at least dozen times since I've known you that he's also like the little brother you never had."

"He is. He can be a real pain in the ass like that."

"I'm sure he can. And yet when I've seen him around I totally understand why he's a popular kid. And even though I don't find him remotely attractive I can see why so many others do," she said.

"Then you're smarter than I am," he said. "Because I've never been able to figure that one out. He's a total slob. He's not as dumb as he thinks or says he is but I wouldn't call him smart either so... I don't get it."

"It's because...and don't tell him I said this...but it's because he's a mutt. He's like a loveable mutt you see at the pound with a sweet face who leaps on you too much and growls but doesn't bite and he does some funny things. And you just know he's going to poop in the house and destroy your furniture. But you take him home anyway and he does all those things," she explained, waving her arms around the still very messy house the two of them were sitting in to demonstrate her point.

"I am *absolutely* telling him you said that," Cal said. "That's the best description of Doug I ever heard."

She knew he was joking and wouldn't relay it to Doug at all but was compelled to say more.

"But you know what makes the mutt okay? Makes him stop ruining the house or doing something stupid or running away?" she asked.

He shrugged his shoulders.

"Love," she said. "A lot of love. And training and patience but mostly just having people who love the mutt enough."

"What's your point?" he asked.

"You know my point," she said. "That's the infuriating thing about you sometimes, Cal. You always know the point. Deep down. You always know what's right or at least the right thing to do. I see that in

269

you all the time. It's the thing I like about you most. And sometimes I like how you can ignore it in favor of something fun or silly, especially when I know nothing truly bad will come from it. Like when we went to Berkeley or when you've talked me into taking a break from studying to go with you somewhere. I envy that about you. But while you were giving those other kids a ride home I sat in there with Doug and thought about the ways you've described him: Friend, drinking buddy, partner in crime...and then the little brother type thing."

"And you think I should look out for him more," he said. "Like a brother."

"Yes. In a way that...from some things you've told me, Tyler *didn't* do for you. Or you wish Rachel had done. I remember you told me how you met Doug. Tutoring him, helping him with...?"

"English," he said. "You think I could tutor anyone in anything else?"

They both laughed, which she welcomed as their conversation was turning serious.

"Anyway," she continued, "I sat in there with him while you were gone and I thought about... and please don't laugh...but I thought about my faith. And I know that's not your thing but it's how I handle challenging moments. I thought about why I was staying in this house. And I realized it was to help Doug. And that's how *you* came into his life. As a helper. A tutor. A guide. If he's like the little brother you never had that also makes you the big brother he doesn't have. If you really think of him that way then you are, whether you like it or not, your brother's keeper."

She watched him taking in her words. She worried that trying to pass on something from her religious beliefs might hit his ears like the parents in Charlie Brown cartoons, just sounds off screen with no meaning. But he appeared to be taking it seriously.

"I get what you mean."

"I know you do," she said. "Like I said... you always do. You always get it. Somewhere in there."

She got back up, grabbing more messes from the couch and the hallway, moving her shirt from the washer into the dryer, and peering in to make sure Doug was still okay. She looked again at the picture of his family and especially the one with his father. She looked at it for several moments, pushing a tear off her cheek as she thought of the smiling little

270

boy and his bat and the huge grin on the face of his Dad behind him. Then she looked at Doug on his bed, still on his side, his stomach moving up and down and a little bit of snoring coming from him.

When she came back out Cal was still sitting on the couch, looking lost in thought. She sat down next to him and put her head on his shoulder.

"You look really tired," he observed. "Once your shirt is dry you should head home. I wouldn't want you to get in trouble with your parents over this. I'm going to crash on this couch and help out cleaning tomorrow with the walking hangover in there."

She knew he was right and didn't want to break curfew. But she felt guilty for leaving him there alone, especially with all the things she'd said to him.

"If it's okay with you I'd like to come back tomorrow morning," she said. "If you guys are going to be here. Help out with the mess and maybe talk to Doug."

"I don't know what condition he'll be in but we'll be here," he said. "What do you want to talk to him about?"

"Faith," she said.

He shook his head and let out his familiar laugh for when he thought she was crazy.

"Good luck with that," he said.

"I know it's probably a long shot," she said. "But I think he's worth it, don't you?"

--

Cal woke several times in the night, as though his own instincts were acting as an alarm clock to make sure he checked in on Doug. Each of the three times he went into the bedroom Doug was in the same place, on his side and sleeping like a grizzly bear.

Cal had been up about 30 minutes the next morning, straightening up the kitchen enough to find Mrs. Fowler's coffee filters and Yuban to make a pot. He figured if Doug wasn't a coffee drinker yet it was a good time to start. He was drinking a cup when Doug came stumbling out of his room, still in the shorts he'd worn the night before, no shirt, and a blanket draped over his shoulders like a cape.

271

"Good morning," Cal said.

Doug just raised his hand to signify he heard him.

"Jesus, what a mess," Doug said as he looked around

"It was worse last night," Cal said. "Anna and I made a pretty good dent in it before she left."

Doug fetched a glass of water from the kitchen and walked back out toward the living room couch.

"Was she in my room?" Doug asked. "I remember her being in there with me."

"Yeah, we tucked your ass in," he said, lifting his coffee mug and tipping it toward Doug. "Do you want some of this?"

"No. Caffeine will kill you."

"Not as badly as your cocktail of weed, beer and Bacardi," Cal said dryly.

Doug had made his way to the couch and had his back to a cushion, spreading his legs across the rest of the furniture.

"Yeah, that was a bad fuckin' idea," he said.

"I warned you," Cal said. "Don't drink at your own party."

"I know you did," Doug said quietly.

Cal was still thinking about his talk with Anna, about what or who he should be in Doug's life. He wasn't sure if she was right but watching Doug's pained movements and what he could only imagine was a headache worse than anything he'd ever experienced he felt sorrier for Doug than anything else. If Cal was angry it was with himself.

"Why did you drink that much anyway?" he asked. "I mean...I've seen you drunk, I've seen you loud and I've seen you get in a fight with someone, but I've never seen you blitzed to pass out plastered. People told me you were howling at the moon on the diving board or some shit."

"I was having a rough night," Doug said.

"Why? What happened?"

"I don't want to talk about it," he said

Doug was now flat on his back on the couch as they talked.

"I'm going to give you, like, 10 minutes to get your bearings," Cal said, "but then I need you to get up and help me clean this place, especially outside."

In a mocking tone Doug replied with, "Okay, Mom. I'll be ready for school in a few minutes. I promise."

Cal went outside to inspect for damage. On the lawn he found assorted bottles, a few cigarette butts, an abandoned bong, and some other trash. All in all it wasn't that bad.

Doug eventually made his way outside, still moving slow but upright.

"There's some lovely dried up puke you deposited over there by the lounge chair. It should just hose off," Cal informed him.

Again Doug lifted his arm to signal he heard him, then unrolled the hose attached to the house and made his way over to the mess, spraying it off.

"Fuck, I just remembered puking on your girlfriend," Doug said.

"Yes, you puked on Anna and, no, she's not my girlfriend."

"I know. I'm just giving you shit. I was surprised she came with you last night. She must have been freaked."

"A little," Cal said. "But she also made sure you were okay. She's a trained lifeguard, ya know. It came in handy."

"Yeah, that was a shitty plunge," Doug said.

"What the fuck were you thinking?" Cal asked.

"I wasn't. I was wasted. And high."

"Any cocaine or LSD or crack or anything else?" Cal asked sarcastically, positive that at least 2 of those things had never entered Doug's system.

"Dude, I got fucked up," Doug said a bit louder. "And I'm paying for it now so please stop ragging on me about it."

Cal walked around the pool over to the lounger Doug had sat down in. Normally he would have been willing to let a wild Friday night roll into a calmer Saturday morning and not say another word but he didn't want to let this one go.

"No," Cal said. "I *am* going to rag you about it. You scared the fuck out of me. And Anna. And everyone else that was here."

"It was a party. That shit happens. I'm sorry. I know I had too much."

"You always have too much," Cal said. "Maybe not as bad as last night but you never get *just* drunk. You get loud drunk or go-pick-a-fight drunk or yell-at-some-ex-girlfriend of yours drunk."

"That's how I am," Doug said. "You know that."

"I do. And I know I've drank right up there with you sometimes. But you always take it another drink farther, or you add some weed to the booze. And I've ignored it and I haven't said anything because I've either been a little drunk myself or I didn't want to come off all judging or get all big brother on you. But this morning? I'm worried."

"I can tell," Doug said. "And I'm telling you not to. I'll be fine. Last night was just… I shouldn't have thrown a party in the first place. I'm obviously not meant to be a party host."

"Probably not. But that's the second time you've said something about last night that you're not telling me. What the hell happened?"

Cal sat in the folding chair next to Doug, who was sitting in the lounger, shaking his head.

"Do you really want to know?" Doug asked.

"Yes, if it'll explain why you went full fucking Lizard King on your diving board."

"Yesterday was my Dad's birthday," Doug said. "That's why my Mom's out of town. She always takes us somewhere to celebrate it but this year I told her it was fine if she wanted to go to Reno with her friend, because it's no fun for me. And I thought I'll throw him a party and that'll be good. It'll be a happy thing. Because I've been trying to not have everything about him be this sad, black cloud. But then I drank and I *didn't* think of his birthday. I thought of what I always end up thinking about. Why he took out his .45 and killed himself. That's why I drank so much last night."

Cal sat quiet and took in what he'd heard.

"Aren't you glad you asked?" Doug said, adding, "You fucking asshole."

Doug put his hands on his temples and Cal was reminded that his friend must be nursing a brutal headache.

"I'm sorry," Cal said, reaching his arm out and putting his palm on Doug's shoulder.

"Fuck you, man," Doug said, pushing the gesture away.

"I'm sorry," he repeated.

"I don't need your fuckin' pity," Doug said.

"I know you don't. But I'm still sorry. I didn't know yesterday was his birthday."

274

Cal looked at Doug and saw the pain and the red eyes from both the hangover and maybe from almost crying, though he couldn't be sure about the latter.

"I really wish I knew what to say to you," Cal said. "But all I can say is that I'm sorry."

"I know. Everyone is sorry about it. I've heard 'Sorry, Doug' for nearly 9 years. It's gotten to where it doesn't really mean anything."

Cal was searching for something else to say when he heard the knocking sound coming from inside the house, followed by the doorbell.

"Someone's at the door," Doug said. "It's hurting my head and it's probably an angry neighbor or a cop. Since you're an asshole could you go get it?"

Cal had a better guess on who it was.

"Oh, it might be even worse than a cop but I'll get it," he said.

He made his way inside and opened the front door to find Anna. She was in summer shorts and a blouse, her hair pulled back and no makeup. She looked all business, like she'd come to clean up a mess or was on a mission.

"How is he?" she asked.

"Hungover. We've been talking a bit. I at least know now why he went overboard last night."

"That's good," she said. "What happened?"

He knew if he told her it would instantly make sense to her why Doug behaved the way he had. But it wasn't his story to tell. He thought about how many people at Crestview, many who called Doug a friend, didn't even know he had lost his father at all. Even fewer knew the reasons why. He'd told Cal almost by accident when they'd first met and he'd never heard him speak about it with others. If it came up Doug would readily say, "My father died:, but never much more than that.

"I can't tell you why," Cal said to Anna. "I know that sounds lame but I just can't. But maybe he will."

He led her to the backyard where Doug was now sitting by the pool dangling his feet in the water. Cal hadn't mentioned she was coming over so Doug looked very surprised to see her.

"Hi, Doug," she said cheerfully.

"Hey," he greeted her. "I'm sorry about last night."

275

"I know you are," she said, walking over to the side of the pool. Cal watched as she kicked off her shoes and asked, "May I?"

Doug pointed to the spot next to him and she sat down, throwing her feet into the pool. Cal kicked off his shoes and was ready to join them when Anna turned to him.

"Cal, is it okay if I just talk with Doug alone for a bit?" she asked.

He felt a little left out by her request and had no idea what she was up to but he obliged just the same.

"Sure, I'll go inside and put some things away," he said.

"Thank you," Anna said, giving him one last look that he took as her saying, 'Trust me'.

And he did. Completely.


--


Anna moved her feet back and forth in the water, not saying anything at first and hoping that Doug wouldn't mind her talking to him if she did say something. She knew she'd find out soon enough but wanted to give him a few seconds to get used to her sitting there. She'd never talked with him before person-to-person, just the two of them.

"I came over because I wanted to check on you," she said finally. "I was really worried."

"I'm okay," Doug said. "Bad hangover but I'll be fine. Thanks for helping get me back inside last night. And Cal said you helped clean up, too."

"Mm hmm," she said.

She stayed quiet, again gently moving her feet in the water and waiting to see if Doug would talk. But he stayed quiet. She knew he had a hangover and guessed that could be the reason. But she also knew he was not even remotely shy as a person. She thought maybe he was embarrassed or ashamed.

"Doug, I have to confess to you that when you were passed out in your room I looked at some of your things," she said. "I shouldn't have because it's none of my business so I really do apologize. But I saw the pictures on your dresser. Can I ask you about those?"

"I guess," Doug said.

"When did your sister graduate?"

"4 years ago," he said. "Class of '87"

"What's her name?"

"Crissy."

"Are you guys close?" she asked.

"Sometimes. Kind of a big age gap," he said.

"My sister Jackie is 4 years younger than me," she said. "She'll be at Crestview next year."

"Cool," Doug said.

She wanted to add, 'And if you go anywhere near her with you sweet mutt behavior I will come back from Northwestern and kill you' but she knew it wasn't the moment for that.

"And the other picture. That was your Dad, right?" she asked.

Doug nodded.

"It's easy to tell. You look like him," she said.

"People tell me that all the time," he said.

She took another pause, readying herself for what she wanted to say next.

"Can I ask what happened to him?" she asked.

"I'm sure Cal's told you," Doug said.

She shook her head. "He hasn't, actually. I asked him but it's the one time I haven't been able to get him to talk on and on and on about something."

Doug made a noise that she thought, if not for his hangover, would be a laugh or a chuckle in agreement about their mutual friend.

She didn't want the conversation to drift away from his father, but she didn't want to force it either. She had a reason for why she wanted to talk to him, stemming from a moment of inspiration that had come the night before.

"He killed himself," Doug said. "But please don't tell other people that, though, okay?

"I won't," she said. "You don't know me very well but I'm pretty good about keeping things private."

She hesitated for a moment as she reached over and held Doug's hand. She thought he might jerk his back but he didn't. And she was confident that despite his reputation with girls that he wouldn't misinterpret it as a come on.

277

"I can't even imagine what that must have been like for you and your Mom and Crissy," she said.

. She took a deep breath and closed her eyes, lifting her face a little toward the late morning sun.

After several seconds of silence Doug said, "He was depressed. Clinical depression. That's what they said it was. I didn't know what it meant because I was 8. I'm still not always sure what it means."

She kept her eyes closed, still holding his hand, telling herself to be patient. To not talk. She didn't know exactly why she thought that was important but something inside her was guessing Doug expected her to add something more. Instead they sat together quietly for several moments.

"I was telling Cal before you got here that the reason I got so fucking blotto last night is because yesterday was his birthday," Doug continued. "Not the best way to celebrate it, obviously."

"Maybe not. But everybody makes mistakes," she said softly.

"I make a lot of them," he said.

There was an air in his voice when he said it, like he was trying to impress her by admitting as much. She had to stifle the urge to laugh and say to him, 'The bad boy thing isn't going to wash with me.' But she didn't.

Instead she said, "I make mistakes, too. I know people like me come off as though we don't. But we do. Like when I was driving home last night after your party I was thinking how stupid I was to let Cal talk me into coming at all. Because while I'm sure this will shock you... I am *not* much of a party girl."

Doug glanced at her and chuckled.

"I'm not ashamed of that," she said. "So again I asked myself why I put myself in that position trying to be someone I'm not? Was it curiosity or because I want to spend as much time with my dear friend as I can before he leaves next month or was it something else? And before I went to bed... and please don't laugh...but I asked God to help me figure it out. And this morning I was still thinking about it. And then I got in the car to drive over here and I was replaying everything in my head and asking why bad things happen. I thought of you falling in your pool and how much worse it could have been. But then I thought of the two guys whose names I didn't even catch that jumped in the pool to help you

278

before Cal and I came out to see what happened. I thought about why I ever got training for lifeguarding and CPR and all that. And, mind you, I didn't have to restart your heart or anything like that but for some reason, of all people, I was there last night in a place I normally wouldn't be."

She was glad she got it all out. They were things she'd been wrestling with and words she'd been searching to to find since the previous night.

"I get it," Doug said. "Things happen for a reason. I've been to counseling and I've heard that one before. People say that about my Dad but I just don't believe it. So no offense but I'm not sure I buy that."

"No offense taken," she said. "I can't think of a reason for that either. And I won't even pretend to know how much pain that has caused you. I really just wanted to come back over for very selfish reasons."

"What reasons?" he asked.

"I had it in my head that since you threw up on me...and you did...that you owed me a small favor."

"I really am sorry about that," Doug said. "What favor do you need?"

"You might hate it," she warned.

"Probably," he said, with a laugh. "But whatever."

"I wanted you to pray with me," she said.

"I don't believe in God," he said quickly.

She was prepared for that. She'd readied herself for it.

"As hard as it is for me to say this I don't blame you," she said. "But I was still hoping you might humor me. Because, again, you *did* throw up on me."

"Fair enough," he said. "I'll pray with you if you want."

"Good. Close your eyes, ok?"

She watched to make sure he had before closing her own.

"Dear Lord, thank you for looking out for my friend Doug last night and this morning and I ask you to continue watching over him for all days to come," she began. "Thank you for giving myself and Cal and those other two boys whatever tools we needed to be able to be there for our friend, even within our own horrible mistakes and behavior. Please grant us the strength and character to continue taking care of each other as friends. Let us learn from each other as you test us. Forgive us when we question your plans for us, as sometimes they seem so

279

confusing and painful and throw our faith in you into doubt. Please show us the light ahead when we need it. And thank you for giving me this morning and letting me get to know Doug a little. I ask that you hold him and guide him even when he doesn't know you're there just as you guide me and all of us. In Jesus' name. Amen."

She heard Doug whisper his own "Amen", which made her smile as she opened her eyes and let go of his hand.

"Was that horrible?" she asked.

"No," he said. "That was actually kinda cool of you."

She stood up and when he did the same she gave him a hug.

"I'm not trying to convert you or anything but I just thought you should know you really do have people who care about you. I know we don't know each other and I'm probably just Cal's uptight, churchy friend to you but if you ever wanted to talk I would be happy to listen. And I know Cal would too. He cares a lot about you even if he doesn't say it."

"Thanks," he said.

Just as they were opening the sliding glass door to go back inside the house Doug stopped her.

"Ya know, I never quite understood what Cal's thing was with you," he said. "I know he liked you a lot when he met you. A lot. But then there was Melody and all that."

"It's okay. I don't always understand me and Cal either," she said. "Not that there ever has been a 'Me and Cal' if you know what I mean."

"There should have been," Doug said. "If I had a do over on this last year? I would have told him to forget Melody. Like, never ask her out. He should have been after you."

# Chapter Ten - July 1991

## *"Last Perfect Thing"*

It took a bit of back and forth with both his Mom and his Dad but by early July Cal had mapped out the remainder of his last summer before college. For the first part of the month he was going to help his father move into his new apartment and then stay there for a little over a week. His Mom, along with much of their household and most of Cal's stuff, was going to follow the moving van to Eureka. Cal would catch up with her after a weekend orientation and class registration at Southern Oregon State College in the middle of the month. From there and for the rest of the summer he was going to help his Mom settle in and work for his uncle at the property management company until he moved himself into his dorm in Ashland. Cal had worked previous summers on a window washing crew and his uncle told him that would be handy to have for pre-move ins or move-out cleaning and that he could help with some other projects, too. Cal wasn't exactly looking forward to that part of the season but he knew he needed to make some money and it would help pass the days in Eureka.

He was able to drive back and forth from his father's new place in Daly City to Concord if he wanted to and while it wasn't a short drive it at least gave him the option to see friends and get in some final visits and goodbyes before mid-July. He ultimately wound up splitting his time between doing that and finding the upside to his Dad being closer to San Francisco, spending some afternoons on his own visiting record stores in search of CDs. He figured it was time to start acquiring them now that he had a player.

His father's new place was nice enough, or at least better than Cal expected it to be. There was a pool and an exercise room for the residents and, as promised, it was big enough for future visits and stays if he wanted to. But by Cal's calculations of beds and bedrooms he figured if he and Tyler and Rachel were ever all there at the same time someone would be in the guest room, someone on the couch, and someone would be on the floor.

"It's a nice enough place," he told Anna over the phone one evening, "But it's weird. I feel more like his roommate or a visitor than his kid right now. It's not homey. And it's boring as hell. He has the TV hooked up but my Dad doesn't really care about cable so we've been watching a few movies I rented down the street."

On one of his last ventures into Concord he made two visits. The first was to say goodbye to Reed, as his family was going to be leaving on a 2-week trip before Cal was slated to drive himself north. Of all his friends he figured Reed was the one he'd likely see the most once college got started, given that he'd be in Portland. The second stop was one he debated back and forth. Ever since Doug's wild party, when he'd seen her arrive but didn't talk to her, he'd wanted to at least try to say goodbye to Melody. He went to her house unannounced and she thankfully didn't shut the door in his face. But she wasn't especially warm or inviting at first.

"I'm leaving this weekend," he explained. "I'm going up to Ashland for an orientation and then to Eureka on my way back and spending the rest of the summer with my Mom. And I don't know... I just didn't want to leave town for good or a really long time and not say goodbye to you."

"You could have just called," she said. "Even left me a message with, like 'Hey! Bye Mel!'"

"I wouldn't do that," he said, hurt that she would even suggest it. "And I never call you Mel."

She frowned.

"I know you wouldn't...and that you don't," she said. "I just said it because I still kinda want to hate you."

"I saw you at Doug's party a few weeks ago," He said. "But I was--"

"You were with your girlfriend," Melody interrupted. "Anna. I get it. And I was with Jake, who has already turned out to be a royal dipshit."

"Anna isn't my girlfriend," he said, trying not to sound defensive or disappointed by it. "And I'm sorry Jake didn't work out. I mean it."

He wasn't sure if he meant it but it seemed like the right thing to say.

"He said mean shit to me," she said. "You never did that and I kinda got used to it. So thank you for ruining other guys for me. You're like this hard act to follow."

"Glad I could help," he said, appreciative that the ice between them was melting. "Anyway, I'm just visiting all the people I've been close to because with my Dad in toward the city and my Mom hours away and my school far away I don't know when I'll get a chance to see anyone again. And even if you're still mad at me I would never want you to think I didn't care or don't think about you. Especially when I hear certain songs."

She started to smile but didn't quite get there. He understood why. If he was in her shoes he'd find it hard, too.

"That happens with me, too...with songs. I just change the station or throw my boombox across the room," she said. "But not really. I usually just listen."

He opened his arms and she hugged him.

"I do appreciate you coming by," she said, giving him a tight squeeze. "And good luck with everything in Eureka and at college. I'm going to miss you at least a little. Mixtape Club won't feel the same next year."

"It'll have less hair metal," he said, hoping to keep the mood light.

"Thank God," she said. "That shit just needs to finally go away and die it's overdue death."

--

Anna's summer got busy in a hurry, with mid-June turning into mid-July entirely too fast for her liking. In the weeks since Doug's party she'd seen Cal less than she'd wanted because her work shifts at the pool left her so exhausted by day's end she couldn't muster the energy to hang out. She spent hours blowing her whistle at kids that were running, occasionally having to scold some playing too rough in the pool, but also getting to know a few of her co-workers and making some money. When Cal moved with his father out to Daly City she made a priority to at least call him regularly and make sure he was doing okay.

To her surprise she also had a chance to follow up with Doug, who had asked Cal for her phone number, and she talked with him a few more times when he first reached out. He said that something about that afternoon by the pool had struck a chord and he hoped that maybe she would be someone he could talk to.

283

"I just feel like there are things I can say to you that I can't say to other people," Doug explained one evening on the phone.

It got a bit intense, especially when he described what she thought might be a real set of emotional or psychological problems. She was reminded that as much as she liked being of help to him, that she, like Cal, was not a professional and they were both going to be leaving in the near future and then Doug might not have anyone he could confide in.

She told him, "I know it's probably easier to talk to a friend than a counselor and I know you told me your Mom sent you to one a few years ago and you didn't like it. But that was a few years ago. Maybe you should try it again."

The next time they talked he said he'd gone to see someone, and he thanked her several times, asking if there was anything he could do to show his appreciation.

"Yes," she said. "First, please take care of yourself. That's more important to me than anything. And second...I think I told you my little sister is going to be at Crestview next year. Jackie Williams."

"Right, you mentioned that," he said.

"Please keep creepy guys away from her," she requested. "I'll feel better at Northwestern if I know someone is making sure of that."

"Absolutely," he promised. "I won't even hit on her myself."

Mid-summer came and on a Friday evening she got started on a project. It took her nearly 2 hours to complete it, which seemed like such an excessively long time to her, with the process involved being as tedious as anything she'd ever tried to do for the first time. But she stuck to it because she thought the most thoughtful thing she could do was make Cal a mixtape as part of the send-off package she was giving to him. When she looked at blank cassettes at Payless she chose a 60 minute one because she wasn't even sure if she had enough songs in mind to fill anything longer than that. With the tape ready she cued up some songs she liked from cassettes, picked a few from the handful of CDs her family had gotten since adding a CD player to their stereo the previous Christmas, and even dug into some of her father's LP records. At first she was trying to be very careful with what songs she picked, worrying that he may not like a song or not get what she was trying to say by selecting it. But by 20 minutes into the process and having only dubbed off three songs total she stopped being meticulous about it. She said to herself, "If he doesn't like a song, so what, he's going to be driving up the highway when he hears it and if he fast forwards through it I won't be there to have my feelings hurt."

The only part of the mix making process she liked was that at least it was a distraction from the reality of the moment. He was leaving and other than some concert thing called Lollapalooza that he said he was hoping to make it back down for in August he'd told her he wasn't sure when he'd be back.

"I'm hoping I'll be able to make it down as part of the holiday break but obviously I'm going to spend some time in Eureka and see my Dad and brother and sister a bit anytime I'm in the area. But I'll find a way to see you," he promised.

The thought of the goodbye, scheduled for the next day when he had promised he would detour through Concord to pick up the package from her, was enough to make her cry. She was glad he was making a point of seeing her in person one more time but she was afraid that face to face she wasn't going to be able to say what she wanted to. So when the second side of the cassette looked like it had a few minutes left on it she took it out of the stereo and put it into her sister's boombox, which would let her record herself.

She hit 'Record', and started talking but stumbled, so she rewound the tape and started over. The second time she just wasn't getting the words right. On her third try she felt like she said what she needed to and hit 'Stop'. She took out the tape, put it in its case, kissed it just to be silly, and added it to the box that already had some cookies, a juice box that she personally thought was a hilarious gesture, and a quick note she had written.

With the care package done she set it aside and moved on to her next priority. Northwestern had sent her a survey for roommate matching and she wanted to get it finished before she collapsed from exhaustion or started crying all over again from thinking about Cal leaving town.

--

The goodbye on her front porch had been rough and he thought it was also a little rushed. He'd opted to make the trip over to Concord

285

the night before and spend the night at Doug's to save some time for the long drive up to Ashland. He needed to reach the campus no later than 4pm to get checked in for the orientation weekend. He was excited and a bit nervous about it. He was going to get to stay in a dorm room for a night, attend a few information sessions, get some time to walk around campus and explore the town, meet his academic advisor and get registered for his first slate of college classes. It felt very adult and he had wanted to make sure that he got enough sleep to get the early start he needed and to make the quick stop at Anna's to say goodbye and pick up the surprise she'd been promising him. But at around 10pm the night before Doug had suggested they make one more Tower Records run together before the store closed at midnight. That trip out included a second stop to grab ice cream. Doug told him he was going to try to live a little cleaner and calmer and Cal didn't want to be unsupportive.

When he pulled up at Anna's he was on his 2nd cup of coffee, a little jittery, and already very sad. No matter how many times he told himself he was good to go, at peace with the summer plan he'd agreed to with his parents, everything still felt rushed. He wanted more time but knew there was no way to get it. And there was no one he wished he had more time with than Anna.

She came outside with a box in her hands and set it down on the bench on her porch.

"I don't like this at all," she said, giving him a tight hug.

"Neither do I," he said, wrapping his arms around her and holding her closer than he ever had.

"Are you at least excited?" she asked as she pulled back from the embrace.

"I am. For the Ashland part for sure. The Eureka part...meh."

"It'll go quick," she said. "Not as quick as you want but it's just a short stop in the grander picture, right?"

He was going to miss her advice. How she saw things. The way she would look at him, even when it left him confused about what any particular look might mean. Ever since she'd given him a ride home after Doug's crazy party he had stopped himself a good three or four times from saying something or doing something to let her know that while he understood all the reasons why they shouldn't be more than friends he

286

regretted never being more. Especially since he thought it was something she was feeling too.

"Thank you for this," he said, picking up the box. "Can I open it?"

She nodded.

"A juice box? Seriously?!" he said as he looked over the items, loving every bit of it.

A note inside was sealed and he didn't want to open it in front of her. And then there were cookies and to his surprise she had made a mixtape. He held it up to try and read her handwriting and see what songs were on it.

"That was a pain in the butt to make, by the way. I have no idea what joy you get out of making such things but I made one anyway," she said.

"Yes, you did."

"And you'll probably hate the songs but they're ones that make me think of you," she said.

It made him want to say something else, something bigger. But again he stopped himself.

"I love it, " he said. "It doesn't matter if I like the songs. I just love that you made it."

"You do have to promise me something, though," she said. "With the tape. You can't listen to it until you're on the I-5, okay?"

"Fair enough," he said.

"Okay," she said. "Now you're going to hug me again and leave before I bawl."

He gave her one last long hug, and she cried anyway. He held it together and then got in his truck to hit the road. He read her note at a red light, expecting it might be long or full of things she wanted to say but it simply read, "Best of luck on your next Adventures! California's loss is Oregon's gain!" Below that was her phone number and her address.

He tried his best to honor her wishes about the mixtape and not listen to it until he reached I-5 North, which was about an hour away. But he cheated, popping it into his tape deck just past the Benicia Bridge. The first song was Paul Simon's "Kodachrome", which he knew he'd heard before but had never listened to all that closely. He had to give her high marks for opening a mix with a song that's first line was "When I think back on all that crap I learned in high school…" From there it moved to some other fun songs that seemed like inside jokes. Richard Marx, a song by Harry Connick Jr. from *When Harry Met Sally*, and many others. It went on for about an hour, which made the drive feel quicker, before closing with "So Close", a Hall & Oates song they'd danced to at Senior Ball. He thought it was over but then he heard a clicking sound on the tape, followed by Anna's voice.

*"Okay...so I was going to put this in a letter but I thought I'd tell you this way. So here goes... When I met you I honestly didn't know what to make of you. A neighbor, a guy who was debating me in my English class and making me so mad that I wanted to kill you. But I soon learned who you were and I knew I liked you, right from the start. I am still amazed sometimes at how we managed to become such good friends because we are SO different. One of your other best friends is Doug for heaven's sake! But I've always known you were my friend and in these last few months I've become even more aware how much you mean to me and how terribly much I am going to miss you.*

He could hear her starting to cry on the recording, which then made his eyes well up.

*"And I'm so sorry your summer here got cut short. It feels like all our time together has been too short. And that we wasted some of it. But I wanted to tell you that no matter what happens next, for the rest of this summer or wherever you go please know that I love you. Very much. I've never been brave enough to say that to you because I knew you would say it back and mean it and we might have ruined what we have. Even now I know you're going to hear me say that and be tempted to turn around, drive for hours and come find me just so you can say it back. But don't do that. Please don't do that. Because I know you care. I know you love me, too. You need to go where you're going and in a few months I'm going to do the same. And I know all you're going to need to do when you get to Oregon is just be you. I've seen you try to be something else and I've always wanted to tell you not to be. Because I know if you're the Cal I know you're going to find friends, you're going to find love, and you're going to do so great. And when you do I can't wait to hear about it. So drive safe. And thank you for being the first and best friend I made here. And no matter where we both may go I will never forget that."*

He heard an audible click again where she stopped recording and by then he was crying fully.

It turned out she knew him all too well because he'd already looked at one exit ramp before she was even done talking and considered turning around. But he knew he couldn't. Instead he pulled into a rest stop, rewound the message, and listened to it again. It was the most wonderful thing anyone had ever said to him. And in another way the cruelest. He had no idea what he was going to say to her the next time they talked but he hoped whatever he might say would be the right thing.

He put her cassette back in its case, then back in the box. He grabbed a different tape from his bag, one of the last cassettes he'd bought before winning his CD player on grad night. He pushed the tape in and listened from the midway point of one song and then into the next. He was doing everything he could to not think about Anna and what she'd said in her message. And as so often happened for him with music he got the right words at the right time.

*I'm not ready as I'll ever be*
*I climb the walls, I fall into the sea*
*I'm not ready as I'll ever be*
*And I suppose your guess is more or less as bad as mine*
*All over but the shouting, just a waste of time*
*Never mind...*

He drove on, knowing he was a bit behind schedule. Not wanting to arrive late, he pushed his speed just over the posted limit. His Dad had reminded him the roads north of Redding were a bit winding and tougher to drive but Cal figured if he made good time before that then he'd get to Ashland and everything would work out okay.

# Acknowledgments and Notes

While many characters and events in this story are inspired by real events and people it is, at the end of the day, ultimately a work of fiction. Apologies and/or my sincere gratitude to any friends or family who see themselves in any of this.

I need to thank my partner, Allison, for enduring my endless talk about this project as I was crafting it. I also had several test readers of earlier drafts who provided me with both constructive feedback and wonderful support. Thank you to Jessica, Sara, and Tiffany for taking the time and giving me a needed boost.

A special shout out to an old friend, Mike, who gave me a random phone call early in the lockdown weeks of the 2020 Coronavirus crisis. Our 20-minute conversation, the first time we'd spoken in almost 29 years, lit the spark that became this story.

And finally, there are my real-life 'Annas'; the friends who served as inspiration for a character I hope did them justice: Stephanie, Colleen, Julie, Liz, and the rather elusive Andrea. You have blessed my life.

--

Excerpts and/or quotes from the following songs and artists appear in this story:

Chapter One: "Billy Two Rivers" by The Dogs D'Amour, 1988

Chapter Three: "Birthday" by The Beatles, 1968; "Jealous" by Gene Loves Jezebel, 1989; "Never Be The Same" by Crowded House, 1988

Chapter Six: "Three Years Gone" by The Brothers Figaro, 1988

Chapter Ten: "Kodachrome" by Paul Simon, 1973; "Never Mind" by The Replacements, 1987

# Recommended Playlist

Music was vital in creating this story, eventually reaching a point where I crafted some playlists of what I imagined would be in rotation in Cal's stereo or in the forefront or background of certain moments in the story.

If any song references in the story made you curious I would recommend the following, which are all available on streaming services and can be made into a playlist.

Consider these the *Like Cassettes* Soundtrack:

1. "The Last Kiss" by Pretty Boy Floyd
2. "Strangers When We Meet" by The Smithereens
3. "Things She Said" by Toy Matinee
4. "Joey" by Concrete Blonde
5. "Never Be The Same" by Crowded House
6. "Somebody's Falling" by Shark Island
7. "Deeper Shade of Soul" by Urban Dance Squad
8. "Tears Don't Lie" by Little Caesar
9. "Opportunity" by Elvis Costello
10. "Bedspring Kiss" by Jellyfish
11. "Come Back Down" by Toad the Wet Sprocket
12. "Three Years Gone" by The Brothers Figaro
13. "Lost" by Kik Tracee
14. "Emotions In Gear" by Bang Tango
15. "So Close" by Hall & Oates
16. "One More Round" by Love/Hate
17. "Last Perfect Thing" by Wire Train
18. "Never Mind" by The Replacements
19. "If We Never Meet Again" by Tommy Conwell

Made in the USA
Middletown, DE
05 November 2020